DEBBIE HIGHTOWER

Kon-Tiki

Book Three in Raven's Record Science-fiction Series

First published by Amazon 2023

Copyright © 2023 by Debbie Hightower

First edition

ISBN: 979-8-87-000215-6

Cover art by GetCovers

This book was professionally typeset on Reedsy.
Find out more at reedsy.com

Contents

Preface	vi
Acknowledgement	vii
Chapter 1	1
Chapter 2	7
Chapter 3	12
Chapter 4	17
Chapter 5	21
Chapter 6	28
Chapter 7	33
Chapter 8	35
Chapter 9	39
Chapter 10	45
Chapter 11	49
Chapter 12	55
Chapter 13	61
Chapter 14	70
Chapter 15	76
Chapter 16	83
Chapter 17	87
Chapter 18	93
Chapter 19	97
Chapter 20	103
Chapter 21	107
Chapter 22	111
Chapter 23	115
Chapter 24	119

Chapter 25	122
Chapter 26	126
Chapter 27	129
Chapter 28	133
Chapter 29	136
Chapter 30	140
Chapter 31	142
Chapter 32	146
Chapter 33	151
Chapter 34	155
Chapter 35	158
Chapter 36	162
Chapter 37	165
Chapter 38	167
Chapter 39	173
Chapter 40	177
Chapter 41	179
Chapter 42	184
Chapter 43	187
Chapter 44	192
Chapter 45	194
Chapter 46	198
Chapter 47	201
Chapter 48	206
Chapter 49	209
Chapter 50	212
Chapter 51	216
Chapter 52	221
Chapter 53	227
Chapter 54	231
Chapter 55	236
Chapter 56	241
Chapter 57	246

Chapter 58   250

Chapter 59   252

Chapter 60   254

Chapter 61   257

Chapter 62   261

Chapter 63   263

Chapter 64   267

Chapter 65   270

Chapter 66   272

Chapter 67   276

Chapter 68   282

Chapter 69   285

Chapter 70   289

Chapter 71   292

Chapter 72   296

Chapter 73   299

Chapter 74   304

Chapter 75   308

Chapter 76   313

Chapter 77   319

Chapter 78   324

Chapter 79   330

Chapter 80   334

Chapter 81   337

About the Author   342

Also by Debbie Hightower   343

Preface

Like the ancient Polynesian explorers, migrants aboard the mothership Kon-Tiki endeavor to travel great distances using celestial navigation. A sudden cataclysm renders continental United States into a forbidden zone known as The Big Scorch. Believing the danger to be past, the remaining officials attempt to pick up the pieces and conduct the country's business as usual. General Leonard Bardick discovers that instead of one nation, this time an enemy intends to wipe out the entire planet. A trip to establish a new colony on the exoplanet Equinox may be humanity's best chance for survival. Rocket designers must hurdle physical, political and economic barriers before making another warp drive mothership a reality. As if that wasn't enough, a turf war over command of the Kon-Tiki heats up. Given the obstacles that lay before them, humanity's survival may depend on help from a hidden source.

Acknowledgement

The author wishes to express gratitude to the following individuals. Without your input and inspiration this installment would not have been possible.

James Bowen

Betsy Decillis

Jolayne Hain

Ed Hightower

Liam Hotze

Aidan Leinbach

Tabitha Leinbach

Elizabeth Saunders

Tina Sheppard

Barbara Stevens

Chapter 1

In the race to make humans a multi-planetary species, there is no prize for second place.

Early in 2042, Rocket Lab had just sailed into first place among all other launch producers. Five ships designed and built by the production and launch outfit were the first functional spacecraft possessing the faster-than-light technology needed for human exploration beyond the Sol system.

With a dozen other launch entities seeking to gain control of the elusive technology, Rocket Lab would have to speed up their pattern of innovation in order to hold onto the prize. A mistake or fiasco could destroy their reputation. A single technological advance by another provider had the power to reduce all their gains to a pile of rubbish.

At the same time, innovations that included deep-space escape pods and self-sealing hull material would not save Dominique Bertrand Inter-orbital shipyard from every emergency. Including this one. Especially this one.

Station manager Eireann Reid awakened to a pitch-black environment with a percussive sound. She pronounced the words *Lights on* with no response. Her fingers explored until they located her hand terminal, which responded to her touch by illuminating her minuscule domicile. The display read 3:28 a.m. Not yet time for her shift, however the newly-acquired role of station manager meant she was always on call. Everything that could possibly go wrong was potentially her responsibility. And evidently

1

something else had gone haywire at this moment.

The continued banging led to her ejection her from the bunk.

The room she occupied was small—barely six meters square. Detecting the motion, her wall view screen lit up to display a screensaver photo of a sandy-haired, blue-eyed toddler boy clinging tightly to his perch on a man—her husband Joe's—shoulders. Pale light from the screen illuminated her deluxe accommodations. A private toilet and shower plus a micro-fridge unit, in addition to nearly 1-G gravity. Palatial quarters compared to the other occupants of the shipyard. With one eye barely open, Reid rolled out of her bunk and into a set of olive-drab coveralls.

At the door she encountered wide-eyed, open-mouthed technician Nicole Bradley.

"Where's the fire?" Reid demanded.

"We're losing power," Bradley stammered. "I thought you needed to know."

"Why the hell didn't you buzz me on the CommLink?"

"CommLink is down and the power level of the station is dropping rapidly. Random lights aren't working. And the temperature is dropping in the command center."

"Well that's not good. What are we waiting for? Let's go figure it out."

If Reid's quarters had been outside the portion of the station in which a rotating torus supplied gravity at nearly-Earth level, getting to the command center would have presented yet another challenge. Fortunately, the artificial gravity in this instance was a huge time-saver. As the two raced to the shipyard's command center, the station manager tried to imagine possible scenarios that could have led to a power drop of this magnitude.

After the Phoenix fleet of ships departed Bertrand shipyard, Reid returned to Earth to take advantage of the surplus of shore leave the company owed her. A huge accumulated bonus would have fueled months of normal family life. Time spent with her husband and family was precious, especially her step-grandchildren Charlie, 2, and Scarlett, 7 months. Leave time allowed her to putter about in the kitchen, producing epic culinary masterpieces. She bought a swimsuit and with her husband headed to a couples' retreat at a Cook Island resort. The time downstairs only whetted her appetite for normal human endeavors.

Alas, the freedom was not to last. She was once again persuaded to submit to another two years of insanity. Rocket Lab immediately accepted more orders and began construction of two new ships. The initial contract was a massive standard-propulsion behemoth designed to ferry supplies from Earth orbit to Mars orbit. On the opposite side of the shipyard, construction had already begun on a colossal starship. The recent builds were initiated under the supervision of a new construction foreman and interim station manager who were both idiots, according to a Rocket Lab administrator who face-timed Eireann Reid and begged her to accept another two-year contract. Offered her a blank check for her services, to her amazement.

Reid's husband was supportive, to her great surprise. He left the decision up to her, knowing that the signing bonus plus her salary increase would fund his expanded automotive repair shop. On top of that, it would provide extravagant college funds for the grandchildren. With family motivations, Reid put her head down and headed upstairs to construct even more innovative vessels.

After the Phoenix fleet left spacedock, the former chief construction engineer Felix Jäger had been replaced by Hugo Frohm. Like Jäger, Frohm wore his stunning platinum hair tied back. Reid was beginning to get used to his nearly-seven-feet-tall height and piercing blue eyes. He was a proficient English speaker. And as far as space vessel construction, Frohm knew his stuff and that was all Reid cared about.

Five weeks after her return, the station manager found herself in the command center unraveling a catastrophic emergency. Frohm checked in a few seconds behind her. After five minutes of trouble-shooting, they succeeded in nailing down the problem.

"How long has that Universal Shipping vessel been docked to our hull?" Reid demanded with a scathing stare at Dylan Hammond, the technician on duty in the command center.

Hammond nervously raked his fingers through his blonde curls. "Couple of hours. She docked at 1:15."

"And the pilot remains on the station?" Frohm asked.

"Yeah, she's here," Hammond once again affirmed, while looking downward.

Panic still lingered on the face of Nicole Bradley, who still hung around in the door of the command center.

Reid pointed in her direction and barked, "I don't care where she is. Get her. We need her up here BANG."

"On my way," she affirmed.

It was a short process to discover the cause of the current crisis: after attaching to Bertrand's cargo compartment, the docking jets of the transport vessel had failed to shut off. Despite the fact that Bertrand station's tonnage far exceeded that of the Universal Shipping vessel, the force of the parking jets was sufficient to propel the shipyard off-kilter.

Rookie starship operator Inga Oja saw no reason to stand around and watch while her delivery was accomplished. After checking in to Bertrand Station, offloading of her vessel was done by means of a robotic system. Computer programs oversaw check-in, stocking and inventory of palletized supplies. Having completed numerous routine deliveries to Bertrand station as well as Artemis colony on the Moon, Oja knew exactly how much time she had to spend in the quarters of a lonely station technician.

A huge chunk of Bertrand Shipyard's power was produced by solar panels— devices that yielded power, but only when they were aimed at the sun. By the time Bradley returned with Oja in tow, Reid and Frohm had discovered the station's maligned status.

Oja was a redhead with a row of silver studs perched along the lobes of both ears. She was tall by human standards, however dwarfed by Frohm's massive frame.

Before she could recover and say anything, Reid accused, "You left your docking jets on?"

Obviously gobsmacked, Oja paled and backpedaled. "I didn't. The ship docks automatically."

Reid placed a hand on her hip. "Then why is my station spinning in the wrong direction? Our communications are out and the solar panels are pointed away from the sun."

Frohm stepped in with an attempt to diffuse the situation.

"We'll figure out who is to blame later," he said. "For now, we need you to get those jets shut off."

Oja took a step back and slapped her forehead. "I'm trying to tell you, everything that ship does is programmed. I didn't leave the docking jets on; I can't turn them off. I don't control anything. All I do is notify the company when I arrive at the designated delivery site."

Reid was already going through scenarios in her mind. She wished that a certain engineering wizard had not chosen to leave with the Phoenix fleet. If she had remained on Bertrand station, Benita Zapata would most certainly have been capable of hacking into the wayward starship's control panel to alleviate the emergency. As she was long gone, they would have to find another way. Preferably before the station's power level hit absolute zero.

With hands on her hips, Reid stared at Frohm, wondering whether there was a chance he could connect to the Universal Systems vessel from Bertrand Station's command center. The two entities were physically connected, therefore it was theoretically possible. As if their thoughts were connected, Frohm shook his head. There was no way to operate the vessel's controls in time to make an appreciable difference.

Reading the nameplate of Oja's Universal Shipping coverall, Reid demanded. "Oja, is there anyone who could change your vessel's commands?"

Oja considered for a moment. "They can be re-programmed."

For a moment, Reid was hopeful.

"Can you do it? Then get to it, girl."

With a hand on her chest and a shake of her head, Oja said, "I can't do it, but someone from Earth could theoretically step in. The programmers back at Universal Shipping—they're the ones who put in the code."

"Anything. We need those parking jets cut off as quickly as possible. They have caused the station to lose contact with Earth, and we are losing the capability to generate power we need for life support functions."

"Give me a minute," Oja responded nervously. "Maybe my delivery ship can still communicate with them. I'll see if they can make it happen."

Oja beat a path to the loading dock where she discovered offloading was complete. The conveyors had ceased their work, retracted and withdrew into their storage alcoves. She dashed towards the transport vessel where she hoped to contact her headquarters.

During this exchange, Frohm's gaze met Reid's.

Release the docking clamps, Reid heard. Only the command was not audible. It was in her brain. It wasn't the first time she had experienced this sort of communication.

Release the docking clamps. Now, before it's too late.

Sure, it's the only way, Reid decided. If Oja couldn't get anyone on Earth to shut off the jets, they would have to release the wayward vessel.

Everyone in the command center—Frohm, Bradley and Hammond—watched as Reid called up the controls on the view screen and entered a directive that released the Universal Shipping freighter from its moorings. It was the only immediate solution still under their control. The one that required the least effort but made the most sense.

A few minutes later, Oja made her way back to the command center. She had just made it to the cargo hold before realizing that her ship had been released into oblivion.

"What the hell have you done?" she demanded. "You guys are in so much trouble!"

With a fixed glare Reid asserted, "What did I do? I saved our all of our asses. Preservation of life takes precedence over any amount of drama. As soon as the station re-aligns, I'll give your company a buzz and tell them to arrange a pick-up for their piece of shit vessel as well as their slack-assed pilot."

Chapter 2

Rocket Lab Launch Providers
Auckland, New Zealand

No deaths or injuries were reported during the recent incident at Dominique Bertrand Station.

"That's the main takeaway we want to provide for the media outlets," emphasized Bella Brown.

The departure of Rocket Lab press secretary Raven Munoz had left an unmistakable void. As Project Manager Camillo Hoffman always said: *If you don't throw the press a bone every once in a while they will eat you alive. Then you're stuck with whatever they dig up or fabricate on their own.*

The post-accident press conference would be the first for new media coordinator Hahona Timoti. Among his assets, he packed a strong background from an aeronautical manufacturing company in Wellington, New Zealand. Rocket Lab CEO Brandon Kemp was a few years older than Timoti, but felt a kinship with the new hire due to the fact they claimed the same *alma mater*. In addition, the board hoped the selection of a Māori press secretary would stave off criticism from local groups who alleged low numbers of native New Zealanders among the launch provider's employees.

His new position in Auckland was his dream job, however Timoti pushed through a few pre-session jitters. In an attempt to channel Rocket Lab's founder Peter Beck, he wore a white shirt which contrasted favorably with his dark skin. A black blazer with no tie completed his ensemble. He had *Ta Moko*, three verticle lines tattooed on his chin. As further evidence of his

7

ethnicity, he wore his jet-black hair long and tied back.

There was another essential element absent from this press conference. In addition to losing their long-time press secretary, Rocket Lab was also minus personnel manager Claire Montgomery, who had taken a leave of absence while dealing with a difficult pregnancy. In her absence, Bella Brown hoped to steel Timoti's nerves with relevant facts as well as a pre-session pep talk.

A black view screen mounted on the back wall of the boardroom was peppered with iterations of the Rocket Lab logo. With Timoti effectively positioned in front of the wall, Brown pointed to the super-large view screen on the opposite wall.

"Your best bet is to direct your gaze to the camera you see up there," said Brown, pointing to a circular aperture at the top of the screen. "As members of the press click into the Zoom meeting, their names and media identities will appear below their images. A green light next to their names will let you know who is currently asking questions. They have been directed to speak English whenever possible, but that doesn't always happen. If they submit a question in another language, Japanese for instance, you will hear it spoken in Japanese but the data feed will display the translation in English."

Timoti swiveled his seat around to face current Rocket Lab CEO Brandon Kemp. "Don't you feel that this type of press conference is too impersonal?"

Kemp, attired in full business dress, shrugged his shoulders. "No elbow to elbow, so you won't expect to contract any exotic diseases. Oh, and it's a sure bet that you won't be shot at either. In the old-style press conferences, preliminary security could take hours to verify IDs, issue press passes and rifle through camera bags for firearms or bombs." With a wave at the view screen and a pat on Timoti's shoulder, he summarized, "This way is better, Welly. You'll get used to it, mate."

After adopting an expression of resignation, Timoti swiveled around to face Brown, who placed a tablet in front of him.

"No deaths or injuries were reported during the August 10, 2042 accident at Dominique Bertrand Station," she repeated, scrolling to a press release on the tablet's screen. "That's the main takeaway we want to provide for all the media outlets. And control of the station was regained within a minimal period of time."

During Brown's briefing, Kemp stood against the wall with his arms fixed across his chest. After she finished speaking, however, he stepped forward to regard the press representative face to face.

"Cheers, mate. Feed them just enough to keep them satisfied without giving out any proprietary information."

With a nod, Timoti acknowledged, "Don't give away any secrets. Check."

There had been no print newspapers since the early 2030's, of course. It became unpopular to print them because environmental groups felt it was a waste of trees. The real reason, of course, was simply because it was cheaper, faster and more efficient for media groups to publish their stories online. The articles were easier for readers to access via their computers or hand terminals, rather than driving out to purchase newspapers at their local newsstand or paying to have them delivered. Therefore, most large newspapers had either shut down or re-invented themselves into websites with Like, Share and Subscribe directives.

Initially, Timoti explained the status of the station at the time of the incident. Two starships had been under construction there. Sticking to the press release, he revealed the tonnage of the starships as well as the entities who ordered them. Nothing to see here.

Rocket Lab IT Trevor Smith was also tapped to play a role in the press conference. At his nearby station, he regarded a monitor in which media representatives raised electronic hands to have their questions answered.

Dressed in a white shirt, tweed vest and grey Jaxon hat, a representative of the London conglomerate news agency was the first selected to voice his question. "Mr. Timoti, according to your initial press release, a Universal Shipping vessel was the cause of the incident. Can you elaborate on the purpose of the shipping vessel? How long had it been on-site when the incident occurred?"

"Thank you for your question, Mr. Townsend," Timoti responded. After a downward glance at his tablet, he again faced the camera. "Universal Shipping is one of several carriers that regularly dispatch needed supplies and construction materials to our job site at Bertrand Intra-orbital Shipyard. According to our logs, the vehicle in question was docked to the station for three hours seventeen minutes."

"Mr. Timoti, can you please explain under whose command the Universal Shipping starship was released from its moorings?"

"Reverse docking was an emergency decision made by an administrator of Bertrand Shipyard. Our initial investigation revealed that the starship's parking jets continued to fire during its entire visit to the station, resulting in a serious misalignment that triggered a catastrophic loss of power throughout the station. Rocket Lab endorses the decision that was made under life-and-death circumstances."

A green light cued the question of the Hong Kong news agency. In English, a female journalist quickly asked, "May we have the name of the administrator who ordered the unoccupied ship released into the black?"

With an unemotional stare, Timoti responded, "It would be against our policy to divulge that information. Sorry, but I am unable to comply with that request."

With the light still on, the Hong Kong journalist further demanded, "Are you aware, then, of the identity of the Universal Shipping operator who left the jets running for more than three hours? At what point did the pilot become aware of the situation?"

With another glance at his tablet, Timoti answered, "Due to the nature of ongoing legal negotiations between Rocket Lab and Universal Shipping, I am not at liberty to discuss that aspect of the incident."

From his station, Smith selectively cued a reporter who probably wouldn't ask such provocative questions.

"Was there any damage to the station?" inquired a reporter from the Johannesburg news agency. "How serious were the injuries? Was anyone killed?"

Timoti almost smiled, but caught himself just in time. "The incident in question caused no damage to the station. The logs indicate that the station was able to re-align itself within a five-hour window. We are pleased to report there were no injuries, serious or otherwise."

The question of a reporter from Sau Paulo, Brazil required translation from Portuguese into English. Timoti waited patiently until the monitor feed revealed her inquiry: "Does Rocket Lab and Bertrand station plan to continue making space crafts?"

Thankfully, Timoti had memorized Rocket Lab's motto. He quoted: *Rocket Lab is an end-to-end space company delivering reliable launch services, spacecraft, satellite components, and on-orbit management. Space has defined some of humanity's greatest achievements and it continues to shape our future.*

"To answer your question, yes. It's what we have always done, and will always continue to do."

Timoti relaxed and breathed a sigh of relief when he believed the press conference was concluded. Images of participants began to drop out from the view screen one by one.

A lone green light appeared below the image of a woman from Delhi, India. Wearing a purple sari draped with a golden scarf, she made her inquiry in Hindi. A few seconds later, the English translation appeared in the feed at the lower end of the view screen.

"The Phoenix fleet ushered in a new era in space craft building. Do you believe that there will be additional motherships constructed at Bertrand Shipyard?"

Timoti didn't have long to think, but his answer was instantaneous. "Rocket Lab has no immediate plans to construct another warp-capable ship of that size, but we've already done it once. To answer your question, yes, I believe anything is possible."

Chapter 3

Hawaii State Capitol Building

Honolulu, Hawaii

The Uber driver couldn't have gotten him any closer to the Hawaii state legislature building. That is, unless he had driven inside the building.

Although he had lived in Hawaii for ten years since leaving Washington D.C., General Leonard Bardick was still absorbing Hawaii's unique history and landscape. And with Honolulu officially designated as the national capital, it was only natural that the nation's business be conducted within the confines of the existing state capital building.

Since the devastating strike that had erased continental United States, the Americans who were left had been involved in a struggle to survive. It would take nothing short of a miracle to allow the shards that remained to form a cohesive unit. General Leonard Bardick headed into the new congressional session with the intention of doing his part to make that miracle happen.

In 2039, Interim President Roger Hughes opted to set up a new national capital in Honolulu located on Oahu, capital of the State of Hawaii. With the continental United States now a wasteland known as The Scorch, American survivors struggled to pick up the pieces. After six hard-fought years, the wounded country once again attempted to rise to its feet. In November 2042, U.S. officials staged the first election since the devastating holocaust. When Hughes lost the election, he publicly admitted his relief.

U.S. officials took a preliminary census of their military strength and were shocked by the minuscule numbers. Along with the remaining able-bodied military retirees, Bardick had been called back into active duty. The opening congressional session would have been his first chance to show up in his dress military uniform. That is, until he was surprised to discover that it no longer fit. Never to worry, his personal assistant Richard Dalton had matched up an alternative: a navy blue suit paired with a crisp, white shirt and red and blue striped tie.

Built in 1969, the legislature building replaced the former Iolani Palace. Signage outside spoke to the history of Hawaii. Bardick took note of the statue of Queen Lili'uokalani in close proximity to the capital. The governor's residence across the street had been the queen's palace—that is, before it was commandeered by a group of American sugar cane planters.

On the way inside, the general greeted U.S. Army General Paul Rodriguez, the new president's pick for Secretary of Defense. The two men took their place inside the House of Representatives Chamber. First order of business was swearing-in of new officers, which included the newly-elected commander in chief.

While waiting for the session to start, Bardick took note of the representation on the wall. He was not expecting to find a the red-white-and-blue American flag there. Fifty states no longer existed; therefore the former icon had been retired. Instead, the coat of arms of the State of Hawaii remained in its historic place behind the speaker's podium. On the left side of the seal was King Kamehameha. On the right side was the goddess Liberty, wearing a Phrygian cap and laurel wreath. Quite appropriately, below the heraldic shield was a phoenix with wings outstretched. The state motto *UaMau ke Ea o ka 'Aina Pono* translated loosely as: *The life of the land is perpetuated in righteousness.*

There was liberal chatter as citizens took their seats in the chamber along with members of the new legislature.

President-elect Maleko Ho didn't need to move into the presidential palace. As two-term governor of the State of Hawaii, he was already a resident of Washington Place where the royal Hawaiian queen had resided. And just across the street from his residence, he was sworn in as the Commander in Chief of the United States to thunderous applause that echoed throughout the congressional chamber.

Bardick had been somewhat hopeful that President Ho would kick-start a national reform. Hopeful, even, for a season of change. His tentative optimism was not misplaced.

The newly-appointed secretary of defense left the opening session with the monumental task to take stock of the nation's military resources.

On mike, President Ho said, "I feel that it's shameful at this point that we are truly unaware of our resources. I want a report on everything we've got. Document every aircraft carrier and all of our ships, whether they are on active duty or reserve. If it floats, count it. We need to know how many fighter jets and what type we have. How many drones? How many helicopters?"

"There have been significant losses in terms of firepower," explained General Rodriguez. "We have endeavored to restructure the supply chain. May I mention that replacement parts are in short supply."

Ho snapped, "I'm well aware of our difficulties, general. Nevertheless, I expect a complete inventory. If there's any hope we can fix it, count it."

"Do you mean to include all of our equipment here as well as Alaska?"

An audible sigh could be heard. "If it can get off the ground, put it on the list. If it floats, ditto. I expect you to inventory everything. Tank drones, armored personnel carriers, jeeps ... I expect to be apprised of every single piece of fighting equipment. Especially strategic items like stealth planes and spy satellites. Here, Alaska, Puerto Rico, Guam—all the territories. Germany, Japan, South Korea, Italy—all of our foreign bases."

"Yes, sir. I'll get right on it."

General Bardick had spent years involved in the D.C. government. Sat through countless congressional sessions. By comparison, the Honolulu session was much smaller in terms of official representatives present. It was also longer—much longer.

Ho instructed the new secretary of agriculture to take stock of the country's food production. Domestic oil resources were the assigned focus of the new secretary of energy. Ho demanded to know how the country's electric energy was being produced, in addition to the vulnerability of those resources.

The day's business was still incomplete when the last person left the legislative chamber. Ho summoned Bardick to his office on the fourth floor of the legislative building.

The general's training at war college had programmed him with a nearly-instinctive habit of evaluating safety and security. He couldn't help but analyze the security status of the Commander in Chief's office. Upon entering, he noticed there were no windows. Only one other door. And there were only three other men in the office, both of whom had been downstairs in the chamber. One he guessed was an aide of some sort; the other two Secret Service. None of them spoke a word. As far as Bardick was concerned, they could have been flies on the wall.

President Ho took a seat behind a large wooden desk, motioning Bardick into one of several couches facing him.

"This isn't the Resolute desk, but it'll serve," said Ho with a smile.

Bardick swiveled his head around the room, his gaze lingering on an extra-large Seal of the President of the United States behind the desk.

"Do you like it?" Ho asked. "I just had them put that up. I feel that it lends dignity to the office."

"Absolutely, Mr. President. Just what it needs."

"I'll get right to the point. I have a special assignment for you, general. Specifically for you—one for which you are uniquely suited."

Bardick listened patiently, eager to play a role in this newly re-invented America.

"The accepted narrative is that the American holocaust was caused by a volcano."

The general huffed, clucked, then replied, "I'm assuming you don't go along with that."

"Oh, hell no," Ho countered with a snort. "Anyone with two eyes and a three-digit IQ can tell who took us out." He pointed upwards, then added. "Our alien neighbors who feel that we broke a treaty decided to show off their displeasure as well as technical superiority. I am aware of your connections and channels of communication. I need you to test the waters and let me know if they're finished or if they intend to come back and finish the job. Are the rest of us in any danger?"

With an appropriate level of gravity, Bardick nodded. "I'll shake the vine and see what's going on up there."

"And general, another matter. We don't have NASA or Space Force to speak of. Or control of any satellites. Which means that when it comes to the sky, our wings have been clipped. I need you to take an accounting of what everyone else is doing in terms of space launches. What's going on at Artemis Colony on the Moon, who's in control of Mars and anything in between. I need you to be our eyes on the sky."

"Especially with our extraterrestrial enemies keeping tabs on everything that crosses the Kármán line," Bardick agreed.

"That's for damn sure. So can I count on you, general?"

Bardick stood to attention and saluted his new Commander in Chief. "Salute and execute, sir."

Chapter 4

Rocket Lab Headquarters
Auckland, New Zealand

In a large corporation, perhaps the easiest way to disseminate information is via email. That's not always the best method, though.

Rocket Lab was about to make a big change. CEO Brandon Kemp decided the best way to drop the bomb was a face-to-face meeting. Project manager Camillo Hoffman answered the summons on a Tuesday morning.

Always fearing the worst, Hoffman debated the appropriate wardrobe choice for his dressing-down session. Uncertain what lay ahead, he decided that he couldn't go wrong wearing his Rocket Lab blazer with a crisp white shirt, blue plaid bow tie and black dress pants.

A soft-spoken woman in a blue jacket with Rocket Lab logo occupied the office immediately in front of Kemp's. Hers was a familiar face, as she had been Kemp's personal assistant for a few years. After only a brief wait, she escorted him into the executive's office.

Kemp was closing out a video call with another executive. He held up his index finger as if to say, *just a moment.*

"Can I get you anything?" the assistant asked.

"Coffee, if you don't mind. Cream and sugar please."

A wall of windows in Kemp's office, located on the fifth floor of the facility, overlooked the courtyard. From this viewpoint Hoffman noted the ebb and flow of staff and visitors scurrying to and from other offices.

"Thanks," said Hoffman to the woman when she handed him a steaming ceramic mug bearing the Rocket Lab logo. While Kemp finished up his call, Hoffman politely consulted his hand terminal through his wire-rimmed glasses.

The CEO projected an atmosphere of formality in his grey suit, blue shirt and coordinating tie. As soon as Kemp disconnected the call, his view screen displayed the corporate logo.

"Thanks for coming in, Cam."

To break the ice, Kemp began by praising Hoffman's leadership during the Phoenix project. Five ships recently launched from Bertrand Shipyard were a credit to Hoffman's engineering team as well as the Rocket Lab launch provider. And now, only a short time later, the shipyard had begun construction on two mega-ships designed for the sole purpose of delivering freight to the Mars colony.

While Kemp was generous with his acclamation for Hoffman's efforts, the project manager immediately recognized a formula he often used to communicate with his team. Begin with something positive, then on to the distasteful bit, before finishing off with another pleasant agenda item.

Here we go, let's get the medicine part over with, he thought.

"I especially wanted to have a conversation with you about the incident that happened recently at Bertrand Station."

Hoffman smacked himself lightly on the cheek. A brief corporate investigation had revealed the incident in question had been caused by a software error in the delivery starship. It was really no one's fault; however Hoffman oversaw construction at Bertrand Station. And as the overseeing supervisor, the fiasco had happened on his watch. Therefore, he was ultimately responsible.

"Last I heard, Universal Shipping was still attempting a lawsuit," he said. "They expect to be paid damages for the unmanned vessel that was cut loose. That plus the recovery costs to get it back."

Kemp chuckled. "All I've got to say is, hope they have deep pockets. It was their vessel that caused the situation in the first place. End of story."

Hoffman spread his arms out and echoed Kemp's sentiments. "I don't see how anyone could arrive at a different conclusion."

Kemp took a sip from his own ceramic mug. Punctuation. On to the next paragraph.

"That very situation has led to a big change in our organization. I wanted you to be the first to hear about it."

"Sir?"

"I'm certain you are aware how much time elapsed before the situation at Bertrand was discovered."

"The ship was docked for nearly three hours, sir."

"Three hours seventeen minutes, according to the logs. My point is this: although there were people on duty in the station's control center, no one seemed to be minding the store."

Hoffman frowned. "They didn't discover the misalignment until there was a significant power drop, causing the CommLinks to go down."

"Exactly," Kemp agreed. "What's the worst-case scenario? How bad could it have gotten?"

With a gloomy expression, Hoffman said, "The solar panels were focused in the wrong direction, so they weren't generating power. That isn't the sole power source on the station, but the situation did cascade into a significant power drop. Power levels are critical in space. The station would not theoretically have headed out to crash into the Moon. That's not going to happen, however a critical power drop could have caused a shutdown in atmospheric purification, water filtration and heat. Life support, in addition to a shutdown of all construction operations. Yeah, it had the potential to become catastrophic."

"Then you revert to the *thousand ways to die in space.* Here's my point."

Hoffman leaned in, hoping he wouldn't have to take a professional hit due to the incident.

"If the shipyard's systems were continuously monitored, none of this would have happened."

"I agree; it shouldn't have happened. We can do better. We will do better," Hoffman promised resolutely. "I'm already drawing up some new protocols to put in place."

"Since we are all in agreement that a change is needed, I have a solution.

We are going to install an AI-enabled system up there. It will be able to detect minuscule variations in readings with split-second reactions to them. In addition, the new system will be capable of fully managing the influx of materials as well as labor schedules."

Of all the possible impacts that could have resulted from the event, Hoffman could not have predicted that one. No words escaped his open mouth.

"The computer system will also improve security down here. Another factor that provoked this decision is the data breach last year."

Hoffman closed his eyes and massaged his forehead. "Don't remind me. I nearly quit over it. Highly embarrassing."

"Our IT manager Trevor Smith has assured me that Artificial Intelligence is the latest and greatest cyber defense against hacking and data leaks." •

Hoffman was skeptical. "How's that gonna work?"

"Don't worry. I have arranged for Trevor to meet with your team and answer all of your questions. The engineers especially need to understand the AI system as it relates to spacecraft design."

Hoffman gulped hard. "A computer is taking over design of our ships?"

"Change is always difficult, however if we keep doing things the same way, stagnation sets in. The definition of insanity is ..."

Hoffman interjected, "doing the same thing in the same way but expecting a different result."

"Exactly. If we don't want to join the list of companies that shut down each year, we have to raise the bar. Get out of our comfort zone. We're going to have to embrace innovation as a way of life."

Although plenty of potential issues crossed his mind, in the end Hoffman voiced only a single objection.

"Eireann isn't going to like this," he told Kemp.

"I'm depending on you to break it to her gently. If you use the right words, I'm certain you'll have her believing that it was her idea."

Chapter 5

Cybernetic Solution
Rocket Lab Headquarters
Auckland, New Zealand

Science fiction was on the payroll of the ongoing reality at Rocket Lab. As a testament to that fact, Bella Brown showed up to a Monday morning meeting in the Rocket Lab boardroom wearing a futuristic Star Fleet uniform of Next Generation configuration. The petite brunette armed herself for the day's agenda wearing a black jumpsuit with gold torso designed for a member of Starfleet operations team. Before the end of the session, all members of the engineering team would get a taste of what it's like to live in the 24th century.

Joining Brown, around the boardroom table were assembled research and development team members whose combined specialties produced the astronomical advances that kept the launch facility on the lips of worldwide news agencies. Members of the research and development division had a familiarity based on seven years spent elbow to elbow at the launch provider. Next to Hoffman was senior propulsion manager Dave Sutton, who at all times was armed with pencil, pen and notebook. So equipped, he was poised to draw, sketch or notate any and all relevant details. Also present were Jim Freeman, Beth Sommerset and Julia Stempler.

Fully acclimated to his team's likes and dislikes, Camillo Hoffman hoped to diminish the impact of the day's agenda by ordering in a catered feast. It was a sure bet that all members of the engineering team were fans of *Funky*

Fish cuisine.

With an Asian-like bow, he offered Brown a cardboard clamshell-encased vegan entree from a cart borrowed from the facility's cafeteria. "Bella, this is for you."

At the front of the boardroom, Rocket Lab IT Trevor Smith wasn't occupied with claiming a lunch order. Rather, he tapped on his tablet. Hoffman correctly assumed that he was familiarizing himself with the day's presentation to be cast onto the large boardroom view screen when the time was right.

As he distributed meals, Hoffman debated the impact of Smith's impending message on the room's occupants. How would a system-wide switch-over affect Dave Sutton, senior propulsion manager, who configured warp-drive engines? Or hull design specialist Jim Freeman? And Beth Sommerset, who was working together with Julie Stempler on biometric bunks and cabins in all of Rocket Lab's vessels. And, of course, Bella Brown was the team's research consultant on a variety of subjects. Whose futures were secure, and who may be booted to the curb under the new system?

The engineers lived and worked together on the Rocket Lab campus, located on New Zealand's north island. When they weren't working, they attended concerts and had beach picnics. At least until recently. They were less like a team; more like a family. It remained to be seen whether or not Trevor Smith's news would damage the team's cohesive chemistry.

Hoffman strategically allowed time for his engineers to consume their meals plus a few minutes for them to chatter among themselves before giving Smith the signal to start.

A hush fell over the room just before the IT expert began his earth-shattering announcement.

"The keys to the kingdom lie in data encryption," he began. "Without it, all of our digital information would be exposed for anyone and everyone to see, use and exploit. Petty thieves will always be able to pilfer tangible items: cars, jewelry, cash. Thieves know they aren't going to get rich in this manner. In addition, if they get caught with stolen goods they likely will go to prison. Rather than the risky, labor-intensive process of stealing personal valuables, cyber data is a more desirable, big-ticket target."

Brown, who was prone to outbursts, argued, "None of us uses cash anymore."

With a stare, Hoffman silenced her protest.

Smith, who was also familiar with the team, continued, "Your most treasured possessions, your Star Trek memorabilia, are kept in your bungalow. How do you protect your valuables?"

After a few seconds of thought, Brown replied, "I lock the front door, the back door and all the windows when I leave the house."

With a nod, Smith agreed. "Most of us do. But how about the door to your crawl space? Do you lock that?"

With a confused expression, Brown said softly, "I don't think my crawl space has a lock. Only a latch."

"My point is that if thieves want to find a way in, nothing is secure. And you are of course aware I don't mean that someone is targeting your Star Trek collection. I'm using your possessions as an analogy for our cyber valuables. In the real world, we guard our personal and financial information with firewalls and passwords. To translate that into corporate terms, here at Rocket Lab our most valuable cyber treasure is our design data. But black-hat hackers can use certain types of computers capable of breaking through our passwords by detecting patterns. They know your habits. Most people choose passwords based on familiar objects, people, events or dates. But like burglars with lock-picking tools, the cryptography we use today is vulnerable to attacks by quantum computers."

The view screen that previously displayed soothing landscape screensavers switched to a screen that read: *A Beginner's Guide to Quantum Computing.*

"I know you all are engineers. You're tech-savvy and I don't wish to insult your intelligence," Smith continued. "Don't be offended that I'm going to start off this presentation at the fundamental level with the assumption that you are already familiar with these concepts. As you will notice on the screen, the smallest possible unit of information is referred to as a bit, which actually a shortened form of the words binary digit. A bit is usually represented by an electrical voltage or current pulse, or by the electrical state of a flip-flop circuit. In other words, a bit's value can be described by a zero or a one indicating a status of positive or negative. Quantum computers, however, run on subatomic qubits rather than conventional bits. Qubits can exist in super position, like taking on multiple values at once. Computers based on circuits are sequential. Quantum computers are simultaneous. This allows quantum computers to perform calculations at a much faster rate than traditional computers. Are you with me so far?"

While Hoffman was busily scribbling in his ever-present moleskin-covered notebook, Dave Sutton responded, "I'm with you, Trevor, but I already dislike the direction this is headed."

Endowed with splashy graphics, the screen kept up with Smith's continued explanation. "Artificial Intelligence is now the latest weapon in our cyber security armory. Quantum computers are well able to detect and break through your firewall or password-guarded data. AI, however, is incredibly useful for rapidly automating decision-making processes and inferring patterns from incomplete or changed data.

"Let's say a rival company or some unknown black-hat hacker wants to destroy the competition through malware or ransomware. We know from history that most new strains of malware are combinations and re-combinations of other malicious codes."

"What about the antivirus software you installed on our system?" Brown burst out.

Smith nodded. "We've been successful with that strategy in the past, but for demonstration purposes not every system will benefit. Data shows that around fifty percent of all connected devices are not capable of running antivirus software."

"I was not aware of that fact," said Hoffman, before scribbling a note.

"Are you telling us that our crown jewels are exposed?" Brown demanded.

Smith continued, "To someone using a quantum computer, they are. AI algorithms are pattern-detection machines with a significant edge over legacy-list based security systems. They detect and respond to attacks before a human or even traditional software would recognize them. And what's more impressive is the preventive measures taken by quantum computers.

They can subdivide data into separate caches, each with a diverse encryption method. One cache of data being useless without all the others."

"Wicked," commented Stempler.

"In addition to prevention, detection and response to outside attacks, it also guards our data from internal meddling or cyber theft."

Everyone in the room was certain Smith was referring to the devastating cyber espionage that had taken place in their organization the previous year. Despite passwords and firewalls, a member of the engineering team had somehow facilitated the transfer of proprietary plans to a rival company. Marama Fetumale had never confessed to the crime, however her rapid disappearance had left a sore spot among the engineers.

"The quantum computer is aware of all of your habitual activities," Smith went on. "For example, Dave Sutton's virtual sports team leadership. So close to a World Cup victory this year, Dave! And Julie Stempler's obsessive online shopping for home furnishings."

"That was business, not personal. I was selecting the decor for the Phoenix cabins," she protested.

"I neither accused nor condoned your activities. I only indicated that they are habitual," Smith explained. "The patterns of your day-to-day can be used used to detect anomalous activities. For instance, the quantum computer detects a record where a privileged user logs into the system and creates a new account. Then, almost immediately afterward, the user copied all the contents of a database. In a subsequent action, they deleted the new account. Now, each of these activities separately wouldn't necessarily represent a problem, but all of these actions performed within a very short period of time ..."

"That sort of behavior would raise a huge red flag," Sommerset proclaimed.

"Right," Smith agreed. "We have what may be an attack scenario where an insider has taken advantage of the system. Artificial Intelligence can protect, detect and respond. It performs real-time analysis of defenses, with the capability to make corrections or shift the data before an attacker has the chance to locate an entry point. Long before a human user would be able to respond to a threat."

"Let's assume that Jim and I are working on a starship design," said Sutton. "How can we be certain that the computer won't detect risky behavior and shut us down at a critical juncture? Am I correct in assuming that Rocket Lab is going to switch over to a quantum computer?"

With a nod from Hoffman, Smith affirmed the inevitable. "That is correct. And, to answer your question, if the computer determines that a high-risk action is taking place, it may prompt the user to submit a password or even a second factor of identification. All while notifying a supervisor or someone higher in the chain of command."

"You will probably want a biometric method of identification," Stempler surmised. "I'm guessing you would opt against an ID card; something that could easily be stolen or duplicated."

"That is correct," Smith countered.

"Are you going with facial recognition? Or retinal scans?" she probed.

"Some of the time." Pointing at Sutton and Hoffman, he further explained, "People who wear glasses present a challenge to both facial detection and facial recognition software. We're going with precise biometric fingerprint recognition software. You press or swipe your finger on the sensor when prompted to do so."

"Well, that's not going to be a violation of privacy," Brown huffed sarcastically.

An absolute silence prevailed over the boardroom, followed by Sommerset's question, "So when does this curtain drop? When do we switch over to the quantum system?"

Smith let Hoffman answer the question. "We're going to have to shut down everything for a week while installation takes place. Then we'll all experience some corporate training procedures."

Smith countered, "Maybe two weeks. Who knows?"

"What is the name of our ... quantum computer?" Brown asked.

"The HAL 9000," guessed Sutton.

"Or VIKI?" Brown countered gloomily, alluding to the Virtual Interactive Kinetic Intelligence in the *I, Robot* production by Jeff Vintar. "I've got a super-bad feeling about this."

"HAL and VIKI are too sinister. I prefer Alexa," Stempler broke in.

"Or Alice," Sommerset countered. "Artificial Linguistic Computer Entity."

"The system doesn't have a name," Smith assured them.

The festive atmosphere that had existed during the earlier feast had completely disappeared, replaced by a pallor.

Freeman broke the silence. "So this quantum computer, Trevor, it's going to design our ships?"

"Yes," said Hoffman, again taking the helm. "Everything will remain under your control. You'll specify the design perimeters, of course. And you'll still have the power to approve or disapprove the final designs."

"Permission to speak freely, sir," Brown asked.

"Always," Hoffman countered.

"If the computer is taking over the engineering process, what the hell are we still here for?" she blasted angrily.

While Hoffman was formulating his response, Sutton went further to attack Smith.

"This won't be the first time that jobs are lost due to automation. Or the last, I'll wager. Consider the fact that your position may be outdated as well, Trevor. Are you at all worried about being replaced by a computer?"

Chapter 6

Success in creating effective Artificial Intelligence could be the biggest event in the history of our civilization. Or the worst. So we cannot know if we will be infinitely helped by AI, or ignored by it and side-lined, or conceivably destroyed by it.

– Stephen Hawking

"*Iron Man. Terminator. Blade Runner. I, Robot. Eagle Eye. Eastern Storm. Rogue Mars.*

With her usual candor, Bella Brown spouted off a list of movies that included a plot in which artificial intelligence went rogue. "When you peel back the layers, it's a disaster movie with us in the starring roles," she added.

A group of Rocket Lab employees had gathered in the backyard of Jim Freeman and Claire Montgomery's bungalow for a Saturday afternoon barbecue. With the aroma of grilled meat wafting through the air, the backyard was a flurry of activity. Soon after their August wedding, Montgomery had fallen pregnant. Severe morning sickness had confined her to home. She had initially intended to be a gracious hostess, however waves of nausea had already sent her inside the house.

In his wife's absence, Freeman was performing the dual role of host and chef. Wearing a black knee-length bartender's apron, he asked Brown, "Want me to put this on the barbie?"

"Yeet, mate. I fixed up a packet of vegetables. They're already seasoned; just open up the aluminum foil and throw it on the grill."

At the opposite end of the patio, Dave Sutton and his date Tino Aroha were occupied strumming their guitars. Sutton was wearing a Captain Boomerang t-shirt and Crocs with no socks. Aroha's facial tattoos identified her as Māori, a race of people who had been repeatedly kicked off their ancestral lands. Brown correctly identified the tune the musicians were playing— the politically volatile protest tune *Beds Are Burning* as performed by the Australian band Midnight Oil.

Unseasonably warm early-spring temperatures had triggered the outdoor get-together. Brown hoped the 33 degrees Centigrade — mid-60s Fahrenheit — temperatures were an indication of things to come.

She herself was more than ready for spring. Especially if that provoked the Rocket Lab staffers to pack their togs and venture out for regular Saturday trips to any of Auckland's beautiful beaches.

While taking note of Freeman's culinary activity, Brown observed Ieohapata's efforts to organize some afternoon recreation with a number of the shipyard employees. Earlier in the day, he had showed up to mark chalk lines on a cricket pitch formed by the combined backyards of several bungalows.

With everyone else occupied, Freeman turned to Brown and said, "I hate to ask you, but can you supervise the grill for a moment? I need to go inside to check on Claire."

Taking a spatula from Freeman, she said, "Sure. I've got this."

After she heard the patio door slam, she regarded burgers and steaks sizzling above the coals. She said aloud, to no one in particular, "Unfortunately, I have zero experience cooking meat."

Wearing cargo shorts, Ieohapata could be seen out on the lawn taking inventory of his sports equipment: a bright-green Cricket kit. A dozen or more residents of the staff village divided up into teams to formulate their strategies.

Before the game could begin, Camillo Hoffman strolled up. In contrast to his normal business dress, he was wearing a pair of jeans with a plaid button-down shirt and canvas slip-in loafers.

"Hi Cam," said Brown as he claimed a seat on Freeman's patio. "Can you help me with the grill? Jim had to go inside to check on Claire and I know nothing about meat. So, hoping we don't burn all this to a crisp."

"I've got this," said Hoffman. "I'm your man."

"Yeah, you're a meatatarian!"

Hoffman switched out the spatula for a pair of tongs and proceeded to flip the portions.

Iehahopata approached the patio. "Hi Bella! Would either of you be willing to keep score?"

"No way," said Bella emphatically.

"We're in charge here," responded Hoffman. "You guys go ahead and have fun."

With a disappointed expression, he returned to the cricketers.

Freeman returned to the patio with a carton of brown-bottled beverages, which he slipped one by one into an ice-filled cooler.

"Hi Cam, glad you could come. Want a drink?"

"Nah, maybe later. How's Claire?"

With an encouraging expression, Freeman answered, "She said she's feeling better. May come out here for a bit later on."

Taking over the grill, Freeman spouted, "So I've been thinking a lot lately about the turn our company is taking. With a baby on the way, I want to make the world a better place for her to grow up."

"Are you talking about the Artificial Intelligence?" Hoffman asked.

"Exactly," Freeman affirmed.

Then Brown blurted, "You know, whether or not it's lightning-fast or smart as hell, artificial intelligence is more artificial than intelligent."

Freeman continued his rant as he transferred portions onto a platter beside the grill. "Quantum computers can process oodles of material simultaneously. What if you put that type of computing power into a body?"

"You mean like a killer robot?" Brown asked. "Do you mean something similar to the killer robots in *Iron Man*? Or the *Terminator* series?"

With a nod, Hoffman affirmed, "I don't think there's a scientist alive who hasn't considered the historical impact of an invention that gets harnessed for military purposes."

Bella interjected, "I don't believe Wilbur and Orville Wright invented their airplane as an instrument of war, but the Wright brothers' biplane was subsequently purchased by the U. S. Government. In fact, they received a bonus when it was able to exceed forty miles per hour."

"Aerial reconnaissance," inserted Hoffman. "The innovation revolution-ized warfare from that point onward. Then they hit upon the idea of tossing out bombs."

"That's the kind of thing that worries me," said Freeman. "Almost all technically advanced countries in the world are working on these type of developments. There was a senior executive in a Chinese Defense firm who publicly stated that future wars will not be fought by humans. The increasing use of drone warfare in the 2020s proved that using lethal autonomous weapons is not only possible, but inevitable."

"There are positive repercussions as well," Hoffman argued. "People could be spared from physically-demanding, repetitive work in favor of jobs that require strategic, creative thinking. That may mean that people could gain more time to spend with their friends and families."

"Do you mean like the twentieth-century animated television series *The Jetsons*?" countered Bella. "The one in which George Jetson had a ten-hour work week? And a floating car?"

Freeman nodded. "Who knows what the future may hold?"

"But on a personal level, VIKI may go rogue and use us in an attempt to take over the government," Brown countered. "Like in the movie *Eagle Eye*."

"The new computer system doesn't have a name. Why do you call it VIKI?"

"Why not? If we're going to work with it, we will eventually slam some sort of moniker on it. It's called the ELIZA effect. There is often an innate human desire to find humanity in everything, much the same way you would talk to your cat."

With a sly grin, Freeman asked, "Bella, do you talk to your cat?"

With a playful shove, Brown clarified, "Don't pretend you wouldn't talk to an animal if you had one. I've crept into the design lab and heard you stage fake battles between your sci-fi model spacecrafts."

"That's different," said Freeman defensively. "But logically thinking, how intelligent can a computer grow without becoming sentient? In any case, if an AI should become sentient, it may lose the capacity to operate within the assigned perimeters."

Hoffman selected a burger and transferred it to a paper plate. "So you're saying the AI we need to fear is one without a moral sense of good or evil?"

Going for her vegetarian foil packet, Brown nodded. "I still believe we need to install a trip-wire failsafe. Or a kill switch. In case it goes rogue, you know."

Chapter 7

"You see, this is why we can't have nice things."

Shipyard manager Eireann Reid ripped a pair of virtual reality goggles off Abdul Khan's face.

Transfer of materials throughout Bertrand Station was accomplished by means of conveyor belts much in the same way it happens in airports on Earth. The conveyors were modular in the sense that materials could be directed to various areas of the station by modifying the configuration of the conveyors.

The astonished technician awakened to the realization that he had neglected to connect some of the components of the conveyor. Boxes filled with supplies shot off the unconnected end of the conveyor and piled up on the cargo bay's floor.

"I'm sorry, boss. It'll never happen again."

"What was it this time Abdul?"

With a sheepish expression, he admitted, "Sandbox VR. It's really a banger."

"If you're an action-adventure fan, that would be great activity for your off hours. Just not while you're on duty."

"I'm sorry, boss. I'll clean it up."

With her hands on her hips, Reid surveyed the pile of boxes on the cargo bay floor. "You bet you're going to clean this up. Let me know when you're finished. Then I'm going to relieve you of duty for one shift."

"I'm really sorry. It won't happen again."

"Yeah? If it does I'm going to send you back to Earth. Maybe you can find your niche playing VR video games down there. Up here, we have too much work to do for that sort of bullshit."

On the way back to the command center, Reid wished there was some way to determine whether technicians were accessing games on the Internet during shift time. She needed to find a way to curtail that sort of malarkey. Hopefully before someone made a worse mistake that killed them all.

Chapter 8

Sutton residence
Auckland, New Zealand
Late November, 2042

"Didn't anyone bring any Anzac biscuits? Or pineapple lumps?"

It was a calendar day for David Sutton. It was a Saturday, but not just any Saturday. With the first month of summer on the horizon, kiwis were looking forward to a monumental occasion. In addition to the holidays, this year there would be a World Cup preliminary match set in their own backyard.

The All-Whites, a New Zealand football team, were facing off against Chelsea, a prestigious British team in a Round 16 FIFA World Cup match. Although the game took place at Athletic Park in Wellington, Sutton had invited a crew of mates to watch a live pay-per-view on his super-large home view screen.

"No biscuits, but I brought a case of Lemon & Paeroa," said Ieohapata.

"Beauty," Dave remarked. "She'll be right."

"Did I miss it?" Noah Smith announced, showing up with a takeaway box of brisket and cheese sliders.

"We're on final countdown," said Sutton with a broad-sweeping gesture. "Come on in. Find a seat anywhere."

Last to arrive was Jim Freeman carrying an Instant Pot in one hand and a pastry holder in the other. "Hi, guys! I brought wings."

"My wing man!" Sutton rejoiced. "How's Claire?"

"She's holding on. Gained a few pounds, although every time she leaves the house she gets dizzy and nauseous. I thought I would come hang out for a bit. She sends her love."

A prime position on Sutton's couch was occupied by Ian Campbell, also a technician in the Rocket Lab shipyard. "Chelsea's going to be a fickle bitch to beat," he predicted. "Were you aware that Chelsea holds the record for the longest string of unbeaten matches at home in the English top-match?"

"Damn skippy — 86 matches from 20 March 2004 to 26 October 2008," countered Sutton.

"You cheated!" Campbell countered.

"Guilty as charged," admitted Sutton while mining additional Chelsea stats on his hand terminal.

Some of the guests argued whether or not Chelsea's away uniforms were appropriate. For the 2042 season, the color chosen for away uniforms was yellow.

The gathering itself, especially the hot wings, reminded Sutton of American days. Specifically, Super Bowl Sunday with friends gathered around the television. Ironically, this was a turning point in his life. One that would hopefully change his status from that of an American refugee to something more permanent.

"Hey, Jim, I've got something to show you."

Sutton jubilantly waved a sheaf of papers under Freeman's nose.

"Your New Zealand citizenship? Congrats, mate!"

"*Kia ora!*" said Ieohapata, raising a brown bottle. "Good on ya, mate!"

As New Zealand's footballers took their places on the pitch, Sutton's guests competed for the most strategic seats to watch the match. On the view screen, they watched Chelsea players taking their positions. For a moment, the camera focused on the antics of someone wearing a lion costume.

"How did you manage that?" Freeman wanted to know. "Citizenship, I mean."

"You mean you never checked into it? There are four ways to gain citizenship. Mine was by grant, based on the fact that I am gainfully employed, haven't committed any crimes and have been a resident for more than five years."

The room grew quiet. All eyes were on the view screen with team captains midfield for the coin toss.

"Chelsea is receiving!" Campbell announced.

After initial play was underway, Ieohapata spoke aloud. "I don't know how you blokes feel, but I think it's high time we had a World Cup round down here. Most preliminary rounds happen in the Northern hemisphere. Canada round is at BMO field in Toronto."

"There's going to be one in Qatar next."

"Yeah, my schedule says it will be at The Khalifa International Stadium."

"What's the location of the finals?"

Sutton tapped on his tablet. "It says the 2042 World Cup is to be held in late December at Estudio Azteca in Mexico City."

It was deep into play when a cheer erupted among the guests in Sutton's bungalow. The All Whites had slipped one past the Chelsea keeper.

"Cheers, mate!" said Sutton. "It's a good omen, that one."

"You know what I think?" asked Freeman. "You're starting to think of yourself as a New Zealander.

With a smile and a nod, Sutton agreed. "It's been that way for a while now."

"Are you still seeing Tino?"

Sutton's girlfriend Tino Aroha could tolerate sporting events in small doses. She had declined an invitation to watch a World Cup preliminary that could go on all afternoon.

With a sly grin, Sutton said, "Yeah, she's part of the equation. But there are advantages to citizenship. I recommend that you check into it."

"What advantages?" Freeman wanted to know.

"A higher security clearance. If the technology we are working on is a matter of national security, then it stands to reason that citizenship should afford a higher security clearance?"

Freeman thought for a moment, then countered, "Unless we ourselves are the source of said classified information."

"You may want to take another path to citizenship," said Sutton. "Perhaps

Claire would be willing to adopt you."

Freeman began to playfully pummel Sutton's arm, until he announced, "Oh, I forgot to tell you. Claire also managed a Bananas Foster cake."

That announcement instigated a scrimmage of sports fans who vied for position at the buffet sidebar.

Chapter 9

Inside the science of Exopolitics
Honolulu, Hawaii

The existence of a United Federation of Planets is a known fact. Unlike the Star Trek science-fiction alliance, however, its members does not include any Vulcans, Andorians or Tellarites.

During twenty years spent as an extraterrestrial military liaison, General Leonard Bardick had absorbed a wealth of knowledge about Earth's intergalactic neighbors. He was appointed to the position back in the 2020s by a secret subcommittee of the United States Congress. He was not, in any case, the only human with such knowledge.

Overlooking downtown Honolulu, the Bardick's historic home in the prestigious Pacific Heights district had been purchased early during his out-processing for retirement. After years of public life in Washington D.C., General Bardick appreciated the home's privacy; at the same time his wife Gladys enjoyed easy access to Honolulu's social circuit as well as proximity to shopping venues.

Before the American Apocalypse, the Bardicks had owned a home in New York as well as another residence in Bloomingdale within three miles of the capital building. As luck would have it, the Bardicks had been in Honolulu when their family and their other residences had been wiped off the map.

Their Honolulu household ran smoothly with the expertise of essential staff members that included their Greek chef Filipe Sanninikone.

Attired in a white chef's coat with double rows of buttons, Sanninikone knocked twice on the door frame of the general's office.

"I wanted to inquire about your dinner order," he asked. "Would you prefer fish? I can prepare some beautiful Kumu. Or perhaps steak?"

Bardick blanked his viewscreen while responding to the chef's request. "The beef for me, Felipe. Filet mignon wrapped in bacon. With a baked potato on the side."

"Sour cream or butter topping on your potato?"

"Both."

"Very good, sir. Do you plan to dine with Mrs. Bardick this evening?"

"I'm afraid that won't be possible as I have tons of work to finish up here in the office. Just bring it in here, if you don't mind."

"Service at the usual time?"

"That will be fine, Filipe."

Like other countries, the United States had appointed ambassadors whose purpose was to maintain positive relations with other nations. General Bardick's area of expertise was Exopolitics, which meant contact with an ambassador to Earth's neighbors who, by and large, could not be considered human.

The vast majority of humanity had been taught to deny the existence of extraterrestrial life. Exopolitics is a well-concealed paradigm which deals with the wide range of implications of extraterrestrial life. It is the domain of elite members of the Exopolitics Institute Strategy Committee that includes representatives from India, Hong Kong, the United States, Italy, Germany, South Africa, Spain, Australia and Canada. On October 15, 2009, the Institute defined Exopolitics as an interdisciplinary scientific field, with its roots in the political sciences, that focuses on research, education and public policy with regard to the actors, institutions and processes associated with extraterrestrial life, as well as the wide range of implications this entails through public advocacy and newly emerging paradigms.

Science-fiction fans are aware of the United Federation of Planets: a large coalition that at its peak included 350 member worlds spread over eight thousand light years. In order to qualify for membership, candidate worlds were required to embrace the principles of universal liberty, rights and equality.

The reality however, is that humans on Earth have not yet acquired the maturity to link arms and sing *Kum Ba Yah* with the extraterrestrials.

Retired head of Israeli military's space division Haim Eshed went public with the fact that Tel Aviv and Washington were in contact with a Galactic Federation of extraterrestrials. The ETs, however, advised them to keep the relationship as well as their existence under wraps.

"The UFOs asked us not to advertise that they are here, [because] humanity is not ready yet," said Eshed. " ... The aliens in the Galactic Federation say: wait, let the spirits calm first. They don't want us to have mass hysteria."

After the attack on the United States, and given his skill set, Bardick had once again been summoned to active duty. He was in agreement with Eshed's statement that the governments of Earth's nations had a long way to go before they reached galactic adulthood. Peace would be impossible with rival space programs such as Russia and China vying for superiority. In addition, there existed an unknown number of space programs in possession of reverse-engineered alien technology.

During the present period of planetary development, Earth remained under the sponsorship and supervision of Nordic extraterrestrials whose origin was from the stars that made up the constellation Pleiades. Historically, many of the technological achievements of the twentieth century had resulted from shared alien technology. The circuit board appeared suddenly and with no apparent evolution, as did lasers, fiber optics, cordless technology, remote controls and microchips.

This technology had all been provided under the terms of a treaty.

As a military official, Bardick was keenly aware of the consequences of breaking a treaty. U. S. officials had been warned to adhere to a strict schedule for the release of technological advances as well as obscure public knowledge regarding Unidentified Aerial Phenomena, formerly known as Unidentified Flying Objects. The U.S. had chosen to cast away the terms of the Human-Alien Alliance, in effect biting the hand that fed them. Whether or not they were the ones who pulled the trigger, the general was convinced that their former benefactors had sanctioned the October 13, 2035 annihilation of the United States.

After a multi-media campaign to wipe out the evidence, the vast majority of people on Earth believed the destruction of America resulted from the Yellowstone volcano. Members of the military, however, were familiar with the facts. With the U. S. annihilation in the rear-view mirror, it was a known fact the aliens possessed technology that could potentially wipe out the rest of humanity. It was Bardick's task to effectively represent Earth in extraterrestrial relations, hopefully without repeating the mistakes of the past.

Bardick had met with his Nordic liaison on multiple occasions. Lukas Berg seemed nice enough. Humanoid in appearance and tall—extremely tall—he had steel grey eyes and white-blonde hair. Berg lived on Earth, in fact in a sanctuary on Hawaii's largest island. His current assignment was to familiarize himself with Earth language and culture.

Bardick weathered military threats before, but he didn't want to witness another annihilation as serious as the destruction of continental United States. During a video call with Berg he tested the waters.

"Right now, we're not your worst nightmare," said Berg. "Not even close."

The Nordic ambassador described a new threat from the Cenos, an insectoid species that originated from Alpha Centauri.

"The Cenotians have locked their sights on Earth. The Federation is aware of their intentions and has attempted to intervene, but they have refused all attempts at negotiation."

Briefly, the general excused himself with, "I feel I'm at a disadvantage due to the fact I'm unfamiliar with this species. Let me do some research on them, Lukas. I'll call you back shortly."

During the next half hour, Bardick buried himself in a file on his computer with the title *Known Intergalactic Species*. From it, he familiarized himself with the Cenotians, an insectoid species with long legs, a brown or green exoskeleton and red compound eyes. Bardick noticed their close resemblance to Earth's praying mantis species. The writer of the article described them as six to seven feet in height. High-status Cenotian individuals wear black robes, however those of lesser rank are typically naked. Their method of communication is described as clicking noises, although their species is also known to communicate telepathically. Cenotians also possess the ability to shape shift, temporarily convincing witnesses that they are human. Technologically speaking, they are skilled space travelers with formidable weaponry.

In a short time, Bardick assessed that Earth was far outmatched by the Cenotians. He held no hope they would be able to defend against them—if and when they arrived.

A brief time later, Bardick again rung up Berg. On the screen, the general scowled while taking a few more sips of his Ancient Age whiskey. "Lukas, are you at all aware what the Cenotians are after? With their capabilities, they obviously have their pick of target species. What can they obtain from Earth that they can't get anywhere else?"

"I'm sorry, general. We have not been able to ascertain their motivations. Only that they are massing for an attack."

Following their conversation, Bardick rang for his personal assistant. Wearing a grey suit with matching teal shirt and tie, Richard Dalton reported to his office. As usual, his hair was recently cut and styled. Even his eyeglasses were top of the line.

"You need something, sir?"

"Yes, I need for you to lay out something for me to wear to a meeting tomorrow. I'm thinking the navy suit with a crisp white shirt and the red-and-blue striped tie."

"Do you want to pair with the Alessandro Demesure leather oxfords?"

"Obviously the black ones, not the brown. And I will need for you to arrange for the arrival of an Uber at the front door at 0830 sharp."

"Yes, sir. I'll make all the necessary arrangements."

The Exopolitical climate revealed storm clouds on the horizon. Bardick planned to deliver the information to the President of the United States in person and as quickly as possible.

With storm clouds on the horizon, he needed to get his own house in order.

Chapter 10

Bardick Residence
Pacific Heights neighborhood
Honolulu, Hawaii

"I don't have a single thing I can wear."

Wearing a short pink Versace robe, Gladys Bardick regarded her image in the mirror of her Pacific Heights boudoir. She scowled at the black sequined formal gown suspended from a clothes hanger held up against her somewhat rotund torso.

"This would have been perfect—if I were thirty years old, that is."

Standing at her elbow was a slim woman with Asian features wearing a simple white blouse and black skirt. In her arms she displayed two other hangers.

Gladys traded the black evening dress for a white pants suit offered by her personal assistant Su Lee.

"Su, what do you think about the white?"

Rather than looking her employer in the eye, she looked downward. She suppressed her own opinion, instead offering carefully considered comments based on what she felt her employer desired to hear. "Here in Hawaii, white is acceptable at any time of the year. The white ensemble enhances your features to best advantage. Also your eyes and hair."

In the months following the American disaster, Gladys had undergone a transformation of her own. One that she didn't necessarily like.

In the mirror, she scrutinized her own image as well as the preliminary

45

wardrobe options. Her hair, arranged in short waves, had recently been transformed with a treatment her stylist referred to as Silver Fox. Her blue eyes were framed by a deepening set of bags and crows feet. A face lift was rising to the forefront of her personal agenda, but the proximity of the upcoming gala event eliminated anything but a quick-fix cosmetic treatment.

She felt like anything but a silver fox.

A final option existed. A Robin's-egg blue Ann Taylor sheath dress passed under the scrutiny of Gladys' full-length mirror.

"If I were ten pounds thinner, maybe ..." Gladys swiveled her body covered by the dress to the left and then to the right. "My upper arms aren't in any shape for sleeveless exposure. Do you think you could find a jacket that would coordinate with the Ann Taylor?"

"I could coordinate, but it would be difficult to match exactly," Su replied truthfully.

"You're right," said Gladys, tossing the Ann Taylor atop a stack of wardrobe rejects on the bed.

Su began obediently gathering up the garments, returning an armful at a time to their places in the walk-in closet.

"The obvious solution is to order something completely new. Something uniquely suited to the occasion. An entire outfit that practically screams *Hawaiian luau.*"

When Su returned to the bedroom to retrieve more outfits, Gladys instructed, "You know what I mean, right? You're so good at coordinating ensembles. Of course I'll need shoes to match. Plus a purse—oh, and don't forget coordinating jewelry."

Su nodded. "I will make all the necessary arrangements."

Gladys' master suite the size of a small house was furnished with a cozy seating area brightened by leafy green and yellow upholstery. With a wave, Gladys took a seat and said, "You can put all those away later. Let's go over the checklist again."

"Where's my tablet? Oh, I put it here," said Su, rescuing her electronic device from the makeup vanity. She rested in a wicker chair facing her employer.

"Have you confirmed our appointment with the caterer?"

"Not yet. He can meet with us on the thirteenth or the fifteenth."

"Tell him to pencil us in for the fifteenth, then."

Regarding the calendar on her tablet, Su shook her head. "You already have a hair appointment on the fifteenth. Followed by mani-pedi. You want to cancel?"

"No, tell the caterer we'll meet on the thirteenth, then."

Gladys had never owned a computer, or even a hand terminal. It was thanks to her personal assistant's technological expertise that she was able to make the connections to organize her current project.

The American holocaust had left hundreds of people homeless. Seven years after that apocalyptic event, many survivors still struggled. Gladys visited with them in refugee camps, homeless shelters and on the streets of Honolulu. She had difficulty believing that despite living in one of the most beautiful tropical paradises on the planet, people could still be living in squalor.

Months ago, Gladys had commiserated the plight of the homeless during an afternoon tea at Temple Beit Shalom. Together, the women hit on a solution to host a fundraiser gala. Hopefully the proceeds from the event would be sufficient to improve the status of the refugees.

Spearheading the benefit had served to take Gladys' mind off the losses in her life. The American holocaust had robbed the lives of her four adult children, to say nothing of her five precious grandchildren. Although the billionaires previously owned several homes, the one in Honolulu was now their sole residence.

As if that weren't enough, she feared that her marriage was over. She and Lenny lived in separate wings of the house; led separate lives. And although they were billionaires, there were some things that all the money in the world couldn't fix.

Gladys spent her early life in New York. She logged a few decades with her husband in Washington, D.C. After the annihilation, their previous social and familial connections were lost. The whole continent had been converted into a wasteland now dubbed The Big Scorch.

She couldn't go back. Not even for a visit. No one could.

Chapter 11

Heading off a mass exodus
Rocket Lab Headquarters
Auckland, New Zealand

"It's been a difficult transition, but we'll have to see what happens when the chemistry settles."

Two months after the switch to quantum computing, Camillo Hoffman once again met with the CEO of Rocket Lab in his office. Brandon Kemp as usual was optimistic; Hoffman not so much.

"Is this a feeling you get?"

"No. Each member of the engineering team, individually or in groups, has clearly informed me in no uncertain terms that they are exploring other options. All of them."

"Even Bella Brown? I thought with her futuristic science-fiction predisposition that she would ..."

"Especially Bella. She persists in referring to the quantum computing system as VIKI. She keeps saying that the BORG are alive and well and poised to take over. She continually insists that we need to create and install a kill switch."

While speaking, Hoffman took the liberty of examining the sole memento on the table beside his seat. The kiwi statue was heavy, evidently designed to serve as some sort of paperweight. For the moment, it would serve as an effective representation of Rocket Lab's home base in New Zealand.

Kemp tilted his head upwards and checked out the suspended ceiling tiles.

"I recently installed an extra fire extinguisher under my desk. Do you know why?"

One of Hoffman's eyebrows arched quizzically. With a slight head tilt, he said, "No clue, sir."

"It's because I've been putting out fires every day for the past month. Every single department is struggling with this new system. Supply, accounts payable, personnel ... even the shipyard here on Earth. At first blush, no one likes change. But I'm convinced that if we push through the transition, it will be worth the effort."

Hoffman studied the carpet for a moment. "Not if all the engineers quit. Designing and building rockets is, in fact, our bread and butter."

"The new system bears benefits that have yet to be experienced. For example, I had to deliver a speech for a Chamber of Commerce meeting last week."

"I was unaware. Sorry I missed it. I'm certain you were well received."

Kemp's lips curled. There was a twinkle in his eyes as he revealed in a quiet voice, "Can you keep something under wraps? An Artificial Intelligence application wrote that speech."

With a sharp intake of breath, Hoffman burst out, "Seriously? I didn't know it could do that."

Kemp leaned back in his comfortable office chair for a moment, then said, "I have another AI revelation, and you're especially going to like this. But first, why do you believe the engineers want to walk away?"

"Because they've clearly told me they're unhappy. They're eventually going to quit, Mr. Kemp. They told me as much."

"No, that's not what I mean. I know they are dissatisfied, but why?"

"They feel that the AI-driven designs are taking liberties beyond the specified parameters. In addition, I figure they're bored. Their skills and talents are no longer coming into play. I guess what I want to say is they're not being professionally challenged."

"What if I had a new challenge for them? Each of them?"

It was now Hoffman's turn to lean forward in his seat. He whipped out his moleskin-covered notebook. "I'm all ears. Tell me more."

"It is my understanding that Jim Freeman excels in hull design?"

"That is correct."

"We have discussed the ever-present eventuality of meteor strikes. You and I also discussed the possibility of self-sealing hulls. You remember?"

Hoffman brightened, and said, "Yeah. As long as the area involved is fairly small. Say, pea-sized on up to bowling ball size. It's possible, we just haven't chosen to focus on that yet."

"They say necessity is the mother of invention. And, for safety's sake we definitely need to come up with something like that. Could you put Freeman to work on that project? I would love to see some prototypes that could be incorporated into our ship designs in the near future."

"I'll have to admit, Jim would likely need some help with that project."

"Whatever resources you need, you've got them. I'm sure any of the shipyard technicians would be willing to cooperate. And I have an idea for another innovation. We need some sort of refuge device that could save lives in the event of a catastrophic emergency."

"The AI can't design the escape pods?"

"If there's no precedent, this type of innovation would require human collaboration."

"Oh, I see."

"You have two staff members whose area of expertise is life support and ergonomics, is that correct?"

"Julie Stempler and Beth Sommerset."

"We have discussed the need for lifeboats on short-term space missions and the intra-orbital shipyard."

"Lifeboats?" Hoffman scratched his head. Then he brightened. "You mean the escape pods, don't you?"

"Miniature life-support pods that could allow personnel to escape in the event of a catastrophic failure. For instance, a meteor strike that's bigger than a bowling ball. It would provide life support until the refugees could be picked up. I'm thinking the target time for life support could be twenty-four to forty-eight hours?"

Hoffman scribbled furiously in his notebook at the same time acknowl-

51

edging, "I'll get them right to work."

"I have a brief for another project, whenever you're ready."

On the view screen, Hoffman recognized Jim Freeman's presentation designed for the Phoenix fleet's dedication ceremony.

Kemp opened a desk drawer to extract a device that Hoffman recognized as a combination slide clicker and laser pointer. With the aid of the pointer, Kemp described the scene depicted on the screen. "At the bottom of the screen here is Exoplanet Equinox. Above it is the *Phoenix* and her associated fleet of four other ships, remaining perpetually in geostationary orbit. And here is the space elevator, connecting them."

Hoffman watched as a compartment pictured on the space elevator cable descended to the planet's surface.

Kemp continued, "With our current mission, the space elevator is our only method to exchange goods and personnel between orbit and the planet."

Afterwards he rose and approached the view screen. With his elbow, he made a sweeping motion which in effect erased the space elevator.

"I've hit upon the realization that our space elevator is crap. It's very precarious. In the event of a major malfunction, the whole system shuts down. Does anyone besides me see a problem with that?"

Hoffman reluctantly nodded. His natural apologetic personality kicked in, as he had played a role in the design of the space elevator.

"I also wanted to show you why a propulsive starship landing is not the way to go, either."

Kemp clicked into a new presentation. "You see here a representation of the *Magellan*, SpaceCorp's starship designed for a propulsive landing on the planet's surface. Now watch this."

Under Kemp's direction, the *Magellan* animation descended from orbit towards the planet's surface, eventually kicking around to line up with the planetary surface. In preparation for landing, a propulsive plume shot out from the rocket's lower end which effectively slowed its descent. As the starship approached the planet's surface, the force of the plume hollowed out a trench in the surface below. Hoffman watched as the little animated rocket pirouetted before collapsing down on its side.

"Propulsive landing is also crap. We want to scrap that concept in the future. And if the *Magellan* had survived the jump to warp speed and the trip to Proxima Centauri, this is what would have happened. Either way, there would have been a catastrophic failure."

Hoffman frowned. "So either way, we're screwed. I'm guessing you want to go in a new direction?"

With a huge grin, Kemp clicked into a third presentation. "Now watch this," he said.

On the view screen, a representation of a giant mothership entered into an orbit pattern around the planet Equinox. From an open compartment in the ship, a tiny vessel emerged. It flew back and forth in space before descending gently down to the planet's surface.

"We need an anti-gravity shuttlecraft," said Kemp, placing his elbows on his desktop and lacing his fingers together. "I'm convinced it's the best way to go. We need something capable of delivering freight and personnel at will from our ships to the planet's surface."

"You want a small vessel that has dual capabilities? One that has the ability to navigate in space as well as make a descent to the planet? And go back up again?"

"We're looking beyond heavier-than-air flight."

Hoffman's eyes lit up.

"You're asking me for an anti-gravity vehicle?"

Brightening, Kemp nodded his head up and down. "You've got it. That's exactly what we need."

"You're asking us to research, develop and build a shuttlecraft. That is what you're asking, correct?"

Kemp held up two fingers. "We will need at least two of them, don't you think?"

With a blank stare, Hoffman voiced, "Mr. Kemp, you are aware, of course, that you are asking us for a miracle. Two miracles, in fact. Vessels that the quantum computer can't design or produce because it hasn't been done before."

"Your team has produced miracles before. And I'm convinced they will once again hit pay dirt. By the way, did you like the renderings?"

"Yes, very descriptive presentation. The animation was sharp and colorful."

Kemp shut down his tablet. Slid his chair back to the center of his desk, face-to-face with Hoffman. "I'm glad you liked it. VIKI put it all together. She's already been a huge time saver."

Chapter 12

Design Lab
Rocket Lab Headquarters

The head-and-shoulders image of an Asian woman appeared on the wall view screen in the Rocket Lab design lab. Endowed with British pronunciation, she quoted:

According to Wikkipedia, an escape pod, escape capsule, life capsule, or lifepod is a capsule or craft, usually only big enough for one person, used to escape from a vessel in an emergency. An escape ship is a larger, more complete craft also used for the same purpose. Escape pods are ubiquitous in science fiction but are only used in a few real vehicles.

"Until today," countered Beth Sommerset. "Hopefully, the escape pod prototype we design will soon become an accessory on all space stations or deep-space missions."

With a glance at Sommerset, Stempler added, "There was rumored to be an escape pod on Air Force One."

Julia Stempler, who headed up biometrics, and Beth Sommerset, whose area of expertise was ergonomics, rarely ventured up to the fourth-floor design lab that was usually the domain of team members Jim Freeman and Dave Sutton.

In addition to the computer stations, the lab contained eclectic décor with a common theme of flight design. The walls contained prints of the Wright Brothers and their 1903 Wright flyer on down to the 1981 United States Space Shuttle Columbia parked next to a design rendering of the *Phoenix*, the first warp-capable ship to leave the Sol system.

Members of the design squad were well aware that Freeman was a member of the New Zealand Model Aircraft Association. Shelves throughout the lab bore evidence of his expertise that included the *Millennium Falcon* from Star Wars, *Battlestar Galactica*, *Serenity* from the Firefly series and of course the *U. S. S. Starship Enterprise* from the original Star Trek television series.

"Welcome to the design lab?" The question in his voice revealed how unmistakably surprised Freeman was to see them enter.

"Hi, Jim, hi Dave," said Sommerset.

"We need to use some of your equipment," Stempler explained.

With a sweeping gesture, Freeman invited. "Not my stuff. Be my guest. *Mi casa es su casa.*"

"What are you guys working on?" Stempler asked. "We don't want to interrupt anything."

"Oh, it's no problem," said Freeman quickly. "We already have a design."

With disbelief in her voice, she asked, "So soon?"

"VIKI is already running test simulations," Sutton replied. "We're only monitoring. And trying to figure out possible scenarios and how the ship and crew will endure them."

With a snicker, Sutton remarked, "Dream it. Design it. Build it. And then try to break it. It's what we do."

"How can we help you?" asked Freeman helpfully. "Need to design a star ship?"

"No, a boat," explained Sommerset. At their confused expressions, she grinned and added, "A lifeboat. The escape pods that we talked about in budget meeting."

Freeman observed that both of the newcomer engineers were searching for a computer station. He instructed them to stand in front of the large view screen on which was displayed the Rocket Lab logo. "If you're looking for a keyboard, you won't need one. VIKI?"

The image of the Asian woman spoke. *How can I be of assistance, Dave?*

"I need you to help Julie and Beth with a project."

Fine. I'll need biometric verification. Please place your hand on the terminal.

Stempler and Sommerset in turn placed their hands on a tablet-sized surface near the desktop terminal.

The computer spoke in an unemotional tone.

Verifying Julia Stempler. Verifying Elizabeth Sommerset. Please proceed. How can I help?

With a look at Stempler, Sommerset stated her request. "We need to design escape pods for use in deep space emergency situations."

After quoting the Wikipedia definition of escape pods, VIKI played a recording of a scene in the 1997 film *Fifth Element*. Patrons of the flying hotel planet Fhloston took refuge inside escape pods that were ejected in response to an alleged bomb threat.

Do you wish to design a similar device?

"Yes," Sommerset confirmed.

What materials do you wish to use?

Sommerset had to scratch her head for a moment. "Hmmm."

She looked at Freeman, who volunteered, "It's your project. If it were me, I would start with a titanium mesh skeleton."

"Sounds good," said Sommerset. "Titanium mesh skeleton. All right, Mr. Hull Design expert, what should we put on the outside?"

"My first choice would be SPAM," was his answer.

"What??!!"

"It's an acronym," Freeman explained.

VIKI responded in a deadpan tone.

I am unable to ascertain what substances made up SpaceX Proprietary Ablative Material, also referred to as SPAM. I can provide a close approximation in your design. Incorporating a titanium mesh skeleton with an outer covering of amalgamate material. What capacity is the target for your escape pod?

"Let's go with a two-person size," said Sommerset. "VIKI, we need a design for an escape pod large enough for two adults. One hundred eighty pounds each."

Consulting her tablet, Stempler added, "Eighty-one point six four kilo-grams."

The Asian female's image contracted into a square at the side of the viewscreen.

All right. Here's a preliminary diagram.

The display on the view screen showed a diagram with two seats, one on each side of the compartment.

"Safety first," said Sommerset. "Add a three-point harness for each seat."

Sure. Here you go.

"I don't mean to intrude," said Freeman.

"What do you have, Jim?" asked Stempler.

"As far as hull design, you will need something strong enough to withstand conditions in deep space. That means outside you will have a negligible pressure, with an inside pressure of roughly 14.6959 pounds per square inch."

You are correct, Jim. I will make the necessary modifications to the design. Anything else?

"Are you going to put in a window?" asked Sutton.

With her hand on her hip, Stempler clarified. "Our assignment is to create an escape pod capable of sustaining life for twenty-four to forty-eight hours for use in the event of a catastrophic event. I don't think our refugees are going to be particularly interested in getting a bird's eye view of their space craft blowing up. And remember the Titan submarine that experienced a catastrophic implosion in 2023? They found out it was caused by a problem with the view port."

"OK, no windows," Sommerset verified. "The compartment will require sufficient filtration ... "

You are correct. Air filtration and purification will be required to allow humans to survive for twenty-four to forty-eight hours within a limited environment.

After a moment of thought, Sommerset continued.

"Let's assume we have the typical space environment, with outside temperatures that approach absolute zero. VIKI, can you provide mechanics that can keep the interior of the escape pod at a comfortable level?"

Of course. For healthy adults with adequate clothing, recommended settings would range between 18 and 24 degrees Centigrade, or 64 and 75 degrees Fahrenheit. For infants, elderly and those with significant health problems ...

Sommerset interrupted, "Maintain temperature settings between 18 and 24 degrees."

I have taken the liberty to include controls which will allow the occupants to modulate interior temperatures as well as the light settings.

"If I was inside one of these things for a prolonged period," Stempler began, "there would need to be a power source inside. Sufficient lighting and recharge ports that would allow them to use their tablets in there."

"Huh?" Sutton objected. "Their tablets?"

With a look at Sutton, Stempler confirmed. "Yeah. So they won't go crazy in the interim. They have to have something to do, right?"

Providing battery power for the occupants' use.

"Yes, sufficient for time period."

Tickety-boo, VIKI remarked.

As the AI made the changes, the engineers could observe modifications being added to the design diagram.

Sutton tapped Stempler on the shoulder. "What about propulsion?" he asked. "The refugees may need to escape to a safe distance."

With a little sigh, she acknowledged the need. "VIKI, add a propulsion system that would allow the escape pod to eject from the original vehicle to a distance of one kilometer."

Installing a limited-distance propulsion system. Parking jets only.

Sommerset made a face, then added, "VIKI, add an emergency beacon. Give the escape pod the capacity to send a shout-out that will alert any possible rescuers of their position."

With only a split-second of pause, VIKI affirmed, *Including electromagnetic wave transmitters in the design. Encoded transmission of distress messages will be sent on specified bands of communication automatically triggered by the pod's departure from the main vehicle.*

"Anything else?" asked Freeman.

With a sigh, Sommerset said, "VIKI, make sure the seat is comfortable. If they're going to be in it for more than a few hours, make sure it doesn't chap their asses."

VIKI's response was, Sure. According to SeatGuru, all airline seats are not created equal. Including recliner-cradle aircraft seats with three-point harness.

With her arms folded across her chest, Stempler said, "The only thing I want to know is, where is the *Print* button? Make it happen."

With what the designers perceived as an annoyed tone, VIKI said, *I can't do that.*

Regarding the design on the screen, Freeman assessed, "It's pretty amazing, isn't it? Big time-saver on design. The rest of the process, however, is pretty normal. Probably be easier to build the prototype out in the shipyard and then launch it out to the intra-orbital shipyard for testing."

"That's our plan," Stempler assured him.

Chapter 13

Rocket Lab boardroom
Auckland, New Zealand

With her brown hair gathered into a high ponytail, Bella Brown stood at the front of the Rocket Lab boardroom wearing her first-season Star Trek uniform: a red and black scoop-necked mini dress with black stockings and boots. In fact, her choice of wardrobe was conducive to a study of their current focus: the science of anti-gravity.

Brown's position on the Rocket Lab engineering team was research manager. Today she was slated to inform the team members of her findings when she poked about to discover definitive evidence that anti-gravity technology is not a new science. In fact, far from it.

As an introduction to the day's topic, she had brought along her personal 1/32 scale model of the *Galileo*, the anti gravity shuttlecraft from the first season of the science-fiction series Star Trek. Inside were seven small figurines representing the bridge crew of the Starship Enterprise. The vehicle's identification was NCC-1701/7.

Camillo Hoffman had known Bella Brown since 2035, as she was an original member of Rocket Lab's second engineering team. With a photographic memory and a keen understanding of both science and science fiction, she was unusually confident in presenting facts, dates and history. But today, if he didn't know better, Hoffman would have sworn that she was nervous about something.

"Bella, are you all right?"

"Yeah, I'm fine," she asserted.

Around the board table were the other members of the Rocket Lab team: Julie Stempler, David Sutton, Beth Sommerset and Jim Freeman. Each possessed a set of specialized knowledge and experience that provided valuable assets to the design and launch facility.

"Just in case you didn't know, Bella is going to give us some information regarding anti-gravity vehicles," Hoffman said.

Brown dived straight into it. "Of course as you can see, this is the *Galileo*. We're going to start with the Star Trek version, since it does exactly what we are attempting to do. It is named for Galileo Galilei, an Italian astronomer and scientist who lived in the 1500s and is considered as the father of modern science. The *Galileo* was built for short trips in space, such as a commute between a ship in orbit to a planetary surface."

"That was before the transporter came into common usage?" Sommerset asked.

"Uh huh. The crew of the *Enterprise* used it during the first season," affirmed Brown. "The set model was 23 feet, or seven meters, long and 1.7 meters high. You couldn't stand up in it that is, unless you were under five-and-a-half feet tall. In 2013, the original restoration of the life sized spaceship prop from the 1960s science-fiction television series was moved to the visitors' center at NASA's Johnson Space Center in Houston."

Hoffman stood up and said, "Apologies, Bella. All of you haven't had the chance to become aware of our current assignment. If it's not too big of an interruption, I would like to give some clarification of what we have been asked to do."

Brown seemed happy to give up the floor for a moment.

Hoffman located the file he first viewed in Kemp's office on his tablet. With a single sweep, he transferred it to the view screen. Before them was pictured the conjoined Phoenix fleet above a yellow planet. In the distance was the Proxima Centauri red dwarf star. "Before you is an illustration of our Phoenix fleet in its geostationary orbit above Proxima Centauri B, a planet we dubbed Equinox," he said. "Between the planet and the ships is our space elevator, which our settlers currently depend on to move freight and passengers from orbit to the planetary surface."

Julia Stempler asked, "Jim's diagram, I presume?"

"It's the representation they showed at the *Phoenix* dedication," he said, crossing his arms across his chest.

Wiping his elbow across the view screen, Hoffman erased the space elevator. "As you know, we are planning a return trip-slash-resupply mission to the planet. At this point, we want to improve our method to transfer freight and passengers to the planetary surface via an anti-gravity vehicle."

Hoffman continued, "The space elevator is a time-limited technology. In a future mission, we plan to include cargo bays in the design of our new warp-drive vehicle. By including anti-gravity shuttlecraft—more than one, hopefully—we offer a more reliable method to transfer goods and passengers to the planet's surface. Hopefully, we can work together to come up with vehicles that would answer this need."

Beth Sommerset and Dave Sutton exchanged a look. "Standard propulsion is a concept that works against gravity. An anti-gravity vehicle," explained Sutton, "would incorporate a technology that would, when applied to an item or place, allow it to cancel gravity rather than compensate for it."

"May I proceed?" Brown asked, to which Hoffman made a sweeping gesture.

"Please continue," he said.

"By the way, Bella, were you able to discern what type of propulsion or forces were behind the science-fiction shuttlecraft?" Sutton wanted to know.

"As you are aware, the concept of an anti-gravity spaceship drive doesn't actually exist. Officially," she added. "According to *The Star Trek Encyclopedia* by Michael Okuda and Denise Okuda the *Galileo* used highly pressurized mercury accelerated by nuclear energy to produce a plasma that creates an anti-gravity field around the ship. Conventional thrusters positioned at the tips of the craft theoretically allowed it to perform complex, rapid high-speed maneuvers along all three axes."

Although it wasn't his presentation, Sutton couldn't resist breaking in. After all, propulsion was his area of expertise. "Gravity and electromagnetism are linked phenomenon. If you could in fact control gravity or inertial forces, you would have a propulsion breakthrough. Thrust without rockets, so to speak. It would mean a way to create synthetic gravity environments for space crews in addition to a means to create zero-gravity environments here on Earth."

"Whoa, you're running way ahead of us," cautioned Hoffman. "Let Bella have the floor."

In front of the boardroom view screen, Bella took a deep breath and then pressed on. "I uncovered multiple references to the use of anti-gravity technology in the past. So the question is not whether it exists, but which path is the most desirable?

"UFOs that employ anti-gravity technology existed in ancient times, as documented by the Madonna of the UFO." Brown explained, "During the Florentine Renaissance, an artist by the name of Domenico Ghirlandaio is credited with painting the Madonna and Child with the infant St. John during the 15th century. Check out this strange painting and decide for yourself whether you think the object is of alien origin."

Exclamations of shock and surprise met the ancient painting that included a background image that resembled a flying saucer.

"As you can see here, we have multiple historical witnesses that anti-gravity technology is nothing new," Brown continued.

As Brown spoke, the slideshow kept pace with her narrative.

"While the entire modern world promotes the idea that the Wright Brothers were the pioneers of aviation, there are images of ancient flying saucers contained within ancient Egyptian hieroglyphic carvings. "There exist ancient documents that point to the fact that ancient civilizations were familiar with the concepts of levitation and anti gravity. In many parts of the world there exist enormous monoliths that no modern, advanced crane of our era could raise. How do you think the pyramids of Egypt were built? Or the stonework at Machu Picchu? In addition, ancient writings from India point to the existence of flying vehicles called *Vimanas*. References to flying chariots or flying palaces are common in ancient Sanskrit texts. As you see in this slide, there are bas-relief sculptures depicting strangely-shaped vehicles flying through the air. In fact, United States NASA program purchased a translation of the ancient Sanskrit manuscript *Vymaanika-Shaastra*, or, in English, the Science of Aeronautics. This book produced certain mind-boggling details of construction, engine mechanics, gyroscopic systems and such that are commonly presumed to be developed much later in aviation development. The pilots were referred to as *Rahasya gnyanadhikari*—sorry, I'm probably butchering that pronunciation—with a rough translation as *he who has the secret knowledge of flying.* Thirty-two proprietary secrets were contained in the training manual for pilots."

"Bella, I suppose you didn't have sufficient time to procure a copy of these translations?" Hoffman broke in.

"No," she said sadly, then brightened. "NASA actually undertook an experiment of construction of mercury vortex engines very similar to those described in *Vymaanika- Shaastra*. According to the book, *Vimanas* possessed the ability to become lighter than air and therefore could levitate and travel freely through the atmosphere. There were many different types of *vimanas*. Some could travel from country to country; others from planet to planet. Eight chapters in the book deal with the secrets of indestructible aircraft that cannot be broken, cut or burned."

"Do you know if the United States ever did anything else with those plans?" asked Sommerset.

"The U. S. military was rumored to have five flying saucers reverse engineered from alien technology," Jim Freeman broke in. "You guys know that I'm from Ohio, right? They conducted secret experiments in a special restricted area at Wright-Patterson Air Force Base in Dayton. The National Archives and Records administration holds records including the Avrocar, initially intended to be a vertical takeoff and landing vehicle that could travel at speeds up to Mach 4. Its saucer shape and ability to levitate would remind you of a flying saucer."

"If it goes up and goes down on a consistent basis, then that aligns with our needs," Hoffman commented.

With a glum expression, Freeman added. "Their initial efforts weren't entirely successful. When Wright-Patterson didn't succeed in perfecting the concept, they handed it over to Canada's Avro Aircraft Limited. According to their narrative, it never succeeded in getting above a height of about three feet and speeds that never consistently exceeded 35 miles per hour."

In an attempt to steer the conversation back to the topic at hand, Hoffman asked, "Bella, didn't you tell me that the Nazis built flying saucers?"

"Yes," she replied. "There were some UFO sightings during World War II, particularly of the sort referred to by witnesses as foo fighters. They were thought by the Allies to be prototype enemy aircraft. According to descriptions, they measured 72 meters across and contained a crew of 32. The Nazi craft could achieve speeds of 7,000 to 40,000 kilometers per hour, could also fly in space and stay in the air for 55 hours. The mysterious Nazi Flying Bell is rumored to have allowed the Third Reich to visit the Moon, Mars and even distant star systems by making use of an unexplained, gravity-defying propulsion system. According to conspiracy theory legends, that is."

"Any photos, plans? Witness testimonials?" asked Hoffman hopefully.

"No, all the evidence probably destroyed just before or during the Nuremberg Trials."

"You got anything else?"

Brown continued. "Serbian-American inventor, futurist and mechanical engineer Nikola Tesla, who lived from 1856 to 1943, claimed to have discovered the secrets of anti gravity. He is best known for his contributions to the design of the modern alternating current electricity supply system. Tesla aimed to create the ultimate flying machine, powered by energy that is found all around us. In 1928, Tesla registered patent number 1,655,144 for a flying machine that looked like a cross between a helicopter and an airplane."

Brown clicked to another slide including a blueprint diagram of the classic flying saucer sort including interior mechanics.

"Bella, can you describe the mechanics of this diagram?"

"I can probably get you as deep in the weeds as you want to go."

Brown had the engineers' full attention. Sutton whipped out his tablet and proceeded to take photos of the view screen while Hoffman scribbled furiously in his ever-present notebook.

"Tesla believed that there is no energy in matter other than that received from the environment. During the infancy period of heavier-than-air flying vehicles, he hoped to create the ultimate flying saucer—a vehicle that would utilize electromagnetic fields which would allow his invention to travel upwards from the ground to the sky with extreme speed and facility."

With a skeptical expression, Hoffman asked, "The important question to consider is whether or not Tesla's designs were built and were functional?"

"There is no evidence to prove that he actually succeeded; however during his lifetime Tesla was extremely close to achieving his goal. He performed numerous tests and experiments by applying high-voltage, high-frequency alternating current to objects. In one of his tests, when he applied high-voltage high-frequency alternating current to a pair of parallel metal plates, he noticed that the space located between the plates turned into what he called *solid-state*. This means that the area located between the plates exhibited attributes of mass, inertia and momentum, transforming the area into a state where a mechanical push could be exerted.

"In his last lectures, Tesla described revolutionary propulsion system that would use the ether's force to mobilize objects. Although many people of the early 20th century thought him a mad scientist, Tesla discovered that powerful electromagnetic waves could be used to push against — or pull away from —what appears to be empty space. The drive principle is based on the Hall-effect used in semiconductor magnetic sensors, and is called the magnetohydrodynamic, or MHD effect."

"Tesla discovered that the electrostatic emission surface of a conductor will always concentrate where the surface is curved, or where it has an edge. The steeper the curve, or corner, the higher the concentration of electron emission is. His experiments revealed that an electrostatic charge will flow over the surface of a conductor rather than penetrate it. This is referred to as the Faraday Effect or skin effect discovered by Michael Faraday."

Hoffman once again broke in. "Where are Tesla's scientific notes and papers now? If we wanted to review copies, would that be possible?"

"There was a thick black notebook with several hundred pages that went missing immediately after his death January 7, 1943," Brown answered. "It was never located."

"Do you think the Nazis ever spoke with Tesla?" Sutton asked.

Brown shook her head. "No way to tell." With a humerus eyebrow wiggle, she added, "No way to determine whether the United States government was ever interested in Tesla's investigation into a death ray."

"Death ray?" asked Sommerset with incredulity.

With a palm held to the side of his face, Hoffman shook his head. Yet another rabbit trail had cropped up.

"He was into all sorts of stuff ranging from free electricity for all to particle beam weaponry," related Brown. "Copies of Tesla's papers on particle beam weaponry were sent to Jim's old neighborhood: Patterson Air Force Base in Dayton, Ohio. An operation code-named *Project Nick* was heavily funded and placed under the command of Brigadier General L. C. Craigie to test the feasibility of Tesla's concept. A project that was later discontinued, or so they said."

Directing a roomful of brilliant people was similar to herding cats, as Hoffman had discovered. The trick was to entice the cats to go in the desired direction without scaring them off.

"We're getting seriously off-topic," Hoffman warned, making a steering motion. "What we all want to know is whether or not anyone in recent history was successful in harnessing anti gravity technology. If so, we want to see the evidence."

Brown nodded. "Of course. You will be pleased to know that in 2019, the U.S. Navy was granted a patent for an advanced aircraft which resembles a flying saucer UFO. Military inventors utilized complex technology to reduce the aircraft's mass and thereby lessen inertia so it can zoom along at high velocities."

"Sounds like we've figured out where Tesla's scientific notes went," Stempler smirked.

Brown continued. "The patent describes a UFO-style craft that uses the generation of gravity waves that can be used in water, air or even outer space."

The large view screen displayed blueprint diagrams for the U.S. Navy patent.

"As you can see, the patent craft features a cavity wall filled with gas, which is then made to vibrate using powerful electromagnetic waves. This then creates a vacuum around the craft, enclosing it in a vacuum plasma bubble/sheath. The hybrid craft would be able to move with great ease through air, water or space."

Hoffman whistled and pointed at the screen. "Put in an order. I want two of those."

Sutton's mouth dropped open. "Me too. I didn't realize anyone had gotten this close."

"Unless..." Sommerset began. "the technology was lost when the United States was destroyed."

Hoffman shook his finger at her. "Negative Nancy! If the United States built it, then five other nations have probably succeeded in copying the technology by now." Turning to Brown, he said, "Great job, Bella. See if you can get any more information on patent applications. Diagrams and blueprints would be great; working models would be even better."

"I'll get right on it."

After some of the engineers had already dispersed, Hoffman muttered to Brown, "And if you need to pay out any bribes, I will need an itemized budget."

Brown swallowed hard, then said, "I'll keep you informed."

Chapter 14

Rocket Lab Boardroom
Auckland, New Zealand

"Bella missed a spot."

"Or two," acknowledged Bella Brown.

First thing on a Monday morning, Rocket Lab engineering team assembled once again to drool over tenable evidence regarding the use of anti-gravity technology.

Leading the discussion, project manager Camillo Hoffman shared startling information regarding innovation and use of anti-gravity technology leading from the 1950s up to the twenty-first century.

"Bella got us started in the right direction," he said with a smile at Brown, who wore a a sheepish expression.

"But I was unable to dig up any plans we could use. Or prototypes upon which we could base our designs," she apologized.

With a flourish of his finger on his tablet, Hoffman located a photo on his tablet. There were multiple intakes of breath when an image came to life on the boardroom view screen.

Julia Stempler tilted her head to regard the grainy black-and-white photo pictured a circular disk of a shape and size conforming to classic UFO descriptions.

"It looks like a flying saucer," she observed.

"It is," Hoffman affirmed. "I believe human being-operated anti-gravity vehicles were behind many reported sightings of Unidentified Aerial Phenomenon during the twentieth century.

"Reverse-engineered alien technology?" Beth Sommerset wanted to know.

"Let's back up for a moment and get the whole picture," Hoffman continued. "If you will grant me a few moments of your time, I'll try to give you a complete education on this suppressed technology."

Sommerset's curiosity was about to burst. "American technology? Kept under wraps?"

Hoffman clicked to the next slide. Above the caption Otis T. Carr (1904-1982) was pictured a middle-aged man in glasses wearing a dark suit with white shirt and tie.

"Otis Carr — wasn't he Nikola Tesla's prodigy?" Brown asked.

"Yeah," Hoffman affirmed. "I guess now we figured out where Tesla's papers and diagrams went. The most important information we need to obtain are plans and technology used to create anti-gravity vehicles. Now we have those plans. We have a paper trail, photographs, diagrams, eyewitness accounts and ..."

"What else, Cam?" asked Bella.

"We have a money trail. Have you ever heard of black budget?"

"Yeah," affirmed Dave Sutton. "In the early 2000s, the American public was made aware that a portion of the federal budget was outside of Congressional oversight."

"The overages were publicly blamed on wasteful military spending," said Jim Freeman.

"That wasn't the whole picture," said Hoffman. "A Michigan State University working with a former secretary from the Department of Housing and Development along with a team of PhD students tracked down approximately $21 trillion USD that went missing and unaccounted for from the Department of Defense and the Department of Housing and Development."

"Holy shit!" burst Freeman. "How did they conceal $21 trillion?"

Hoffman continued, "They discovered that the diverted money was used to fund government black budget projects, off the books, with no Congressional oversight. These black budget projects were ongoing for many years."

"I can see where this is going," said Sommerset. "Unlimited funding used to produce secret technology that could be exploited for nefarious uses."

"Political money laundering," countered Stempler.

Hoffman nodded and took a sip from his ceramic mug. "You guessed it. One of the avenues of exploration were efficient energy-generating devices that could eliminate the use of oil, or any fuel source for that matter. In the 1970s, patents for solar photovoltaic generators were suppressed due to a potential national security threat."

Sommerset crossed her arms over her chest and huffed, "Free energy isn't a threat to national security. It's a threat to the energy industry. Coal and oil corporations are big business and subsequently wield a great deal of power."

With a steering motion, Hoffman said, "Let's segue back to the topic at hand. This guy Otis Carr took up where Tesla left off. Carr catapulted into the public eye when he founded OTC Enterprises in 1955 in Baltimore, Maryland." Hoffman clicked to the next slide. On it was a clipping of a Baltimore Enterprise newspaper article documenting Carr's declaration that his company was making preparations to build a flying saucer capable of traveling outside the Earth's atmosphere. "Carr went public with his plans, stating he needed $20 million in funding."

Sutton wondered aloud, "I'm curious whether or not this flying saucer built by Carr's company was capable of achieving his claims."

Hoffman shrugged wistfully. "We may never know. Federal agents claimed that Carr's project would bring about the ruin of the monetary system of the United States. The Feds confiscated all his equipment in addition to any documentation that existed. In 1961, Louis J. Lefkowitz, the Attorney General of New York, accused Carr of swindling his investors out of $50,000 USD."

Now it was Freeman's turn to cross his arms. "Obviously, the United States government would have benefited from a strategic invention that had the potential to put them head and shoulders ahead of their enemies. I don't understand why they blocked Carr's research, though."

At that point, Hoffman voiced his own theory. "If he was a crackpot, I don't think they would have bothered with him. I think they only shut him down at the point at which he achieved a level of scientific development from which they could benefit. Such developments are reserved only for the black budget world. Carr was convicted and denied an appeal for his alleged crimes. He served a fourteen-year jail term. His craft never flew again."

"That we know of," muttered Stempler bitterly.

"Nepotism," Sommerset proposed. "Cronyism. Carr didn't have the right pedigree. Or know the right people."

"Tesla claimed that he was using alien technology," said Stempler. "I wonder whether Carr was in possession of any alien tech?"

Hoffman countered, "Whether or not the aliens had anything to do with it, the United States government wanted this type of research kept under their control and at the same time under wraps."

It was Bella's turn to voice her own opinion. "The global elite had always promoted their own superiority by ridiculing concepts they don't want made public. Extraterrestrials, for example. There is no denying that anti-gravity technology has been around for a long time. Although public research activity seemed to disappear by the mid-1950s, reported scientific findings and technology show that the technology is alive and well and is, in fact, very advanced."

With a nod to Brown, Hoffman acquiesced. "I know you're holding back something."

With a twinkle in her blue eyes, Brown acknowledged. "Damn skippy."

With a gesture, Hoffman surrendered the view screen.

At Brown's coaxing, a text document appeared on the viewscreen. She subsequently narrated, "Patent #6,960,975 was granted November 1, 2005 to Boris Volfson of Huntington, Indiana. It describes a space vehicle propelled by a superconducting shield, which alters the curvature of space-time outside the craft in such a way that it counteracts gravity. The device builds on a claim by Eugene Podkletnov, a Russian physicist, who avowed that superconductors can shield the effects of gravity."

With a smile on his face and a wiggle of his eyebrows, Hoffman alleged, "Bella, please tell us that you have evidence of a flight-capable prototype."

"You read my mind," she said, clicking to another text document.

"The U.S. Navy filed a patent for a hybrid craft they called an inertial mass reduction device. The craft was actually approved in 2018 with credit for the invention given to Salvatore Cezar Pais. In January 2019, Pais published a paper named *Room Temperature Superconducting System for Use on a Hybrid Aerospace Undersea Craft* that would provide the means for powering this hybrid craft. The inventor himself warned that *the achievement of room temperature superconductivity represents a highly disruptive technology, capable of a total paradigm change in science and technology.*"

Pointing at the screen, Jim Freeman burst, "Now that's something we can use."

Brown had accumulated energy — nervous energy that had to break out in one way or another. She stood and paced up and down the elongated end of the boardroom table.

"It never ceases to amaze me that the topic of anti-gravity is thrown into the conspiracy theory bin," she said. "In reality it isn't a fringe science; rather it's the domain of reputable scientists and inventors."

"I did a little poking around on my own," said Jim Freeman. "In the 2020s, there were as many as a dozen companies who produced prototypes for supposed anti-gravity vehicles. Some of them were hybrid vehicles that could operate on the road as well as in the air. They were electric vehicles that could fly anywhere from one hundred forty to four hundred kilometers on a single charge. A few were more like helicopters or quad copters but some used actual anti-gravity concepts. Advertisements focused on the vehicles' ability to eliminate the problems of fossil fuels as well as inner-city traffic."

With a glance at Freeman, Sutton interjected, "I've seen photos and read about the one that looked like a fat Tic Tac."

"The point I wish to make is that it can be done because it has been done," Hoffman announced. "At this point, we have credible witness testimony. We have photos, plans and more than one patent. Do you have enough information to convince you that the science is real?"

"Fair dinkum," said Dave Sutton.

Sommerset echoed, "She'll be right."

Brown remained standing.

Hoffman cued the Phoenix logo to return to the view screen.

"Do we have sufficient evidence of anti-gravity technology?"

Several voices murmured their assent.

"Do we have enough information to determine how the system works?"

"Not only photographs, but patent diagrams," affirmed Jim Freeman. "We know what materials to use as well as the configuration of essential components."

Pointing in the direction of the door, Hoffman issued a charge.

"Ladies and gentlemen, let's go build a shuttlecraft."

With his tablet tucked under his arm, Dave Sutton said, "Find the secret sauce and then work like stink."

Chapter 15

Temple Beit Shalom
Honolulu, Hawaii

The noonday sun shone through a sliding glass door in the community room of the reformed synagogue where twenty-three women chatted over the remains of a catered salad luncheon.

"You're finished, ma'am?"

"Thank you," Gladys said to a white-coated woman who was in the process of collecting glass plates.

Naomi Kaplan's tan skin contrasted with her pink blouse. Golden curls spilled onto her neck from a delicate scarf ponytail binding.

"Ladies, ladies," she announced, tapping on her empty water glass with a fork. In response to the sound, the wave of conversation immediately died down.

"First of all, I would like to welcome everyone who came out and braved this intense weather."

At this comment there was polite laughter. The majority of them had vivid memories of snow and ice that prevailed during the winter months over the continental United States. Below-freezing temperatures were expected, especially in the northern states. On sunny Oahu, however, daytime December temperatures currently were 81 degrees F, with an expected dip into the sixties at night. Nothing a light sweater couldn't remedy.

Kaplan continued, "As you are well aware, during today's meeting we will review our tzedakah. Rivkah, that's over to you."

Rivkah's silver hair was arranged into a bun at the nape of her neck. She slowly arose before retrieving a pair of reading half-glasses which she perched on the end of her nose to regard a document on her tablet.

"During the past quarter, we delivered a total of 433 kits," she read from a tablet. "The breakdown is 181 hygiene kits, 86 farm worker kits, 63 infant and 103 school kits. We will continue to collect items for the school kits, as they will be necessary for the second semester. Most needed item for the school kits is the one-subject, spiral-bound notebooks. They are in short supply and in addition, the prices have gone up considerably. If you don't like to shop and would prefer to donate coin, you can do that and we will handle all the shopping."

"Why don't they do their assignments exclusively on their tablets?"

All eyes turned to the back of the room where the comment was made. Wearing a teal hibiscus sheath dress, Miriam Schneider continued, "As we all know, the schools use electronic tablets in order to eliminate the use of paper. It's better for the environment, you know."

While Kaplan looked flustered, Gladys Bardick could no longer restrain herself.

"We are talking about refugees, Miriam," she explained. "They are homeless, which means they don't have tablets either. However, if you wish to purchase electronic tablets for these students, that would mean another project entirely. And if they live in tents, I wonder where they will charge them? Hmmm?"

Gladys' comment cued low conversation breaking out in a couple of different places throughout the room. Perhaps unfortunately, she overheard one of the comments that were made.

"Next she'll be taking them home with her, naming and feeding them."

Gladys scowled. Her first impulse was to lash out at the ignorant women who were unaware of the refugees' plight. Comparing them to the hoards of stray animals that hung out behind seafood restaurants. Instead, she took a deep breath and raised her hand.

Chairwoman Kaplan glanced at Schneider to ask, "Are you finished with your report, Rivkah?"

With a positive indication, Kaplan nodded and asked, "Gladys, you have something to say?"

Gladys stood, cleared her throat, and regarded the women in the room.

"It's one thing to throw coins into a tzedakah box. In the spirit of tzedakah, however, it is better to make contact with those less fortunate than ourselves. Put a face to their needs, so to speak. I have not only visited the refugee camp, there are some whom I consider my friends."

As she spoke, she overheard more whispered comments. Kaplan took charge with a stern, "Ladies, Gladys has the floor."

With a nod to Kaplan, Gladys continued. "First of all, I would like to ask any of you to raise your hand if you live in a home with a roof that doesn't leak."

Virtually everyone in the room raised their hand.

"Margaret, we are keenly aware of your current situation with your additions and renovations."

With a sour expression, the woman identified as Margaret added, "Yes, and we are putting in a new HVAC system. Our air conditioning wasn't working so we had to move into a hotel."

With a sympathetic nod, Gladys said, "We feel your pain. At the same time, I want to share a short story with you. As you know, I make frequent visits to one of the refugee camps. I have friends there. One of the camp residents by the name of Paula Gonzalez happened to be here on vacation in October, 2035."

The room fell silent as all were aware of the implications of the infamous date.

"Paula's husband Antonio was a software engineer. She was a stay-at-home mom. To celebrate their twentieth anniversary, they left their two children in California with her mother and flew here for a much-needed, week-long vacation. Paula and Antonio lost more than their home and their bank account. Their children, parents—every single member of their family was gone." She snapped her fingers. "In one day."

Gladys paused for a minute to let that sink in.

"Want to know what hard-working, college-educated professionals have been doing since the American holocaust? Want to know why they are still living in a camp? They started out staying in the shelters. As you are aware, the homeless shelters have limitations on the amount of time patrons can stay. Most of them kick you out after 30 days. Paula and Antonio hired themselves out. Paula has worked continuously since then. Right now, she is a waitress at a restaurant near the camp. Antonio is a farm worker. That's right, a software engineer is now a farm worker because the island has more people wanting to work than it has jobs. That goes for a number of native Hawaiians as well. Want to know why they are still in the refugee camp at this point? None of the banks will give them a loan on a house, as they are living hand-to-mouth. There are more people wanting to rent than available apartments, plus the rent is astronomical. They would prefer to buy a home, however they don't have what it takes for a down-payment. Certainly nothing to offer as collateral. They have been working and saving coin the entire time, hoping to buy a pre-fab home. Or a tiny home. Or maybe a house trailer, if they can afford it."

She paused again, then punched, "From a ten-room home in an up-scale California neighborhood to a tent. They have no home to renovate. No electricity, no running water. And certainly no air conditioning. And I forgot to mention, for now, they are still sleeping in a tent on a cot."

There was dead silence in the room. A pause only broken by the chair, who said, "According to my calendar, we have only three months until the gala to benefit the refugees. Gladys, would you like to give your report on the ongoing preparations?"

Haunted by the reality of the refugees, Gladys returned to her home in Pacific Heights, one of Oahu's richest neighborhoods. It was conveniently located between Honolulu and the east side of the island. As Gladys made her way home, she considered the huge upward climb, geographic as well as financial, from the refugee camp to her neighborhood.

Although some of the richest people on the island lived in her neighborhood, the older twelve-room, ranch-style home where the Bardicks lived could not be considered by anyone as a mansion. Still, the front of the house overlooked a calm, turquoise bay below where swimmers could be seen every day. In the early morning, if you were patient you could catch dolphins playing there.

As she circled 'round back and parked the Mercedes in front of the garage, she noted a van bearing a logo parked next to the fence. A native Hawaiian man wearing a logo-embellished t-shirt was servicing the swimming pool.

Like many Pacific Heights homes, the Bardick's property had come equipped with a pool. Sometimes Gladys sat out on the deck, but never entered the water. And her husband always seemed too busy to swim.

Often other vehicles parked back there. Her personal assistant Su Lee frequently showed up. General Bardick's assistant Richard Dalton had a dedicated parking space. Professionals from a cleaning service showed up on a rotational basis. Vans came to deliver food at the behest of household chef Felipe Sanninikone, who kept the Bardick's kitchen stocked with sufficient culinary items to meet their gastronomic whims.

People visited her home every day, but it wasn't the same as having family who lived there.

The rear entrance to the home led past the kitchen where Filipe Sanninikone was taking inventory of items in the chrome double refrigerator. As usual, he was attired in his chef's hat and white coat with two vertical rows of buttons. When Gladys walked past, the chef approached her.

"Good afternoon, madam," he said. "May I offer you a bite to eat?"

With a smile and wave, Gladys declined his offer. "I lunched with the ladies' group today. But thanks anyway."

With a little bow, the chef inquired, "Would you like anything special this evening for dinner?"

After a moment of thought, Gladys responded, "Have you spoken with the general yet?"

Felipe shook his head. "General Bardick left early this morning to attend a meeting at the legislative building. He has not returned."

With a wistful smile, Gladys said, "When you see him show up, ask him what he wants. And if he's not too busy, serve it in the dining room please."

Sanninikone nodded. "Understood madam. I will notify you of the general's wishes. I did, however, see your assistant come in earlier. She is waiting for you in the lounge."

"Thank you, Felipe."

Gladys loved her lounge, which she had ordered set up as a sun room. Filled with tropical fabrics and plants, she found it soothing and relaxing. Rather than hot and humid, though, the sunlight that filtered through its floor-to-ceiling windows was offset by air conditioning.

"Sorry to keep you waiting, Su," Gladys apologized. "Our meeting ran long today."

Her personal assistant arose. Today's wardrobe was no different than any other day. Su Lee found it expedient to own a wardrobe built around only two colors—black and white. It was an efficient system, as there was never a need to purchase new wardrobe items or accessories in order to match an outfit.

"It's no trouble," she told her boss. "I have prepared some choices for your gala attire. I took the liberty of placing the items in your bedroom where you can view them as a unit. The purse, the shoes, the whole ensemble."

"That would be wonderful, Su. I'm certain you have taken care of everything."

As the two women traversed the hall that led to the bedroom suite, Gladys fished a tablet from her extra-large purse. It wasn't the electronic sort of tablet. It was a ruled, spiral-bound notebook of the sort that her women's group collected for the refugee children's school kits. Gladys never needed to scramble for folders or documents on a computer. And sometimes those electronic things went *poof*. In contrast, her neat handwritten notes were at her fingertips at any hour of the day or night.

Gladys' mind wandered while Su described the new outfit—an Ann Taylor design with matching accessories that were part of the designer collection. Everything was the right size, the right color. Black and white, with silver-accented accessories. It even coordinated perfectly with her new silver fox hairstyle.

Gladys mind was going in a hundred different directions at once.

Su repeated her question for the third time, "Do you like this style? There's still time to replace these if you're not pleased."

Gladys realized that she was a billionaire with the ability to procure anything she wanted to eat. Have anything she wanted to wear—a brand-new outfit for every day of the week, if that was her desire. And people who pandered to her every whim.

"Mrs. Bardick, if you don't like them, do you want me to take them away?"

"No, no," Gladys insisted. "It's lovely, dear. All of it. I absolutely love it. You've done a great job."

Chapter 16

Bardick residence
Pacific Heights neighborhood
Honolulu, Hawaii

Like his wife, General Leonard Bardick had a wardrobe problem, but it was nothing that money could fix.

The general's personal assistant coordinated a navy suit, blue shirt and striped red and blue tie for his private meeting with President Maleko Ho. His dress blues Army uniform was outdated in addition to being a size too small. Or five. And, in addition, all branches of the United States military had recently merged as in pre-World War II days. With huge amounts of personnel and weaponry lost in the American holocaust, it made sense to combine resources.

In a previous age, the United States Army would have insisted on a spectacular new uniform design. Equipped all the soldiers with new uniforms paid for with an infusion of freshly-printed United States dollars.

The collapse of U.S. dollars meant that rather than being the world's strongest economy, the nation's finances were among the shakiest. And right now, they had bigger problems than wardrobe. Much bigger.

Upon entry to the legislature building in downtown Honolulu, General Bardick was quickly escorted to the fourth floor by four men wearing black suits with white shirts and black ties.

Bardick, who always kept his eyes open, noticed that two of the men were wearing bluetooth earpieces. The same two men stuck to him like glue as he entered the president's office.

The general recognized the aide who had been present during his last meeting with the commander-in-chief. Following protocol, the general shook hands with the president first, then his aide.

"Good morning, Mr. President. Daniel, nice to see you again."

The general made no attempt to greet the Secret Service before or after entering the president's office. He knew they would not acknowledge him, either. They were on duty, constantly observing each person's behavior. Heads on a swivel, scanning the room for possible threats.

President Ho gestured to the seats in front of his desk. The general chose the one closest to the door.

"I like this new White House," said Bardick, attempting to start the conversation.

With a scowl, the president quickly countered, "As you know, I spent an extended period of time in Washington when I served in the Senate. As they used to say in the states, this ain't the White House. And I hope it never is."

Bardick sat down, saying, "No offense intended, Mr. President."

"None taken. However, when it comes to certain topics, I plan to divert from the behavior of previous administrations. I think you know exactly what I'm talking about. Who killed Kennedy, and why. What the Earth space programs are doing. What's going on at Artemis colony on the Moon. By the way, news travels more slowly than it once did. Are you aware of what is happening at Aires Prime on Mars?"

General Bardick's brows furrowed. His research focused on Exopolitics — the alien civilizations that existed beyond the solar system. He had as yet focused little attention on humanity's activities on the Moon and Mars. "No, what's shaking out there?"

President Ho looked down, then propped his hands together in a triangle. "Owing to your specific area of expertise, you are of course aware that the Mars colony was established by an American corporation? As of last week, they have declared themselves a sovereign nation."

"Wow," commented the general. "Didn't see that coming."

"I guess it makes sense. They can make all their own rules and call all the shots now."

Bardick slowly shook his head. "Just because they are self- governing is no guarantee they are self-sufficient. If they want to give it a shot, good luck to them. Just how many permanent citizens does this new nation have?"

"At last report, ten thousand and change." President Ho picked up his hand terminal as if to check the time. "Thank you for taking the time to report in person today. I was hoping you have some information for me."

Bardick said, "I just wanted to pass along the intel I have gleaned regarding the various space programs that exist. I checked into military operations as well as private start-ups. I went from national programs on down to anything with a set of diagrams and a press release."

The president leaned forward. Daniel Lokela, who doubled as the White House press secretary, set up his hand terminal on a kickstand.

"If you want to hear the weirdest thing first, let me tell you about what's going on in Beijing. They pulled out a Long March rocket on a trailer and just left it out there. It's not in the high bay where they make 'em. Not on the launch pad for testing. They just left it where the satellite cameras can easily see it."

Ho smiled and shook his head. Held out his right hand and said, "Look at this right here." He then shook his left hand and countered, "But don't look at what's going on over here. Nothing to see. I think we both can recognize this sort of bullshit as a distraction."

Bardick continued, "As you know, the Chinese have the capability to launch stuff to the Moon. They have some funky satellites that have the capability to snatch things out of orbit."

"We have a pressing need to regain contact with our satellites in orbit. Check to see what would be the best way. In the past, England had uplinks. I believe Australia had them as well. With the U.S. dollar collapse, some of our paid-for friends may have crossed us off the list and may possibly be trying to take over our satellites.

Ho continued, "And general, another matter. I need you to take a deeper accounting of what everyone else is doing in terms of space launches. What's going on at Artemis Colony on the Moon, who's in control of Mars and

85

anything in between. I need you to be our eyes on the sky. Since our last meeting, we are becoming aware of how badly we have been hurt."

"Especially with our extraterrestrial enemies keeping tabs on everything that crosses the Kármán line," Bardick agreed.

When the president stood up, Bardick followed suit. "Hopefully we will talk soon."

Chapter 17

Bertrand Intra-orbital Shipyard

"Nobody likes change."

In a rare opportunity, Eireann Reid had allowed film maker Hans Günther into the inner sanctum of Bertrand Shipyard. The You Tuber wanted to obtain a first-hand look at operations following Rocket Lab's public switchover to the AI system. And Rocket Lab officials had given the interview a nod hoping for a positive public relations opportunity.

With a Go Pro camera attached to a helmet, Günther followed Reid as she pointed out changes in the shipyard operations. Not the proprietary ones, mind you. Or the glitchy stuff. She was careful to show off the shiny, smooth fabrication procedures that would make the company proud. And customers happy they had chosen Bertrand Shipyard to build their starships.

Like many You Tubers, Günther was hoping to uncover snags in company operations. A little drama — or a lot, for that matter —would entertain and thus increase the number of viewers who liked and subscribed to his channel.

Reid had been open with the You Tuber. With company approval, she loaded him up in the school bus for a ride to the various job sites. Nothing top-secret to leak out there, as press releases had already revealed the types and capacity of starships already in production.

Bertrand Shipyard was the first to construct ships in high orbit, but others would certainly follow. Reid had been careful to steer the reporter away from new, innovative construction methods that competitors would love to get their hands on.

As usual, the station manager was wearing her olive coveralls bearing the Bertrand Shipyard logo. An explosion of black, curly hair framed the feminine freckled face that visably expressed the relief she felt upon their arrival to the docking collar which spilled them out into the cargo bay.

"I just wanted to clear up a few questions before we wrap up today," said Günther. "When exactly did Bertrand Station incorporate the AI system? And was there any push-back from your technicians?"

Before answering his questions, Reid glanced around at the dozen or so technicians scurrying through the bay. None of them scrolled on their hand terminals. In fact, no electronic devices of any sort were within sight.

"We've been using the system full time for about six weeks. The AI computer fully manages building materials and supply inventories. It controls shifts and duty assignments. In answer to your question, there were a few staff members who initially objected to it. We lost three technicians in the first week after converting over to the new system. Evidently, they weren't willing to adapt to the change. But in an off-world job site like this one, you have to expect heavy turnover. It's not a good fit for everyone."

"There's something else I wanted to know. I saw your welding robots at work on the ships out there. What's the relationship between the AI and the robots?"

"As I explained previously, the AI creates the duty roster with tasks for each shift. There is a smooth interface between the system and the robots. It is no longer necessary to manually change the robots' programming for each assigned task. In terms of human labor, it saves us tons of time and effort."

"That's good. Time is money."

With a mischievous smile, Günther paused before asking a provocative question. "Eireann, I can't leave before asking this question. The AI obviously has a mind of its own. Are you at all afraid that it might go rogue and do things beyond your control?"

With a grin of her own, Reid finessed the question. "Like becoming self-aware and going beyond the perimeters we give it? Or making a determination that human beings make mistakes and start eliminating everyone? Yeah, that has entered my mind, but do you know something that's even more scary?"

"No, what?"

"What scares the crap out of me is the constant possibility of finding a pink slip in my employee portal. Up here in space, there's not a lot to do for fun. In my free time reading, I made a deep dive into the history of technology, specifically as it applies to manufacturing and the space program. Very revealing, especially for someone in my position. And do you know what I discovered?"

By his expression, Reid could tell that the You Tuber was off balance due to the conversation's off-script direction. "I'm not sure."

"New technology can be responsible for the creation of jobs, and also for their elimination. You would have plenty of company if you believe that industrialist Henry Ford created and utilized the first assembly line in manufacturing. You'd be wrong, though, because by 1900 the H.J. Heinz company had adopted a continuous flow system and assembly line techniques in the production of ketchup, pickles, mustard, olives and vinegar."

By this time, a deer-in-the-headlight expression was spread across Günther's face.

"The point is that I'm playing the long game, Hans. When the company told me they would be installing the AI system, I could have said, sod it all, it's going wrong. Like any good entrepreneur would, Rocket Lab opted to embrace a technology that will allow them to continue on into the future. You see, manufacturing is and always has been an equation of labor and production. It's a matter of giving consumers what they want and reducing costs. Do you understand?"

Wishing to retain the illusion of control, Günther lied, "Yes, I believe I do."

Reid continued, "When our generation was growing up, there were plenty of kids who wanted to work in space. Many of us had big dreams, but few of us actually got the opportunity. During the early years of the United States space program, seven astronauts were chosen as part of the Mercury program. Only seven. All seven of them got to go into space. The Gemini program had sixteen pilots. Still a relatively small number. Back then, being an astronaut was the only possible way you were gonna get to cross that line. But today, it isn't only astronauts who are going into space."

"My uncle went on vacation to the Moon."

Reid crossed her arms over her chest and nodded. "The Artemis Experience®. I'll bet he's loaded, right?"

Günther nodded. "One of the ten richest people in Europe. Said he had a really great time up there. Got to suit up and walk on the Moon's surface, as I understand."

Standing next to the observation window, Reid pointed at one of the school bus flights, taking technicians out to a starship job site.

"Take a close look out there. Do you know what I see in the future, Hans?"

Günther only shook his head.

"In the future, there will be more space vehicles actually constructed in space. These technicians you see here will probably become obsolete within the next generation. Traveling to the exoplanets will require more motherships with warp drive capabilities. Space colonization and resupply will require ships with enormous capacities. I see more motherships being built in space in an automated fashion using materials sourced off-world. That will require more rotating-torus orbital shipyards."

Günther couldn't repress an elated, "How cool would that be?"

"Since the Heinz assembly line, the manufacturing business has never been about providing a decent wage and taking care of the employees. It's about this," said Reid, rubbing the thumb and fingers of her right hand together. "It's about the manufacture of innovative products built as quickly as possible with the lowest possible cost, producing the highest amount of profit for investors. And as the cost-per-launch goes down, more people will take advantage of space opportunities."

"I see what you mean. But Eireann, what does that mean for the workers?"

Reid put her hands on her hips, swiveling around to take stock of operations. "As I said before, I'm in this for the long game. Workers, and managers such as myself, need the ability to adapt and overcome. We need to do our jobs and do them better than anyone else. We need to exceed standards whenever possible in order to outshine the competition. And when AI eliminates the need for my job, I will be forced to to re-invent myself."

"What's going to happen to these workers when automation eliminates the need for their positions?"

Reid swatted the air and said, "Pfffft. No problem. By that time, there will be even more jobs for people who need or want to work in space. I'm imagining an orbital civilization with rotating toruses that provide artificial gravity. Pilots will be needed to drive space taxis and space trucks. There will probably be hotels in space, on the Moon and Mars. That will mean a slew of service jobs: stewards and cooks as well as construction workers and plumbers. And someone will have to provide media coverage."

Reid paused with a nostalgic expression, once again looking out the observation window at the ships under construction. "I had a friend up here not too long ago. You may have heard of her. Raven Munoz was the Rocket Lab press secretary for a few years. Anyway, she always wanted to be an astronaut ever since she was out of diapers, she said. Huge space fan. Her career path took a different turn. She made her living doing photography and journalism. To her surprise, however, she was selected as a member of the Phoenix program. Not as your typical sort of astronaut. They sent her as the mission historian. She was over the Moon that she finally got to go into space. Pun intended." With a little chuckle, Reid concluded, "Don't you find that ironic?"

"Pretty sweet gig. I'd go, wouldn't you?"

Reid tilted her head, then countered, "Hans, wouldn't you like to go to Mars to produce You Tube programs?"

The You Tube blogger looked down at the deck and responded. "Nah. It takes too long to get there, and the planetary restrictions are ridiculous. Did you know they don't allow alcohol? And certain recreational substances?"

The station manager continued to stare out the window, although whether she was monitoring station operations or lost in her own imaginary dreams, Günther couldn't tell.

"The world of the future is going to take movers and shakers, creators and innovators. And I plan to be one of them. How about you?"

Chapter 18

Rocket Lab residence campus
Auckland, New Zealand

"It's a baby bump basket. I thought it would cheer you up."

Rocket Lab personnel manager Claire Montgomery had been absent from her duties at the corporation facility for the past two months due to pregnancy complications. Under doctor-ordered restrictions, she had been placed on leave. She was super-pleased when Bella Brown requested to make a mid-afternoon appearance.

Brown showed up on Montgomery's doorstep wearing a blue one-piece Star Trek Uniform of the type worn by the Betazed character Deanna Troi. Her brown hair swept in waves over her torso.

"Rocket Lab is quite generous with their maternity leave policy," Montgomery explained. "They provide twelve months of leave, although I was hoping to save it until after the baby is born rather than right now."

Bearing the wire basket, Brown entered the Auckland residence Montgomery shared with her husband Jim Freeman. From the outside, she noted that this bungalow was slightly larger than the one she occupied on the Rocket Lab campus. Easily large enough to accommodate a growing family.

"I came to check on you today," said Brown. "You are, of course, aware that everyone asks about you. How are you feeling today?"

With an expression of disgust, Montgomery placed her hand on her stomach and replied, "I drank some tea earlier. Hoping it stays down. Won't you have a seat?"

"I brought over some things for you hoping they would cheer you up. You are the heart and soul of Rocket Lab. I know it's hard for you to stay away."

Brown picked up peaceful vibes from the den's sunny yellow walls and the green upholstery of furnishings. Montgomery chose a perch on the love seat with green upholstery. Brown installed the wire basket on a low coffee table before taking a seat in the green recliner.

Montgomery brightened as she picked through the basket's contents. "My family is already sending gifts for the baby. The doctor confirms we're having a girl."

Picking up her hand terminal, she scrolled to a sonogram image. "I just passed the twenty-six-weeks milestone."

Regarding the sonogram image, Brown explained, "I figured you and Jim will get plenty of baby stuff. I brought items that are just for you. It sounds as if you have had a rough couple of weeks."

With a nod, Montgomery acknowledged, "The doctor is calling it *hyperemesis gravidarium*. My second trimester is nearly over but I'm still having killer morning sickness. And on top of that, none of my clothes fit any more."

Although Brown didn't mention it, Montgomery's current disposition varied greatly from her office presence. In the past, the personnel manager wore high-end ultra-matched outfits with coordinating accessories and jewelry. Today, though, she was barefoot and wearing sweatpants paired with one of her husband's t-shirts. Her hair, usually sleek and professional, was bundled into a messy bun.

"Check it out," said Brown cheerfully. "There's some nausea tea in there. I wasn't sure if it would help, but there's nothing in it that would harm the baby."

Positioning a pink plastic bracelet on her wrist, Montgomery held her hand out and commented. "Oh, this is stylish, for sure."

With a chuckle, Brown explained, "It's an accu-pressure nausea bracelet. There's some Belly Rub cream in the basket, as well as a water bottle and a pregnancy journal. I thought that would help you pass the time, as well as provide a memento of your journey."

"You beauty! Thanks, mate."

"And I knew you would be able to use the wire market basket. Perfect for fruits and veggies. We vegetarians have to stick together, you know."

Beside the loveseat, Brown observed a yarn tote containing balls of grey yarn. She admired Montgomery's swirly circular crochet afghan project that was nearly complete.

"It's for the baby," Montgomery explained. "Hey, thanks for the tea. I'll just be happy when I can eat something that stays down. But can I get you a bite to eat? Some regular tea or a Bikkie? Certified vegan-friendly."

Brown shook her head. "I don't expect to stay long. I know you aren't feeling well."

"I can maintain normalcy for the most part as long as I don't move around too much. Listen, I'm pretty much confined to quarters, so I wonder if you can confirm a rumor, yeah?"

"What did you hear?"

"First of all, I caught the recording of Welly's first press conference. He did a good job keeping it level. I heard a rumor, though, that he wore beach shorts."

With a huge grin, Bella's nod was enthusiastic. "Business on the top. Party on the bottom. Cargo shorts with beach sandals. I think he'll do all right, though."

"No one can replace Raven."

"It's a fact that we all miss her. Especially our Saturday trips to the beach."

Montgomery leaned in for a moment, then became serious and asked, "What are your thoughts on Rocket Lab's new computer system?"

After a half-moment of thought, Brown responded, "VIKI definitely takes some getting used to. Rather than using a keyboard to input your inquiries, you speak to an image of an Asian female on the view screen. *Good morning, Bella. What would you like to do today?*" said Brown with an affected British accent. "There are a plethora of responses that spring to mind. But of course, she's a computer program and it's impossible to hurt her feelings."

"What else? How is the AI doing on rocket design?"

"The design team was somewhat overwhelmed at first, but I believe they're coping well. VIKI has already designed the next mothership to be built up at Bertrand station. But you already knew that was coming, right?"

With a nod, Montgomery acknowledged, "I understand they've already laid the keel and production is proceeding at an unprecedented rate. Yeah, but I didn't expect the design would be complete so soon."

"It's fast, all right. In fact, VIKI is rapidly completing the process of hiring for the next warp-drive mission."

Montgomery's eyes opened wide, "Oh, sorry for bailing on that. I wanted to personally screen the candidates."

"I'm certain you did. Make certain there were no Sawyer Kilpatricks in the bunch. Screen out the people with stellar resume skills while concealing serious character flaws."

She shrugged. "Once they are on their way to Proxima Centauri B, it will be too late to kick out any bad apples."

There was a long pause during which Montgomery sorted through the contents of the Baby Bump basket. "Thanks so much for this, Bella. It was so thoughtful of you. And for taking your lunch hour to visit me. That is how you were able to tear yourself away in the middle of the Arvo, yeah?"

Brown looked downward, then fidgeted in her seat. "We're sort of in the same boat now."

With wide eyes, the expectant mother asked, "Oh? You're not preggers, are you?"

With a giggle, Brown confirmed, "Oh, heavens no! I mean, you're on leave. And ..."

Now it was Montgomery's turn to lean forward.

"I'm not working right now. VIKI fired me. She didn't think my educational resume was prestigious enough to serve on the engineering team."

Montgomery couldn't restrain an explosive, "Crickey!" Deep inside herself, she scraped up the energy to rise and deliver a much-needed hug for Brown.

"Well if you're job hunting, Jim and I are in the market for a nanny."

Chapter 19

Rocket Lab campus
Auckland, New Zealand

"What are we doing here? Why all the skullduggery?"

In the middle of a planning session for Rocket Lab's newest mothership, Camillo Hoffman pulled rank and drew Jim Freeman and Dave Sutton away from the design lab. His explanation involved language that would make any engineer's heart go pitter-patter.

"There's a problem in the shipyard. I will need you both to come with me."

With tremendous apprehension, Freeman and Sutton accompanied Hoffman downstairs where they were invited aboard a company golf cart. Their suspicions were heightened by his request to leave their hand terminals in the design lab.

With Hoffman at the wheel, the golf cart motored past the high bay where technicians were preparing to transfer an electron orbital rocket designed to carry scientific payloads to the launch pad. It was a familiar sight, as they had both been involved with the project's design.

Hoffman ignored their protests when he continued to drive past the high bays and rocket garden. His route took them past an abandoned warehouse.

"I thought you had to show us something," Sutton finally asked. Hooking his thumb in the opposite direction, he said, "Everything's back there. Exactly where are we headed?"

"Yeah, I've never actually been to the back lot before," said Freeman.

"Does anyone still do anything back here?"

With a wiggle of his eyebrows, Hoffman said, "Let's find out, shall we?"

At the absolute end of the unpaved road behind several heaps of fresh gravel was a two-story metal building. Inside, Hoffman brought the golf cart to a stop inside the center of an empty cargo bay. While Freeman and Sutton stepped out, he walked back to controls located beside the bay doors. Bright lights came on and the bay doors creaked closed.

"Why all the skullduggery?" Sutton repeated.

"You have it all wrong," said Freeman. "It's not my birthday. Or yours, Dave?"

"We're on a tight schedule working on the mothership, Cam. We're due to begin production in a few days. We really don't have time for all this cloak-and-dagger bullshit."

Hoffman had returned to the center of the bay where the two engineers stood. With a two-handed sweeping gesture, he said, "Wouldn't this make a great place to design a shuttle craft?"

"No," said Sutton, right off the bat. "It's stuffy, and dusty. And it smells a little bit like ...."

"Don't worry about the smell," said Hoffman. Pointing to a pair of doors at the end of the cargo bay, he explained, "Your new design lab is in there. And all this cargo space is big enough for the equipment needed to construct an anti-gravity shuttle."

Sutton nodded, then said, "So you're planning to go dark for this project. You want to keep it away from prying eyes."

Hoffman's chin bobbed. With two fingers, he adjusted his glasses. "You, my very perceptive friend, are exactly right."

"What does Mr. Kemp have to say about this?"

Unexpectedly, Brandon Kemp in the flesh emerged from one of the doors.

"In fact, this was my idea," he said.

Kemp was accompanied by Ieohapata, a Māori man wearing a Rocket Lab coverall, who was foreman of the ground-level shipyard.

The CEO exchanged handshakes with the engineers, while continuing to explain, "It's difficult to convince a board that they should invest a big pile of money on a project when I can't describe it to them," Kemp explained. "My thoughts were, if the United States could conduct research under a black ops budget, Area 51, no-fly zone, then by George, so can we."

With his hands on his hips, Freeman ventured to ask, "No disrespect intended, but I think it's time for you both to clue us in. What are the perimeters for this project?"

"You have been hand-picked for a top-secret project," Kemp announced with a smile. "I asked Cam to borrow a couple of his top engineers to create a couple of anti-gravity vehicles. Come with me."

Freeman followed Kemp into a laboratory located on the ground floor at the back of the warehouse.

"We don't use this warehouse or the lab anymore, which is why I selected this location."

As he entered the facility, Sutton soaked in the environment. High ceilings featuring direct centralized lighting gave the space the aura of an airport hanger. Off to the side was a bank of cubicles. A couple of ancient computers—the sort with a separate hard drive in a tower—occupied the desks. There was no way to tell how long the diagrams fastened to cork boards along the wall with stickpins had been there. A dust-covered beverage machine advertised drink options that had long ago become extinct. Against one wall was an ancient printer as big as an SUV. Sutton took note of a drafting table freshly stocked with drafting tools and super-sized graph paper.

"Oh my God, those cathode ray tube monitors are dinosaurs. Why hasn't someone put them in a museum?" Sutton exclaimed.

"Here's an even bigger surprise," said Kemp. "Trevor Smith came out here for a couple of weeks. Ta daaa! Everything works, including the computer-aided-design software."

Hoffman took over by saying, "Mr. Kemp here asked me for my best engineers. You guys will work on the anti-gravity vehicles here. All of these computers are off-grid. Not only are they off grid, as a matter of fact, they don't have Internet capability."

"I get it; they're not connected to the Internet so there's no way they can be hacked," Freeman guessed. "It certainly puts the kibosh on international espionage."

"You will have unlimited access to materials and technicians. Any experimentation is strictly top-secret. No photos or recordings of any type are allowed."

"Just to be certain of the project perimeters, I'd like to know who exactly is in the know?"

Kemp and Hoffman exchanged a look, after which Hoffman replied, "Trevor Smith, of course. If the need for additional resources arises, he will see to it. The shipyard foreman Ieohapata will be your project builder." With the index finger of each hand pointing downwards, he said, "All builds, of course, will take place out here. Ieohapata can fabricate components in his shop on a limited basis, but we will have to take extraordinary precautions to keep everything under the radar."

Ieohapata leaped into the conversation with, "I am available to fabricate components on the off-shift. I have a couple of technicians who can assist, and we can always arrange for a camera glitch to crop up when we're working on this particular project."

Sutton had finally succeeded in firing up one of the older-style computer screens using keyboard commands. Upon opening the program, a grid diagram was visible on the view screen. "I don't suppose this one has voice interface, does it? Or touch screen?"

"Nope," said Hoffman. "But there's one other person who will be helping you. Off grid, of course. You can't leak out she is still working for Rocket Lab."

A squeaky door at the top of the stairs opened, followed by Bella Brown's inquiring expression. After a beckoning gesture from Hoffman, she skipped down the wooden staircase.

After a dramatic pause, Hoffman added, "Bella will procure any data or schematics you need."

After a glance at Sutton, Freeman said, "Thank God. I was worried we had lost her."

She had a little side hug for both engineers. "Good to see you, guys."

There have always been prying eyes in the sky. There will be satellite telemetry of the Rocket Lab campus. Corporate as well as international spies are interested in finding out what we're doing. You will need to coordinate your trips out here so as not to arouse attention," said Hoffman. "I realize that your workload just doubled. We are in the process of hiring another engineer who will assist with your regular projects. Under your direction, of course."

"In the interests of secrecy," Kemp glanced at a set of stairs leading to the top story. "There's a sizeable apartment up there. I was hoping you two would be willing to sequester during this project. But Hoffman here informed me of Jim's delicate situation."

With a slow head swivel, Freeman said emphatically, "Yeah, my wife is having a difficult pregnancy. Long hours won't be a problem but any overnight absence is a no-go."

Kemp crossed his arms and said, "I understand. And Jim, how is Claire?"

With a smile, Freeman replied, "She is feeling better. At her last exam she gained three pounds. But still on home rest. Doctor's orders."

Kemp continued, "So I must insist on top-level secrecy. In order to sign on to this project, all of you must keep to the protocols necessary to prevent any other entities from gaining knowledge of your activities out here. This is all dark ops. Jim ..."

With a huge sigh, Freeman acquiesced, "Yeah, don't discuss work with Claire."

With a serious expression, Kemp emphasized, "With your cooperation, none of you will have any financial difficulties for the forseeable future."

"I'm going to work upstairs," Brown explained. "I'll do all your research with a dark computer and a fake IP address using a mobile Hotspot. While I'm working on my aerospace engineering degree. In Brussels — theoretically."

"We will have to leave our hand terminals and tablets inside the main building each time we come out here," Freeman observed. "If they were out here, they could track our location."

"Yeah, it would throw up a red flag," agreed Sutton.

"So you're in?" asked Hoffman.

"Yeah. Golden opportunity. History in the making," said Freeman.

Sutton pointed at the old drinks machine and said, "Stock that thing with some Gatorade and you have a deal."

Chapter 20

Why did I choose aerospace? Why? Why?

Suited up in a white light-duty pressure jumpsuit, Julie Stempler attempted to suppress the reality that she felt green around the gills.

"Almost there now," reassured Beth Sommerset, strapped into the next seat in the crew compartment.

Stempler drew her head as far back into the helmet as space would would allow, trying not to speak or think at all.

Rather than wait for the next supply delivery, the two engineers had chosen to head in an intra-orbital direction in the crew dragon. Bertrand Station was the perfect location to try out the prototype for their new emergency escape pod.

There was no need for a pilot, as the vessel was fully automated.

"We are separated. The rocket that brought us here is now on its way back to Earth," announced Sommerset helpfully.

"Oh, God," remarked Stempler softly, her eyes closed..

There were two more seats in the crew dragon. Currently strapped into the remaining seats were the engineers' companions — two anthropomorphic devices, otherwise known as crash test dummies. Unlike Stempler and Sommerset, the life-sized devices were dressed in red jumpsuits with breast patches that identified them as Gus and Ethel.

From the interior monitor, the passengers witnessed their approach to the enormous bulk of Bertrand Station. Two cargo ships were visible under construction in the shipyards' bays as well as the monstrous keel of a new mothership recently underway.

Stempler was aware of the signs and symptoms of her own anxiety attack. Quietly, she initiated self-soothing strategies to ease herself through the ordeal of space travel. Motion sickness was a gravity response, but out here there was no gravity. Therefore, the nausea was an illusion perpetuated by her own mind, not sensations of her inner ear.

A slight bump followed by a series of clicks provided an unmistakable indication that the crew dragon was at last connected to Bertrand's cargo bay. Inside, they witnessed a symphony of motion being performed by technicians and robots who procured and manipulated materials from the cargo bay.

"Hey there!" The engineers were greeted in person by Eireann Reid herself. Like the other Bertrand occupants, the station manager was wearing olive coveralls that featured the station's logo. "Welcome to Bertrand."

Sommerset had her own helmet off within seconds of stepping into the cargo bay.

"Phew!" she said after breathing in the coolness of the station's interior.

While assisting Stempler to remove her helmet, she said, "My friends over here have a case of stage fright. Could we get some assistance, please?"

Reid had to stoop over to gaze into the crew dragon's interior. "Gus? And Ethel? Hmmm. Precious cargo, I presume?"

After a brief interlude of station hospitality, Reid introduced them to a technician also wearing station coveralls.

"This is Clayton Lee. He was in charge of the installation of your device here."

As Stempler and Sommerset looked on, Lee, who wore his dark curly hair cropped short, explained the escape pod's set-up. They would later learn he was a former submariner who made a natural transition to the intra-orbital shipyard.

"Bertrand Station is experiencing growing pains," Lee explained. "In the future, G ramp will serve as the location for the construction of yet another high-tech miracle. As you can see, access to the escape pod is two-way. You have to spin the dog on this side to open it."

Stempler nodded. "If the station were under a state of emergency, the power supply could possibly be cut. In that case, manual access would be the best plan of action."

Reid stepped back and allowed Lee to lead the way. He spun the wheel, which granted access to an additional barrier door.

"There are two ways to gain access to the interior of the device. You can punch the code into your tablet like this."

Lee tapped on his own tablet. Beyond the interior door, a set of sliding panels opened to each side. "In the event that you didn't bring your tablet with you ..."

He indicated a control panel beside the hatch. "You can key your access code in right here."

The interior of the escape pod was now visible beyond the hatch. Lights inside revealed Gus and Ethel already strapped into the three-point harnesses. They weren't at all intimidated by the simulation, as evidenced by the perpetual Sharpie-marker grins imprinted on their faces.

"Hi, guys! Are you comfortable?" said Sommerset brightly.

"The pod is all set up," said Lee. "Just say the word."

While the rest of the entourage took a moment to check out the pod's interior, Sommerset extracted her own tablet from her satchel and tapped commands into it.

To Lee, she said, "You may begin the simulation whenever you're ready."

With tablet in hand, he said, "I've now given the pod a false command that the station is under a state of emergency."

Both interior and exterior doors slid closed. A few seconds later, Lee glanced down at his tablet and added, "And the escape pod is away."

"Now we wait?" asked Reid.

"Yes," confirmed Sommerset. "The plan is to leave them out there for forty-eight hours."

Stempler added, "Then fish them back inside and check out their vital signs."

The pair of engineers lagged behind Reid and Lee on the long walk back to the main part of the station.

"I feel like a nervous parent," said Stempler. "We haven't left them on their own like this for a hot minute."

With a nod, Sommerset affirmed. "Remember the *Comet.* They were out there for two days as well as traveling to the edge of the solar system."

With lowered voice, Stempler acknowledged. "I'm not so much worried about our test subject as my own stability. Look around you, Beth. I'm nearly losing my shit just being out here for a couple of days. These technicians are out here for months at a time. They are vulnerable to power failures, meteorites ... all kinds of catastrophic failures. All day, every day."

The station manager slowed her pace, mirroring the engineers' whispers. "Thanks for coming up with this, you guys," said Reid. "At least if we can make our way to an escape pod, it gives us a fighting chance of survival."

Chapter 21

Rocket Lab boardroom
Auckland, New Zealand

"Do you think this is overdoing it?"

The display on Julie Stempler's hand terminal read *Brass Fanfare.*

A symphonic introduction made up of French horns and kettle drums met the disapproval of Beth Sommerset, who shook her head.

"The Internet providers will each insert their own preferred sounds," she sternly told Stempler.

The two engineers had just finished conducting a briefing with Rocket Lab press secretary Hahona Timoti. For the occasion he was wearing a traditional grey suit—including matching shirt and tie, pants and dress shoes. He straightened his tie before taking his position in the Rocket Lab boardroom, closely regarding a digital countdown in the lower right-hand corner of the large view screen.

"Five minutes," Sommerset announced. "Ready, Welly?"

Timoti scowled as he regarded the press release once again. "I have the press release memorized. But none of us has any idea what sort of rubbish questions they will ask."

"You'll do fine," Stempler reassured him.

On the view screen, zoom windows began to open up with images of press representatives from around the globe. Each participant had signed in, supplying their names and organizations now displayed below their images.

Seconds after the clock reached 00:00, Timoti spoke into the screen:

"This is Hahona Timoti from Rocket Lab in Auckland, New Zealand with an exciting announcement. Rocket Lab recently tested and patented a new device that will greatly enhance the level of safety for individuals traveling and working in deep space. A prototype escape pod was recently tested at Bertrand Intra-orbital Shipyard. As you can see, this device will provide a safe means of escape and survival in the event of a catastrophic emergency."

All of the press members' photos disappeared, replaced on the screen with a video clip diagram of the escape pod with dual seats. A narration described the pod's exclusive features. The scene switched to a live recording of the recovery of Nicole Bradley and Clayton Lee, both volunteers who took part in a live demonstration of the escape pod's use at Bertrand Station.

After the clip played, the screen returned to images of the media representatives. Half of the images displayed green lights beside their names, indicating reporters with specific questions.

On her tablet, Sommerset scrolled to the image of a reporter from Beijing who led off the question portion of the press conference. "Yes, I understand that this is a prototype device. How soon do you expect that functional escape pods will be produced?"

"That's a great question." Timoti said, with a comment that is useful to gain a few seconds when he needed time to regain his bearings. "We expect to go into production of these devices for installation and use at Bertrand Station as soon as four to six weeks."

"Yes?" said Timoti as Sommerset recognized a reporter from a Toronto, Canada television station.

An auburn-haired woman wearing a bright green sweater asked, "I'm certain you are familiar with the historical narrative of the Titanic. Do plans for installation include enough lifeboats to accommodate all occupants of Bertrand Station?"

"I'm going to be brutally honest with you," said Timoti. "Initial plans include the installation of a limited number of devices for testing and refinement. But eventually, we intend to manufacture sufficient devices for distribution throughout the shipyard—enough to save everyone in the event of a catastrophic emergency."

"What sort of emergencies would warrant the use of an escape pod?" was the inquiry of a reporter from India.

Sommerset was pleased to note that Timoti was rapidly gaining his sea legs. His confident reply was: "Sure. The escape pod would come into play after any event that caused a significant drop in pressurization. This could be caused by a meteor strike or hull failure for any other reason."

A journalist from Kenya was the next to forward a question. "I saw from your clip that the escape pod provides accommodations for two individuals. Assuming they are able to gain access, for what length of time will they be safe?"

In advance of the interview, Timoti had memorized responses to a list of expected questions. His answer to this one was: "The new escape pod will provide sufficient heat and air filtration for twenty-four to forty-eight hours. An emergency beacon is designed to activate upon departure from the mother vessel, allowing any vehicle attempting rescue to quickly locate and acquire each of the emergency pods."

"It would appear that the pods have their own propulsion system?" A representative of a Brazilian news agency asked his question in Portuguese. The computer interface provided an English translation on the ribbon at the bottom of the boardroom view screen.

"That is correct," Timoti chimed in. "Sufficient propulsion to allow the pod to escape from the primary vehicle to a distance of one kilometer. You may compare the propulsion system with a starship's parking jets."

Timoti's on-screen performance met the scrutiny of Sommerset and Stempler within the boardroom as well as CEO Brandon Kemp who watched the feed from his office.

As the conference wound down, a London newspaper reporter asked, "Congratulations on your recent achievement. With this one in the bag, what's next for Rocket Lab?"

The press agent was ready with a reply for this question as well. "It's not official yet, but we have some engineers working on self-sealing hull technology for the smaller meteor strikes that are a constant threat in space."

The London reporter nodded his approval.

A lone green light remained on the screen. Sommerset allowed a single question from a brand-new press agency. She activated the feed of Rebekah Hekikia from WUSA out of Honolulu, Hawaii. Wearing bright, tropical clothing and a flower in her hair, Hekikia asked, "I heard from somewhere that Rocket Lab is involved in the design of an anti-gravity flight device. Can you confirm those rumors?"

With a wistful expression, Timoti rolled his eyes. "Wish it were true. Along with a dozen other space-launch providers, we at Rocket Lab dream of the day when we will be able to launch vehicles into space while bypassing standard propulsion. For now ... "

Sommerset and Stempler held their breath, hoping Timoti's pause was for dramatic effect. Hoping he wouldn't spill any information he had accidentally acquired regarding Rocket Lab's black ops project that had slipped onto the radar of far too many employees.

"For now that dream remains in the realm of science fiction."

Chapter 22

Junk Works

Rocket Lab Launch Complex

Auckland, New Zealand

Our mercury is triple distilled, ACS instrument grade. It is commonly used in the mining and refining of gold and silver, as well as in the production of other metals. — Vector Chemical Distributors

Over the years, Bella Brown had been tapped to name various projects. After naming their team's first warp-drive prototype the *Comet*, Camillo Hoffman realized he didn't posses a flair for cranking out memorable nomenclature.

Officially, Brown named Rocket Lab's new computer system VIKI. She was among three members of the engineering team who were tapped to harness a new form of energy at a throwaway facility. All of them vowed to put their heads down and make the best of it. In spite of Camillo Hoffman's protests, Brown dubbed the black operations design and manufacture center *Junk Works*.

The facility had its drawbacks, however. In its infancy, Rocket Lab didn't feel it was necessary to install air conditioning—or heat—in the design bay. Installing an HVAC system in the unused facility at this point would attract unwanted attention. As a result, the engineers labored away to the droning whine of a couple of box fans. Utilizing the CAD computer programs in combination with the drafting table, Sutton and Freeman had managed to achieve a preliminary design.

During the second week of work in the off-grid facility the engineers navigated through the next challenge: locating materials required to fabricate a small-scale prototype.

Another of Brown's duties included the location and acquisition of materials necessary to the top-secret project.

"I'm embarrassed to ask, but what does ACS mean?" Sutton wanted to know.

Regarding her off-grid tablet, Brown replied, "It's an industry term. It's a gold-standard indicator in chemical manufacturing meaning greater than 95 percent purity."

"OK, but are you able to get it? Because our design concept requires highly-pressurized canisters of mercury. We need to procure some right now, but we will eventually require large amounts of it."

"Yah, but I'm going to have to keep looking around for a local source," said Brown, scraping through her tablet entries.

"Oh? Why?"

"Evidently mercury is classified hazardous materials Class 8. It's a corrosive substance so it's not allowed to be shipped via air. This listing also says customers should expect additional duties, taxes and customs clearance service fees incurred during delivery."

"Bloody hell," said Freeman. "Keep looking, Bella. We've got to have it."

Sutton wanted to know, "How are you able to order our stuff without attracting unwanted attention?"

"I'm using a faked IP address for this tablet as well as the computers up in my Junk Works quarters. Plus, I'm in Incognito Browser mode. But that doesn't mean that someone out there might get their knickers in a knot over the fact that we're ordering large amounts of mercury. Or uranium. Or plutonium, or anything else you guys may need."

Freeman was seated in a vintage office chair in one of the Junk Works cubicles, with Sutton peering over his shoulder at the computer view screen. On the opposite side of the room, Brown braced both arms on the drafting table, studying a series of diagrams clipped to it.

"Mind if I take a look?" she asked.

"No drama," said Sutton. Turning to Freeman, he asked, "I'm curious; what's the size for the initial prototype?"

"About two meters for the AGV-X1."

"Are you going to slip it away to Model Club for a show-and-tell session?"

Freeman was unable to suppress a snort. "Wouldn't that be a hoot? They would love it, no doubt. Especially when I staged an in-house demonstration."

Brown's voice projected from across the room. "Is it supposed to look like a flying saucer?"

Freeman sighed before joining Brown at the drafting table. "The small-scale model we're going to build initially is mostly Otis Carr with a side helping of TR-3B."

"Huh?"

Sutton joined them, explaining, "Did you ever hear of black triangle anti-gravity vehicle sightings? That was the TR-3B. No one really knew who made it, so it didn't officially exist. In theory, it used highly pressurized mercury accelerated by nuclear energy to produce a plasma that creates a field of anti-gravity around the ship. Conventional thrusters enable it to perform all manner of rapid high-speed maneuvers along all three axes — pitch, yaw and roll. Interestingly, the plasma it generates also reduces radar signature significantly. So a device of this sort will be almost invisible on radar and in this manner remain undetected."

By her expression, Freeman perceived that Brown was annoyed.

"So it can go anywhere without being detected by air traffic control? Or air defense systems? You're telling me I may have unknowingly helped create a military weapon?"

Freeman switched gears, explaining: "Not necessarily. By the way, we also used Tesla's diagrams. He spent most of his adult life fiddling with what he called the Dynamic Field of Gravity. His concept incorporated a disc idle capacitor with gyroscopic stabilization system and electric drive control. We did actually procure the design plans for Nikola Tesla's anti-gravity vehicle patent. He never actually built a working model, though. But we have photographs of Carr's working model."

"How similar was Carr's design to Tesla's?"

Freeman scratched his head. "Not at all. A patent for Tesla's final invention, issued in 1928, was for a flying vehicle that looked like a cross between a helicopter and an airplane. Otis Carr's craft, however, bore a strong resemblance to a flying saucer."

"Much like your diagrams on the drafting table?"

"Yeah," said Sutton. "The spin is part of the process. When the outer hull rotates counter clockwise, the inner ring spins in a clockwise direction."

"Am I correct in assuming that anti gravity is an electromagnetic process?"

Locked into explanation mode, Freeman reverted to an oversimplification. "When the craft is functioning, it is charged to a high voltage. But technically, the process has nothing to do with anti-gravity and everything to do with mass and field alteration by electromagnetic waves of specific frequencies."

"So you're creating negative mass," said Brown.

With a look at Freeman, Sutton explained, "It's a function of your basic quantum physics."

"Something like the Casimir effect?" Brown wanted to know. "A concept that is theoretically impossible in regular science, but has been proven in quantum field theory."

After determining that the conversation had taken them miles away from the task at hand, Sutton added, "Now we're getting sidetracked into wormholes and time travel stuff. By the way, do you want anything for lunch?"

"Hmmm," said Brown. Her black ops status came with a prohibition against showing her face in public. Meaning, she couldn't run out to grab lunch as in the past without a suit of armor.

"Yeah, think you could snag a Veggie Burger? And make sure you tell them no mayo."

"You got it," said Freeman.

Sutton added, "We'll be back in about an hour."

Chapter 23

Rocket Lab boardroom
Auckland, New Zealand

"I tried to get a variety of sandwiches. Hopefully there's something in here you like."

During the top-secret project ongoing at the Junk Works facility, engineers had to give the appearance that things were moving along normally. That meant hiring a new engineer to complete the research and development team.

It was Brandi Red Feather's first appearance at a budget meeting in the Rocket Lab boardroom.

"First things first. Food is an essential part of our culture," Camillo Hoffman told the new member of the engineering team. "Today's budget meeting is likely to run long, so I ordered in. Federal Delicatessen is one of our favorites. There's a Veggie Smash Bagel if you are by any chance vegetarian."

"No, I'm really not picky," said Red Feather, selecting one of the packets wrapped in deli paper. "Oh, looks like I got the Reuben. My favorite, if it doesn't go to someone else."

"No, you get first pick today. Who wants the Street Dog?" asked Hoffman. Freeman reached out and grabbed. "That's mine."

"You should have a Tuna Melt somewhere in there," said Sommerset.

Hoffman fished through the delivery box imprinted with Federal Delicatessen logo to retrieve a packet. "Here ya go. Who had the Spit-roast chicken? The Best Ugly?"

With lunch portions distributed, Hoffman proceeded with Item One on the agenda.

"Brandi, we are super-pleased to have you join us. Before you dig in, why don't you tell us a little bit about yourself?"

VIKI hand-picked Brandi Red Feather for the engineer position from among several hundred qualified applicants. The new engineer was comparatively short, heavy-set and dark-skinned with deep brown eyes and black hair arranged into two braids. Proudly, she wore a navy Rocket Lab jacket.

"I'm a Canuck from Canada," she said. "I guess you could call me a snowbird. Like the Canada geese I migrated south to escape the long, brutal winters in search of sand and sun. Couldn't have migrated much farther south than this, eh?"

Team members laughed politely.

"I guess not," said Stempler.

"I grew up in Saskatchewan but earned my undergraduate degree from Embry-Riddle Aeronautical University. I have an Aerospace Engineering degree with a specialty in hull design."

"Did you study at the Daytona Beach, Florida or Prescott, Arizona campus?" Freeman wondered.

"What do you think?" Red Feather grinned. "I'll take the beach over the desert any day of the week. Daytona Beach, of course!"

"And you went back to freezing-ass Toronto to work?"

"Had to. As soon as I graduated, I got a sweet job offer with Canadian Armed Forces. Traded my bikini for a parka. Twenty years of experience in aerospace design. I started looking around last year. As a function of time, the demand is shifting from aircraft design to spacecraft design. At forty years old, I plan to finish out my career designing stuff to be used above the Kármán line."

With VIKI's assistance, Hoffman brought Red Feather up to speed regarding concepts currently in development by members of the design team. Only the projects that had been made public such as Beth Sommerset and Julia Stempler's efforts on the emergency escape pods. Hoffman gave a rundown of the rocketry under construction on the facility's campus, with design by VIKI under the supervision of Jim Freeman and Dave Sutton.

"We had a special purpose in mind when we hired you," said Hoffman.

"I would hope so!" she interjected. "I look forward to a challenge."

"VIKI, open presentation XC83," Hoffman instructed.

The visual representation of the woman answered, "Opening file XC83. Here you go."

VIKI's image contracted into a small square in the lower right side of the screen. Instead, a rendering of a starship appeared against a starry outer space background.

Hoffman took the lead, narrating, "This is a super heavy starship, the kind used to transport passengers and freight from the Earth and the Moon to Mars. Let's say for the sake of argument that there are one hundred souls aboard with twenty-seven tons of goods in the cargo compartment. On the way to Mars, let's say the ship experiences a meteor strike. It's somewhat like a gunshot wound; typically with an entry wound and an exit wound."

Red Feather crossed her arms and leaned back in her chair to regard the presentation. An AI-animated rendering enlarged to focus on the animation in which a meteor pierced the exterior skin of the vessel, passed through, then exited out the hull on the opposite side.

"What size is the entry wound?" Red Feather asked. "Theoretically speaking, of course."

Hoffman responded, "For our initial project, we want the capacity to deal with anything bowling-ball size or smaller."

"Self-sealing hull," Sutton piped up. "We want to give the hull structure the capacity to detect the strike and immediately respond to it. Seal it up in a spontaneous reaction."

"Oh, you want me to work a little magic, eh?" Red Feather smirked. "Is that all?"

On the view screen, the engineers watched as the entry wound spaceship hole quickly shrank and sealed up completely."

A commercial paper cup sat on the table near Hoffman. On it, a barista had written *Cam* in Sharpie marker.

"We don't ask for much," said Hoffman, taking a sip from the cup. "Necessity is the mother of invention. It's a cliché saying, but it's true. Beth and Julie are working to perfect their emergency escape pod prototype. While they're working on that project, I'm going to put you in charge of research and development of the self-sealing hull. If we're going to build rockets that travel in space, meteors will be a risk we run into each and every day. Of course, you'll be working closely with Jim and Dave."

Sutton reached across the table to offer Red Feather a handshake. "Welcome aboard. If you're free right now, I'll take you up to the design lab."

As the other team members greeted her in turn, she remarked, "Cool. Finally, something I can sink my teeth into."

Chapter 24

Rocket Lab Design Lab
Auckland, New Zealand

"I always wanted to be a part of Star Fleet."

The first thing that caught the new engineer's eye in the design lab was a recruitment poster hung on the wall that pictured William Shatner as *Enterprise* Captain James Kirk pointing at the camera. The inscription on it read *I want you. Apply now for Starfleet academy.*"

Beyond the poster, Brandi Red Feather took stock of the expansive facility. An Asian woman's image appeared on the side wall view screen. For the moment, the image was frozen. When activated, she seemed to come to life.

"This is home," said Jim Freeman. "We design stuff in here. Some of it gets built out in the high bay. The really huge stuff gets constructed out in space at Bertrand Shipyard. Dave and I spend a lot of time out in the production facility."

After placing his palm on the touch ID sensor, VIKI said, *Welcome back, Jim. Who's your friend?*

To Red Feather, Freeman instructed, "Here's the touch screen."

She placed her palm on the touch screen, cueing the computer to respond, *Welcome to the design lab, Brandi Red Feather.*

Dave Sutton was welcomed to the facility in like manner.

How can I help you today? VIKI asked.

"I don't need help right now. I just want to look around," replied Red Feather.

A tour of the facility revealed the engineers' fascination with both science-fiction and historical forms of craft designed for use above and below the Kármán line. On the wall were prints that ranged from a grainy photo of the Wright Brothers' first flight to a picture of Buzz Aldrin in front of the Apollo 11 lunar lander.

On shelves and suspended from the ceiling were models of science-fiction and historical vehicles.

Side by side on one shelf stood 3-d printed metallic models of SpaceX Falcon and Superheavy rockets. Nearby was a completed model of NASA's Space Shuttle Discovery along with the Apollo Saturn 5.

Red Feather also took note of science-fiction representations including the Babylon 5 *Starfury* spacecraft. The Johnny Quest *Dragonfly. Firefly.* A clear lucite stand supported a model of the Star Wars *Millennium Falcon.* Rounding out the collection was a model of the *U.S.S. Enterprise.*

"I was wondering whether you guys geeked sci-fi," she said.

Sutton quickly responded, "Most of us do. Starfleet Academy's motto is *Ex astris, scientia* meaning *From the stars, knowledge.*"

Red Feather acknowledged, "The science of space discovery has gleaned much from the annuls of science fiction. How about cosplay? Do any of you ever dress up as sci-fi characters?"

Sutton looked at Freeman. Should they mention Bella Brown? They decided to keep her existence under wraps for the present.

With a grin, Red Feather admitted, "I went to a Star Trek convention a while back. Accidently wore a Chewbacca costume."

Sutton snickered, "That was a Wookie move."

She continued testing their knowledge of the subject with, "Did you know about the door prize you get when you attend a Star Trek convention?"

His eyebrows raised, arms crossed, Freeman countered, "Yeah. It's called the Enter Prize."

With an intake of breath, Red Feather approached the work table. "I guess you've heard them all before. Oooh!" she exclaimed suddenly. "Whose toys are these? And, more importantly, who gets to use them?"

On the table was an unopened Kidz Labs Anti-Gravity Magnetic Levitation

Science Kit. Sutton's eyes got bigger, as he had ordered the kit weeks earlier to explore various methods of producing anti-gravity. Using supplies in the kit, it boasted that junior scientists can make a pencil float, levitate a screw and build a maglev, a device that causes objects to levitate by means of two electromagnets. He had meant to haul the kit out to the Junk Works where the team conducted research and development of anti-gravity concepts.

"We stay pretty busy, but I was hoping to have the time to play around with it," said Sutton. "Physical forces are our favorite toys. I just wanted to see what we could learn from it."

Red Feather's curiosity was piqued. "Have either of you ever fooled around with anti-gravity? The concept is theoretically possible though the specific technology is elusive. If you could expand the application into larger craft, the discovery would be a game changer. And quite lucrative, I would imagine."

With a look at Sutton, Freeman said, "For now, let's concentrate on our immediate assignment. After we perfect the self-sealing hull, you can start work on anti-gravity technology. In the meantime ... "

Sutton countered, "If you have any ideas, though, feel free to toss them our way."

Chapter 25

Gogo Music Cafe
Downtown Auckland

Weird place for a suicide bomber to show up.

Camillo Hoffman was pleased when he was able to lay claim to a small round table at Gogo Music Cafe in downtown Auckland. For a brief moment, he worried that a bombing was imminent when an individual wearing a shapeless black robe with a burqa that covered most of her face plunked herself down in the vacant chair in front of him.

The room was full, with customers claiming their seats for the free late-evening concert. Patrons were expected to order something to eat, of course.

Thankfully, he recognized the voice as Bella Brown. "We never go to the beach anymore. Why don't we ever go to the beach on Saturdays?"

With a raised eyebrow, Hoffman said, "Bella?"

"Shhh!" Brown raised an index finger to her black-shrouded face. "Don't say my name. I'm supposed to be in Brussels pursuing my degree. You hate the beach, anyway. Marama and Raven are gone. Jim is practically glued to his expectant wife. Julie and Beth are busy orchestrating a baby shower for Jim and Claire, oh, and Dave is neck-deep in this." She gestured in the direction of the makeshift stage.

Hoffman, who had been digging into an order of Xinjiang chicken, said, "Oh, of course. Your disguise is a strategic way to avoid the satellite facial recognition software. Very clever. You want something to eat?"

The project manager couldn't discern Brown's facial expression, but from her tone he discerned her irritation. "It's a barbecue place," she snapped. " Have you forgotten I'm a vegan?"

"You want some chips?" he offered. "You are supposed to order from your seat using your hand terminal. I can get something if you like."

"No, but thanks. There's no guarantee what sort of oil they fry those things in."

For a moment they were silent, watching as yet another amateur gig launched their Musick Point career. They took note of the entire performance of the colorful trio whose instrumental debut included a didgeridoo, a flute and a native drum with Māori engravings.

"I thought they were good," assented Hoffman amid a round of applause.

"I don't think I thought this through," said Brown beneath her disguise. "I smuggled in some vegan crisps and a bottled Kombucha in this super-large movie purse, however I won't be able to eat anything without showing my face."

Hoffman clicked his tongue. "That's unfortunate," he said before shoveling in another forkful.

Rather than food, Brown extracted a hand terminal from her purse.

"I thought you were trying to stay off-grid," said Hoffman.

"It's OK; I've disabled the location feature. Heads up, Dave's up next."

"I'll bet his partner in crime wishes he could be here to witness Dave's musical debut."

With an air of smugness, Brown said, "Jim will see and hear. Claire too." She adjusted the kickstand to position her hand terminal to provide a less-than-optimal view of Dave Sutton's guitar performance.

In conjunction with a Māori guitarist introduced as Tino Aroha, Dave wowed the audience with a medley of guitar tunes. The duo's song set included *Weather With You* by Crowded House, *How Bizarre* by OMC, *April Sun in Cuba* by Dragon and *Don't Forget Ya Roots*, an overwhelmingly popular hit originally released by Six60. After whipping the crowd into a frenzy, the duo finished off with *God of Nations*, the New Zealand National Anthem finished off with an energetic series of guitar rifs. The duo bowed and waved as the crowd rose to its feet.

Brown was forced to wait until the applause died down before holding up the terminal's microphone and asking, "Did you guys catch that?"

The face of Jim Freeman appeared on the device's view screen. Claire Montgomery squeezed in next to him. "Thanks to you, we heard it all."

"The view wasn't so great, though," added Montgomery.

"Thanks, Bella," said Jim. "Wouldn't have missed that for the world. Dave put in an excellent performance, didn't he?"

"I was pleasantly surprised," Hoffman admitted. "I knew he was good, but I haven't had the opportunity to hear him play in quite a while."

"Miss you, Claire!" said Brown. "Good night to you both!"

With the evening winding down, some members of the audience were abandoning their seats to head home.

"I had better toddle off to practice my piety, modesty and hospitality," said Brown, rising from her seat as well. "By the way, how is my replacement working out?"

Hoffman replied, "She strikes me as a Vulcan with a sense of humor. And although VIKI hired her, she fits in with our design team rather well."

"How so?"

"She's a Trekkie."

Brown couldn't repress a belly laugh. "What are the odds of that? Hope I get to meet her soon, then."

"Not until you guys wrap up your assigned project. And by the way, VIKI assigned Brandi to your quarters."

With a frown, Brown assessed, "I left all my Star Trek stuff there. But my last housemate's room is empty. You know, the one after Raven."

"I'm sure Brandi will take excellent care of your memorabilia. She thinks you're in Brussels."

Holding up her hand terminal, she said, "I am in Brussels. Working on my engineering degree."

With a glance to his left and right, Hoffman said, "After he finishes up here, Dave is heading out to our secret facility to assist Ieohapata and his team. We're hoping to present the illusion that he has time for a life while you guys are actually working your asses off."

"I do have one question about work," Brown leaned in and whispered to Hoffman.

"OK, shoot. What do you have?"

Through her black mask, she whispered, "Since your black ops design team is nearing completion of our little miracle, I wanted to make certain that our legal team ticks the boxes for the patent application."

"I'm way ahead of you. Everything is fair dinkum."

With an elbow nudge and a lapse into her best New Zealand accent, Brown teased, "I think you've been here too long, Cam."

"No wuckas," was his reply.

"Do you think we're going to manage to keep our little project off the radar until time for the big announcement?"

With a smile and wiggle of his eyebrows, Hoffman said, "They'll be so surprised!"

Chapter 26

Junk Works
Rocket Lab campus
Auckland, New Zealand

"Who's Thomas Martin?"

Bella Brown confronted Dave Sutton and Jim Freeman as they arrived at the Junk Works facility one morning. Her inquiry was so urgent it couldn't wait until they had a moment to switch over from business casual to work coveralls.

"He left files on your ancient computer in here," Brown protested.

"I don't have any idea what you're talking about," Freeman protested.

"And the name isn't familiar. Thomas Martin? Tell me where you found it," Sutton responded.

Brown immediately went over to the cathode ray tube computer terminal that Freeman and Sutton were using to design anti-gravity vehicles. She fired up the computer oh-so-slowly, then pointed to a folder icon on the view screen.

She had access to state-of-the-art computers upstairs in the apartment she was using. Tired of isolation, however, she crept downstairs to snoop into project plans on the old design computer. That's where she found the first folder labeled Thomas Martin.

"It's just something that one of the early Rocket Lab designers left here," said Freeman. "It shouldn't affect our work here."

"Besides," added Sutton, "we couldn't check it out even if we wanted to.

I'm pretty sure all the old stuff is encrypted."

Brown placed her hand on her hip and cocked her head at an angle. "Please?"

"Okay, I apologize. You were able to open it up?"

With a serious nod, Brown affirmed, "Yah. Piece of cake."

"What was in it?"

After a pause for dramatic effect, she said, "Thomas Martin was performing experiments with acoustic levitation."

With a glance at Freeman, Sutton said, "Probably built a TinyLev."

"What's that principle?" Brown asked.

"If I had my phone, I could show you a diagram," Sutton lamented. "Basically, it's a single-axis standing wave levitation device. It has a piezoelectric source on the top and bottom, rather than a source and a reflector."

Freeman nodded, "It's cool. You can float small objects. Or a mouse."

The latter comment drew a glare from Brown.

Sutton added, "It's a fun lab experiment, but impractical if you want to make it much bigger."

"But what I'm telling you is that he was having a measure of success making the field bigger." She spread her hands out as far as they would go. Then, with her two index fingers, she pointed downwards. "Much bigger. And his experiments happened right here. Dave, do you know anything about far field acoustic levitation?"

Sutton shook his head.

"Thomas Martin was mucking about with larger objects and a longer field," she confirmed.

"Do you have any diagrams that we could look at?"

"There was only that one encrypted folder on the desktop, but if I poke around, I'll bet there are more in the Documents file."

Sutton blew out a breath, then said, "It would be interesting to find out, but we have a lot of stuff to work on here today that take priority over this sort of playing around."

Brown looked disappointed. "Jim, can you at least ask Claire to look up the dates Thomas Martin was at work out here?"

"She'll probably want to know why," he said.

Sutton warned, "If you tell her anything at all, you'll spill the beans on our little black ops operation out here."

"My poker face sucks," said Freeman. "Claire can read me like a book."

"Even so, if you ever have the opportunity, I'd love to find out who Thomas Martin was and to what project he was assigned. Maybe we're not the first team Rocket Lab has had running after anti-gravity technology."

Chapter 27

Junk Works
Rocket Lab Launch Complex
Auckland, New Zealand

"Why can't I pilot the craft?"

A small group who had taken part in constructing the anti-gravity prototype gathered to witness its first test flight.

Although the full-size prototype would be covered with a more expensive, durable material, Ieohapata covered the two-meter wide prototype with aluminum. A shop buffer whined as he endeavored to polish the surface to a metallic gleam.

"There are people out there who will pay oodles and gobs of money to anyone providing visual proof of alien life," said Bella Brown. "I'm going to record your first flight, just in case we need it."

"No, Bella!" Sutton nearly shouted. "It will void our top-secret contract, if not force us to go job hunting."

Brown pouted and slammed her hand terminal face-down on one of the cubicle desks.

She critically regarded the prototype model poised at the center of the Junk Works terminal — the results of weeks of work. The sleek metallic device did in fact resemble a flying saucer.

"Can you explain to me how it works again?" she asked. "Hoping I'll be the one to brief Welly when he makes the announcement about our anti-gravity discovery."

"You'll absorb more of the process as we get closer to the full-sized version," said Freeman. "The basic design for the prototype is two circles. The outer circle spins in a clockwise direction. The inner circle spins the opposite way. The pilot's capsule remains stationary."

"What makes it pitch, yaw and roll?"

"Do you see the little jets positioned equidistant around the center axis? The anti-gravity effect makes it go up. The little jets steer it."

"OK, I get it."

"Thanks for loaning us your Mr. Spock as test pilot, Bella," said Sutton. "I promise we'll take good care of him."

Through a clear window in the top, the engineers could see a bobble-head figure seated inside. The science-fiction pilot seemed well-suited for a futuristic vehicle.

With a sweeping gesture, Brown admitted, "This one is my Funko Pop Spock. He already has his own chair. But if you had asked for my Barbie doll Ken as Captain Spock twelve-inch action figure, the answer would have been a definitive *No*."

Jim Freeman had linked up the model's drive to a joystick controller.

"Once again, I volunteer to operate the AGV1," said Iehohapata. "How difficult can it be?"

With his hands on his hips, Sutton added, "At least do rock, paper scissors."

With a serious expression, Freeman explained, "Have either you operated any radio-controlled aircraft or rocketry? Have you, Bella? Any of you?"

No one said a word. Heads swiveled back and forth.

"What's the last thing you flew, Jim?" asked Sutton.

With no hesitation, Freeman answered, "I piloted a Gulf Stream small business passenger jet. Want to see?"

"Yeah, as a matter of fact," said Iehohapata.

Can you pull up You Tube on your black ops tablet, Bella?

"Sure," she said, handing the device to Freeman. "Just press the microphone and say the name of the recording you wish to view."

"Underwood Airfield. Time stamp 6.12.41."

Team members crowded in to observe and assess Freeman's piloting skills. Another member of the aircraft modeling association held up the device that recorded Freeman's exploits during which he successfully took off and landed his model jet aircraft on the landing strip, even managing a series of barrel rolls during the twenty-minute flight.

"That flight took place last year, before Claire and I were married." As an afterthought, he mused, "Don't have the time or the money for that sort of stuff anymore."

"All right, I admit you're the man for the job," said Sutton. "I'll stay here and turn the wrenches."

"Keep the blue side up, Jim." Ieohapata agreed.

Although none of the team members were allowed to bring their personal electronic devices to the development area, they used a designated tablet to initiate operations. With a huge grin, Freeman took the tablet in hand. "If this were a normal research and development project, I would state the project name, date and time for the record. But since it's all off-grid, I'll just say ... fingers crossed."

He raised the tablet and entered a code to access the vehicle's controls. "Initiating anti-gravity drive *now*."

Frowning, he re-entered the code and pressed the *go* button. Nothing happened. No sound, no motion.

"Buggar!" he said in frustration.

"Are you certain you have the right code?" inquired Brown.

Freeman gave her a look that would melt lead. "Yes, I entered the proper code. She's locked up and I can't figure out why."

Ieohapata approached the test craft. With his hand, he attempted to hand-prop the spin process.

"Careful!" Freeman cautioned. "The surface is high voltage when the process is active."

Ieohapata rubbed the aluminum surface with his hand. "No electricity here."

Freeman slammed the tablet down on a desk in one of the side cubicles. He paced back and forth a couple of times, then grabbed the tablet and once again entered the code.

Ieohapata gave a running commentary. "Nothing, Jim."

Scowling, Freeman plopped down on the concrete surface with his arms across his knees. "Fanny dickhead bloody hell! Bollocks and ass!"

With a swatting gesture towards the garage doors, Sutton suggested, "Why don't you guys give us a minute?"

Brown raised her black neck gaiter and donned a black hoodie for good measure.

"Ieohapata and I are going to grab some lunch," said Brown. "Be back later."

Sutton plopped down on the concrete floor opposite Freeman. Several minutes and a few dozen more curse words later, Freeman exhaled, worn out. "I thought by now we would be celebrating. Enjoying a couple of coldies. Letting Hoffman know the good news. *We have proof of concept, sir. You may pass along the good news to Mr. Kemp.*"

"A minor detail went wrong," said Sutton. "We'll get it right tomorrow, or the next day."

"I know, but I was looking forward to crossing that proof of concept bridge today."

Sutton thought for a moment, then said, "Are the coldies you're talking about in the chilly bin over there?"

"Nah, I put them in the back of the drinks machine. It makes a great 'fridge."

"The field of engineering means we have good days and bad days. Why can't we toast a bad day, and chalk it up to experience?"

"Great idea, Dave. Why not?"

Sutton went around to the back of the machine and opened it up. He handed a brown bottle to Freeman and took one for himself.

"To tomorrow?"

With a clink, Freeman said, "Tomorrow. It's gotta be better."

Chapter 28

Junk Works
Rocket Lab Launch Complex
Auckland, New Zealand

"In fact, it is rocket science. We are rocket scientists."

Jim Freeman and Dave Sutton stood in the test bay where the anti-gravity model stood. Ieohapata was also present. The model was poised on a test stand, allowing the engineers to make some last-minute adjustments.

"The canisters that hold the mercury have to be equidistant," said Ieohapata.

With his hand slapped against his forehead, Freeman said, "My bad. I'll have to pay the stupid tax."

Sutton said helpfully, "Things in the physical and mechanical realm don't always cooperate. I've discovered that Humble Pie tastes a lot better alongside a scoop of vanilla ice cream."

After a few brief pre-flight checks, Freeman announced, "OK, guys. Clear prop!"

Sutton cupped his hands, imitating Tower audio feed. "AGV1, you are cleared for takeoff."

This time when Freeman initiated the anti-gravity process, onlookers witnessed the rapidly increasing spin of the craft's outer ring, coupled with the opposite-direction spin of the inner ring.

He looked at Sutton, took a huge breath, then touched his tablet again. Switching over to the joystick, he pulled back the lever just before the saucer-like craft floated up to a waist-high elevation.

Brown emerged from her upstairs apartment. "Did I miss it? Oooh, it's working!"

Sutton whooped joyfully, then said, "When you want something done right, call a construction technician. Plus a couple of insane engineers in a smoking hot design hangar."

Sutton had a fist bump for Ieohapata and another for Freeman.

Brown skipped downstairs. "She's up! She's up! Stopping mid-stair, she turned around and started to go back up. "Where's my phone?"

With a cutting motion across his throat, Sutton reminded her of the filming prohibition. "No, Bella. Let's make sure she is operating correctly first."

An expression of concentration on his face , Freeman manipulated the joystick. In response, the craft moved higher, then down. Cautiously, he practiced a series of horizontal moves.

"Want me to open the door?" asked Ieohapata.

"No," answered Freeman. "Let's do a thorough set of tests inside first."

A few tense minutes later, Freeman directed the craft downwards. It came to rest at the center of the hangar.

There were screams of celebration along with a few high-fives and fist bumps.

"And the crowd goes wild!" Sutton rejoiced. "All right, Jim, see if you can do a barrel roll in that!"

"Not right now," said Freeman, calmly taking a sip of his soda.

"Bella, did you ascertain that Captain Spock in fact survived?"

"Oh!" Brown interjected. After checking to make sure the electrical field had dissipated, she clicked opened the dome to retrieve her Funko Pop bobblehead figure. "Yeah, Spock's giving it a thumbs-up."

Someone located a few cold beers and a bag of crisps that provided the essential elements of a celebration. This time a *bona-fide* celebration. In addition, the coldies provided a welcome respite from the mid-afternoon heat.

After downing half of his beverage, Sutton asked Brown, "So, Bella ... how would you describe the process by which our prototype operates?

Bella thought for a moment, then said, "The basic concept used is a Tesla gravity engine. To be precise, it doesn't produce anti-gravity; instead it causes a situation of negative mass. The anti-gravity Tesla coil is comprised of a ring of superconducting Yitrium-barium-copper oxide spinning at a rate of 5,000 revolutions per minute. High voltage in combination with the spinning components would normally produce catastrophic heating. To counteract that, the entire device is cooled by liquid nitrogen. Horizontal motion is provided by means of standard-propulsion jets."

Sutton sucked down more beer, pointed at Brown and said, "Bella, you are an absolute jewel. I'm tapping you to do our project write-up."

Freeman joked, "Are you absolutely certain you don't want VIKI to do it?"

"No, I don't trust VIKI. I want Bella. But I definitely need to be there to see the expression on VIKI's face when she finds out."

Chapter 29

Junk Works
Rocket Lab Launch Complex
Auckland, New Zealand

"We're going to have to work our socks off."

Proof of concept is not the end of the road: it's the beginning of an even longer road. The successful build and testing of the anti-gravity miniature model didn't mean the end of the engineering team's long hours. In fact, it meant that the design and production of a full-scale working prototype began in earnest. Rocket Lab had gotten wind of intelligence that there were other launch companies currently in pursuit of the technology. And there was no prize for second place — a fact that kicked the black-ops project into overdrive.

Using an ancient cathode-ray tube computer equipped with computer-aided design, Sutton and Freeman attempted to map out the specifications for a futuristic full-sized vehicle capable of making a trip from the sea level facility at Auckland to Bertrand Intra-orbital station. The technology would make an earth-shattering impact on space launches. It also held the potential to make Rocket Lab administrators, and the engineers themselves, wealthy beyond their wildest dreams.

Sutton was prohibited from bringing his hand terminal out to the remote facility, however he remembered the presentation in which Camillo Hoffman issued their mission perimeters. On the screen in an animated rendering, a tiny anti-gravity vehicle launched upwards from a planetary surface. As it rapidly gained altitude, the scene shifted from blue sky with clouds to black with a background of stars. Once the transport arrived at the intro-orbital shipyard facility, the animation gave over to a cheers, balloons and confetti celebration.

When Freeman pressed the print button, slowly, the ancient printer gave birth to a wide graph sheet with a two-dimensional representation of their full-sized design.

As the inkjet slipped back and forth over the full-length graph paper, Sutton asked, "Jim, do you think that the U. S. government possessed anti-gravity technology that they sequestered and kept from public knowledge?"

"Well, yeah," said Jim. "Air Force Research Laboratory Headquarters were a short distance away from Wright-Patterson Air Force Base. I lived not far from there."

"I mean, how much of that conspiracy theory do you go along with?"

Freeman straightened up and stretched. "Conspiracy theories are painted with a broad brush. The rumors say that President Dwight D. Eisenhower negotiated a treaty with extraterrestrials in 1954, which supposedly allowed the aliens to abduct humans and conduct tests on them in exchange for technological assistance. And President John F. Kennedy was supposedly assassinated because he was about to reveal that extraterrestrials were in the process of taking over the Earth."

"What do you think?"

During the years since their employment by Rocket Lab in 2035, the two engineers had discussed a variety of topics. Nothing was regarded as taboo.

"You have to look at the source, Dave. I have my personal copy of *Behold a Pale Horse.* The author, Milton William Cooper, was a longtime American conspiracy theorist. He had delusions of a secret world government in addition to the coming ice age. He believed that the extraterrestrials were in cahoots with the United States government."

"So you don't swallow all of that?"

"Nah. I believe in aliens—multiple species, in fact. But I don't believe they're all out to get us. I'm just spitballing here, but I think that conspiracy theorists' works are fifty percent true and fifty percent clickbait."

As the graph paper ticked off the printer, Sutton regarded the image.

"This is a totally different design from the circular model."

"Yeah," Freeman acknowledged. "In Tesla's flying-saucer design, the only cargo capacity is in the central area. That's not sufficient for our mission brief, which is transportation from a planet's surface up to a starship, shipyard or starbase out in space. We're going to need room for more passengers in addition to a lot of cargo capacity."

"In these designs, it looks like you are going more for the black triangle design."

"I thought that would be best, for several different reasons. The crew compartment of the craft is pressurized, providing a suitable environment for a dozen or so passengers. The back has pressurization as an option. I'm figuring that the cargo hatch can probably transport up to ten thousand pounds."

"Do you have the mechanical components figured out?"

"Yeah," said Freeman. "We're going to need separate systems for above and below the Kármán line. Do you remember when we watched that old 1983 disaster movie *Starflight One: The Plane That Couldn't Land?* They theoretically had a hypersonic Concorde shuttle that's capable of making the trip from Los Angeles to Sydney in two hours. An in-the-air disaster causes the plane to fly above the Kármán line."

"That sort of shit left you hugging the edge of your theater seat way back when."

"There are so many impossibilities in that movie that it's funny to watch now. For instance, the last I checked jet engines require oxygen to burn, but there's none of that out in space. And the script said they achieved an orbital path. Escape velocity from Earth's gravity is 25,000 miles per hour, but Starflight was only supposed to go Mach 2. Plus a ton of other issues."

Sutton surveyed the interior of the Junk Works hangar, empty except for the AGV1 vehicle. "I love your design."

"I feel a *but* coming on. What's your chief complaint?"

"Looks like it's going to be bigger than we originally planned," Sutton pointed to the emerging vehicle on the sheet of graph paper, "If you expect to build it in here, I'll say good bloody luck."

Chapter 30

Junk Works
Rocket Lab Launch Complex
Auckland, New Zealand

"I've been weightless before. Really, I have."

Bella Brown was the only person in the Junk Works garage who wasn't clamoring for a seat on the anti-gravity prototype.

As proof, on her tablet she located a much-younger picture of herself seemingly suspended in the air inside the fuselage of a Boeing 727. Her long brown hair floated out on both sides of her face. Her expression gave witness that it was her best experience ever.

"My parents got me a ticket on the Zero-G Experience® as a high-school graduation present. Living near Cape Canaveral, it was something that the astronaut candidates loved to do. It didn't last long, but the weightlessness allows you float and do flips in the air. It had a reputation as the closest thing to a trip to outer space. I wonder if a ride in our anti-gravity shuttle will feel anything like it."

"You don't have to fly in it, Bella," said Dave Sutton.

"At this point, we'd just like you to name it," Jim Freeman added.

Brown had been a partner in this creature's development from concept to prototype to final product. A glass windshield allowed her to see into the vehicle's cockpit. Two seats were positioned immediately inside. Pilot and copilot or navigator, she surmised. Beyond that were a dozen or so passenger seats with three-point harness with a little bar on the floor in front of each seat. Iehohapata was trying out the rear hatch. Once raised, it revealed a toy-hauler compartment suitable for any type cargo.

Although its white surface appeared similar to fiberglass, Brown had inside knowledge that the shuttle was covered with an amalgamate material designed for durability both below and above the Kármán line. The interior compartment was rated for ten thousand feet of elevation or more as well as space travel. It could be pressurized and was equipped with air purification for longer missions. Secretly, she wondered whether the craft would be successful in traveling not only through the atmosphere, but all the way to Bertrand Shipyard.

"Hey guys, I have a few questions," she mused. "What about the pebbles and dirt beneath the shuttle? Will that stuff fly up when you activate the anti-gravity effect?"

"No, don't worry, Bella," said Sutton. "Only the shuttle and the people and cargo inside are subject to the anti-gravity effect."

Sutton raised the side entry door again, allowing Brown a peek inside.

"It has that new-car smell."

"Probably from the aircraft seats," he guessed. "So what are we going to name this one?"

"I don't have a bottle of wine. And don't expect me to smash my Kombucha."

"It's OK," said Freeman. "It's not a proper dedication. We're not recording it."

With a pat across the smooth, white surface, Brown said, "I christen thee the *Griffon*."

Ieohapata nodded appreciatively. "I like it," he said.

Brown explained, "The griffon is a legendary creature with the body, tail, and back legs of a lion; the head and wings an eagle with it's talons on the front legs. According to tradition, griffons were the guardians of golden treasures."

"Did they fly?" asked Sutton.

"They sure did," Brown answered.

"Just wanted to make sure."

Chapter 31

Rocket Lab campus
Junk Works
Auckland, New Zealand

"What if intelligent extraterrestrials are watching us and refuse to communicate or share technology with us because we haven't earned it for ourselves? If people suddenly were given near unlimited energy and resources and the ability to travel to the stars without the responsibility learned from developing at a natural pace we could become a plague on the galaxy."

When Jim Freeman was nervous, he had a tendency to rattle on. He and Dave Sutton were inside the brand-spanking-new shuttlecraft, making final configurations for the first official test flight.

While seated in the shuttlecraft cockpit, Freeman continued his speculative narration. "Maybe one particular civilization acts as the great filter. Maybe they actively curb attempts by other species to become space-faring civilizations, thus preventing them from becoming threats. Less resources to share and less future conflicts to resolve sounds like a good enough reason. They don't even have to resort to violence, they just need to keep us in the dark about certain technologies until we doom ourselves in their absence."

"Like anti-gravity technology?" asked Sutton.

"Yeah, that," he confirmed. "Rock, scissors, paper. One, two, three, go!"

The two men made three cutting motions, then both paused in a gesture with two fingers extended.

"Damn," said Freeman. "Scissors tie. Go again."

This time, Freeman made the symbol for paper. Sutton went for the rock. "Buggar!" said Sutton. "Have a nice flight!"

The shuttlecraft they named the *Griffon* was everything they hoped it would be. At fifty-three feet in length, it filled the interior of the black ops cargo bay. Only Rocket Lab employees within Junk Works' small top-secret circle were allowed to witness the preliminary test flight.

Ieohapata crawled in and out of the vehicle in a last-minute preflight check. After a lengthy inspection, he emerged from the side door to give the vehicle a thumbs-up. "She's ready," he said.

Afterwards, he handed the *Griffon* off to a newcomer wearing red coveralls. He also made a thorough preflight inspection over, under and around the prototype.

At that precise moment, Camillo Hoffman entered through the side door. Sporting a navy Rocket Lab jacket with plaid bow tie, he was the only person in the hangar not wearing a red jumpsuit. "Good morning, all. Are we ready for take-off?"

Grumpily, Sutton said, "I didn't expect to see you here this early."

At 0 dark-thirty in the a.m., Hoffman was uncharacteristically cheerful. "The coffee has worked its magic. This is the day we've worked for. Why so glum, Eeyore?"

With a frown, Sutton replied, "I know this bucket inside and out. I figure I'm the most qualified to fly her."

With a pat on Sutton's back, Hoffman explained, "But you don't have a pilot's license, Dave. Not yet, anyhow. You understand that we have to tick the boxes. That's why Viktor here will take her up. Besides, I need you on the ground to monitor the *Griffon's* telemetry."

Bella Brown at last emerged from her upstairs apartment. Momentarily, she whipped out her phone. Hoffman shook his head, which triggered an annoyed expression on her part. She replaced the phone back in her pocket, then announced, "And, according to our plan, there is currently a computer network error that will prevent any aircraft in the vicinity from venturing anywhere near us."

Turning to a platinum-haired pilot in red coveralls, Hoffman asked, "Are you ready, Viktor?"

With a certain degree of apprehension, Camillo Hoffman had gone through VIKI to select Viktor Akermann for the test pilot's job. He had been chosen based on his stellar resume that included an impressive number of flight hours on various types of aircraft. Coupled with his flawless safety record, VIKI had hand-picked him.

"Pilot is go," he said, climbing inside the pilot's seat. With Jim Freeman strapped into the front passenger seat, Viktor added, "Test pilot is go. The *Griffon* is ready for launch."

Into his forward console, Akermann said, "Auckland Tower, Rocket Lab *Griffon* is ready for departure. Heading east from Mahia Spaceport over the Pakuranga Basin."

Over the vehicle's CommLink, Hoffman said, "Air traffic control is shut down, and, thanks to the radio chaos instigated by Bella, there will be no one else in the air. *Griffon*, you are cleared for takeoff."

The eager engineers watched as the *Griffon's* outer lights activated. In conventional fashion, there was a green light on the right and red on the left, supplemented by other exterior lighting. Onlookers detected a whirring sound.

Hoffman nodded to the Junk Works team, who eagerly awaited the results of the day's demonstration. "Proof of concept. That's our goal for today."

Akermann and Freeman both donned the helmets and goggles, as per the company medical team's orders. Inside the *Griffon's* cockpit, the pilot and copilot regarded evidence that the anti gravity effect was functioning within normal limits.

When the *Griffon* levitated to knee-high altitude, Brown screamed and jumped up and down. "She's up! Whoo! We're airborne!"

Watching from the entryway of Junk Works, Ieohapata, his team of technicians and the engineers applauded, a few giving the others high-fives.

"You are clear to proceed with the flight plan," Hoffman said into his hand terminal.

In response, Akermann gave Hoffman a salute and a thumbs-up. At that point, Iehohapata remotely cued the outer doors to open.

"Better step back," cautioned Hoffman.

Everyone in the garage backpedaled while the vehicle scooted towards the doorway. A good ways outside the structure, the *Griffon* gradually increased in altitude until it was well over the tops of the trees. Freeman eyed the altimeter until it read 185 feet.

"You ready?" Akermann wanted to know.

"Hell yeah!" Freeman responded without a moment's hesitation. "Punch it!"

"Here we go," said the pilot as he urged the craft forward. Even though it was long before sunrise, moonlight lit the surface of Pakuranga Creek as they skimmed above the surface.

"Did you get the tutorial on the ejection seat?" Akermann asked a short time later.

"I designed this thing. Who built an ejection seat in? None of the technicians told me about that."

Akermann's voice grew serious. "Here's what you need to know. When you feel the RPMs deteriorate, you may experience quite a bit of turbulence. It will feel like there's a pair of elephants dancing on the wings. If I yell *Eject, eject, eject* I want you to reach down and pull the ejection lever."

Freeman did a momentary search around the perimeter of his seat, until Akermann erupted into laughter.

"Gotcha!" he said. "There is no ejection seat. And no parachutes. But as long as the anti-gravity feature is activated, we aren't likely to fall out of the sky."

"That was cruel," Freeman fired back.

The moonlit ride was somewhat surreal. As they rounded Pakuranga Creek, there was no prop wash on the water and very little sound.

There was indeed an elephant, but it wasn't dancing on the wings.

Freeman took a moment to address the elephant in the room. Would this monumental innovation ever be used as an instrument of war? And still another question smoldered in his brain. How would the aliens feel about humans once again gaining the capacity for anti-gravity technology? And would this innovation activate another intergalactic trip wire?

Chapter 32

U. S. Capitol Building
Honolulu, Hawaii

The guest list was short.

General Leonard Bardick reported to a special committee meeting in the upper floor of the U.S. capitol building. Only a few officials were allowed to attend; no one else was even aware that it took place.

Upon entry, the interior of the room didn't strike him as a stronghold of democracy.

Bardick figured that President Ho had focused far more time and energy into transforming the timbre of the governor's office into a respected center of presidential authority. He had attended meetings in the new Situation Room, with its long table lined with seats on each side. A large view screen at the short end.

In contrast, the room that had been chosen for top-secret small group meetings didn't in the least resemble the Situation Room, or the legislative chamber. In fact, it looked more like a file room from pre-computer days that had been recycled into a meeting room. In fact, imprints made by filing cabinets that had been removed still scarred the walls.

Along with Secretary of Defense Paul Rodriguez, Bardick was escorted upstairs by two men he assumed to be Secret Service. The two officials were directed to a half-dozen seats lining the outer walls, closely followed by special defense committee members Gabriela Sanchez from Puerto Rico and Guatapang Camacho from Guam. The ever-present men in suits stood at attention on either side of the interior door.

Everyone in the room exchanged pleasantries for the next few moments. Five, maybe ten minutes. All realized that Maleko Ho was late to his own meeting. He didn't need to apologize. After all, he was the president.

To himself, Bardick assessed that whatever Ho was doing in the previous hour, or even all day, was less important than the information to be served up in this meeting.

"Good afternoon, Mr. President," said General Rodriguez.

The moment the commander-in-chief entered, everyone stood.

President Ho acknowledged each participant before letting Rodriguez take center stage.

"Paul, this is your show. What are our chances of getting overrun, muddy or bloody?"

For the first half of the meeting, Rodriguez enumerated the United States' earthly enemies. For the moment, the wounded nation had achieved a delicate balance. Although there was a long list of nations with superior technology and weaponry, few gripes and complaints had come to the surface.

"Thanks to satellite telemetry, any and all of our potential enemies know essentially what weaponry we possess and where we have it," Rodriguez said. "Normally that would be placed in the minus column, except in our current situation it means not only that our capabilities are limited, but also we aren't perceived as a threat. None of our earthly neighbors has us in their crosshairs right now.

"Unfortunately, no one in authority on the new space station is willing to offer us a place up there.

"Regarding the topic of spying eyes in the sky, I will let General Bardick speak to the status of our alien neighbors."

Bardick cleared his throat and pulled out his tablet.

"Thank you, Paul. As you are all aware, there is a Galactic Federation of planets and exoplanetary species. Thus the term Exopolitics. Planet Earth isn't a member—officially or unofficially. Nevertheless, we have a Federation liaison residing on our planet. The ambassador is a member of the

Nordic species. If you met him coming down the street, you wouldn't know that he's not human. In any case, I have recently been in communication with him regarding our current situation."

President Ho spoke. "What is his name, just for future reference?"

"He calls himself Lukas Berg. I think it's a Swedish name, although he is definitely not Swedish. In light of our current status, I asked him to check around to determine the intergalactic climate. It's stormy. Cloudy with a chance of Category 5 hurricane. As in, not good."

With his brows furrowed, President Ho asked, "I'm hoping you can provide us with details. What species specifically is the focus of your gloomy forecast?"

"Just in case any of you are not familiar with it, I brought along a file of *Known Intergalactic Species*."

With a sweep of his hand, an image from the general's tablet blew up on the view screen. A sharp intake of breath could be heard from Sanchez when she saw a rendering of the insectoid species. She quietly crossed herself.

"The Cenotians are an insectoid species with a brown or green exoskeleton and red compound eyes," Bardick began. "Physically, they are six to seven feet in height."

"Oh, God. Looks like a praying mantis," said Camacho. "Something out of an old Japanese horror flick."

"That's not our biggest problem," Bardick announced. "Technologically speaking, they are skilled space travelers with formidable weaponry."

President Ho made an inquiry. "I'm assuming you are about to tell us why the Cenotians are pissed at us."

"Yes, I was getting to that. If you are a student of world history, I'm certain you would be aware of the ancient Assyrians. Their conquests weren't a matter of their anger. Conquering other nations was simply what they did. And they did it with style and brutality. Such that other nations would surrender once they saw them coming."

"So do they want to conquer the Earth, or destroy it?" asked Ho.

Bardick shook his head. "I wish I could tell you. Lukas obtained positive evidence that the Earth is in their path of destruction. They can and will annihilate it."

"Could I venture a question?" asked Camacho. "Among our alien allies, is there no one in our arena? Hopefully at least one species, or a league of them, who will be inspired to defend us?"

"Forgive me for being brutal, but due to the Cenotians' reputation, I don't think anyone else wants to mess with them."

"Has every effort been made to negotiate with them?"

"As far as negotiations, we can only communicate through channels. While they can shape-shift to appear human, they communicate by means of telepathy. And currently, they continue in their path of conquering other civilizations without making any treaties."

President Ho took a few long breaths. Crossed his arms over his chest. "So there will be no quarter. How far off is Cenos, exactly?"

"They hail from a planet in the Alpha Centauri system. Pretty damn close in galactic terms."

"Pretty close, huh? How fast do you imagine this territorial conquest might take place? How long before we start stacking up bodies again?"

General Bardick hesitated for a moment before answering. "If it's any indication, Lukas is in the process of getting his family off-planet."

Amid the pallor that had fallen over the room, the president asked, "Can we discuss the status of any off-world colonies? Did you gather any intel on any of them?"

With a scowl, Bardick summarized, "Artemis colony can be described as a research station with a nearby mining facility. As for Aires Prime, you probably know more about them than I do. They are functioning on a rudimentary level however they have yet to achieve food production equal to the needs of their population. Therefore, they are dependent on Earth supplies."

The president ventured, "Don't we have a new colony on Proxima Centauri?"

General Bardick continued, "Yeah, there was a mission to settle a habitable planet there. The vessels were built by Rocket Lab at Bertrand Shipyard. They launched last year, but there is currently no way to determine whether or not they survived. In case you wanted to know, the Chenghuang Corporation from China footed the bill for this development."

"Are there any further plans to build other ships? A re-supply mission?"

Bardick cleared his throat. "As of this time, you are aware of the financial status of China. They are experiencing an economic downturn. Chenghuang Corporation is struggling to keep the lights on."

"My God!" Ho interjected. "Does the facility that built the ships have the capability to produce additional vessels?"

"Yes sir, Rocket Lab is in the process of building another mothership at Bertrand Shipyard. It is my understanding that a colossal vessel was ordered some time ago by the Chenghuang Corporation, but they recently backed out of their contract."

"Would this be the re-supply mission?" asked Ho.

"Yes, that's my understanding."

"Without Chenghuang's funding, will Rocket Lab be able to complete this mission?"

Bardick hesitated. "Unknown, sir."

President Ho straightened himself in his office chair. "Well, somebody better find out. Because at this point, it sounds as if this colony may be humanity's best chance for survival."

Chapter 33

Rocket Lab administrative offices
Auckland, New Zealand

"I wonder if VIKI knows anything about fundraising.""

Project manager Camillo Hoffman rarely had a reason to step into Rocket Lab CEO Brandon Kemp's office. In the past, each summons to visit had meant a serious challenge to him and the engineers.

While he waited to discover the reason for the summons, a knot grew in his stomach. Kemp's office staff were usually quite hospitable, however. And whatever challenges Hoffman would encounter would be offset by a fresh cup of coffee.

As soon as he entered the administrative suite, he was greeted by Kemp's personal assistant. She always wore the Rocket Lab uniform — a navy blue blazer bearing the company logo. This would be no occasion for anxious waiting. She immediately waved Hoffman straight through to Kemp's office.

"Mr. Kemp is expecting you. Would you care for some coffee, Mr. Hoffman?"

"Yes, please. Cream and sugar."

Hoffman discerned that Kemp was definitely less jovial than usual. He guessed he would discover the reason soon enough.

"Good morning, Cam. How are things in the research and development department?"

A moment later, Kemp's assistant brought in a steaming ceramic cup which she placed on a napkin beside Hoffman's seat.

"I'm pleased to report things are going well," Hoffman reported. "Of course, you are aware of the progress we're making on the emergency escape pods. Our new research and development engineer is acclimating to the challenge. She is making progress on self-sealing hull design."

Kemp nodded his head, waiting until his assistant had closed the office door. "How about our top-secret project. Is that going well?"

Hoffman grinned. "Our team is hard at work. At this point, we just had a successful test flight."

"Was that the full-sized prototype?"

"Yeah. It goes up and it flies. We have a few kinks to iron out before we take it all the way up to Bertrand Station."

"Good. No video, as yet?"

"No, sir. As per your orders. When we become confident concerning the reliability of the technology, we'll have to back into development videos."

"You can't hack what isn't there," Kemp nodded.

"Of course you haven't invited me up here to discuss the weather."

Kemp took a sip of his own coffee, then scowled. "I guess I was dreading this conversation."

At this point, Hoffman was really worried. Right on the heels of the AI crisis, something else had gone sour.

"What is the status of the mothership under construction at Bertrand Station?" Kemp inquired.

Hoffman thought for a moment, then said, "I can give you all the specifics if you like. But in general she is about halfway finished. With the station running on AI and the robots doing the bulk of outer construction, work is proceeding at an unprecedented pace."

"Excellent! That's superb!" Switching gears, he added, "But who is going to pay for it?"

The question felt like a gut-punch.

"Sir?" Hoffman interjected in disbelief. "The Chenghuang Corporation ordered the vessel. And although they didn't say it in so many words, they are eager to be first in line for the mineral rights on Proxima Centauri B."

"Just when we're chugging along at a reasonable pace, something sets us back. Have you kept up with the economic crisis in China? Because it's likely to blow back on us."

"Not specifically."

Kemp's desktop view screen displayed the Rocket Lab logo. Once active, he one-tabbed it to an audio news file. The newscaster on the screen described China's gloomy economic crisis:

Hong Kong's Hang Seng Index slid into a bear market on Friday, having fallen twenty percent from its recent peak in March. Last week, the Chinese yuan fell to its lowest level in 16 years, prompting the central bank to make its biggest defense of the currency on record by setting a much higher exchange rate than the estimated market value. Consumer prices are falling while discretionary spending —food, travel and recreation — are in a twenty-year slump.

At that point, Kemp stopped the audio feed. "I'm sorry, I can't stand to listen to any more."

Although he hadn't yet determined Kemp's direction, Hoffman attempted to contribute to the conversation. "I'm somewhat familiar with China's situation. In the past 50 years, their economic model has taken the country from poverty to a world economic power. I'm not a news hound, but I did hear that there is a growing real-estate crisis."

"What you've heard is only part of the crisis. The housing boom contributed to an overabundance of construction. At the same time, the income of Chinese consumers is buying less and less. Are you ready for the bomb drop? All that has contributed to a huge impact on large businesses. The Chenghuang Corporation has backed out of their contract."

"Holy fuck! Oh, my apologies, sir. Wouldn't that constitute a breach of contract?"

"It would if we chose to pursue a lawsuit. At this stage, there's no point. Chenghuang is struggling to keep the lights on. Can't get blood from a turnip, you know."

Hoffman experienced a brief panic attack. "How are we going to meet our costs without their funding?"

Kemp rocked back a few times in his office chair. "We have a few options. As this technology is a matter of national security, I have looked into seeking federal funding."

"That's actually a great idea."

"Do you have any idea of the size of the New Zealand national budget?"

"Comparitively not huge, I imagine. Have you considered crowdfunding?"

Kemp rolled his eyes. "Do you have any idea of the cost of this project?"

Hoffman nodded, "Actually, I am aware."

"We are nearly out of options. Which leaves one more alternative."

"Which is?"

"We're going to put the word out, as in advertise. Find someone in the private sector to purchase our mothership. And as far as Rocket Lab funding, I'm going to ask you to expedite our top-secret project. Once the prototype is reliable enough to make a trip out to Bertrand station, we'll shout it from the mountaintops and sell the shit out of it."

"Only when the patent clears."

"And, Cam, please do me a huge favor. Don't mention this funding glitch to Eireann. As you are aware, she has plenty on her plate already."

"No worries, sir. You can count on me."

Chapter 34

Anawhata Beach
Auckland, New Zealand

When Bella Brown got the all-clear to move back into her bungalow, she wasn't surprised to find someone else living there as well.

During her years of living in a company bungalow on the Rocket Lab campus, housemates had come and gone. Some of them worked out better than others. Some tried to convert her away from veganism. Others dared to re-arrange her sizable collection of Star Trek memorabilia. Unfortunately, when she did manage to find a housemate who was a good fit, they always found a reason to move out. Her first housemate Marama Fetumale, who had also been on the Rocket Lab research and development team, left amid rumors of international espionage and a suspicious data breech. And the year before, her longtime favorite housemate Raven Munoz left to accept a position as historian for the first exoplanet colony.

Brown and Munoz had often enjoyed Saturday trips to the north island's many fabulous beaches. And during her six-months' exile at Junk Works, she had been prohibited from showing her face at the beach — or anywhere else, for that matter.

Initially, Red Feather seemed to be a good fit for the bungalow. She wasn't a vegan, but she was respectful of the practice. She was exceptionally fond of the grey cat that Brown had adopted and named Kitty Kitty. And she was, coincidentally, a Trekkie.

It hadn't been difficult to convince her new housemate to hop in her Subaru and head out for a day trip to Anawhata Beach, a fabulous attraction only forty kilometers away.

During the final days of summer, the two sat on the beach in lawn chairs making patterns in the black sand with their bare toes. The beach was a remote location. Signs bore witness to the fact that Anawhata had no beach patrol. That presented no problem, as neither of them were there to swim.

Others who took part in their day-trip were Dave Sutton and his lady friend Tino Aroha. A native of Auckland, Aroha was an avid hiker and member of the Auckland Tramping Club. Sutton was a novice tramper, but he promised to give it a try.

Aroha showed up wearing hiking clothes with her hair bound into a hair clip. A boonie bush hat topped off her ensemble. Sutton wore his Phish Tour 2023 ball cap with a pair of dark sunglasses. Both wore backpacks. Grabbing Sutton's hand, Aroha indicated, "The stream up there is a popular tourist destination. There used to be an old bus that would drop off the trampers up in the hills above the stream. A few hours later, the bus would come down here to collect them from the beach."

"So you guys are going to head up to the stream?" asked Brown.

"Over there is where the Anawhata Stream exits into the Tasman Sea," Aroha explained.

With a wary look, "Sutton said, "We're going to head over that way to see how far we get."

"Have a nice walk!" said Red Feather.

After they departed, the only sound on the remote beach was the sound of the surf. As they watched the two disappear down the beach, Brown asked, "More wine?"

"No, I'm good. What did you bring along to read?"

"As you probably are aware, there are a lot of authors who jumped on the Star Trek train. One of them being Greg Cox who wrote this one: *The Eugenics Wars: The Rise and Fall of Khan Noonien Singh.* This is Volume I, which fills in the story of Khan and the other Children of Chrysalis."

"They were genetically-modified offspring, weren't they?"

"Yeah. They were physically and mentally superior to your average human

156

beings. Superior intellect contributed to their grandiose egos and profound psychological imbalances."

With an offended look, Brown said, "Not always."

Red Feather giggled, then said, "Oh, Bella. I didn't mean to offend you. Khan was insane and power hungry, but you will likely approve of one thing he did."

"What's that?"

"Khan destroyed Gary Seven's Beta 5 AI supercomputer."

"Ah ha! He didn't trust it, either!"

"On second thought, I will take some more of that wine."

Brown replenished Red Feather's cup as well as distributed some fruit for a snack.

"What are you reading?"

Red Feather answered, "*I Am Not Spock* by Leonard Nimoy. Did you ever hear of it?"

"Did you know that autobiography caused a big kerfuffle among Star Trek fans?"

"See, the cover on my copy has the Vulcan hand salute," said Red Feather.

"A gesture usually accompanied by the traditional spoken blessing live long and prosper – *dif-tor heh smusma* in the Vulcan language," Brown added.

"Yeah, I did a little research to discover that Nimoy wrote another autobiography twenty years later called *I Am Spock*."

With an incredulous tone, Brown said, "You know, I've actually never read *I Am Not Spock*. Can I have a go when you're done?"

"Sure. And, by the way, my aunt is coming for a visit next week. I just wanted to make sure it was all right with you if she stays with me?"

"Of course!" said Brown. "I'd love to meet her."

"She's in her eighties and she's never flown anywhere in her life. I'm really surprised that she's willing to make the trip. I just want to have the opportunity to spend some time with her while she's down here."

To herself, Brown wondered what it must be like to have family still alive who could come and visit.

Chapter 35

Rocket Lab boardroom
Auckland, New Zealand

"I think we should name it the *Kon-Tiki*."

Bella Brown stood at the head of the oblong Rocket Lab boardroom table for the first time in six months. In unremarkable clothing, not wearing a hijab or Mandelorian helmet. Or a Star Trek uniform. Instead, she prepared for her presentation in a standard Rocket Lab blazer with her long hair in a single braid.

Surrounding the room were fellow members of the research and development team including Julie Stempler, Dave Sutton, Beth Sommerset, Jim Freeman and Brandi Red Feather.

"Nice to have you back, Bella," said Project Manager Camillo Hoffman with a wink.

"It's super-nice to be here," she replied.

"How was Brussels?" said Dave Sutton, suppressing a chuckle.

Brown ventured a glance at the view screen which displayed an Asian woman's visage.

"Pleased to report success in earning my engineering degree," she replied. "I now have a specialty in Spacecraft Design with a minor in Warp Propulsion Dynamics."

"Congratulations," said Hoffman, extending a handshake. "We're all proud of you."

"And it's been crazy weird while you were gone," said Stempler, with a glance at the view screen out the corner of her eyes.

"Now that the anti-gravity project is complete, let's get back to the business of designing spacecraft," said Hoffman. "Today's agenda is the business of naming the behemoth we have nearing completion at Bertrand Shipyard. Bella, I believe you have done some research?"

Hoffman cradled his usual ceramic coffee mug, while Sutton sipped Gatorade from a plastic bottle. Stempler fueled up with green tea in a travel mug. Brown slaked her thirst with Kombucha. All were well-stoked with beverages. None of the engineers, however, were in possession of a tablet. None were needed, as all files were safely stored in VIKI's electronic brain.

Brown, who had been standing at the head of the oblong table, moved to the side of the boardroom view screen.

"VIKI, access the file labeled Kon-Tiki," she instructed.

"Here you go," the Asian woman said.

On the view screen was displayed a photo of an ocean-going raft made from balsa logs lashed together.

"In the past we have drawn from the fields of science fiction and space exploration to name our vessels," Brown explained. "This time, I thought we could honor the Polynesian explorers who first reached New Zealand back in the twelfth century."

She paused to regard the reaction of Hoffman, who crossed his arms across his chest and said simply, "Let's hear your idea, Bella."

Bella instructed, "VIKI, play the Kon-Tiki Wikipedia entry."

In a deadpan tone, VIKI obliged. "*The Kon-Tiki expedition was a 1947 journey by raft across the Pacific Ocean from South America to the Polynesian islands, led by Norwegian explorer and writer Thor Heyerdahl. The raft was named Kon-Tiki after the Inca god Viracocha, for whom Kon-Tiki was said to be an older name. Photographs also show a topsail above the mainsail, and also a mizzen sail, mounted at the stern.*"

"Pause recording."

Brown continued her discourse. "The Kon-Tiki's journey took place from April to August in 1947. My research revealed the truth of the matter, which was that Heyerdahl's craft was a primitive raft which had no means of steerage. It stood in contrast to the sophisticated double-hulled outrigger canoes and catamarans historically used and in fact still in use by the Austronesian people. Heyerdahl believed that New Zealand was settled by people from South America, in contrast to the archaelogical, linguistic and genetic evidence that supports an Asian origin for the Polynesian and Māori peoples. VIKI, skip to 'conclusion' please."

Rather than drift voyaging, the Polynesian sailors likely used deliberate wayfinding and celestial navigation techniques. The voyage of the Kon-Tiki and a successive series of Pacific voyages by similar craft proved that Polynesian-Māori peoples were capable of navigating long distances.

"Stop recording. Thank you, VIKI."

It's a pleasure to work with you, Bella.

"In conclusion, I feel that we should name our new ship the *Kon-Tiki*. Like the ancient Polynesian explorers, our ship will also have the capability to navigate long distances using celestial navigation. What do you think, Cam?"

"I love the idea," Hoffman replied. "People? Your thoughts?"

"Very creative," said Sommerset.

"I think it's appropriate," said Freeman.

Red Feather added, "Love it!"

"If no one else has any other ideas ... *Kon-Tiki* it is," said Hoffman definitively. "And Bella has an additional surprise."

"VIKI, display logo designs," she instructed.

"I designed the first trial logo as a representation for our exploratory vessel," said VIKI.

The viewscreen displayed a rendering of a double-hulled outrigger canoe crewed by Polynesian sailors.

"You have two to choose from," said Bella. "VIKI, display alternate logo."

"Here you go."

The second design pictured a mask-like representation of the Polynesian god's face.

Sommerset shook her head. "I don't like it. This one doesn't say exploration at all."

"No, it doesn't," agreed Sutton.

"It sort of creeps me out, too," said Red Feather.

"I'm with you guys," said Hoffman. "I think we should use the one with the canoe. Does anyone object?" When silence reigned, he said, "Bella, I think we can adopt Version 1 as our logo. After we get the kinks out, we can have Welly to put out the word that we're one step closer to launching the mothership *Kon-Tiki*."

Sommerset raised her hand. "Just have a quick question. If we have a new customer, then why doesn't the general get to name the new vessel?"

Hoffman wrinkled his nose, then replied, "General Bardick said he had zero interest in naming the ship. He only specified that, and I quote, *make sure the bucket is sea worthy.*"

Chapter 36

Bardick residence
Pacific Heights neighborhood
Honolulu, Hawaii

Divorcing a billionaire is a complicated process. And Gladys Bardick was nearly one hundred percent certain that her husband wanted a divorce. Or that he was once again headed out to the Porgera Gold Mine in Papua New Guinea. Probably the latter. Hopefully the latter.

Despite the distance that had grown between them, in her heart she still loved him.

All the same, it had raised a red flag when Felipe Sanninikone rapped on the doorframe of her sunroom early one morning. First she caught a glimpse of his curly black hair, for the moment minus his chef's hat.

"No, you're not disturbing. Come in, Felipe. I was just reading."

"General Bardick requested that the two of you will be dining together this evening. I wanted to consult with you regarding the menu. Would you like the same entree or should I prepare something else for you?"

Being a military wife, Gladys Bardick understood there would be times when her husband needed to be away. Away from the house or out of the country, he was absent for the purpose of saving the world. Now, he was constantly isolated from her in their own home. By choice, not out of necessity.

It required a handful of staff members to keep the household afloat. People came and went to make deliveries, clean the house, service the pool and provide for the day-to-day needs of the homeowners.

Although she spoke to other people on a daily basis, at this point Gladys rarely saw her husband, much less spoke with him. He kept to his bedroom, office and library located in the opposite end of their home from her bedroom, salon and sun room. Not so much an early riser, nevertheless when the chef consulted with her, she was already dressed in a tropical print blouse, coordinating solid pants and silver wedge sandals.

She cleared her throat, then answered, "What is the general having?"

"He requested Alaskan halibut."

"Well then, if the general is having halibut I will have the same."

"He requested dinner to be served at seven p.m. Will that be suitable, ma'am?"

"That will be fine, Felipe."

It had been more than a month since the Bardicks had dined together in the formal dining room of their Pacific Heights home. As a matter of fact, Gladys didn't remember precisely how long it had been. The previous occasion had been an awkward evening, one in which very few words were spoken. The silence only emphasized how far apart they had drifted. With very diverse lives, they had little in common any more.

Gladys feared the general's motive for requesting a meal together. She could tolerate the silence, or his absence, for any other reason. If he wanted a divorce, however, it would shatter her heart. Plus it would be a very complicated process given the general's massive wealth.

She came to the conclusion that they were both adults. There was no need to squabble. After a moment, she decided that whatever his motives were, the best course of action was to be civil. She didn't want to be pictured in the tabloids among those wives scrambling to collect massive amounts of cash from their rich husbands.

There was another reason she hoped to avoid a divorce. The fallout would cause a lot of talk among her friends at Temple Beit Shalom.

There were, after all, a few hours to prepare for their evening together. Su Lee could help her select a casual ensemble that her husband wasn't likely to forget. And there was time to pop out for a hair and makeup session. Perhaps squeeze in a nail touch-up as well.

If the general wanted a divorce, she would do her best to show him what he would be missing. It was time for the Silver Fox to emerge from her den.

Chapter 37

Bella Brown residence
Rocket Lab campus
Auckland, New Zealand

Sunday mornings came with a welcome absence of schedule. Bella Brown and Brandi Red Feather were puttering about in the kitchen of their bungalow when they heard a rapping at the door.

On the other side of the door they discovered a plump elderly woman wearing a toboggan and a heavy coat.

"Hi! Can I help you?" Brown asked her.

"Auntie!" exclaimed Red Feather, enveloping the visitor in a warm embrace.

"Hello, dear! How nice to finally be here."

Their guest waved at a woman driving a red Suzuki Swift parked immediately in front of the bungalow.

"Thanks for the ride!"

The driver waved back and was on her way.

Their guest arrived with a suitcase, a backpack and a shoulder bag. Red Feather and her housemate pitched in to transfer the items. Just inside, she plopped down in their recliner and raised the footrest.

Brown wasn't at all surprised to note the resemblance between the two women. Each had tan skin and dark brown eyes, though the aunt's face bore creases and smile lines. Red Feather's hair was jet black arranged in a single braid. Two snow-white braids extended down to the elder woman's waist.

"I wasn't certain when you would be arriving," Red Feather apologized. "I would have picked you up. How was your flight?"

"Ummm, several flights. My last flight was from San Francisco. It felt like we were in the air for days. But there was a nice lady on board. She gave me hot tea and a blanket."

She removed her sherpa and fanned her face with it. "It's plenty warm here, though."

"Who was the driver who brought you here? Did you call an Uber?"

"I didn't call anyone. She was a nice lady in the airport who asked me if I wanted a ride."

With a stern expression, Red Feather asked, "Auntie, did you get in the car with a total stranger?"

"She wasn't a stranger. She told me her name."

Red Feather shook her head. "And you still don't have a phone, do you?"

"Yes, I do," she protested. "I left it on the wall. At home, where it belongs. And I trust in the Lord to protect me wherever I go."

The elder lady rummaged in her belongings to find two brightly-colored plastic bags marked with the Air New Zealand logo. "They had a store in the airport. I picked up a little something for you."

Red Feather took the bag and gave her aunt a hug. "The gift shop sucked you in, eh? Why, thank you."

"Just a token of my thanks for your hospitality."

She extended the other bag to Brown. With a tentative expression, she inspected the contents. Inside was a women's prayer journal with a pink floral cover.

"Thanks, but you didn't have to get me anything."

"I came to see you as well, dear."

"Oh?"

"We didn't get a proper introduction, now, did we? We've never met in person; all the same I feel as if I know you. I'm Muriel Santiago."

Chapter 38

Design lab
Rocket Lab headquarters
Auckland, New Zealand

"You want me to do what?"

It was January, hot as Hades at Rocket Lab headquarters. A native of Canada, Brandi Red Feather brought in a box fan to supplement the facility's air conditioning. Otherwise, she threatened to melt.

At 9 a.m. on a Thursday morning, Jim Freeman and Dave Sutton popped in to check on R & D projects before heading out to Junk Works at the opposite end of the Rocket Lab campus. They normally showed up at the administrative building in button-down shirts and dress slacks. After a brief check-in, they headed out to the Junk Works facility at the far end of the campus. A dirty job, for sure. As soon as they arrived at the top-secret facility, they exchanged business casual attire for a pair of well-worn coveralls to get down to business.

To complicate matters, Freeman's wife had insisted on reporting back to work to apply her personal talents to the massive load faced by Rocket Lab personnel. Dressed in a crisp white maternity blouse with navy and white polka dot skirt and matching scarf, the HR manager reported in to the Rocket Lab campus for the first time in months. *Kon-Tiki* crew selection required some human eyes-on, she said.

On the way upstairs, Hoffman had shucked off his jacket, hooking it by one finger over his shoulder.

The drone of the fan was the only sound that could be heard when he reached the design lab to confront the engineers. He began the conversation with the usual pleasantries, complementing Freeman and Sutton on the progress with their projects, especially the *Kon-Tiki* build at Bertrand Intra-orbital Shipyard.

"Our new team member has done a great job overseeing the build," said Sutton.

"I do a face-time call with Eireann Reid every day," said Red Feather. "VIKI, why don't you give Cam a breakdown of mothership construction?"

The Rocket Lab logo on the view screen switched to the Asian female image presence. Hoffman wondered who selected the British accent for the AI computer.

Top of the morning, Cam, said VIKI. *I'm pleased to report that the mothership build is proceeding according to schedule. As you can see, progress is ongoing with outer hull, inner hull and warp nacelles nearing completion. Would you care to see a video record of last week's progress?*

"Yes, VIKI. Please proceed."

The view screen displayed quick closeup views of work details, ending with a long-range stem-to-stern panoramic view.

Hoffman whistled. "Nice work, gentlemen. Smashed it."

"Don't mind me, I'm over here producing your other little miracle," said Red Feather.

"My apologies, Brandi. Any developments on self-sealing hull?"

"I have gained a rudimentary grasp of the concept and will keep you apprised of my progress." Pointing to the print of the Wright Brothers' flyer, she added. "Heavier-than-air flight was once regarded as impossible. I aim to keep working until that hull will detect any sort of breach and seal itself up."

"Good on ya," said Hoffman. Turning to Freeman and Sutton, he dropped the bomb. "General Bardick will arrive next week."

Sutton's mouth dropped open.

Freeman said, "That can't be good."

Hoffman shoved his hands into his pockets, then looked up and said, "Do you remember when Phillip Wong brought in those scientists to inspect the *Comet*?"

"Oh, God, don't remind me," said Sutton, rolling his eyes. "They asked a thousand-and-one questions. Wanted to know what everything was and how it worked. It was a nightmare."

"Who's General Bardick?"

All eyes turned to Red Feather. Hoffman pointed upwards, then answered, "Our mothership being constructed up there was a contracted purchase made by the Chenghuang Corporation."

With her eyes wide, Red Feather said softly, "And the cracks in China's economy are growing wider."

"Chenghuang backed out of their contract," Hoffman explained.

Sutton stepped in to explain, "Brandi, General Bardick is the multi-billionaire who stepped in and bought the *Kon-Tiki*."

"Is he the guy I've been hearing about? One of the richest people in the world? Owns a gold mine in Papua New Guinea?"

"Probably," Hoffman nodded. "In any case, our financial and legal teams are still working to seal the deal. Which may depend on what he sees when he gets here."

With one eye closed in a pirate scowl, Freeman thought aloud. "He's not coming here to see the *Kon-Tiki*. And I'm certain he's not stopping by for afternoon tea. That leaves ..."

"He's making a special trip to get a good look at the world's first anti-gravity cruiser," Sutton guessed aloud.

"I knew it!" said Red Feather. "I knew you two weren't spending all that time in the high bay coordinating rocket builds." Pointing at Freeman, she added, "or sneaking home to have lunch with your wife."

"That only happened one time," admitted Freeman with a sheepish expression.

With his hands on his hips and a stern expression, Hoffman added, "The knowledge that we are making progress in the field of anti gravity will come out soon enough, but only with strategic timing. And it will cost you your jobs if that knowledge goes any further than this room."

"Loose lips will sink no ships on my end," Red Feather promised, making a zipping motion across her lips.

Hoffman continued, "One week from today, you two will be able to present the *Griffon* and its inner workings in great detail."

"But Cam, theoretically it's still in the developmental stage," Freeman argued.

"That's no excuse," said Hoffman. "Then sell him on the concept. You have a week to prepare. I'm depending on you. We're all depending on you. By the way, do any of you play golf? No? Evidently I need to locate a staff member to escort and entertain the general. Make this a trip he will remember."

Hoffman spun on his heel and departed the design lab.

Sutton looked at Freeman and said, "No pressure."

"Are you going to take the lead or will I have to do it?"

Freeman raised his hand and crooked his elbow. "One, two three, go."

Both men made three karate chop gestures. Sutton went paper, covering Freeman's rock.

"Fair suck of the sauce," said Freeman. "Makes me feel like a used car salesman."

"Bring out the old razzle-dazzle," said Sutton. "Selling a vehicle is like writing up any other scientific project. It's eighty percent scientific principle and twenty percent fancy footwork."

With a glance at the view screen, Red Feather said, "Is VIKI aware of this top-secret project?"

"No," said Sutton. "Probably. But at this point, we have one working prototype and the patent application is already in the works. If any other launch facility attempts to copy the design, there is no way they can get a vehicle in operation before we announce ours."

Red Feather playfully slapped Sutton's back, then Freeman's. "You little beauties. You did it. Anti gravity will be as earth-shattering as the Wright Brothers' heavier-than-air flying machine. You'll see."

Freeman sighed, "As it turns out, we're marketing a vehicle that can launch from Earth and go into outer space before we've effectively tested that concept. I guess we've crossed the line of impossibility a couple of times now."

"Found nine hundred ninety-nine ways how not to make a light bulb," said Sutton.

"Now let's see how quickly I can perfect my bullshit skills."

With his upcoming debut to promote the *Griffon*, Freeman felt he deserved a few minutes to look in on his wife.

With a knock on the door of the personnel office, he said, "Hi, Sweetie. How's it going?"

Montgomery looked up from the view screen on her desk. "Bloody oath, it is. We're hiring crew members for the *Kon-Tiki* but the computer has neglected to follow protocol. There are interviews to do; training opportunities to arrange."

He reached over for a brief kiss. "Listen, would you mind a tad bit of research for me?"

"You know I can't give out any private information. And employee reviews and salaries are strictly off limits."

Freeman held up a hand. "No, nothing like that. I just need for you to look up someone to find out when he worked here. Dates of employment is all that I need."

With a shrug, Montgomery said, "That's more or less public information. What's the name?"

"It's a Thomas Martin."

The personnel manager's brows knit as she stared at her view screen.

"What's the significance of this past employee?"

Freeman shrugged and said, "He evidently did some scientific research and development work that I would like to retrieve. If you can give me the dates, it will help us to retrieve his research."

Montgomery sat back in her office chair. "Huh," she said.

"What did you find out?"

"No record of anyone named Thomas Martin during the company's entire history."

Freeman quickly backpedaled. "Maybe I have the name wrong."

Montgomery swirled around to face her view screen. "Go get the correct information and get back to me," she said sweetly. "Then I'll be happy to help you."

Chapter 39

Bardick residence
Pacific Heights neighborhood
Honolulu, Hawaii

The air reeked of Maison Francis. Gladys Bardick had applied and re-applied the high-end fragrance to guarantee the scent would waft across her extra-long dining table.

Freshly coiffed and dressed to the nines, she awaited her husband in their formal dining room. Wine-colored toenails peeked through the ends of her silver sequined wedge sandals. She placed her hands on her knees and spread out her fingers to check her manicure. Her wine-hued fingernail polish was perfect — surprising since she had rushed the nail technician.

Place settings for two and a centerpiece with candles were already laid out on the white-cloth-covered dining room table.

Chef Felipe Sanninikone poked his head into the dining room. "Would you care for a canapé, Madam? Or perhaps a cocktail?"

"No, thanks, Felipe. I'll wait for the general."

As it turned out, her husband was fifteen minutes late for dinner. Though it could have been her imagination, she thought his hair looked freshly cut, his eyebrows less shaggy then they normally appeared.

"Shalom, Bubala."

With a sigh of relief, Gladys realized he started out the evening by referring to her Yiddish pet name. A term of affection.

"Shalom, Lenny."

Sanninikone had been the Bardicks' chef for just over two years. In that time, he had grown keenly aware of their likes and dislikes, especially their expectation of timing.

Seconds after Bardick's arrival, he stepped into the formal dining room with a pitcher of ice water. He filled Gladys' glass first. While filling the general's, he asked, "Would either of you care for a cocktail?"

Shortly after their move from Washington D.C. to Honolulu, the general was hospitalized for a minor heart attack. He had been cautioned to modify his diet and lifestyle. A low-fat diet with less red meat. And limit alcohol. Which would definitely cross off the dose of Ancient Age he so craved.

With a sudden glance at Gladys, the general declined.

This evening, his only goal was to re-acquire a connection with his wife. Not piss her off.

Sanninikone was prompt with the first course — a refreshing salad with orange sections, walnuts, dried cranberries and coconut curls.

Gladys picked at her salad while the general polished his off. He had been involved in meetings at the capitol complex all day, which meant no time for lunch.

They chatted about household matters. A decorator had been called in to redo one of the guest rooms under Gladys' direction.

"Did you do something different to your hair?"

With an unconscious pat to her new hairstyle, she affirmed, "I had an appointment today. Do you like it?"

With a nod and a wink, he affirmed, "Yes, it suits you."

Gladys smiled. Maybe she wouldn't be getting a divorce after all.

"I was just wondering if you and your ladies' organization had already held your fundraiser. I've been so busy at the capitol that I was afraid it had passed by."

At this point, Gladys began to consider that her husband wasn't purposefully ignoring her. There was, in fact, a lot going on. A new national capitol and a newly-installed commander-in-chief. Plus all the details that followed.

"No, Lenny, but as we get closer, more details pop up to be ironed out."

Sanninikone took away the salad plates, replacing them with the main course. Halibut garnished with a lemon slice.

"Why don't you give me a run-down of how it's shaping up."

Gladys couldn't believe the positive direction the evening was taking. The general winked at her hairstyle, then took an interest in her pet project.

"Who are the people that will benefit from this gala?"

By the time the Hummingbird cake was served, the general had learned the reason for his wife's passion.

"And you know, Lenny, that it's not just American survivors who are refugees. There are a growing number of native Hawaiians who are poor and homeless. Before the American holocaust, Hawaii had the highest homeless rate in the nation. Even now, people from outside are emigrating to the islands and taking over more and more positions. That means less jobs are available for the rest of the population. Native Hawaiians are generally nice to tourists, but there is an underlying resentment. As the cost of living increases here, they are getting priced out of their ancestral land."

"I would imagine that more immigration means less resources to go around. Less jobs, fewer apartments and homes for everyone."

"That's right, Lenny," she nodded, taking a sip of coffee with her cake. "Su Lee's grandparents came here from Japan. All the same, she isn't considered a native Hawaiian."

"Oh really?"

It was only when Sanninikone came in to draw the drapes and light the candles on the table that the Bardicks realized that they remained in the dining room long after the dishes had been cleared.

The general pulled out his hand terminal, causing Gladys to fear their conversation was over. Instead, he looked up at her and said, "Now tell me exactly when is this gala you're planning? And what do you think I should wear?"

"Oh, Lenny!"

Gladys got up and ran to the general to give him a hug from behind. He turned around to give her a little smooch on the cheek.

He had never doubted that he would be able to revive their relationship.

Re-connect with his wife — ticked the box.

But finding a ride off the planet and convincing Gladys to board a rocket ship, that would be another matter.

Chapter 40

Rocket Lab boardroom
Auckland, New Zealand

"You seem distracted, Cam," said Bella Brown at Monday morning budget meeting.

In fact, Hoffman made a circular motion when Julie Stempler gave her report on progress for uniforms for the *Kon-Tiki* crew.

"Are you all right?" Stempler asked.

"I'm fine," Hoffman assured them. "I'm a little nervous about meeting the general. This meeting has to go well. Plus we have a 9 a.m. tee time."

With an eye roll, Jim Freeman countered, "I'm the one who should be getting nervous about my anti-gravity presentation. Are you taking him to the Pakuranga Club?"

"No, he's a billionaire, Jim. Everything first class, you understand. I made a reservation for 18 holes at Royal Auckland and Grange Golf Club. Him and his assistant," consulting his tablet, he added, "Fellow by the name of Richard Dalton. Followed by lunch at a restaurant of his choosing."

"Sounds like you are creating a memorable impression," Sutton noted.

Scowling at his tablet, Hoffman continued, "Business men, bankers and insurance brokers were among those who chartered Royal Auckland in 1894. Very prestigious. They have views of each hole on their web site. I'm certain the general will enjoy himself."

"Are you going to play, Cam?" Brown wanted to know.

Hoffman shook his head. "I've played golf only once in my life. That was enough. I'm certain my golf skills would be an embarrassment to all concerned. I have an appropriate outfit and I'm going to walk the course, but Welly has been tapped to defend our honor in this act of hospitality."

Julie Stempler leaned in to Beth Sommerset and whispered, "What I wouldn't give to be a fly on the wall for that game."

Chapter 41

Rocket Lab Launch Complex
Auckland, New Zealand

General Leonard Bardick arrived ostentatiously at the Rocket Lab complex in a rented limousine. Camillo Hoffman's mode of transportation was far more humble: a Rocket Lab golf cart.

The general's arrival coincided with a flight line safety walk by shipyard flight crews across the tarmac that had been selected as a launch pad. Elbow to elbow, a dozen or so workers wearing olive-drab coveralls carried trash bags. Their sole purpose was to eliminate even the most minuscule particle of rubbish. The utmost care was taken to ensure a successful demonstration of the launch entity's prototype vehicle.

At the center of the field, the *Griffon* awaited launch. Rocket Lab officials had chosen the location in hopes of presenting the new technology in the most positive light.

Their initial customer had ordered the huge mothership vessel under construction at Bertrand Shipyard. With ongoing costs for construction as yet to be calculated, Rocket Lab depended on winning the billionaire's favor today. And selling him on the anti-gravity cruiser was their best chance of accomplishing it.

The general was accompanied by a much slimmer man wearing an upscale business suit. Engineers would soon become familiar with the general's assistant Richard Dalton. He mounted one of the rear-facing golf cart seats suitable for additional passengers.

"General, I hope you rested well last evening," said Hoffman as he motored the golf cart. "Richard, nice to see you again. How are you this morning?"

"A little stiff. Your press agent gave us some serious competition on the golf course yesterday."

Motioning in the direction of the sweep team, the general asked, "Is this some sort of pre-flight check?"

"These workers are combing the tarmac to ensure that there is nothing that may interfere with flight operations," Hoffman explained. "No rubbish, leaves, or anything of that nature."

"I see." Bardick appeared calm in the business suit that, for now, served as his dress blues.

Hoffman took one look at the general's attire and gauged that, before the day was over the old codger would be sweating his ass off.

The golf cart ride from the parking lot took five or ten minutes, giving the general time to check out the gleaming white anti-gravity vehicle upon their approach.

"Buffed and waxed?" he asked.

"Absolutely. Ready for your inspection," Hoffman answered. As they neared the vehicle, Jim Freeman stepped out from behind it wearing his official Rocket Lab blazer.

"General Bardick, this is Jim Freeman, one of our top engineers who headed up the anti-gravity project. With him is David Sutton, also a part of our research and development team. They are here to answer all your questions about the *Griffon's* operation."

Another man wearing a red Rocket Lab coverall stepped out to meet the general.

"Allow me to introduce your pilot, Nick Van den Berg."

"A pleasure, general." Attired in a red flight jumpsuit, Van den Berg extended his hand.

Bardick shook hands with his right, all while pointing to the sky with the other.

"Exactly how many flight hours have you logged on this baby?"

Van den Berg had been apprised of the importance of today's presentation.

His instructions were to refer to Freeman if there were any doubts.

Freeman quickly stepped in to answer, "It's a brand-new technology, sir. Nick has a handful of hours on this particular vehicle. However, he has logged an overwhelming number of hours on flight simulators that tested his ability to handle any and all situations with this sort of craft."

Hoffman said, "Jim, do you want to give the general a brief run-down of the *Griffon's* capabilities?"

Freeman was secretly relieved that his presentation was likely to be brief.

In anticipation of the explanation, Van den Berg hatched the *Griffon's* side entry door. The general and his assistant peered inside.

"The exterior of the craft is covered in a proprietary amalgamate that is rated safe for both aerial and inter-spatial operation," Freeman quoted.

"What makes it go? Up, I mean," Bardick asked.

"She actually has separate systems. The anti-gravity drive operates like an electric magnet that can be increased or decreased according to your desired altitude. The anti gravity drive brings us down from space, or up again. And if you will look over here here.... a pair of standard jet engines provide our horizontal propulsion. They can safely give us an air speed of up to two hundred kilometers an hour. About one-seventy-five nautical miles per hour."

"Nice, but I don't smell jet fuel," Bardick commented.

Van den Berg tilted his head slightly in Freeman's direction, who explained, "It runs on hydrogen fusion when we're inside the atmosphere. No fill-ups necessary."

"What are the chances of running out of gas and falling out of the sky?"

"Zero chance, sir."

"And this thing will go up into outer space? And it's going to be our means of getting down to the planet from the *Kon-Tiki?*"

"That would be an accurate statement," Freeman agreed. "The space propulsion system is fully capable of traveling to a star base or ship in orbit, but limited operation in space. You couldn't expect it to fly to the next planet or travel extensively. And the landing gear is similar to that used in recreational vehicles. Starships require paved landing pads but these will not be necessary for an anti-gravity vehicle. We have incorporated landing legs capable of adaptation to any sort of terrain, meaning you can land just about anywhere."

"What's this baby's cargo capacity?"

Freeman was ready with an answer. "As you can see, here are seats and restraints for fifteen passengers, including the pilot, in the front compartment. The cabin is pressurized with air purification similar to a jet plane. In the back, a cargo door hatches upwards. I would compare the cargo capacity to a 26-foot box truck. The storage compartment measures 23 feet 10 inches long and around 7-1/2 feet wide and tall, giving it a total cargo volume of around 1,340 cubic feet. Although we haven't tested the cargo limit yet, I wouldn't hesitate to say it could handle up to 10,000 pounds."

"Do you think you could fit a golf cart back there?"

"Absolutely, sir."

With an appreciative nod, Bardick put one foot on the passenger door's step and paused to ask, "I'm assuming we are going to take her out for a spin today."

Sticking to their pre-determined flight plan, Hoffman had decided that he and Dave Sutton would stay on the ground, leaving Jim Freeman to accompany the general to answer any and all questions.

Van den Berg slipped on a helmet before strapping into the pilot's seat.

"Strap in and tuck your toes under the bar," he instructed the passengers.

Freeman showed the general and Dalton how to fasten the three-point harness. "Do you wish to stow your hat? We want to avoid objects floating around the cabin."

"Oh, yes. Lose the cover, check." Bardick handed Freeman his U. S. Army Veteran ball cap, which he placed into a storage compartment in the side bulkhead.

In the pilot's seat, Van den Berg reviewed pre-flight checks. Then he checked in with Air Traffic Control.

"Tower, this is AGV1 *Griffon* requesting a take-off from Rocket Lab Launch Complex."

"*Griffon*, what is your expected trajectory?"

"Headed east following the route of Pakuranga Highway."

"*Griffon*, you are cleared for takeoff."

The gentle lurch upward reminded the general of a helicopter takeoff.

Occupying the front passenger's position, Jim Freeman absently deposited his hand terminal on the center console. It floated upwards when the pilot activated the anti gravity drive. With a stern look from Van den Berg, he grabbed the device out of the air and shoved it into an interior pocket of his jacket.

The anti-gravity drive made little sound when it was fired up. Sailing over the launch complex, Van den Berg followed the predetermined flight path, taking the craft in a clockwise direction above Pakuranga Creek. During the brief flight, Freeman attempted to impress the general with details about the ground-breaking vehicle.

"And as far as high-end features, we have installed a killer sound system. She can access any song you may wish to play," Freeman revealed. Of all the features in the anti-gravity cruiser, the designer was most proud of the sound system's extensive capabilities.

Initially unimpressed, the general slowly shook his head, commenting, "I'm not really a music lover. Other priorities, you understand."

"With your permission, allow me to demonstrate?"

"Sure, go ahead. Play something."

Freeman accessed a menu from the passenger side view screen. The audio system began to play *Hail To The Chief.*

Bardick's expression brightened just before he said, "OK, you've sold me." Waving his hand in a circle, he said, "But I want two of these. We can't expect to depend on a single vehicle for transportation down to the planet and back. Redundancy, you understand."

Freeman gulped. "Yes, sir. You are aware of our approaching launch date?"

"I have every confidence in your ability to fulfill the need." With his hands, he made a bracket gesture, then moved them to the right and made a downward motion. "Copy this one and make another just like it."

Chapter 42

Rocket Lab boardroom
Auckland, New Zealand

"Flying cars and anti-gravity skateboards may soon become a reality thanks to a new Rocket Lab discovery."

"You're going to smash this announcement. It's going to catapult us into a new era."

Rocket Lab CEO Brandon Kemp popped by the boardroom prior to the launch provider's groundbreaking announcement.

The Rocket Lab logo was peppered over the surface of a view screen. Seated at the boardroom table was media coordinator Hahona Timoti dressed in a double-breasted Tom Ford suit in grey stripe with solid pink tie. He paid close attention to a time countdown in the lower right-hand corner of the main view screen that just passed 05:00.

"Five minutes, Welly," announced Kemp. "Chookas. Oh, and don't give out our proprietary information. Only the facts this time."

Bella Brown adjusted the settings on a tablet which she positioned on the table in front of Timoti. "I didn't give him any proprietary information," she said. "Just enough to tantalize our media representatives."

To the view screen, Brown said, "VIKI, do you have the video recording ready?"

Yes, Bella. Ready to roll as soon as Welly gives the word.

When the countdown reached 00:00, the logo of a Sydney news network appeared on the screen. A fade-out presently revealed the image of a newscaster whose dark skin and hair contrasted with her green sheath dress and coordinating scarf.

"This is Tasha Banks with the Australian News Network. Today we're here with Hahoni Timoti with an exciting announcement about developments at Rocket Lab in New Zealand. I'm going to turn it over to you, Hahona."

"Cheers, Tasha, and welcome. Rocket Lab is pleased to announce the development of the first anti-gravity vehicle capable of a non-propulsive launch from the Earth's surface also possessing the ability to travel short distances in outer space. The following video clip was recorded during the March 20 test flight of our prototype. VIKI, run the clip please."

The clip began with an interview Timoti conducted with Nick Van den Berg standing beside the *Griffon* positioned on the Rocket Lab tarmac.

"I'm here with pilot Nick Van den Berg who has been selected to pilot the *Griffon* during its trial run. Nick, can you describe your flight plan today?"

"Gonna take her from Rocket Lab Launch Complex here in Auckland, New Zealand up to Bertrand Intra-orbital Shipyard."

The camera clip recorded the vehicle's launch, lauded with riotous applause from the workers and observers near the tarmac. A drone camera followed the vehicle's ascent.

"The prototype pictured on your screen is the first truly anti-gravity vehicle. Designers predict this type of craft will revolutionize space travel by providing smooth, reliable passenger-friendly take-offs and landings."

As usual, Claire Montgomery accepted a select few questions from representatives of world news agencies.

A Rio de Janeiro News Agency submitted this question: "What is the cargo capacity of this type of anti-gravity cruiser?"

On point with the facts, Timoti responded, "The *Griffon* is equipped with seats and restraints for fifteen passengers with a sizable cargo compartment in the rear."

A journalist from Edinburgh asked, "How much can you fit in the boot?"

Ready with an answer and without hesitation Timoti responded, "The storage compartment measures 23 feet 10 inches long and around 7-1/2 feet wide and tall, giving it a total cargo volume of around 1,340 cubic feet. It can handle loads up to a maximum of 10,000 pounds."

"When do you expect to go into production to manufacture these cruisers?" asked a reporter from Seoul, Korea.

"I am at liberty to divulge that Rocket Lab is already in production of a second prototype," Timoti responded.

"Here's the question that's on everyone's lips," asked a liaison from the Montreal News Agency. "When can I get one?"

Keeping it together with a neutral expression, Timoti answered, "Rocket Lab has no immediate plans to go into production of this type of vehicle for the general public. However, we will issue further updates as the information becomes available."

At the conclusion of the news conference, Brown cued Timoti to issue a final news clip.

"This just in: There's another announcement I'd like to make. Billion-aire Leonard Bardick and Rocket Lab recently partnered to purchase the SpaceCorp Launch entity. The new division is located in the township of Nhulunbuy near Arnhem Space Centre in Australia's Northern Territory."

Chapter 43

Waikiki Beach
Oahu Island, Hawaii

"I wasn't aware that the gala would be held outside. Is there a possibility I'm slightly under dressed?"

On the afternoon of the gala, Gladys Bardick and the general drove out to Waikiki beach early enough to supervise final preparations for the gala fundraiser.

In a rare breach of protocol, General Bardick trusted his wife's personal assistant Su Lee to order him an outfit suitable for the occasion. He felt slightly out of place in the casual tropical print shirt and khaki pants. He dutifully wore the coordinating straw hat, however he felt naked without his characteristic *U.S. Army Retired* ball cap. He was still getting used to wearing a pair of casual step-in loafers.

Gladys had scrapped all other wardrobe options for a tropical sheath dress with jacket made from the same Hibiscus-print fabric as her husband's outfit.

The carpark was a good distance away from the location where caterers were setting up for the buffet dinner that would take place later on. As Gladys and her husband approached the awning lined with twinkle lights, they were met by hostesses Naomi Kaplan and Miriam Schneider, each of them wearing tropical attire. Over their arms they carried bundles of flower leis.

"Aloha, Gladys! So nice to see you! I don't believe we've met your friend."

Slightly annoyed, Gladys said, "You've met him, I'm certain. This is my husband, General Leonard Bardick.

"Aloha, general," said Schneider, slipping a lei around the general's neck. "And welcome. So glad you could join us this evening."

"Aloha, ladies." Offering his arm to Gladys, he added, "Sorry to disappoint you, but my dance card is completely full this evening."

As they walked in the direction of the event setting, Kaplan called out, "Have fun, you two!"

A short distance away from the greeters, the Bardicks witnessed caterers scrambling to arrange traditional Hawaiian dishes on long tables accented with fruit and flowers.

Beach chairs were already positioned near the water's edge in preparation for the native Hawaiian dance troupe's performance later in the evening.

"Would you like to take a seat, Lenny?" Gladys asked. "I can get you something to drink while I check to make sure the preparations are going smoothly."

"No, if you don't mind I'll just tag along and see what keeps you busy day after day."

With a puzzled expression, Gladys said, "All right, if that's what you want."

The Bardicks traveled down the buffet tables to survey the fare. One of the caterers, a native Polynesian woman, walked with them to identify the delectable dishes that would make up the evening's repast.

"Over here, you have your Rumaki with pineapple, your Hawaiian fried rice, your Huli Huli Chicken and Lomi Lomi Salmon. And, of course, everyone loves macaroni salad."

"Macaroni salad?" the general questioned.

"Yes, of course," said Gladys. "It isn't a native Hawaiian dish, but it is expected and everyone seems to love it. What is this one over here?"

Gladys indicated a dish made up of orange rounds with a coating of white shavings.

"Ah, that's our Molokai sweet potatoes. And you couldn't have a Hawaiian gathering without Poi. Next to the Poi you have your beef and your chicken portions wrapped in taro."

"No pork?" whispered the general. "everyone is nuts about pork around here."

"No, Lenny," said Gladys. "The caterers are very nice about suitability to any special dietary needs. I made certain everything here is kosher. No pork."

The Bardicks stopped by the beverage table to try out the pineapple daquiris.

"This is excellent," said the general, tapping his beverage against his wife's glass.

By the time they finished inspecting the buffet tables, a couple of vans with the Fire and Sticks logo on the side pulled up on the beach. Entertainers quickly and expertly unloaded their equipment.

Gladys grabbed her husband's hand and led him back down to the beach area.

The entertainers arrived dressed in traditional Hawaiian clothing. Female dancers arrived dressed in green grass skirts and red tropical-print bikini tops with flower leis around their necks. Bare-chested male performers wore identical knee-length tropical-print shorts.

The Bardicks stopped by briefly to check on the musicians. Some were equipped with ukelele stringed instruments and conch shell trumpets. A pair of drummers warmed up on a set of sharkskin drums.

The general thought he recognized the traditional ukelele tune *Aloha'Oe*. When he asked the musician, he confirmed the identity of the Hawaiian folk song written by the last Hawaiian Queen Lili'uokalani.

Gladys spoke briefly with a woman who wasn't wearing native attire. The general correctly guessed her identity as the entertainers' manager.

It wasn't until she was convinced that all the elements were proceeding according to plan that Gladys invited the general to be seated.

"When all this was just an idea on the planning board, I booked a Fire and Sticks lu'au package." she told him. "Later in the evening, the native Hawaiian dance troupe will give a hula demonstration. In case you've never seen one, there is a lot of hip-shaking and drum cadence going on. When it's good and dark over the beach, there will be a Samoan fire knife performance.

"

Motioning in a circular gesture that took in the buffet, the guest seating and the entertainers, the general asked, "And you organized all this?"

"Our ladies' group was doing a few little things here and there to benefit the refugees that live in the camp. The amount of cash put into the tzedekah box plus the hygiene kits they put together wasn't doing a whole lot to change the refugees' lives. So I decided to do something a little bigger."

"So you put together a benefit meal. How many guests and what are you charging per plate?"

With a sly smile, Gladys said, "I thought one thousand was too much. Then I realized how fast the reservations were coming in. And I promoted this gala to some of the island's wealthiest residents. My thoughts were, go big or go home."

General Bardick had just one final question. Guests had begun to arrive and select their seats prior to the buffet meal. Each of them was professionally-groomed with tropical attire suited to the occasion. Outfits that were likely purchased to wear only once.

"Bubala, where are the refugees? Are any of them here?"

Gladys shook her head. "I thought about inviting some of them here tonight. Having them stand and introducing them to the other guests. But if they're living in tents or temporary storage buildings, you know they don't own suitable clothing."

"Oh, right," agreed the general. "You wouldn't want to embarrass them."

"If I dressed them up, you know, ordered matching outfits and the like, then they would just look like one of us. That, plus it would be a waste of money that could be used more effectively for blankets, sleeping bags, apartment down payments, utilities or that type of thing."

With a dreamy look in her eyes, Gladys wishfully said, "If I had all the money in the world to spend on these refugees, I would give them jobs that paid well. I would provide the means by which they could borrow a down-payment on a place to live. And when they pay back the money ..."

"It could be paid forward so another family could get a better place to live."

Gladys looked surprised. She and her husband did think alike sometimes. He was good at making money, but by no means did he have a cold heart.

"Right. That's what I would do if I had unlimited resources. But for tonight, we'll have fun and raise funds to help all of them that we can."

"Bubala, you never cease to amaze me. And you have some untapped talents of which I was totally unaware."

"Oh, Lenny!" Gladys snuggled up next to her husband to enjoy the evening's activities.

Chapter 44

Rocket Lab Launch Complex
Central Boardroom
Auckland, New Zealand

"General Bardick wants to talk to me?"

Camillo Hoffman approached Jim Freeman during his routine morning check-in at the third-floor design lab. Freeman momentarily abandoned the model he had been constructing and diverted his attention to Hoffman.

Without his usual burst of positivity, Hoffman dived right into the challenge at hand.

"Our financial and legal teams have ironed out the deal with General Bardick. He now owns the *Kon-Tiki.*"

Freeman's eyes nearly popped. Nearby, Brandi Red Feather and Dave Sutton were monitoring test simulations on one of the view screens.

"It's a done deal? So soon? That's good news, right? Then why does the general want to talk to me?"

"Yeah, why not all of us?" asked Sutton.

With a stern look, Hoffman said, "If the man can shell out billions without putting a dent in his bank account, he can afford to pick and choose his favorites."

Red Feather quickly focused her eyes on her view screen. "And what happens in the design lab, stays in the design lab."

While making a circular motion with his finger, Hoffman said, "I know I can count on you all to keep this information confidential."

There was silence in the room. In response to agreement from all the engineers, Hoffman explained. "The general now owns the *Kon-Tiki*. Legally, the Chenghuang Corporation is still involved, although the portion of their ownership is very minor."

"Hmmm," Freeman commented. "Wasn't expecting that."

Hoffman continued, "Your presentation on the *Griffon* was very positive. He wants to buy it as well, plus he wants us to make a second prototype. And he wants to take them both aboard the *Kon-Tiki*."

"He said words to that effect when he was here."

"While he was here, Welly and I took him to lunch at a restaurant of his choosing," Hoffman said. "Turns out the place he wanted to eat was the Thai Archer Restaurant."

"Great food," said Red Feather. "Just tried it last week."

"The general liked it so much he was inspired to name the second anti-gravity cruiser the *Archer*."

"Not the worst idea I've ever heard," said Freeman. "If the guy wants to buy it, then it's his baby. He can name it anything he wants. But building another anti-gravity craft will create a huge time crunch for all of us."

"Does the general know how soon the launch date has been scheduled?" asked Sutton.

"I think he is keenly aware," said Hoffman. "Your Zoom meeting with the general today concerns modifications he wants us to make to the *Kon-Tiki's* design."

"Get out!" Sutton exploded. "You can't be serious."

"Fanny dickhead bloody wanker," said Freeman. "I'll be dipped."

"Ditto," Hoffman agreed. "Grab your blazer and come with me. You are live with the general in ten minutes."

Chapter 45

Rocket Lab boardroom
Auckland, New Zealand

"Remember, unless his alterations are virtually impossible, the answer is *yes.*"

General Leonard Bardick was no less intimidating on the view screen than he was in person.

Rocket Lab normally took pains to keep their staff out of the public eye. Since he had actually met and laid eyes on Jim Freeman, however, Freeman was the name the potential buyer had requested. When purchasing a car or truck buyers occasionally order upgrades. Satellite radio or navigation systems. It seemed that the general insisted on some last-minute upgrades in order to make the behemoth ship align with his expectations. His specifications, however, were exponentially more involved and expensive than automobile upgrades. All the same, he firmly believed Freeman was capable of fulfilling his wishes.

Dressed in official attire with his hair combed neatly, Freeman showed up in the boardroom with Hoffman alongside him for backup.

"VIKI, ring up General Leonard Bardick in Honolulu, Hawaii."

The Rocket Lab logo on the screen was replaced by VIKI's image.

Calling Leonard Bardick. Leonard Bardick is available to take your call.

On the third buzz, the general's image appeared on the screen.

"Good morning, General Bardick," said Hoffman.

"Good morning, gentlemen," he replied. "Although I am currently tied up and unable to make a visit down there, I wanted to have a face-to-face meeting with you regarding some modifications you will need to make to the *Kon-Tiki*."

"We are prepared to make any and all modifications to your specifications if at all possible. I have here with me Jim Freeman, as you know one of our top engineers. If you can inform him of your expectations, we will try our best to incorporate them into the final design."

"Excellent, excellent. How can we ensure that we are on the same page regarding the design? Is it possible for us to look at the design schematics as we refer to them?"

"Certainly, sir," Hoffman replied. "VIKI, pull up the plans for the *Kon-Tiki*."

Pulling up design for mothership Kon-Tiki now under construction at Bertrand Shipyard.

The image of General Bardick's face contracted into a small square in the lower right of the screen. The bulk of the view screen subsequently displayed the body plan for the *Kon-Tiki*.

With the design particulars visible, Freeman took over the conversation. "This large diagram illustrates the outer bulkhead lines. When I touch the screen, it will be possible to zoom in on any particular area you wish to see. Your view screen should now be showing you this diagram."

"Yes, yes... that will be very helpful. Can you give me an idea of the size of standard crew quarters?"

"The cabins vary in size depending on the shape of the area in which they are located," Freeman explained. "We have continued with the idea that each cabin should have its own toilet and shower facilities. They average between five to six hundred square feet each. I'm certain you'll be most comfortable."

The general shook his head. "Five to six hundred square feet? I was afraid of that. I don't think so, gentlemen."

Freeman looked at Hoffman. Hoffman's expression seemed to say, *whatever he wants, give it to him.*

"Now, I've taken the liberty of having my architect draw up a set of plans for my personal quarters. I fully understand that instead of drywall and such, your ship uses sea-worthy materials. Diamond plate steel, is it? I'm not picky about the materials, but I'm certain you can incorporate our state room without any difficulty."

As if it had a mind of its own, Freeman felt his head bobbing up and down. "Yes, sir, I'm certain we can incorporate your custom designs."

"Now, as far as my staff ... who would I need to speak to regarding quarters for my staff?"

Once again, Freeman and Hoffman looked at each other. "What kind of numbers are we talking about?" Hoffman questioned.

"My personal assistant will be going along in addition to my personal chef. Oh, and my wife wants to bring along a small group of entertainers."

Freeman gulped. "That ... won't be a problem. No problem at all."

Freeman's thoughts at that moment were along the lines that Claire Montgomery had already submitted a final number of crew members who would need accommodations aboard the Kon-Tiki. Any additions would not only increase the number of crew quarters, but place a strain on the equation of food, water and oxygen that would need to be supplied during their journey.

And Hoffman's immediate thoughts went to the reaction of station manager Eireann Reid, who would no doubt be infuriated at the last-minute revisions. It was going to take a lot of fast-food deliveries to assuage the irritation that would no doubt be caused by the general's whims.

"Oh, and there's one more modification I'd like for you to make," Bardick said. "If I put a video image on my computer, will it be visible for you to look at?"

"It should be," said Freeman.

Freeman and Hoffman paid close attention to a video clip in which a light beam shot up from an earthbound facility, destroying an enemy drone in the sky.

"This is a directed-energy weapon," said Bardick. "They are a high-performance means of taking out hostile aerial vehicles, missiles and ships."

With a quizzical expression, Hoffman asked, "General, what exactly are you asking us to do?"

"Isn't it obvious? You can't expect me to fly across the cosmos to set up shop somewhere in an unarmed vessel? How stupid do you think I am? The *Kon-Tiki* needs to have state-of-the-art laser weaponry, no less."

At that moment, Hoffman broke his own *give him whatever he wants* directive.

"But General, laser weaponry for space vehicles hasn't been developed yet."

"Listen to what you're saying, Hoffman, in light of the fact that six months ago, anti-gravity cruisers hadn't been invented yet. And you have the best research and development engineer in the business sitting right next to you. You have three months. I'm certain in that amount of time you can come up with something."

Hoffman was uncertain that his team could crank out what General Bardick wanted in three months, or ever for that matter. All the same, he attempted to appear positive.

"It was a pleasure to talk with you again, General Bardick. We will keep you informed of any and all new developments."

"Thank you, gentlemen. We'll be in touch."

Chapter 46

Bardick residence
Pacific Heights neighborhood
Honolulu, Hawaii

When it comes to romantic gestures, some women appreciate flowers. Others jewelry.

Gladys Bardick loved animals as much as she cared for the poor and homeless residents of Honolulu. And General Leonard Bardick knew it.

"I'll take it from here."

Two crates of wiggling pups were more than he could manage. For this reason, he had enlisted his assistant Richard Dalton's help to carry two animal crates to the entrance of Gladys' sun room. His approach took place when she was at her most tranquil. Mid-morning, reading a book with her feet up on a footstool. A cup of tea was within easy reach by her side.

The glass French doors that stood between the hallway and the sun room allowed Gladys to witness her husband's approach on the other side.

For years, the sun room and rooms beyond it were considered Gladys' personal space. And he was trying to win her heart, not piss her off. For this reason, he sought permission to enter. Rapped lightly on the door frame.

"Come in, Lenny." Gladys beckoned with a come-hither hand gesture.

The general opened the doors and transferred the crates inside one at a time. The puppies inside immediately began to yip and jump about.

"Lenny, what's going on? Whose dogs do you have?"

Pausing for effect, he said nothing while he unlatched one of the crates.

Reaching inside, he retrieved one of the squirmy puppies which he placed in her lap. Tail wagging, the puppy licked her hands.

It had been a difficult decision to move to Honolulu when her husband retired. Then in one day she experienced the loss of all of her children and grandchildren during the horrific American holocaust.

It had been another tough pill to swallow when, more than a year before, she lost her twelve-year-old Schnauzer Bruno. He had been the only living remnant of her past life. Until now, she had been too brokenhearted over the loss to replace her beloved pet.

"They're so tiny!" exclaimed Gladys as the juvenile animal wagged its tail and licked her hands. "Are they big enough to leave their mother?"

While removing the other puppy from its crate, the general explained, "They are both eight weeks old. The breed is called Shih Tzu. Siblings, a male and a female."

Gladys now struggled to cope with two wiggling pups in her lap. She held one up to her face and kissed it. "You're the boy. So that one is the girl."

With a mischievous expression, the general asked, "I picked them, but you haven't yet said whether or not you like them. The breeder said she would take them back if you don't want them."

Gladys seemed offended. "Don't want them? Lenny, I love them. They're perfect!"

"Listen, if you need help managing them Richard said he would be happy to help out. He will come by your room each morning to walk them."

"Oh, you're so sweet!" said Gladys, cuddling the pups.

"Me or the puppy?" asked the general with a sly smile. "The breeder also suggested that we spay and neuter them, although they're not old enough yet. We can use the same vet, if you like. And the same groomer, as well. Do you have names in mind, Bubala? What are you going to call them?"

Gladys paused a moment, then said, "Fifi for the girl. Bobo for the boy."

Her husband appeared contemplative, then said, "Fifi and Bobo. It has a nice ring to it."

Gladys suddenly scooped up one of the puppies and extended it towards her husband. "I'm certain you got the pick of the litter with these two. And they seem to like you. Would you like to pet this one?"

Tolerating a small animal wasn't at the top of his list, but at this juncture he was willing to do just about anything to restore their relationship. He scooped it up and cradled it, stroking its head.

"They appear to be very healthy, but we can make arrangements for the vet to check them out, if you like. Oh, and we'll need to pick up some supplies. Collars and leashes for them. Are you certain you like them?"

Gladys rose from her seat to plant a kiss on the general's lips.

"Lenny, I love them. Thank you so much!"

Chapter 47

Rocket Lab boardroom
Auckland, New Zealand

"I need coffee."

Camillo Hoffman and Jim Freeman stared at each other immediately following their conversation with General Leonard Bardick.

"Coffee? We need need something stronger," said Freeman. "If we're going to get all this done we're going to have to work our socks off. And probably move out the launch date."

"Hopefully not. VIKI, display the architectural designs submitted by General Bardick."

VIKI complied, revealing the plans submitted by the general for the proposed addition.

Hoffman stood and moved closer, peering at the view screen through his new bifocals. "That old curmudgeon really is something, isn't he? But we've dealt with tough customers before, haven't we?"

With an expression of disbelief, Freeman said, "The general doesn't want a stateroom. This is a luxury master suite. From these dimensions, I would guess we're ripping out about six crew quarters to make room for this 2,300-square-foot addition. Looks like two bedrooms, two bathrooms, an interior sitting room and an office."

"The *Kon-Tiki's* crew quarters have already been roughed in," said Hoffman. "Which means we're going to have to say two words that no one up there wants to hear."

"Yeah. Tear out. Which means Eireann will want to do some tearing as well. And then there's the matter of the weaponry."

"Oh, God," said Hoffman while massaging his forehead.

"Spacecraft weaponry doesn't exist yet? Well, no problem. Let's just sit down and have a convo with the Russians or the Chinese and ask them for a set of instructions and a tutorial. I'm certain they won't mind sharing their proprietary top-secret weaponry."

"I've just had another idea," Hoffman added. "Lasers require huge amounts of electricity for operation. VIKI, what do you know about lasers?"

Laser tag is a game played using lasers to tag opponents. Laser hair removal can permanently eliminate hair from facial area as well as legs and armpits. Laser eye surgery ...

"VIKI, narrow the search. Show only entries pertaining to laser weaponry."

A laser weapon is a type of directed-energy weapon that uses lasers to inflict damage. An electro-laser first ionizes its target path, and then sends an electric current down the conducting track of ionized plasma, somewhat like lightning. It functions as a giant, high-energy, long-distance version of the Taser or stun gun.

In Project Excalibur, a United States government nuclear weapons research program attempted to develop a nuclear-pumped x-ray laser as a directed energy weapon for ballistic missile defense.

"VIKI were any plans or patents issued subsequent to Project Excalibur?"

I'm sorry to disappoint you, Jim. The U.S. government canceled the project at an early stage.

"Were there any similar government laser weapons?"

The Polyus spacecraft was a prototype Soviet orbital weapons platform designed to destroy Strategic Defense Initiative satellites with a megawatt carbon-dioxide laser. It had a Functional Cargo Block derived from a TKS spacecraft to control its orbit and it could launch test targets to demonstrate the fire control system. It was launched 15 May 1987 from Baikonur Cosmodrome Site 250 as part of the first flight of the Energia system, but failed to reach orbit.

"VIKI, why did the *Polyus* fail?"

If you want my opinion, I believe the failure was political rather than mechani-

cal. Shortly before the launch, President Mikhail Gorbachev visited the Baikonur Cosmodrome and expressly forbade the in-orbit testing of its capabilities. He was concerned that the West would interpret the technology as an act of war. A shot over the enemy's bow, so to speak.

Hoffman asked, "Were other governments or entities successful in the development of laser weapons?"

Progress on laser weapons was made later by the United States. The AN/SEQ-3 Laser Weapon System or XN-1 LaWS is a laser weapon developed by the United States Navy. The weapon was installed on the USS Ponce for field testing in 2014. In December 2014, the United States Navy reported that the LaWS system worked perfectly against low-end asymmetric threats ...

Hoffman leaned over and said softly to Freeman, "they always say they tested it against drones."

Freeman asked the AI, "VIKI, did USS Ponce survive U.S. annihilation? If so, where is the vessel currently located?"

On October 13, 2035 the USS Ponce was stationed in the Persian Gulf. The vessel was listed among U.S. assets that survived the annihilation. Her whereabouts at this moment in time are unclear.

"Continue listing other examples."

Freeman nodded and listened as VIKI went on to describe Israel's Iron Beam system.

At that precise moment, Dave Sutton knocked on the door.

When Hoffman waved him in, he asked, "How bad is it?"

"Ask me later."

With an elbow bump at Freeman's arm, Hoffman proposed, "Jim, why don't we ask VIKI to give it a go? If she knows how the basic concept works, why can't she design a system that would be appropriate for the *Kon-Tiki?*"

"Didn't think of that."

"It never hurts to ask a computer to do your homework," commented Sutton.

Freeman considered the request, Then he said aloud, "VIKI, cancel current line of research. Pull up the body plan for the *Kon-Tiki.*"

Here you go. Kon-Tiki ship plans.

"VIKI, can you modify the existing plan to incorporate a space-to-surface laser weapon? One in which the power usage level doesn't make the lights go out all over the ship?"

Yes, Jim, I think I can do that. Estimated time for completion of design project is three hours thirty-seven minutes.

"Beauty," said Freeman, crossing his arms over his chest. "And we need to prepare for our anti-gravity test flight up to Bertrand Station."

"Are we going to do rock-paper-scissors, then?"

"No. We have to use a certified test pilot, of course. This flight will be recorded for the record. Accompanied by an engineer who is intimately familiar with the on-board systems."

"So that means you're going up."

"That's a negative, Dave. I can't take any risky chances right now, considering my family's needs. So that means you're getting your astronaut wings."

With an insulted expression, Sutton countered, "I've already been up, remember? When we all went to Bertrand to leave our mark on the *Phoenix*?"

"Last time as an engineer. Anyone and everyone is going up to orbit on a starship as a passenger. This time you'll go as a test pilot. Or copilot, in any case, so you can add a test flight up to Bertrand on your resume."

Sutton had nothing to say, still weighing the benefits as well as the risks.

"I knew we could count on you," encouraged Hoffman.

At that precise moment, there was another rap on the door.

Hoffman opened it to discover a staff member from the personnel department.

"I knew you said you were in a meeting and shouldn't be disturbed ..."

The woman stammered. Freeman was beginning to get a bad feeling. "We're finished in here. What's wrong?"

"We have a medical emergency."

"Go on," Freeman urged her.

"Claire has been taken to hospital. We couldn't notify you while you were involved in a meeting so Julie Stempler and Beth Sommerset packed her up and whacked her out the door."

"Oh, God," said Freeman.

"She'll be all right, Jim," Hoffman assured him. "Go to her."

"It's not that," said Freeman. "I need to get to Claire. She came in the car, and she has the key fob in her purse. I came in earlier on my bloody bike."

Chapter 48

Bardick home residence
Pacific Heights neighborhood
Honolulu, Hawaii

General Bardick awakened in his wife's boudoir.

It wasn't the first time he slept in her room, but it had been a long time. A long, long time. At least before his bypass surgery.

Neither the general nor his wife were entirely certain how they ended up sleeping together. In the beginning, they were sitting on the bed cuddling the puppies. One thing led to another, and they wound up cuddling each other.

Just as the sun came up, the puppies awakened and began whining. At the same time, there was a knock at the bedroom door.

Wearing only his shorts, the general hastily grabbed one of his wife's white terrycloth robes. Regarding his image in the dresser mirror, he regretted the fact that it didn't quite reach across his middle. He didn't know where the rest of his clothing landed and the robe was the only thing within reach that didn't look too feminine.

Gladys opened her eyes and gave him a smile. He planted a kiss on her forehead and said, "I'll get the door."

Richard Dalton spoke through the door. "Mrs. Bardick, I'm here to walk your dogs. Oh!" he interjected when the general opened the door.

"Morning, Richard," said the general. "I'll grab the puppies and their leashes for you."

The general closed the door, leaving Dalton to wait outside, speechless. During the period of his employment, he had never known the Bardicks to sleep together.

The general returned a moment or two later, holding the two squirming animals with the sequined leashes attached to their collars.

"This one is Fifi, and the other is Bobo," he explained. Then he held one of the animals up to the light. "Or maybe it's the other way 'round. Hell, I don't know. What I know for certain is they are overdue for a trip to the backyard."

"Good morning, sir …. ma'am. I'll walk and feed them. I'll have them back in half an hour."

"Good man," said the general. "Better make it an hour."

"Yes, sir."

Returning to his wife's bedside, Bardick's heart was warmed by her rumpled hair. She propped up on one elbow.

The fear that had overshadowed Gladys for so long had lifted. At this point, a divorce was no longer on her radar.

"So, do you come here often?" she said.

"As often as you'll let me."

The general crawled back into his wife's rumpled, king-sized bed and mirrored her position. Propped up on one elbow facing her, looking into her eyes.

"Where have you been all my life, Bubala?"

There was no need to bring up the past. The weeks spent away from home in Papua New Guinea or trips out of the country on top-secret missions. Plus hours of meetings required to set up the new national capital. Her husband was present now, and that's all that mattered.

"Right here, Lenny."

"I guess I'll have to stop by more often."

General Bardick assessed that his relationship with his wife had been repaired. Or headed in that direction, at least. After his temporary retirement from the military, she had been willing to pull up sticks from New York to follow him to Honolulu. The question remained: could he convince her to follow him light years across the universe?

Chapter 49

Auckland City Hospital
Auckland, New Zealand

Carpark B is the closest carpark to Starship Hospital. If you are coming to the Emergency Department, follow the 'Adult and Children's Emergency' signs.

The proliferation of obstacles made Jim Freeman feel like he was navigating through a maze. But he was willing to hurdle any number of barriers to reach his pregnant wife's side.

In spite of Rocket Lab's monumental challenges, Camillo Hoffman did the human thing and halted the wheels of progress to give Freeman a ride to Auckland City Hospital.

Reaching the hospital was a minor issue. Finding a place to park was another problem entirely. Hoffman had to wait in a queue to navigate past ongoing construction at Auckland City Hospital, *Te Whatu Ora* in Māori.

"Thanks for the ride, Cam," said Freeman. "I'll find Claire. You don't have to stay."

"There's Julie," said Hoffman, pointing to a seat in the crowded Emergency Department waiting room. He waved across the crowded waiting room.

Stempler rose. Freeman assessed that she looked worried, but not in a trauma kind of way.

"Is Claire in labor? Where is she?" he asked.

"Walk and talk," she replied. "I'll take you straight up to her. She's already been taken up to Maternity."

Stempler speedily led them through a series of winding corridors to an elevator. Freeman kept pace with her, with Hoffman trailing close behind.

"Is she in labor?" Freeman wanted to know.

"Not right now," Stempler answered as the elevator ascended.

His eyes moist, Freeman said, "I should have been there for her."

Stempler reached out for a side hug. "You're here now. That's all that counts."

The elevator opened onto an upper floor. Just beyond the door, a sign read *Maternity*. A sign below it bore an arrow indicating the route to the Labor and Delivery ward.

"She's in a treatment room for now," said Stempler. "She sent me downstairs to make certain you could find her."

Stempler led them to one of the side rooms where she rapped on the door.

"Come in," said Claire. "Jim!"

Beth Sommerset was crowded into the super-small maternity monitoring room in along with a woman Freeman had never seen before.

Freeman rushed in, grabbing his wife's hand. "I was worried I would never find you."

He took in Claire's form, still in her work clothing but barefoot with a white pack applied to her left ankle that read MEDI-FIRST COLD COMPRESS. Her hairstyle was wet and mussed in the area where a white cloth was spread across her forehead. A fetal monitor was hooked up to her belly. Freeman was comforted to hear a robust fetal heartbeat thumping on the monitor.

"What on earth happened? Are you in labor?" There was concern in the expectant father's voice.

With a glance toward the woman standing at the head of her bed, she said, "Jim, this is Dr. Moore."

The on-call obstetrician was a slim woman wearing a surgical green scrub outfit with a matching scrub cap and mask.

"I'm the father," he announced.

Freeman couldn't asses the doctor's expression due to the mask she wore. She said, "Good to meet you. Mr. Montgomery, I just checked out your wife's x-rays and am pleased to report that nothing is broken."

The doctor had assumed that the couple shared last names. Both the patient and her husband felt it wasn't the right time to tell her otherwise.

In response to her husband's confused expression, Montgomery explained, "The whole thing started when I fell in my office. I didn't trip over anything and I wasn't wearing heels. I just got dizzy, twisted my ankle and fell. I was worried I had broken something. Beth and Julie pushed me outside in an office chair, loaded me up in Beth's car and got me here in record time."

Dr. Moore continued, "Her ankle isn't broken, but she does have a rather severe sprain. I'm just getting ready to wrap it. If we can keep her off it for a week or two, the swelling should go down and the inflammation will heal. It's lucky she reported in today, though, as we were able to discover that her blood pressure is dangerously high."

Freeman's eyebrows knitted in an expression of concern.

"We monitor maternity patient's blood pressure closely as elevation could be an indication of a condition known as pre eclampsia."

"Is it dangerous?" Freeman asked. "I mean, could it hurt Claire? Or the baby?"

With a frown, Dr. Moore said, "At this point, we don't know. We need to keep a close watch on it. All the same, we are six weeks out from expected date of confinement."

Montgomery added, "Dr. Moore said every day we can keep this bun in the oven is one more day of development our baby will have. Jim, Dr. Moore wants to admit me to the hospital on bed rest to try and prevent having to induce labor."

Freeman, who appeared slightly lost, glanced at his supervisor.

"Your family comes first," said Hoffman. "Your number one priority is to stay here and take care of them."

Looking at Stempler and Sommerset, he added. "Don't worry, Jim. Stay and take care of Claire. We'll manage everything else."

Chapter 50

Rocket Lab Launch Complex
Auckland, New Zealand
March 20, 2043

Dave Sutton guessed that he was the most likely candidate to be selected from the research and development team to accompany a pilot up to Bertrand Shipyard in the prototype anti-gravity vehicle. He wasn't expecting that flight to take place so soon, though.

By March 20, he found himself with a prep team on a countdown.

The central tarmac of Rocket Lab's Launch Complex had been selected as the location for the vehicle's first manned launch into outer space.

Jim Freeman had torn himself away from his wife long enough to do a pre-flight check with pilot Nick Van den Berg. Currently they were both working with a loading team to ensure that cargo placed in the rear compartment was properly distributed and adequately strapped down.

Wearing red coveralls, the pilot who had been hand-picked for the *Griffon's* first space voyage had racked up more space hours than flight hours. Sutton especially endorsed Van den Berg's selection because he was an enthusiastic backer of the All-whites, the New Zealand men's football team.

Biometrics consultant Julie Stempler immediately summoned the pilot back into the complex, insisting that he wear a white light-duty pressure suit.

Van den Berg had evidently not received the memo. In fact, almost everyone else on site was wearing red jumpsuits. A notable exception was project manager Camillo Hoffman, who showed up in his usual black dress pants paired with Rocket Lab blazer, white shirt and plaid bow tie.

Sutton had a couple of decades' experience working with design and launch entities. And according to his past experience, most launches involved a precise schedule of launch procedures. Today of all days, he had the feeling that Rocket Lab officials were flying by the seat of their pants. The thought was seconded by the next thing Hoffman said to him.

"What could go wrong today?"

Wearing his white light-duty pressure suit, Sutton swiveled his head around to give Hoffman an incredulous stare.

"You can't seriously want to know that now? With an ongoing countdown two hours before launch? Son of a bitch, Cam!"

Hoffman bobbed his head. "Yeah, but in your professional estimation, what's the best-case scenario? And, on the other end of the spectrum, what's your worst nightmare?"

Sutton took a deep breath to keep from hitting Hoffman, despite the fact that he wanted to.

"Obviously, I wouldn't take part in this trip if I weren't ninety-nine percent certain that the *Griffon* will perform to our expectations. If I'm correct, Nick and I should reach Bertrand Station by this time tomorrow. I'm not certain of the exact timeline ..."

"That is understandable because this is theoretically the *Griffon's* maiden space voyage," Hoffman interjected, pushing up his glasses with an index finger.

"Yeah. Now we come to the major malfunction category," Sutton continued. "As far as possible glitches, I would identify the critical point as when the vessel crosses the Kármán line."

"One hundred kilometers," Hoffman added. "Roughly, three hundred twenty-eight thousand feet."

"Negative mass effect should carry us out that far without any problem. After we cross that magic line, though, Earth's gravity will lose its effect. Then we go into a standard outer space propulsion situation. The jets used for maneuvering in the atmosphere require oxygen to function, which is why we designed our alternative system for use in the black."

Hoffman took a deep breath. "Dave, what if the outer space unit doesn't work? Or it doesn't function as well as we thought it would?"

With a shrug, Sutton said, "As I said, it should function within our perimeters. If something happens or we have a systems malfunction, we have the ability to abort mission and head back down again. The *Griffon's* landing procedure is similar to the old American space shuttle. We've even installed drogue parachutes if we need them to slow her down. But do you know what concerns me the most?"

"What's that, Dave?"

"Eireann Reid with her feathers ruffled. She's still perturbed because of the changes demanded by the general. She won't blame Nick; he had nothing to do with the design or the rip-out. So there's a distinct possibility I will find myself targeted in her crosshairs. If she kills me, Cam, just be aware of my final wishes. I want my ashes scattered over Anawhata Beach."

"If it's any consolation, you and Nick will deliver gifts for Eireann and her immediate crew. Make sure to point out the Yeti hotbox to her first."

"What's in it? Will she like it?"

"Funky Fish. All her favorites."

The launch site was becoming more crowded by the minute. Sutton gauged that was good for public relations, but a possible security nightmare if there were a terrorist among them. He then noticed that Hahona Timoti, affectionately known as Welly, was now in front of a woman holding a camera. Rocket Lab's media coordinator had seized the last-minute opportunity to interview Van den Berg just before the *Griffon* liftoff.

Out of the blue, Julie Stempler appeared to recheck the pilot and co-pilot's flight wear. Wearing goggles with her blonde hair styled in a bun, she was also dressed in a red coverall embellished with the Kon-Tiki logo. All members of the engineering team were aware that there were cameras rolling, as the administrators wanted to record the launch in the best possible light.

"How are you feeling, Dave? Any butterflies?"

Sutton lowered his voice to answer, "Those anti-nausea tablets you gave me are kicking in. They won't make me sleepy, will they? Because it's essential for me to be awake and alert for the next twenty-four hours."

"No, they're the non-drowsy kind," Stempler assured him. "And you'll need to keep your lid on as long as you're in the atmosphere. After that, you can take your helmet off if it makes you more comfortable."

"That directive seems backwards to me. I would worry more about depressurization occurring out in the black. And if the cabin should suddenly depressurize at any time, I'll initiate the procedure to let the oxygen roll into our helmets."

"And Dave?"

"What?"

The engineering team had been living and working in close proximity for a number of years now. Stempler wanted to offer him a hug of re-assurance. She didn't dare, though. Not with the cameras rolling, as it would appear unprofessional as well as ominous.

"Be careful up there. We need you to come back safe."

Chapter 51

Bardick residence
Pacific Heights neighborhood
Honolulu, Hawaii

Gladys was a poised hostess wearing a turquoise silk kimono. Three of her friends — Naomi Kaplan, Miriam Schneider and Dina Feldmann — had come over for a weekday afternoon Mah Jongg session.

Kaplan arrived wearing a red fitted sheath dress with black piping trim topped off with an Asian conical hat. Schneider and Feldmann followed suit with their own Asian-themed costumes.

Gladys owned a Hong Kong Mah Jongg ivory set of the sort played by enthusiasts in China. A sentimental treasure, it had belonged to her grandmother. It was not for everyday use. The well-worn tiles were safeguarded in a glass curio cabinet in the parlor.

Today she and her friends played with an American Mah Jongg game that came from Amazon. The online store, not the river.

"Felipe, we're ready for luncheon," she announced.

Gladys escorted her guests into the formal dining room. The table had been downsized and adorned with a pastel tablecloth and a Japanese-style floral arrangement. Wearing his traditional white chef's coat and hat, Sanninikone served each guest a chilled glass plate with artfully-arranged fruit salad. He also brought in a platter containing an assortment of tea sandwiches from which the guests could choose.

A cup and saucer had been positioned at each place setting in the event that some guests may wish to drink tea. As she delicately dunked a bag of Earl Grey, Kaplan said, "My mother belonged to a league of Mah Jongg enthusiasts in upper Manhattan."

"Mine did too," remarked Schneider. "Our club was in Babylon, a little over an hour away from Manhattan. I used to watch my mother and her friends play. They used Asian Pacific rules."

"Thank you, Felipe," said Gladys, nodding at the chef. "Is Asian Pacific style played differently?"

Schneider elaborated. "They use a hundred forty-four tiles. And the players don't keep score, an official has to do it. And under AP rules, honor tiles aren't played."

After lunch, the players were eager to get back to their favorite pastime.

"Sik wu!" announced Feldmann.

"You have Mah Jongg?" sighed Kaplan. "I was so close. I only needed one more meld."

Out of the blue, Schneider asked Gladys, "Are you nearly ready to give your report on the funds raised from the Gala?"

As she replaced the tiles in their box, Gladys replied, "Even after expenses, we raised forty-four thousand."

Fanning herself with an oriental fan, Schneider said, "I believe we can chalk that up as a huge success. How are you going to distribute the funds?"

"I expect we will finalize our plans at the next afternoon meeting, but here is what I was thinking. If we contribute the proceeds to our local shelter facility, it will keep them in operation for a few more months. That wouldn't do anything to lift families out of poverty, though. If we focused on a few truly needy families, it could impact their lives for the better. An allowance to cover the deposit on an apartment would at least give some of the children a roof over their head."

With her hand on her hip, Kaplan smirked, "Don't be silly, Gladys. There are just some people who are always going to be poor. Like there are some who are wealthy. That's just the way life is, so you might as well get used to it."

Gladys could feel her blood boil within her, however giving in to a meltdown would achieve nothing. Instead, she tried a different approach.

"All the same, I'm going to have my assistant draw up some alternative plans. That way, the group could have exact figures to determine the best course of action."

Gladys was uncertain whether she would be able to make any further headway at the next ladies' group meeting, but she had to try. For her own sake, as well as theirs.

After her guests departed, Gladys headed to her bedroom to change out of the kimono.

Instantly, she detected something strange. Lined up along the wall outside her room she spotted a five-piece set of Samsonite luggage in charcoal with leather trim. Sizes ranged from an extra-large wheeled case with extendable handle on down to a carry-on makeup case.

On close examination, Gladys perceived that the luggage smelled new and still bore the tags. Puzzled, she headed outside where Su Lee was watching the puppies.

She cuddled her animals, then said, "I noticed a luggage set right outside my bedroom door. Do you know anything about it?"

"The general brought them by while you were occupied with your guests," she said.

Gladys picked up her pets for a quick snuggle, then asked, "Can you watch Fifi and Bobo for a few minutes more? I need to speak to the general to find out what's going on."

Su Lee thought to herself, when someone receives luggage, she may have a trip abroad in her future.

Gladys was having a different set of thoughts. Does my husband want me to pack my bags? Her heart was beating furiously as she made her way to his library on the other side of the house.

"Bubula," exclaimed the general, whom she found seated in his library. "Did you get my gift? The suitcases?"

Puzzled, Gladys asked, "I did. Interesting gift. What are they for, Lenny?"

The library was furnished with a leather sofa, loveseat and recliner. Settled in the loveseat, the general patted the cushion beside him. Unsure of herself, his wife joined him.

"Care to join me for a few moments? I didn't want to disturb you while you were entertaining visitors. By the way, you look lovely in that color."

Warmed by her husband's flattery, Gladys was still worried that he was going to ask her to jet off to Papua New Guinea. Between their rekindled relationship, her work with the refugees and her new little dogs, she was just beginning to feel happy with her life again.

"You look a little worried, Bubala."

The general's library provided a place for his numerous pictoral reference books. The volumes on military strategy and aerial warfare fascinated him. He had called in a decorator to furnish the space with prints of airplanes, jet planes and a photo of Clément Ader's Avion III.

Taking in her surroundings, Gladys opened up. "I don't really come in here much. It makes me feel as if I'm an intruder in the boys' clubhouse."

With a chuckle, Bardick linked elbows with his wife and took her hand. "If it makes you feel any better, you're the only girl allowed in this clubhouse. Other than the housekeeper who comes in to clean."

Gladys looked into her husband's eyes and asked, "Now are you going to tell me all your secrets? Such as the purpose for these suitcases?"

The general held up his hand terminal, tapped it and began to scroll. "I was just thinking it might be relaxing for us to take a trip together. Will you indulge me for a moment? Perhaps check out some websites with me?"

Gladys nodded and allowed the general to show her promotional photos of vacation locations.

"We've never been to Tahiti. I hear the water is just as blue as the sky."

Gladys tried to relax, but in the end she felt the need to express herself.

"Lenny, these are beautiful places, but I have a lot on my mind right now."

Bardick felt the urgent need to get his wife in a traveling mood. That would be the first step in getting both of them safely off planet. He was just beginning to pick up on her anxiety, though.

"Why are you worried? Is it the refugees?"

Gladys nodded. "The women's society is content with handing them a bag of toiletries. That helps them for a day but it does nothing to alleviate their living situation. If I don't lead the charge to help them, I'm not certain anyone else will. And it's not just the refugees, it's the puppies."

General Bardick slipped his arm around his wife. "Don't worry, Bubala. I won't take you anywhere you don't want to go. Not anymore. But consider this: what if you could travel and take the dogs with you? Just think about it, will you?"

Chapter 52

Bertrand Intra-orbital Shipyard

It was not until they approached Bertrand Station aboard the *Griffon* that Dave Sutton realized just how much expansion the shipyard had undergone.

Van den Berg turned to catch Sutton's reaction to the colossal station, especially the massive *Kon-Tiki* reflected in his glasses.

"Must see to believe," said Sutton. "It's one thing to see it laid out on a computer screen; quite a different experience to see it nearly completed out here. Bang-on job they did, that."

"No more awe-inspiring than this little beauty we're riding right now," quipped the pilot. "Ah, wait. There's our cargo bay. Cargo Bay 3."

The pocket cargo bay doors slid to each side upon their approach revealing a well-lit compartment inside.

"Switching to parking jets now," Van den Berg reported. "Fifty meters 'til entry. Forty … thirty …"

"Sweet as!" exclaimed Sutton when they touched down inside.

"Bloody ripper!" agreed Van den Berg. "We have a countdown to observe while the station re-pressurizes the compartment."

Sutton experienced a flood of simultaneous emotions that included relief when the anti-gravity cruiser functioned as expected. Anticipation of the upcoming task of reproducing one more little miracle in time for the *Kon-Tiki's* launch. That added to the dread of Eireann Reid's anger ignited by the time-consuming tear-out the general ordered.

At the precise moment the numeric countdown on Van den Berg's dash reached zero, a flood of Bertrand shipyard technicians wearing olive-drab coveralls spilled into the cargo deck. All were cheering and applauding wildly.

While shutting down the shuttlecraft's systems, Van den Berg commented, "Our adoring fans await us."

Sutton instructed, "We're making the official film, remember? The mission brief states all you and I need to do is exit the craft, smile and wave."

As the engineer and pilot followed the script, familiar faces appeared in the crowd. At the center of it was Eireann Reid flanked by Julie Stempler.

Van den Berg diligently endured a sea of handshakes and fist bumps.

Reid finally wove her way through the crowd to give Sutton and his pilot each a pat on the shoulder. "Well done, mates! Smashed it!

Stempler had a hug for her fellow teammate. "*Ka Pai!* Good on ya, Dave!"

The adoring Bertrand technicians didn't stay in the cargo bay for long. When most of them had departed to finish their duties, Sutton glanced around and asked, "Are we off camera now? Do we need to check in with our handprints anywhere?"

With a sweeping gesture, Reid answered, "No, it's all facial recognition up here. VIKI has eyes and ears all over the station. Nothing escapes her attention." She paused for a moment, then said softly, "Is there by any chance a chilly bin in your cargo hold?"

With a huge grin, Sutton said, "Damn Skippy."

"Anything alcoholic in there?"

"You know it. And we brought along a hot box as well. Do you suppose we could locate a picnic table somewhere?"

Reid looked around the cargo hold where only a small remnant of the coverall-clad technicians remained. "If you will be so kind as to retrieve those items? The shipyard has changed a lot since you were last here, Dave."

Still wearing the light-duty pressure suits in which they arrived, Van den Berg and Sutton dragged the wheeled coolers and trailed behind Reid and Stempler. The route took them past crew quarters.

"If you'd like to get out of those pressure suits for a bit, you'll find some clean coveralls in the employee locker room," said Reid, hooking her thumb in that direction. "Come on, I'll give you a tour before you have to head back.

But first, let's have a bite to eat."

"We're not going to eat here?" asked Sutton softly as they filed through the mess hall where a number of off-duty technicians were eating.

With a wave, Reid answered equally softly, "Nah. I've worked hard for my reward. I don't have to share it with these clowns." Pointing to the hall ahead, she explained, "It's up here. The door at the end of the hall."

Sutton and Van den Berg's curiosity was satisfied when Reid opened the door to a small-scale chow hall. "It's much nicer in here. You can eat your Ramen Noodles in peace."

The smaller dining room was furnished with a metal table with attached benches on either side. The floor was equally high-end: aluminum diamond plate sheeting.

"Nice!" said Van den Berg. "This place needed an officer's mess."

Sutton shook his head. "I didn't bring you any Ramen Noodles, if that's what you're after."

Reid laughed out loud. "Thank God for that! Whatcha got?"

Sutton looked around. "Are we on camera?"

"That's a negative," said Reid. "But VIKI can still hear us. VIKI, raise the lights ten percent, please?"

Is that sufficient, Eireann?

"Yes, VIKI. Okay, Dave, where's the chow?"

While raising the hotbox clamps, he said, "I have two words for you: Funky Fish."

Reid pumped her elbows and knees up and down in a little happy dance. "Beauty!" Afterwards, she fished in the hot box to retrieve a packet. "Chicken. This must be yours," she said, handing it to Stempler."

Shortly she located her desired entree. "This is it! A fish and chips Butty!"

"What's that?" asked Van den Berg.

"It's new. It's beer-battered fish drizzled with their tartar sauce. Comes with hot, salty chips with tomato sauce."

"Fish and chips are best paired with beer," said Sutton. "I brought along a case of Lion Red. None for you, Nick, as you'll be driving soon."

Reid did an encore of her happy dance. "She'll be right, mate."

Tearing into their takeaways yielded a few moments of relative silence, punctuated by Sutton who ventured, "Are you and your staff still getting used to the Artificial Intelligence?"

"Love it!" said Reid between bites. "The astronaut robots were always efficient; the humans not so much. VIKI monitors all the activities that take place during duty shifts. There are precise logs of work assignments plus an assessment of how daily expectations are fulfilled. Plus she makes sure that when they're on duty, no technicians are able to play video games or watch movies. Or listen to music. In this way, They're not distracted."

"Do the technicians think that's too strict?"

With a shrug, Reid answered, "Productivity is up twenty percent, which means I don't care how they feel about it. They can like it or lump it. And, provided they turn off their audio feed, they are allowed to hum softly to themselves. And, on top of that, VIKI has ironed out quite a few supply chain issues."

"If you're not pissed about the AI, does this mean you're not going to tear me a new one over General Bardick's tear-out?"

"Phhht," said Reid, swatting the air and taking a seat with her culinary bonus. She raised a hand up, then swiveled it downwards. "Being station manager has its ups and downs. I was initially slightly irritated, but that's not your fault. The alterations dropped a grenade into our timetable, but with VIKI's help, we were able to catch up. Do you know what they call General Bardick?"

Hearing the request, VIKI supplied pertinent information. *General Leonard Mordecai Bardick, age 65, resides in Honolulu, Hawaii. Married to Gladys Goldstein Bardick. Other nomenclature: General Bardick is also known as The Old Shark.*

"Thanks, VIKI. Shut down research mode."

Shutting down research mode, check.

"As I was saying, the installation of his state room was initially irritating to the point that I was considering a few modifications of my own. Namely, putting his chef, butler and other staff members' quarters at the opposite end of the ship."

Sutton snickered, nearly blowing out a mouthful of beer.

With a glance at Julie Stempler, however, Reid admitted, "I decided not to, because he would most likely insist that the mistakes are torn out with subsequent updates. In the end, Julie and I gave him all he asked for, and more."

Stempler stepped into the conversation with, "If I'm in charge of decorating the crew quarters, I'm giving Bardick and his wife a tropical paradise. When they get a peek inside their living quarters, hopefully they're going to believe they're in Tahiti instead of outer space. I hope Mrs. Bardick is fond of wicker furniture and tropical prints. Their quarters even smell like pineapple and coconut oil."

Reid volunteered, "Julie continued the topical theme for the entertainers' quarters. The décor is definitely high-end."

Wadding the Funky Fish packaging into a ball, Reid asked, "Which leads us to the upcoming shit job. Dave, when should we expect to play host for the dedication ceremony?"

In response to her question, Sutton leaned back in his chair and crossed his arms over his chest. "I can think of plenty of adjectives that describe General Bardick, however there's one thing he's not. You can't call him indecisive. He told us in no uncertain terms that there will be no dedication."

"What?" said everyone else in unison.

"The ship already has a name that suits him just fine. It's already gone out in a press release. A naming ceremony is therefore ridiculous at this point. Plus Bardick thinks that having all those officials and guests up here is a security risk."

"Well, he's right, you know," said Reid. "It's a nightmare when you consider how precarious our atmosphere, electricity, gravity and water filtration is up here. Add fifty to a hundred additional bodies and you have a disaster waiting to happen."

"I think the general is concerned about terrorists," Stempler guessed.

"Whatever his reason, General Bardick wants no unauthorized visitors on the premises before launch date," said Sutton.

"I expected that he would have his wife up here to smash the champagne bottle, at the very least," Reid mused.

Shaking his head, Sutton explained, "That was Brandon Kemp's suggestion, but he wasn't going for it."

"I guess the old shark is too smart to take the bait," guessed Van den Berg.

"It isn't that," Sutton answered. "I heard him tell Cam that he doesn't want his wife up here until the boat is ready to set sail."

"Why do you suppose he doesn't want to let her come up to have a look around?"

"Why do you think?" Stempler wondered aloud.

"Dunno," said Sutton. "They're billionaires, and I suppose he doesn't want her to find out that there isn't a single bathtub with gold faucets in the whole place."

Chapter 53

The prayer journal was pink. It was pretty. She appreciated it. But Bella Brown was no more capable of using it than she was of composing a symphony. Or speaking Swahili.

Shortly after her arrival to the bungalow, Muriel Santiago discovered Brown seated in the small den, turning the gift over and over as if she were attempting to figure it out.

With an impish grin, Santiago said, "It works better when you use a pen."

Prompted by her guest, Brown opened the cover to examine the inside. Each pastel page bore a Bible verse. She normally moved on from anything that had to do with religion, but it was a sweet gift and she didn't want to offend the giver.

Santiago leaned over the arm of the recliner, turning the pages as she read, "Romans 12:12: *Be joyful in hope, patient in affliction, faithful in prayer.* And the next page, 1 Thessalonians 5:16-18: *Rejoice always, pray continually, give thanks in all circumstances; for this is God's will for you in Christ Jesus.* And here's another good one: Philippians 4:6: *Do not be anxious about anything, but in every situation, by prayer and petition, with thanksgiving, present your requests to God.*"

Brown furtively read one of the verses. "Mark 11:24: *Therefore I tell you, whatever you ask for in prayer, believe that you have received it, and it will be yours.*"

She unconsciously shook her head.

"You don't like it?" asked Santiago.

"I really do," said Brown. "It's just that ... I don't understand how you use it. Or why."

"Well, it's basically a journal in which you write down your prayer topics. If you receive any blessings, you can record prayers of thanksgiving. If you or anyone else is sick or going through trials, write down your concerns. It shows the power of prayer when you record that someone who was sick or injured got better. Prayer is a dialog between you and God. It's like a spiritual diary in which you can record your conversations with Him."

Santiago was just beginning to realize there was a disconnect. A serious one.

Bella Brown believed in God. Her belief was quite unlike Muriel Santiago's, though. She believed that God was manifested in the everyday miracles of science, but she didn't believe that God dealt in the affairs of humanity. Especially not individual people such as herself. Furthermore, she could not wrap her brain around a reason anyone would revere somebody like Jesus. Who — or what — was Jesus, anyway?

When science can explain everything, why was there a need to believe in anything else?

Muriel Santiago was gifted in reading people, a skill derived from years of daily visits to a hospital praying over the patients. She accurately picked up on the fact that Brown was unfamiliar with the concept of prayer. Ultimately, the problem went deeper than that.

"Bella, you believe in God, don't you?"

"I don't actually go to church," she confessed, looking up to determine Santiago's reaction.

"The idea makes you uncomfortable, does it?"

"Ummm," Brown nodded.

"The church is just a building," Santiago explained. "You can experience God wherever you are. You aren't required to attend church, although the support of fellow believers is helpful."

The topic of discussion was causing Brown a certain amount of discomfort. In her mind, she was pressing the brakes. If it wasn't for the extreme kindness that Santiago had lavished on her former housemate, she would have completely avoided this line of conversation.

"I don't mean to be nosy. Were your family Christians, Bella?"

Brown shook her head. "My parents were scientists. They never took us to church. Once a neighbor girl invited me to attend a summer Bible school. I liked the crafts and Bible stories. But one day they were singing *Jesus Loves Me* and the teacher noticed that I wasn't singing. She asked me why, and I told her I didn't know the song. She ridiculed me and said, *Everyone knows Jesus Loves Me.* And all the kids laughed at me. I felt stupid."

Santiago had a little hug for Brown. "I'm sorry you didn't have a good experience at Bible School. But whether or not you know the words to the song, what's important is that you know that Jesus loves you."

At that point, the elder woman read her hostess accurately. Bella Brown was fluent in numerous scientific concepts. The theory of relativity as well as the principle behind anti-gravity and warp-drive propulsion came easily to her scientific mind, however it was obvious that she lacked a basic understanding of God.

There was work that she needed to do in New Zealand. A purpose for her trip in addition to a visit with her favorite niece.

Santiago could easily have pulled out her own prayer journal to show as an example. Hers was a simple, spiral-bound notebook. Pages upon pages were filled with prayer topics in her own neat handwriting. Her prayer topics included Mercy hospital patients who had been seriously injured in car accidents. A man from her church who had recently loss a spouse. A child who had been diagnosed with cancer. She didn't show her personal prayer record to Bella Brown, though, because it would have overwhelmed her. She was nowhere near ready to see or understand its significance. The blank pages of her new journal were a perfect place to start.

"There's a verse in the Bible that I believe you will appreciate. Isaiah 66:2 says *We can see God reflected in the world He created.*"

"I'm with you on that one," Brown agreed.

Santiago longed to share her faith with Bella Brown, but she realized that most topics relating to religion repelled her. For this reason she would need to temper her zeal with patience. Take it slowly.

This situation would require a ton of prayer coupled with an equal amount of sensitivity.

Chapter 54

United States government complex
Honolulu, Hawaii

After they had solved all the world's problems, one more impending crisis remained.

At the conclusion of their weekly session, the volume in the United States congressional hall escalated. General Leonard Bardick watched closely as the delegates milled around the room. Small groups were involved in conversation. Some were speakers, others listeners. A few waited on the outskirts of those conversations, hoping for their ideas to be heard as well.

President Maleko Ho remained seated at the podium. General Bardick watched as an aide bent down to listen to what the president was saying.

The general remained rooted to his seat. It was a feeling he had.

A man in uniform worked his way over to the general's elbow. From his dark complexion and stocky build, it was evident that he was of native Hawaiian descent.

"General Bardick, the president wishes to speak with you. If you will come this way, please."

Enroute through the congressional chamber, General Bardick noticed that General Paul Rodriguez got the same memo. Both of them wove their way past the seats in the chamber to a hallway linking the chamber with the rest of the building.

Bardick assessed that the two men who escorted himself and General Rodriguez were young — probably in their twenties. Despite the disparity in their ages, all four of them instinctively walked in step down the long passageway, up the stairs to the new Oval Office.

By the time they entered, President Maleko Ho was already seated behind his desk. It made sense that the commander-in-chief would have an alternate route to exit the legislative room and navigate the building.

Two Secret Service men wearing dark suits were positioned on either side of the door, ever watchful to eliminate any human threat that might breach the chamber and attempt to harm the president. The commander in chief revealed he called the meeting, however, to discuss a threat that wasn't human.

"I think I can shed some light on our enemy's motivation," Bardick began.

The president nodded and gestured for him to continue.

"I'm certain you are familiar with Hawaiian history. After being isolated from the rest of the world for a number of centuries, King Kamehameha I established a kingdom that united the islands. Although it was intended to protect Hawaiians, their numbers continued to decline. After the Americans annexed the islands and took over, the number of native Hawaiians was reduced even more to around 37,000."

With their full attention, President Ho added, "I am aware there was a coup during which Queen Lili'uokalani was forced to abdicate the throne and placed under house arrest. The native Hawaiians are still resentful. I'm descended from Chinese sugar plantation workers. We've been here five generations but they still don't classify me as a native Hawaiian."

"The hoards of wealthy immigrants coming in are pumping cash into Hawaii's economy," said Bardick. "That's driving up the cost of living, which is pricing the native Hawaiians out of their ancestral homelands. My wife heads up an organization that focuses on the homeless."

Perhaps not so helpfully, Rodriguez announced, "And I'm from the Phillipines. First generation."

With a sigh, General Bardick continued. "The background we need to grasp here is the significance of the Hawaiian islands, specifically Pearl Harbor, during the World War II period. Why do you suppose the Japanese wanted it?"

"During that period one-quarter of the Hawaiian population claimed Japanese ancestry," President Ho recalled. "Over the course of Hawaiian history, Japan had sent ships to Hawaii to protect the Japanese citizens who lived there."

"Now I get you. Military Strategy 101," said General Rodriguez. "The Hawaiian islands, specifically Pearl Harbor, are centrally-located in the Pacific Ocean. Very strategic location."

"You're both right," said Bardick. "It was a refueling and repair station for ships crossing the Pacific, but it was more than that. Pearl Harbor has a deep-water lagoon capable of accommodating large ocean-going battleships. For this reason, it was a strategic shipyard that could harbor United States naval vessels. As such it was the perfect deep-water home base for the U.S. Pacific fleet. Japan was aware of its strategic value as gateway to the Pacific Ocean. They wanted the Pacific, but the United States was aware how much power it would give them if we let them have it."

"Just a short hop over to California," Rodriguez figured.

"Bingo!" said Bardick, pointing an index finger. "Now we come to the reason why we're here."

He left President Ho an open door to ask the critical question. "Why is an alien enemy so bent on conquering the Earth?"

"It's the same exact reason," said Bardick, stretching his arms out on either side. "It has to be. Habitable planet with abundant natural resources. The only planet in the vicinity that will support life without extensive terraforming effort. Oxygen-nitrogen atmosphere and an optimum distance from the sun. And, who knows, it may offer them a strategic military home base. What I do know for certain is that Lukas Berg assured me there is nothing this species will accept in negotiation for leaving us alone."

With his head in his hands and his elbows on the table, President Ho shook his head back and forth. A moment later, he looked up.

"General Rodriguez, is there any hope that we have strategic weaponry that we could use to defend ourselves against such an attack?"

Bardick and Rodriguez looked at each other.

"No, sir," Rodriguez answered. "I have no personal knowledge of this particular species, but I conducted extensive research on them and their capabilities. Strategically and intellectually, we have assessed that the species' technological knowledge is light years ahead of us. You saw what happened to the United States. Due to their shape-shifting capabilities, they may already be here. If they decided to press the button, it would be that fast." He snapped his fingers.

The president thought for a moment, then said, "Lenny, is there any hope that Lukas Berg can secure an alliance with any advanced civilizations who would be willing to come to our aid?"

General Bardick pulled off his gold wire-rimmed glasses, and with the fingers of his other hand massaged the bridge of his nose. "I've already pursued that avenue. The other alien species are smart enough to know when to fight and when to back away. And right now ..."

"They're staying out of it. I was afraid you would say that."

"And, as I've already informed you, the Nordic ambassador has been ordered to get his family off this planet. They have already departed, sir."

There was dead silence while the commander-in-chief struggled to come up with other options.

"How long, Lenny? How long do we have?"

Bardick shook his head. "Absolutely no way to tell. And, sir, concerning the other part of my assignment. I have assessed the capabilities of other nations on Earth. The short version is a handful that are manufacturing and launching starships, mainly to the Moon and Mars, plus a limited number of asteroid mining projects. They're toddling around fighting over their toys."

"Ummm," said the president, processing.

"Recently I have been in communication with Rocket Lab, a launch provider in New Zealand. They were in the process of constructing another warp-capable mothership when the Chenghuang Corporation backed out of their contract."

"So I heard. The Chinese economy is in a crap cycle."

It was then that Bardick dropped the unavoidable bomb. "As you may or may not have heard, I purchased the *Kon-Tiki*."

"The hell you say!" Rodriguez interjected, staring at him.

President Ho was silent, his eyes large.

General Bardick continued, "If Rocket Lab didn't come up with some cash, there was the possibility that construction would be halted. Anyway, they are nearing completion of the vessel. And, sir, I'm headed off-planet as well. I'd like for you to consider this as my official notice."

"You?" demanded the president. "You're leaving us?" After a few seconds, he added, "Of course, the colony at Proxima Centauri."

"I wouldn't blame you for doing the Texas two-step right about now," Rodriguez remarked.

"How many people will be aboard the *Kon-Tiki?*"

Bardick shrugged. "Four hundred and change."

Locking his gaze with Bardick, General Rodriguez asked, "Does Gladys know? How were you able to convince her to load up on a spaceship?"

With a furtive expression, he admitted, "No, she doesn't know yet, but we are rapidly moving in that direction."

Chapter 55

Bella Brown residence
Rocket Lab campus
Auckland, New Zealand

"Oh, no!"

Brandi Red Feather and Bella Brown headed home after a stressful day at work. Red Feather was grilling some meat for herself and her aunt; Brown was seasoning some vegetables to throw on the brazier later on.

For an unknown reason Brown's house cat had imprinted on Miriam Santiago, curled up on her lap in the den.

While they were attempting to relax, Brown received a text message.

"What's wrong?" asked Red Feather.

With a frown, Brown answered, "I have a friend who is the spouse of an engineering team member. She's had a really difficult pregnancy. Right now she's in the hospital with pre eclampsia. I just got a text from her saying her doctor plans to induce labor in a few hours. If her blood pressure spikes, she is worried they will have to do an emergency Caesarean delivery."

"Oh, my!" remarked Santiago. "What hospital?"

"They have her in Starship Hospital. They were trying to keep her on bed rest to lower her blood pressure, but I guess that didn't work."

"Brandi, is the meat ready?"

"Yeah, I think so."

"Then wrap it up and put it in the refrigerator. Bella, you can drive us to the hospital. There's no time to waste!"

The crisis threw Santiago into action. Brown didn't think showing up at the hospital would serve a purpose, however she didn't know what else to do.

Santiago was already seated in Brown's Range Rover while Red Feather and Bella Brown were still wrapping up things in the house.

There was no denying the fact that Muriel Santiago was a praying woman.

Red Feather explained, "Ever since she retired, my aunt has gone nearly every day to Mercy Hospital to pray over the patients. I'm certain that's what she intends to do for Jim and Claire."

"I know," said Brown. "My housemate Raven said she came and prayed over her while she was recovering at Mercy Hospital."

In her mind, Brown was wrestling with a dilemma. She was willing to do anything that would alleviate Claire Montgomery's suffering, or ensure that her child would be healthy. She was uncertain how to pray to God, though, or whether any actions Muriel Santiago took could affect the precarious circumstances.

In the elevator headed up to the maternity ward, Brown said, "I'm not certain whether a visit to Jim and Claire would be appropriate right now. After all, they've already got a lot going on."

Regarding Brown, Santiago said, "You mean whether or not they would be open to someone praying for a healthy delivery."

Red Feather looked at them both but remained silent.

"All right," said Santiago, with an expression of resignation. "All right. When we get there, there is a possibility may refuse to see us. It happens from time to time. If they ask us to leave, then we will respect their privacy." She paused for a moment and then added, "In that case I will pray for them out in the waiting area."

Brown breathed a sigh of relief. "I don't think we should butt in on an intimate family moment."

"If nothing else, we can give them a show of support," said Red Feather.

Brown had been a regular hospital visitor since Montgomery had been admitted. All the same, she stopped at the nurses' station to verify her location.

"Claire Montgomery?" she asked.

A grey-haired woman wearing a surgical green scrub outfit searched until she found the name on her computer screen.

"She's in 327. It's straight down the hall," she told the women, pointing in the direction of the room in question.

Brown led the way. She rapped lightly on the door that was nearly closed. "Claire? Jim?"

"We're in here," answered a weak voice.

The room was small; not much larger than the hospital bed and a monitor stand. Outside the window the visitors got a good look at the setting sun. Seated at his wife's elbow, Jim Freeman wore a worried expression.

Staff at Rocket Lab were accustomed to seeing Claire Montgomery in top-of-the-line business fashions. Matching outfits with coordinated jewelry and pumps. Today, she lay nearly motionless in the bed in a rumpled hospital gown. Her hair was mussed; her skin pale without makeup. An IV line extended from her arm; a wire from a monitor led to her her enlarged belly. She winced when a blood pressure cuff on her other arm suddenly tightened.

Santiago had never been medically trained. From her time at Mercy Hospital, though, she knew what blood pressure numbers were supposed to look like. And Claire Montgomery's numbers were much higher.

"Bella, I'm so glad to see you!" Montgomery said.

Brown approached and asked, "How are you feeling?"

"You got the text I sent you," she answered. "They are going to induce my labor just as quickly as they can get everything set up. So I'm a bit overwhelmed right now."

"I believe you have both met Brandi Red Feather," Brown began.

"Oh, yes, I set up your introductory training just before I had to leave. Nice to see you again."

"And this is her aunt, Muriel Santiago."

Freeman nodded with a puzzled expression.

"Nice to meet you," said Montgomery.

"I'm so happy to be here this evening. May I ask whether you are expecting a little boy? Or a girl?"

"A girl," verified Freeman.

"I realize that this is an uncertain time for you both. I would like to ask your permission to pray with you."

There was a pregnant pause during which Freeman and Montgomery looked at each other. Montgomery nodded; Freeman said, "It's all right. We would appreciate it."

Santiago approached the bed. She extended her hands to the expectant mother and father. "May I?" she asked.

The couple joined hands with the elderly woman who bowed her head and closed her eyes. Everyone else in the room did also, except for Brown, who kept one eye open to observe.

"Heavenly Father, we come before you this evening with thanksgiving in our hearts," Santiago began. "We give you praise for the gift of this little one who is about to enter into the world. Please wrap your loving arms around this mother and father during this critical time. Comfort them with your presence, Lord. We ask you to gird up the doctors and nurses with wisdom and a steady hand. And above all, Father, we petition you for the safety of this child and a healthy delivery for this mother. Thank you for listening to our prayer for it is in Jesus' precious name that we pray."

Brown opened both eyes and blinked. "Is that it?" she asked.

"Yes, dear. All we can do is voice our request to the Almighty."

At that moment, a man wearing green surgical scrubs pushed a cart into the room. He checked out Montgomery's hospital bracelet, then verified her date of birth.

"I'm here to get you ready for the delivery room," he said.

"My prep team is here," said Montgomery with a little smile.

Brown reached over to give Montgomery a hug. She took Freeman's hand and gave him a parting squeeze.

"I understand. You're going on stage," said Brown.

"He's here to do my hair and makeup," Montgomery joked.

"Please let us know when you have some good news," said Santiago. "I'll keep praying."

"We'll keep you informed," Freeman promised.

"Thank you so much for coming," said Montgomery, giving Santiago's hand a final squeeze.

Chapter 56

Bella Brown bungalow
Rocket Lab campus
Auckland, New Zealand

"She's here. Six pounds three ounces."

Bella Brown and Brandi Red Feather had been at work when they first heard the good news that spread rapidly throughout the Rocket Lab facility.

A skillful personnel manager, Claire Montgomery had been missed during her absence. And although the AI computer was fully in charge of recruitment, certain personnel matters needed a human touch.

Jim Freeman did his best to focus on Research and Development projects, but due to his frazzled nerves, his supervisor had granted a parental leave of absence.

While the good news spread among Rocket Lab staff, Brown and Red Feather took an early lunch hour to inform the prayer warrior Muriel Santiago.

"Auntie, Jim and Claire have a daughter! The baby is here and she's healthy!" she rejoiced, almost before she crossed the threshold of the bungalow they shared.

Santiago was seated at the kitchen table. One hand on a Bible and the other on a cup of tea in front of her. She clapped her hands together and raised them slightly. "Thank you, Lord. All praise goes to you!"

Brown and Red Feather took seats at the table where Brown retrieved a series of photos on her phone to share with Santiago. A picture of the brand-new baby wrapped in a hospital blanket. Claire Montgomery with the new infant cuddled up to her chest. Jim Freeman, Montgomery and the baby girl together.

"She is absolutely beautiful," said Red Feather, admiring the photos on Brown's phone.

"Have they given the baby a name?" asked Santiago.

"I don't know. I'll ask them." Her fingers tapped lightly across her hand terminal.

In the meantime, Red Feather served up fresh blueberry scones and a selection of fruit for lunch.

"Did you know," began Santiago, "that there is a bright spark that happens at the precise instant when a baby is conceived?"

Brown was skeptical. "Who said that? And how do they know? That's a pretty intimate moment ..."

"An electron microscope can capture it during *in vitro* fertilization," she explained.

"Oh," Brown remarked, "I never thought of that."

"Have you ever studied chromosomes?"

Red Feather began to heat water for tea, listening all the while to Brown and Santiago's conversation.

"No," Brown replied, wrinkling her brow. "Not really."

"That isn't my area of expertise, but it is an area of interest."

"Auntie Muriel is a chemist," added Red Feather. "She retired from a fertilizer plant in Saskatchewan."

"I didn't know you were a chemist!" Brown remarked.

"Yes. A fellow scientist. Back to the chromosomes. As you are no doubt aware, human beings have twenty-three pairs of chromosomes; with each pair having one from the mother and one from the father. And thousands of individual genes on each chromosome."

"The electron microscope was invented in 1931, with the devices commercially available since 1939," Brown contributed.

"It's good that you have a scientific mind as well," said Santiago. "Scientific research tells us that a human baby has twenty-three chromosomes. A dog, however, has more. They have thirty-nine pairs of chromosomes, for a total of seventy-eight."

"You are correct. But where is this going?"

Santiago continued without answering. "A mother dog will always give birth to dogs. It isn't scientifically possible to cross species. A Great Dane is a dog. A Chihuahua is a dog, at least she thinks she is!"

"Oh hello, Kitty Kitty," Santiago said as Brown's house cat leaped into her lap. Stroking her fur, she continued, "A domestic cat has nineteen pairs for a total of thirty-eight chromosomes. It's marvelous, really."

Brown normally put on the brakes when it came to conversations about religion. Scientific principles, however, drew her in.

"What all this means is that a cat will always give birth to cats. If Kitty Kitty had kittens, they will always have nineteen pairs of chromosomes."

"Kitty Kitty can't have kittens," Brown interrupted. "I had her fixed."

Ignoring Brown's comment, Santiago continued, "If human beings wanted to manipulate a specific population, they could breed for specific characteristics. Grey fur or green eyes, for example. While natural selection may produce the desired characteristics in individual populations, it will never, ever, never change the number of chromosomes within a species."

Brown volunteered, as usual, more than anyone else needed or wanted to hear. "Abnormalities in human chromosomes cause serious diseases. Down's Syndrome is caused when the offspring has an extra copy of chromosome 21. Sickle cell anemia is caused by an alteration of chromosome 11."

"Is it?" asked Red Feather. "Bella, do you want Earl Grey?"

"Yes, please. There are multiple examples of lethal genes that show up in poultry chickens—especially in show breeds. The creeper gene that causes short legs in Japanese bantams also causes the loss of one-quarter of their offspring."

Bella Brown stopped quoting facts. Her mouth fell open in an expression of surprise. She took a sip of tea, then said, "Each species of animal has a specific number and type of chromosomes that never changes. The loss or damage of any of those chromosomes would mean serious abnormalities or a non-viable offspring. Which means ..."

"You've figured it out, my dear," said Santiago. "Nice work."

"The theory of evolution is impossible."

Bella Brown suddenly began to feel uncomfortable. Her brain had already applied the brakes. "There's a simple scientific explanation for every process in nature."

"Like the Big Bang Theory?" asked Red Feather.

"Yeah," agreed Brown. "Except now the scientific community is referring to it as the big Bounce."

"Oh, I'm familiar," said Santiago, backing off for a moment. "Something at the center of the universe triggered an explosion of energy, causing a domino-like effect. Cosmic dust came together, forming stars and planets. But what caused it? It's my understanding that scientists still haven't identified what was at the center of it all."

Red Feather grinned at her aunt, aware of the direction in which she was headed. Still, she said nothing.

"They're calling it a Singularity," said Brown.

"If you are interested in learning more about the cause of that occurrence, I am in possession of the log book of that precise event."

Brown paused in mid-bite. "No way! You're not saying you were there!"

A chuckle escaped from Santiago's lips. "No dear. I'm old. Nowhere near that old, though."

Santiago wet her finger, then used it to turn the thin leaves of her Bible to the book of Genesis, all the way back at the beginning.

"Did you know that the sun, moon and stars didn't come about until the fourth day of creation?"

Brown still wanted to object, however she was too curious to stop the explanation.

Santiago found the place for which she was searching and began to read:

Genesis Chapter 1 verse 14. *And God said, Let there be lights in the firmament of the heaven to divide the day from the night; and let them be for signs, and for seasons, and for days, and years: And let them be for lights in the firmament of the heaven to give light upon the earth: and it was so. And God made two great lights; the greater light to rule the day, and the lesser light to rule the night: he made the stars also.*

"That sounds an awful lot like the sun, the moon and the stars," said Brown slowly.

"That's because it is," Santiago admitted. She held up her Bible and said, "This book describes how God spoke the universe into a state of existence. God is your Singularity. And science," she pointed at Brown, "science merely attempts to explain how it happened."

"Hmmm, like the male sperm and the female egg unite in the test tube, but there is a little something extra added that plays a mysterious unknown role."

"It's not unknown. It is the spark of creation; the breath of life."

Brown was silent, chewing her bottom lip.

Santiago held up both her hands, bring her two index fingers together. "Science and religion, true religion, do not cancel each other out. They are one and the same thing. Now think about this. If I were to place an ice cube on this saucer and leave it there for an hour, what do you suppose would happen?"

"It would melt," Brown answered.

"That's right. But what if I believed that it would remain in a frozen state regardless of the room's temperature?"

"It would still melt at the same rate."

"The process of liquification does not depend on your belief that it exists. Truth is truth, whether or not you believe in it."

Brown paused, then sprang into motion when she heard a beep alert from her hand terminal.

She picked it up and said, "Claire and Jim named the baby Avia."

Red Feather searched the name on her own hand terminal. "It says Avia is a girl's name of Hebrew origin. It means *My father is Yahweh.*"

Chapter 57

Bella Brown residence
Rocket Lab campus
Auckland, New Zealand

"I have to leave. It's time."

Rocket Lab's rather remote launch complex meant that many employees took advantage of on-campus housing.

During Bella Brown's time in New Zealand, those who shared her company-owned bungalow had made a significant impact on her life. You can live in the same house with someone without becoming friends. But sometimes, housemates just click.

Housemates came and went, occasionally leaving an indelible mark.

During their period of living and working together, she had easily formed a bond with her first housemate Marama Fetumale. It had been a shock when Fetumale abruptly disappeared under suspicion of treason and corporate espionage.

Brown vowed to be more cautious when she formed a friendship with her second housemate Raven Munoz. Two years of living and working together along with frequent beach picnics contributed to an amiable synchronicity. Unfortunately, she was forced to let go of Raven when she was selected as mission historian for the Phoenix flight to Planet Equinox.

Yet another housemate had moved in. Since her arrival, Brown gauged she had a lot in common with Brandi Red Feather. They shared a love of the beach and all things science fiction. It had presented a different sort of challenge when Red Feather's aunt arrived, though, and not just the issue of three women living in a small space.

Santiago read her Bible a lot and prayed even more, facts that made Brown uncomfortable. In spite of those concerns, she found herself dreading the hour of Muriel Santiago's departure.

"You forgot this one," said Brown, lugging one more duffle bag to the door of the bungalow.

Santiago was already dressed to embark aboard New Zealand Airlines. Wearing a coat and toboggan, she took the bag, then abruptly plopped down in the den.

"Ah!" she exclaimed. "I nearly forgot. I have something I want you to deliver."

Brown sat next to her, uncertain what to say.

"Auntie, do you want me to take that last bag and load it in the boot?"

"Not yet," she said with a smile. "Give us a moment, won't you please?"

"All right," agreed Red Feather before disappearing out the front door.

Brown waited expectantly while Santiago rummaged in the knapsack. "Here! I found it!"

Brown was uniquely familiar with the sort of brown cardboard box that Santiago pulled out of her luggage, as it was of the sort used to package books for shipping.

"I know that the *Kon-Tiki* will launch soon. It's headed for Planet Equinox. That's where Raven is right now."

"As far as we know."

"I want you to get this to her," she asked.

With a puzzled expression, Brown asked, "May I ask what it is?"

Santiago nodded. "It's already opened. Go ahead, take it out."

Inside, there was a hardcover book. Brown first looked at the back where she spotted Santiago's photo. A blurb that read *About The Author.* She flipped it over to reveal the title: *Faith and Prophecy in the Space Age.*

"You wrote a book?" asked Brown incredulously.

"I did," she admitted. "With a little help."

"It's about the destruction of the United States, isn't it?"

While Brown flipped through the pages, Santiago explained. "For years before it happened, I tried to get people to listen to the message that Babylon had been judged and was heading for destruction."

She looked up from the pages and asked, "How did you know that it was going to happen before it actually happened?"

"Much of the Bible's content concerns prophecy. A prophecy is like a watchman on the wall warning the people who live inside that an enemy is approaching. Certain events are written in advance of the time when they will actually happen. Very helpful, that is, if the people the prophecies are written about will listen to the warning. Which they usually don't."

Still flipping through the pages, Brown said, "Raven wrote her book to let readers know that an alien species was responsible for the elimination of America in a single day. It wasn't an earthly enemy or a volcano that brought about their destruction."

"I know," Santiago said. "She visited me in Canada to bring me a copy of her book. It was then that I realized the story needed to be told from a spiritual standpoint."

"You believe that America was destroyed because they were evil people?"

"God blessed the nation of America with prosperity. They had great riches, but they forgot the Creator who had judged them worthy to receive those blessings. In the beginning, they acknowledged God and studied the Bible to learn the path of righteousness. In the end, they forgot Him and turned to wickedness. They not only refused to repent, but they also accepted and taught abominable practices. Because their wickedness exceeded that of any other nation, they were punished by an enemy that was unlike any other. An exceptionally powerful, ruthless enemy."

Brown closed the book and re-inserted it into the box. "So you wrote your side of the story."

"I wrote the story from God's point of view. I got a little help from a ghost writer and an author coach. Even put in some reviews. Since Raven was the one who provoked me to write it, I felt that I needed to send her a copy. There's a letter inside, if that is allowed. I figured you knew how to get it packed away on the *Kon-Tiki*, yes?"

"Sure," said Brown, "I'm pretty sure that I can get it boxed up and placed with the supplies that are headed out there."

"And Bella, I got a book for you as well."

"Oh? You didn't have to do that."

"The purpose of a gift is to get you something you wouldn't normally buy for yourself."

Santiago once again rummaged in the duffle, fishing out another cardboard box. "This is for you. In appreciation of your hospitality. I know it has been a challenge for you to share your house with two other women."

This box had not been previously opened. Brown ripped open the seal to extract a tablet. "What's this?"

"It's a Bible. Now you have your own. I thought you would appreciate this technological marvel."

Brown had never owned a Bible. All the same, her conversations with Santiago made her want to become familiar with the ancient narratives, if merely to be informed. She wasn't ready to approach Santiago's religion. But she had always found the Bible stories interesting.

She opened the tablet's cover, plugged it into a charger and fired it up.

"It's like an electronic reader," Santiago explained. "The tabs at the top allow you to select which Bible version you want to read. There is a commentary tab that can open up on the right side which gives explanation of the passage you are reading. Like the story of the Big Bang in Genesis Chapter one."

"Thank you, Muriel," she said while giving Santiago a warm hug.

"Now I must return to my home," she said. "You are an engineer. Your purpose is to design spacecrafts. I need to get back to my mission as a prayer warrior. There are patients at Mercy Hospital who need intercession."

Brown placed a hand on Santiago's shoulder. "Before your flight leaves, Claire and Jim wanted you to stop by and meet Avia."

With a zip of finality, Santiago closed her tote. "Well, let's get going!"

Chapter 58

Residence bungalow
Rocket Lab campus
Auckland, New Zealand

Jim Freeman returned home from work to find Claire Montgomery bathing her infant daughter in the kitchen sink. It was a comforting sight after a long day.

"Hi, baby!"

"Are you talking to me or Avia?" Montgomery asked.

Freeman slid around behind her for a kiss — one for the mother and a smooch on the forehead for his tiny daughter. "Both of you. How was your day?"

Montgomery used a spray attachment designed for dishes to rinse her baby's body. The infant made cooing noises, staring at her mother's face.

"There was a lot of dirty diapers and spitting up involved, but we both made it through."

"Do you remember when we took that instructional class on how to bathe your baby? You aced it."

Montgomery asked, "Oh, Jim, could you hand me the towel just over there?"

"Sure, hon."

"Was your day the usual stuff?"

Freeman hesitated. "Some stuff on the personnel end. I really don't want to talk about work right now."

With the baby bundled in a bath towel, Montgomery headed to the nursery with Freeman in tow. With expert motions, she placed Avia in her crib where she had strategically positioned a clean diaper and pajamas.

"Let's hear it. I got good numbers on my blood pressure again today."

Her husband breathed a sigh of relief. "That's good to hear. Anyway, the launch date is approaching and there is a scramble to get everyone prepared."

Montgomery rolled her eyes. "Do you think? Welcome to my world."

"It's my understanding they have the big stuff out of the way. Technical training and EVA experiences. Boxes all ticked. But it seems at the last minute, someone forgot to assign basic launch training for the non-skilled personnel."

"What a surprise!" Montgomery remarked. With an imitation of VIKI's British accent, she said, *"Welcome to outer space. Strap in to your three-point harness and for God's sake don't walk out of the airlock. Have a lovely flight!"*

"Yeah, that's the one. Today, there was a certain amount of discussion — let's be honest. There was a heated debate over whether to ask General Bardick to submit to the training."

"Oh, Jim, you can't be serious? It's a matter of safety for everyone aboard the ship."

"Yeah, but that would mean giving orders to a multi-billionaire. And if you've ever met General Bardick, he doesn't strike me as the type who takes orders. In fact, it's the other way 'round. He's the one who orders everyone else around."

Montgomery's eyes grew larger. Her hand flew up to her mouth. "And Jim, what about his wife? I heard a rumor that Gladys Bardick doesn't even know she's on the *Kon-Tiki's* passenger list."

Freeman threw up his hands and said, "Who understands how the general's mind works?"

Chapter 59

Bardick residence
Pacific Heights neighborhood
Honolulu, Hawaii

"And just up the passageway, your chef will have access to a full galley in which to prepare your meals."

This time, Rocket Lab team member Julie Stempler had been tapped to create and promote a product to *Kon-Tiki* buyer General Leonard Bardick. Representing the Rocket Lab Launch Services in a bright red *Kon-Tiki* jumpsuit, she conducted a virtual guided tour of the Bardick's stateroom within the *Kon-Tiki's* bulkheads.

General Bardick watched the facility tour from the comfort of his Pacific Heights office. Due to the fact that the presentation had been recorded in advance, Stempler was of course unable to respond to any of the general's questions or comments.

In a live call at the conclusion of the presentation, the head, shoulders and bow tie of Camillo Hoffman appeared on the screen.

"Good afternoon, General Bardick," he said. "I'm just calling to make sure that the modifications to the *Kon-Tiki* suit your expectations? I would be happy to arrange for a personal tour if you would like."

"No, that won't be necessary," he replied quickly. "Everything seems to be ship-shape and Bristol fashion."

"Then you approve of the modifications? And the decor?"

"Absolutely, Hoffman. Top-notch. How are the developments on the laser cannon?"

Hoffman swallowed hard. "Coming along nicely, sir. I will get back to you shortly with a report on our progress."

"We'll be in touch, then."

The general was convinced that Gladys would be satisfied by their VIP suite, provided she was onboard with their plan to depart from Earth. That feat may prove to be just as hard as the diamond-plated decks beneath their quarters.

Now was the time for his own sales pitch.

Their lives depended on his ability to convince his wife that they needed to move light years away at the right time and for the right reasons.

Chapter 60

Bardick residence
Pacific Heights neighborhood
Honolulu, Hawaii

You agreed to follow me to the ends of the Earth for as long as we both shall live. Now that promise includes a move across the galaxy. What do you say, Bubala?

It was mid-afternoon when General Bardick took his wife's hand and once again invited her to make a trip to his library.

"I need to have a serious talk with you and it needs to be on my turf."

Gladys Bardick had been indulging in her favorite activity — reading in her sun room — when her husband had unexpectedly showed up.

"Just indulge me for one hour. Please."

Gladys was worried by his final entreaty. The general was accustomed to giving orders. He never, ever said *please*. That alone threw up a red flag.

At that precise moment, Filipe Sanninikone rapped on the sunroom's entryway. "Begging your pardon. Will you be dining together this evening?"

With a nod, the general affirmed, "Yes, Filipe."

"May I presume you wish to dine at the formal table?"

Gladys regarded her husband as he answered for both of them. "Not this evening, Filipe. We will eat in my study tonight."

The chef's eyebrows went up. He was accustomed to serving the evening meal to the general alone when he was working late, but never had he served the couple together there. While considering the issue of place settings, he ventured his final inquiry. "Do you have anything special in mind with regards to the menu?"

With a sideways glance at his wife, the general answered. "Whip us up your best Chicken Cordon Bleu, if you don't mind."

Gladys added, "With the vegetarian ham, Felipe. And one of those salads with the oranges and coconut."

"Very well. Dinner will be served at seven."

Bardick waited a moment, then said, "Now that he's out of the way, come with me, if you please."

Gladys managed a sideways glance at her dogs, snoozing away in their dog beds positioned by her chair.

"Tell Fifi and Bobo they can come too," the general added. "If they pee on the rug, I will ring up Monica."

The general led the way through the house, trailed by Gladys with her two dogs trotting along behind.

As soon as they reached the study, Gladys asked, "Lenny, this isn't your way of telling me you're sick, is it? You're not going to have surgery again, are you?"

Motioning to the leather loveseat, he protested, "No, I assure you I am in perfect health."

Close proximity was a necessity due to the love seat's small size. Gladys closely regarded her husband's face to see if she could discern his motives.

"I have some thoughts I wanted to share. I'm most comfortable on my home turf. Too much estrogen in that end of the house, you understand."

Gladys couldn't suppress a giggle. "You are welcome in my boudoir any time you like."

With a wink and a nod, the general assured her, "Love will have to take a backseat to some ideas I wanted to share with you. First of all, what are the names of that couple you visit all the time in the refugee camp?"

"Do you mean Paula and Antonio Gonzalez?"

"Is he the one you said was a software engineer?"

"Yes, he had a solid background prior to the holocaust."

"I have an idea. You and your ladies' committee were able to garner an unprecedented amount of funds through the gala. Is that correct?"

Gladys was beginning to feel unsure of the direction their conversation was taking. Her husband once again reached over to take her hand as a gesture of reassurance.

"We decided to start a fund that provides down-payments for residence rentals and purchases," she replied. "If we can get a few families out of the slums, it will give them a new start."

Once again, General Bardick patted his wife's hand. "It's a good idea, Bubala. What if we could expand your fundraising idea? Make it bigger with a higher return? More funds to help more people, right? I want an opportunity to speak with Gonzalez to get his take on the possibility of a new foundation. We could invest seed money into certain ventures that would likely garner piles of coin to help the refuges obtain housing, start new businesses ... the possibilities are endless."

"Oh, Lenny!" said Gladys, enveloping him in a huge hug. "I think it's a wonderful idea."

Chapter 61

Bardick residence
Pacific Heights neighborhood
Honolulu, Hawaii

"There's something I want for us to discuss. Something we've never talked about before."

There was no earthly enemy that provoked fear in General Leonard Bardick. Tense negotiations with lethal consequences didn't provoke any panic attacks for the Old Shark. But all the same, for months he had been dreading this particular conversation with his wife.

He decided that the best course of action was to tell Gladys the truth and, for better or worse, rely on her wisdom and maturity to carry them through.

"Gladys, you're a very perceptive woman."

Gladys withdrew her hand from his and said, "Now you're scaring the hell out of me, Lenny. What's going on? Just spit it out."

The general swallowed hard, then continued, "You are aware, of course, that the American holocaust wasn't brought about by a volcano."

Gladys snorted, then said, "Give me a little credit. It was the aliens, wasn't it?"

"Yes, you're right. The United States had a treaty with some galactic neighbors of ours and it didn't work out well. The Americans violated the terms and subsequently the aliens insisted on them paying a high price."

"No, you and I never discussed it, but there are some women at our synagogue who have it figured out. It was quite tragic the way so many lives were lost."

Bardick breathed a sigh of relief. Gladys didn't question the existence of at least one species of aliens. That was something, at least.

"There are not many people on the planet who are aware that there are multiple species of extraterrestrial civilizations," he admitted. "Some are benevolent and just want to govern themselves and get through the day. Others, well ..."

"The United States was too proud for our own good. Lenny, are you telling me that there are other alien species who want to do us harm? And are capable of carrying out their threats?"

General Bardick had to think for a moment. He had underestimated Gladys who was now three steps ahead of him.

"There is an intergalactic league of nations that wants to protect us. There is also a species of aliens who want to wipe us off the board. They want to take over a strategic intergalactic position and we are the only thing in their way."

From her demeanor, Bardick determined that she was flustered. "Isn't there someone who can negotiate a treaty for us?"

"No, Bubala. There is no way they will ever make peace with Earth."

Gladys looked as if she were going to cry. "These aliens want to assimilate us?"

General Bardick slowly shook his head. "No, their goal is to wipe us out. And they have the technology to do it without breaking a sweat."

Understandably, Gladys looked miserable. "Is that what you've been working on at the legislature building?"

With a nod, Bardick assented. "Trust me, we have been trying to find another way. It seems the United States government has come to the conclusion there is nothing they can do other than wait and hope. But as it turns out, I have an assigned mission and so do you."

"Me?" asked Gladys skeptically. "What's our mission?"

The general rose and went over to a teak cabinet beneath a bookcase. He brought out a couple of glasses and a bottle containing an amber liquid. "Would you care for a cocktail, my dear?"

Suddenly overtaken by stress, his wife quickly said, "Why yes, pour me one, Lenny."

Bardick poured out a double dose of Ancient Age, one for himself and one for his wife.

"Here you are."

Her husband's health had taken a backseat to an even bigger, more immediate concern. She gauged the shot of bourbon would take the edge off the news of their doomed planet.

He clinked his glass against hers, then continued, "The United States government wants me to travel to their exoplanet to take an up-close look at the new colony. They named it Equinox, because it is always daytime on one side and night on the other. The powers that be want me to analyze the colony's safety and security systems."

Gladys downed her dose of whiskey, then made an unpleasant face. "Go analyze their defenses. That's your area of expertise. But what can they possibly want me to do?"

"I told them you were an expert when it comes to organizing a party. That's exactly what they want you to do. They want you to travel with me to Planet Equinox so you can throw a party for the new *Kon-Tiki* settlers."

"Whatever for?" she objected. "What's the strategic value of a party?"

"A party would be very beneficial, both for the legacy colonists and the new settlers we are bringing there on the *Kon-Tiki*. It would boost their morale, so to speak. And add to a cohesive community of new settlers. Think of it as a USO show."

Gladys thought for a moment, and then said, "What sort of a party would you want me to organize?"

She's nearly onboard for a trip to outer space, the general gauged.

"What's the best way to boost camaraderie, do you think? The gala was well-received, I gathered. High-end food, quality entertainment — I'll let you decide."

"Do you think we should have a theme?"

With the planet going to hell in a handbasket, General Bardick didn't mind throwing any amount of money at a venture to get his wife off-planet. "I enjoyed the gala; the other guests seemed to as well. No point in re-inventing the wheel. Why don't you do something similar?"

Deep in thought, Gladys mused aloud. "A Hawaiian luau. I'm not certain we could book Fire and Sticks on such short notice, but I'll bet we could find a similar outfit. And Hawaiian sous-chefs could create the menu. Oh, and Tiki huts would be nice as a station to serve food and beverages."

In his mind, the general was now convinced he could get Gladys on board the *Kon-Tiki*. If she could convince the entertainers to endure a five- or six-month journey out and back, he wouldn't mind paying them for their time.

It would be a monumental undertaking to get their household packed and aboard the *Kon-Tiki*. With her organizational skills, he was convinced that Gladys could get the task accomplished.

If, and only if, she remained onboard with their mission.

Chapter 62

Bardick residence
Pacific Heights neighborhood
Honolulu, Hawaii

"As usual, I don't have a thing to wear."

Flanked by her assistant Su Lee, Gladys Bardick stared at her image in the full-length mirror of her walk-in closet. It was early spring, three months before the *Kon-Tiki's* launch.

The white pants suit she currently tried on somehow seemed inappropriate. Gladys had never been on a space journey. Never booked passage on the Moon walk flight, or even experienced anti-gravity in a parabolic arc flight. Therefore she was uncertain about appropriate attire for a space traveler. What sort of climate would she experience on the planet? And the length of time that they would remain there was as yet uncertain.

As the collection of rejected wardrobe items grew higher on Gladys' king-sized bed, Su Lee doggedly retrieved and submitted additional wardrobe possibilities.

"If you would please explain the circumstances of your vacation, I will be happy to obtain the needed items for you."

With a heavy sigh, Gladys surveyed her surroundings. She didn't think it wise to reveal her destination to Su Lee. Not right away, anyhow.

"Let's just say I'm headed to a tropical paradise for an extended period of time. We haven't definitively decided where we're going or exactly how long we're going to stay."

Su Lee retrieved her tablet and made some notes. "With your permission, I will order the necessary additions to your wardrobe. What color choices would best suit the occasion?"

Gladys thought for a moment, then answered, "Tropical theme. Lots of separates. Heavy on the reds and greens. And I will need footwear to match."

A moment later, she added, "The general gave me a set of luggage. Five suitcases. We're going to fill those up in nothing flat. What's the best method to transport an entire wardrobe?"

Su Lee continued to tap on the tablet before showing an Internet website to Gladys. Pictured on the tablet's screen was an upright cardboard box bearing the logo *U-Box Moving & Storage Solutions.* She scrolled through alternative box configurations.

"If you will take note of the options on the website, these clever little boxes may provide the best means to store and transport your clothing. See, this type of container has a bar running across the inside so you can hang your blouses in it as you would use a clothing closet. And this style has compartments for your shoes. Or accessories like scarves, belts and purses."

"All right. Order some of those as well." With a sweeping gesture, she added, "Enough boxes for all of this. Who knows what the future may hold. Oh, and I may wish for you to order a few items for the general. Tropical attire is not his strong suit when it comes to his wardrobe."

Wearing her simple white blouse and black skirt, Su Lee's eyes got bigger. She was often amazed at the excesses to which her employer was willing to go.

But she took notes and said nothing.

Chapter 63

Rocket Lab Launch Complex
Auckland, New Zealand

Ensure that four hundred forty-two people were fully qualified, trained and disease free before launch date. Shake down the *Kon-Tiki* and smooth out the bugs. And stock her with food and supplies needed for a six-months to one-year-long voyage.

These were a few of the major miracles that would need to take place during a rapidly-shrinking number of weeks remaining until launch day.

The weight of all preparations rested squarely on the shoulders of Camillo Hoffman.

The project manager certainly had the power to delay the launch. In a recent conference with Rocket Lab CEO Brandon Kemp, Hoffman had been informed of the negative international impact of such an announcement. It would cause the reputation of the launch provider to drop significantly in the eyes of potential customers, an eventuality administrators wished to avoid at all costs.

The research and development team's nightmare schedule was the topic of conversation at a Monday morning budget meeting attended by Hoffman, Dave Sutton, Beth Sommerset, Bella Brown, Brandi Red Feather and Jim Freeman. Absent was Julie Stempler, who was still up to her neck in *Kon-Tiki* cabin installations.

"How much training remains for the crew — and passengers?" wondered Hoffman.

During Claire Montgomery's absence, Rocket Lab had attempted to hire temporary help. There are some positions suited for temporary help; others not so much. None of the temps had remained in the personnel manager's position for long, however, given the demands of the job and the break-neck pace. Other staff members had stepped in to fulfill her duties, however there were noticeable gaps in the workload.

"Preliminary physical exams have been accomplished for all of our regular crew," said Sutton. "There are some entertainers on the passenger list, however. As they will remain in Hawaii until the last minute, I'm making arrangements for them to receive their medical screening locally."

"It is my understanding there are some outstanding procedures needed for officers and bridge crew," said Red Feather. "I went through the crew files and discovered some of them who were actually hired without having an official interview. None of the new hires have experienced any isolation testing and there are still some simulations they need to experience."

"Not much time left for that," Hoffman lamented. "Did you ever have one of those days when everything blows up in your face?"

With a frown, Freeman said, "We need Claire. You'll be pleased to learn that she and I have discussed the possibility of her coming back to work part time. It would certainly help with some of these last minute fiascos."

"What about the baby?" asked Sommerset.

"Claire is able to perform some of her magic remotely; however we plan to let Ieohapata's wife take care of her when Claire is here in the office."

There was a rumble during which engineers mumbled, "Ieohapata has a wife?"

"Yeah," Freeman assented. "They had been dating for a while and got married a few weeks ago. She was a teacher before she moved here. Hasn't found a job yet, so this will work for all of us. For now, at least."

Hoffman's eyebrows went up when he said, "We will respect your family decisions. All the same, please tell Claire we will welcome her back with open arms." He checked his tablet and moved on to the next agenda item. "Who was the last person to touch base with Eireann Reid?"

"That would be me," said Red Feather. "She said the *Kon-Tiki* is on track to be prepared for the space trials. Haven't scheduled the run yet, though."

Sutton voiced, "Got to identify all the bugs before you troubleshoot."

Red Feather countered, "We'll get that on the schedule ASAP, Cam. I'll keep you informed as to the date."

"Did anybody ever get General Bardick to go through Basic Launch Training?" Freeman wondered aloud.

"Surprisingly enough," answered Sommerset, "Our Old Shark said that if he was going to make us jump through hoops, it was only fair that he jump through a few himself. I don't think his wife has reported in, though. Oh, and by the way, I heard the general has put in a request to tour the facility."

With a glance at Hoffman, Freeman added, "I'm assuming you mean the *Kon-Tiki*. I'll guarantee he wants to make sure his laser cannon fires effectively."

Taking a sip of his morning energy drink, Sutton said, "Shall we staple a target onto an unwanted satellite and test our accuracy?"

Brown chose that moment to insert an unsolicited comment. "VIKI has my vote of confidence on the laser cannons. She positioned them correctly, considering the *Star Trek Encyclopedia*. They are nowhere near the nacelles."

"If the general wants to check out the equipment, there's a simple solution," said Beth Sommerset. "Put him on board during the space trials."

"I could list quite a few risks," Hoffman assessed. "But if the Old Shark is going to sail off into the universe on the *Kon-Tiki*, he might as well be on board for the trial run."

Sommerset nodded. "If we sent him out with the Bertrand engineers and collected video footage…"

"It would make a great PR tool," Hoffman completed her thought. "That's the best option. But here's a worst-case scenario we need to discuss. What if the general attempts to veto the space trials altogether?"

"He can't," said Sutton. "It's not possible. Legally, we can't hand over the *Kon-Tiki* without thorough testing. Can't present a customer with a product unless it is certified in top-notch operating condition."

As a group, the team realized they were going to have to expend all the resources they could dig up in order to be prepared for the upcoming launch date.

At the conclusion of the meeting, Sutton and Freeman waited to corner Brown. Quietly, Freeman looked around the corner to make certain that none of the engineers lingered.

Brown rolled her eyes. "Whether or not anyone else is listening, you of course realize that the walls have ears."

"Huh?"

Pointing at the view screen, Brown said, "Remember our Big Brother VIKI?"

Still speaking softly, Freeman told her, "We need for you to check out something in the old test facility."

"What is it?"

Sutton volunteered, "We found some video footage recorded by Thomas Martin. If you can unlock it, we'll look at it together."

Brown's eyes opened wide. "Can we go out there right now?"

Sutton looked at Freeman. "Since our off-grid project is closed out, I see no reason why we can't hop into a golf cart and motor on out there."

"Give me a moment to run to my desk and grab my purse. I'll be ready to go momentarily."

Chapter 64

Junk Works laboratory
Rocket Lab Launch Complex
Auckland, New Zealand

After the dark operations anti-gravity experiment was closed out, Dave Sutton was tasked to copy and remove project information from the Junk Works computers.

While he was picking through the Documents folder, he located an AVI file labeled MARTIN. With his curiosity aroused, he cornered Brown to help him investigate the encrypted file.

The Junk Works garage had recently been cleared of debris left over from building the experimental anti-gravity models. And Bella Brown's personal belongings and computers had long been packed up and moved out of the upstairs apartment. As soon as the computer files were removed, no traces would remain that their off-grid project had in fact taken place in the facility.

Bella Brown slid off the golf cart's passenger seat nearly before it came to a complete stop outside the garage. The petite engineer lightly skipped into the building, reaching the ancient computer three steps before her fellow team members.

She then parked herself in the cubicle's office chair.

"I almost left this guitar out here," said Sutton, retrieving a guitar case from under a desk in one of the cubicles.

"How could you forget your guitar?" inquired Freeman in amazement.

"I have like seven of them," he answered, removing it from the case and strumming a few dystopian minor chords.

Meanwhile, the outdated computer fired up slow-as-molasses. Once the screen activated, Brown snooped around in the My Computer icon to locate the Documents file.

"It's that one," Sutton pointed out.

"I can see that," Bella said. "Give me a moment to decrypt it."

A moment later, she said, "Okay, I am now going to claim this as a personal file. I will next uncheck *Encrypt contents to secure data.* Run the *Cipher* command and voila, your AVI is open. Want me to run the file?"

"Of course," said Sutton, strumming another minor chord. "Go for it, Bella."

Sutton and Freeman both leaned in.

As the video recording began, they could easily see that they were looking at the inside of the Junk Works test lab. Inside the garage, a man with blue eyes and black hair gathered at the nape of his neck spoke into a camera. Brown wondered whether the recording had been taken on a mobile device. Given minimal evidence, it was impossible to tell.

"My name is Thomas Martin. It is currently 11:10 a.m. New Zealand time, Wednesday, April 19, 2023. This recording will provide verifiable documentation for the first run of project RL-129. My team has made progress in the field of acoustic levitation in an imitation of the technology used by ancient civilizations to construct stone megaliths. In this experiment, the test device will be used to levitate a subject weighing one hundred twenty-five kilograms. If you will observe."

Martin stepped away to reveal a saucer-like device with an opening large enough for a seat in the very center. Propped up in the seat was a super-sized man with pale skin, shoulder-length platinum-blonde hair and steel-blue eyes.

"Lukas, ready for takeoff?" Martin's voice could be heard in the distance.

"Proceed when ready," the pilot answered.

An eerie whining sound could be heard as the experimental device lifted off from the hangar floor. The pilot appeared to remain calm while it continued to rise until his head nearly reached the ceiling.

The project coordinator wasn't nearly as reserved. Martin's voice rejoiced, "Air time two minutes nineteen seconds! Hot damn!"

The recording stopped abruptly with the test subject still in the air.

Brown pushed out her lips in a pout, then said, "Something's not adding up."

With a sarcastic tone, Freeman asked, "You think? This Thomas Martin guy obviously did experiments out here in our garage twenty years ago. And whether or not they contributed to a successful technology, Claire should have a record of his employment period."

"That's not all that bothers me. What about this computer? If he conducted his research in 2023, they had much better computers at this time. Why were they using this fossilized dinosaur?"

Sutton's face lit up in a light bulb expression. "Do you know what, Bella? Martin may have been assigned to do his anti-gravity experiments in the same way we were. With the same out-dated equipment, even. Black ops, off-grid. And when the project fizzled out or shut down, they wiped away all the data. And since Thomas Martin was black ops, off-grid ..."

"He was never listed as official personnel."

"Why did they erase all the data except for this one file?" said Freeman, his brows knit. "Did they miss one?"

"Or was it left here on purpose?" wondered Bella.

"Like a breadcrumb?" asked Sutton. "In any case, we don't have the time to play Scooby-Doo right now. I'm uploading this file onto a device and erasing it. We'll figure out who Thomas Martin and his magic flying saucer is at a later date."

Chapter 65

Pacific Heights neighborhood
Honolulu, Hawaii

I'm headed to Australia, Bubala.

"But why, Lenny?"

"In these times, you can't assume that everyone is going to do their job. I am going into outer space to make sure that our quarters are satisfactory. And that the *Kon-Tiki* is sea worthy."

An airport shuttle was parked in their driveway, waiting to take General Bardick and hiss assistant Richard Dalton to the Daniel K. Inouye International Airport. Gladys didn't relish the idea of her husband being out of town, especially since the recent rekindling of their relationship.

"How long will you be gone, Lenny?"

With a little hug, he told her, "The purpose of this trip is to run the ship through her paces. If anything breaks, you want it to happen within close proximity of a repair station."

From her expression, the general could discern that his wife was overwhelmed.

"I hope nothing breaks while you're up there." During his trips away from home, Gladys calmed her nerves by involving herself with projects. "You want me to go ahead and pack up the house? There's not much time until the launch date and we have so much to do."

The general had gotten wind of a mandate limiting the amount of personal items the *Kon-Tiki's* crew could bring along. As the ship's owner, he could probably demand more space, but certainly not everything in their twelve-room mansion.

"Everything you can handle while I am gone would be helpful," he said. "But do me a favor. Please."

"What's that, Lenny?"

"Just pack up our clothing and personal items and nothing else. No dishes, no furniture, no knickknacks. Just clothing."

With a confused expression, Gladys replied, "All right, Lenny. I'll miss you."

"Me too, Bubala. But just think about it. It won't be long until we're on a space cruise together. Like an extended honeymoon."

Gladys giggled. "Oh, Lenny," she said, blushing.

Chapter 66

Rocket Lab boardroom
Auckland, New Zealand

"This guy is a solid administrator, but he's only been above the Kármán line three times. And here's one who has an extensive career in space, but there are notable complaints regarding his people skills."

The crew roster for the *Kon-Tiki* had long ago been completed. Rocket Lab had selected their choices from among the world's elite with regards to education, experience and physical condition. Candidates had been well-tested and trained.

Only one slot remained; undeniably the most important position of all. The captain's seat had yet to be filled.

Claire Montgomery, Camillo Hoffman, Julie Stempler and Beth Sommerset put their heads together in the Rocket Lab boardroom. As they considered each possibility, various files along with the corresponding 3-d head-and-shoulders images were projected on the viewscreen.

The image of a brunette woman was brought under consideration.

"Amelia Jones," Montgomery read. "She has walked on the moon, has EVA certification. In addition to her aerospace skills she has logged an illustrious career with the South African National Defense Force."

Hoffman tilted his head to regard the candidate's image. After taking a sip of his coffee, he asked, "But how much experience does she have in command? Can she manage the operations of a mothership along with the people it takes to keep her going?"

"Why don't we find out? Put her in the *Kobayashi Maru* simulation and see how she holds up."

All eyes in the room turned to stare at Sommerset.

Shaking his head, Hoffman said, "We can't, Beth. We don't have a *Kobayashi Maru* simulation. Or any other simulation, for that matter."

"Why not?" Sommerset argued. "If we are going to do any more of this type of thing, we need to asses our candidates' ability to navigate a no-win situation."

At that moment, Bella Brown burst into the boardroom. "Sorry I'm late, guys. Do you even know what *Kobayashi Maru* means?"

In response to their blank stares, Brown explained. "It's Japanese for little wooden ship. It refers to the inevitable vulnerability of a no-win simulation. Charge of the light brigade, so to speak."

Due to her total recall of details, it was easy to get Bella Brown off-track. Not so easy to maintain her focus.

It was Claire Montgomery who spoke up. "Bella, we have narrowed the field down to three candidates for the captain's position."

Brown pointed at the screen. "Can you pull up this candidate's record again?"

Montgomery obliged, flipping the screen quickly from one text file to another.

Looking at Stempler, Brown asked, "How did she do on the physical and medical?"

"Pretty good," Stempler answered. "No significant medical issues. She's in exceptional health, but she's not what I would call an athlete."

"We shouldn't expect her to run marathons to fill the captain's positions."

"All the same, past age fifty it's even more important to keep in shape. You know, if you don't move it, you may lose it."

Brown, who hadn't yet passed the thirty-year mark, scrunched her nose into a scowl. "She's fifty?"

"Will be next year," answered Hoffman. "If we want experience, we're going to encounter age."

After a pause, Brown asked, "Who else are you considering?"

Montgomery gave Brown a brief summary of the other two candidates. The first was an experienced starship pilot who moved up the corporate ladder of a space transport and delivery service. The other was an astronaut who had briefly been in command of the Artemis Space Station.

Suddenly, Brown interrupted Montgomery's explanation.

"When all else fails, pass the buck," she burst.

Looking offended, Montgomery said, Bella, I wasn't finished comparing the data between these two candidates."

"It doesn't make sense," Brown began. "None of us have ever conducted a spacewalk or ever been in command of anything? Well, have you?"

She looked in turn at each person seated around the boardroom table.

"Are you saying that we should let VIKI choose?" Hoffman inquired with concern.

"Oh hell no," said Brown quickly and emphatically. "Why don't we ask General Bardick to make the selection? He's been in command before. He was in charge of military personnel including hiring and firing. He's probably be a good judge of character as well as the command skills we want our captain to have."

Hoffman looked around the room. "Bella is right," he said. "Let's ask the Old Shark. We could at least take his choice under consideration."

In fact, General Bardick was delighted when he was consulted. In fact, so much that he made an immediate recommendation.

With an early career in the Japanese Air Self-Defense Force, Kazuki Hihara was among the original astronauts who took part in a lunar landing at the Artemis Space Station. He was an excellent physical specimen. As far as command was concerned, he always managed to get the job done.

What General Bardick hadn't been made aware of, though, were a series of complaints regarding Hihara's management style. A tendency to push his own authority meant a tendency to push his subordinate's buttons. Occasionally rubbing them the wrong way.

As a post script to his recommendation, General Bardick had said, "I would look forward to an in-person meeting with Captain Hihara at the earliest opportunity."

Hoffman had sent a reply back to the general.

A personal meeting with Captain Hihara may have to be delayed due to our tight pre-launch schedule. Captain Hihara will be in command during space trials of the Kon-Tiki vessel scheduled to take place soon.

Chapter 67

Personnel office
Rocket Lab administrative complex
Auckland, New Zealand

Claire Montgomery's first day back in the office was sufficient to make her long to be back home to deal with with spit-up and dirty diapers.

Crew preparations for the Kon-Tiki were woefully behind schedule. The only solution was to list inadequacies and tick the boxes one by one, starting at the top. Some of the reasons that certain crew members were selected were readily apparent; others not so much.

The face of Julie Stempler was first to appear on Montgomery's view screen.

After brief pleasantries, Montgomery went past personal to address the outstanding professional issues.

"I see that General Bardick finally underwent his Basic Space Training, but I don't see that his jumpsuit has been manufactured or issued."

Stempler looked uncomfortable. "There is a matter of getting him fitted. Then I expect we will have a challenge getting him inside the coverall."

Montgomery couldn't help but release a very unprofessional snicker. She quickly regained her composure and stated, "It's our policy that everyone in space gets issued a jumpsuit. I suggest you send him a message to ask that he submit to a virtual fitting."

"Do you mean I should ask a general to stand in front of a computer screen in his underwear?"

In this instance, Montgomery maintained her businesslike expression. "That would be one way to achieve your objectives, yes. Another way would be to ask him or a member of his staff to submit his shirt, pants and shoe sizes."

"Didn't think of that," Stempler replied.

"We need to tick this one off the list, Julie. Make sure it gets done. We also need measurements for Mrs. Bardick."

"I know, I know," she acknowledged.

"Our policy is to issue the uniforms. Whether or not they are willing to wear them will be someone else's responsibility."

"Oh, right."

"Let me know just as soon as those jumpsuits are in the works."

"Will do. And Claire, it's great to have you back in the office."

The next order of business was to complete official interviews for the *Kon-Tiki* crew, beginning with colony administrator Jack Armstrong.

Montgomery was surprised to greet the designated administrator whose aura of authority was augmented by his prematurely grey hair.

"Mr. Armstrong, for the purposes of our records, this conversation is being recorded."

"Right-o," he responded. "I would expect no less."

"Would you be so kind as to confirm your educational background for the record?"

"Yah, no worries, Love. Attached to my application are certifications in municipal administration as well as education administration."

"You also submitted some ideas to construct shelters for your new colony?"

"Right. We have already mapped the general layout but the final design will somewhat depend on the terrain. As far as habitations, there is a device I'd like to use that extrudes concrete along a framework. It's an automated shortcut way of building individual cabins. I hope you will consider including that sort of equipment in the *Kon-Tiki's* manifest. It would be sturdier than wood construction and much quicker than making bricks or concrete blocks."

After conversing with Armstrong, Montgomery proceeded down the list to contact a married couple who had been selected. Keith and Maxine Pettigrew, both in their late twenties, hailed from Alaska where they raised cattle.

"My specialty is bovine science," said Maxine.

The woman's hair was neatly combed and she wore makeup. Montgomery doubted that cattle farmers looked like that every day.

Seated beside him, Keith Pettigrew quickly chimed in, "I'm a third generation cattle rancher. And I'm also a certified machinist. I'm guessing that in a remote location, we will need the ability to repair just about any type of equipment. Whatever the need, I'm your man."

"I'm super pleased to hear it, Mr. Pettigrew. I see a note on your application that indicates that you're bringing cattle on board?"

"Yes, my wife has selected the best specimens from her personal herd as breeding stock for the planet."

"Are they meat or dairy cattle?"

"Holsteins are the best dairy cattle. The breed is known to produce up to nine gallons of milk per day."

"Have you coordinated with Bertrand Station on the logistics?"

"Oh, absolutely," said Maxine. "The twenty cows and two bulls we plan to bring on board the Kon-Tiki will provide the basis for a domestic herd on the planet. That's in addition to a flock of Rhode Island Reds."

"Have you already arranged transportation for these animals?"

"Of course," Maxine replied. "They will be transported up to the Kon-Tiki via starship. The poultry will make the trip out in stasis, but all of the cattle will be awake during the entire journey. I coordinated with Beth Sommerset regarding feed and water requirements."

"Thank you for sharing your skills and expertise with us," said Montgomery. "We will be in touch."

Medical personnel were of utmost importance for the second colony on Equinox. Among her plethora of last-minute directives, Montgomery was tasked to make certain there was a solid foundation of healthcare workers, some of whom planned to transfer down to the planet's surface and others who would remain on the ship throughout the return journey.

Before ringing him up, Montgomery checked out the 3-d head-and-shoulders file of Dr. Raja Patel. She noted he was wearing a lab coat with the insignia of a Pakistani hospital.

"Good morning, Dr. Patel. I wonder if I might have a moment of your time to iron out some details of your employment."

The medical doctor spoke excellent English with a British accent.

"Easy Peasy. As you will discover from my resume, I am a medical doctor with a specialty in infectious disease control. I spend my holidays volunteering abroad, and over the years I have gained a great deal of experience in disaster relief efforts in third-world countries. If you wish, I can provide numerous references that you are welcome to contact."

Montgomery discovered that Nurse Practitioner Judy Brown was a little older than the average crew member — in her early forties.

"I'm looking forward to space travel," she said. "I've always dreamed of being a part of a space colony."

"What has your experience in medicine been like up until now?"

"Just so you re aware, my specialty is pediatric medicine."

Montgomery couldn't restrain herself from giggling. "I'm certain you are aware of the average age of our crew?"

"I am," said Brown. "But I am confident that my skills will be useful, regardless of my patients' ages. And I'm certain the colonists will produce children later on in the timeline."

"All right, Ms. Brown. I believe we have you set up at this point. You'll be hearing from us shortly."

Montgomery couldn't help staring at the 3-d image of Conner McPherson at length before phoning him. His educational background was basic law enforcement training. When she consulted his employment history, it revealed eighteen years of experience as a sworn special constable with SAPOL, South Australia Police.

Although she was required to conduct his interview, McPherson was already a designated crew member. With his handlebar mustache and Boonie bush hat, she opined that he looked more like a criminal than a member of law enforcement. And why would an exoplanet colony need law enforcement? Which country's laws would they follow?

If one more bloke refers to me as Love, I'm going to throw something at the monitor, she thought.

"Conner McPherson?" she inquired when he accepted the call and his image appeared on the screen.

"In person, Love," he answered.

Forcing herself to put on her professional pants, she responded, "Claire Montgomery, personnel manager at Rocket Lab. I'm contacting you today regarding a few questions concerning your upcoming period of employment. I was just checking over your educational background."

"You will find that I am a certified graduate of Modern Defensive Tactics Australia," he began.

"Could you please describe your employment experience?"

"Happy to. As a constable, I dealt with drug interdiction, theft, embezzling ... I coordinated some armed and dangerous and hostage situations. The occasional shoot-outs, quite a bit of routine drunk and disorderly conduct."

"Mr. McPherson ... "

"Call me Mack, Love. Everyone else does."

"Very well, Mack. It is my job to ascertain any training or expertise you possess that may enhance the colonization effort. Could you describe any of your special skills?"

"I have extensive firearms training and am a certified range instructor. My field experience has been with a Glock semi-automatic pistol, although I am well versed with the .38 as well as .357 Smith & Wesson revolver. In the field, we also carried pepper spray, batons and conducted energy weapons."

With a head tilt, Montgomery asked, "Conducted energy weapons?"

"Oh, sorry," he apologized. "You will most likely be familiar with the term Taser."

"I see. Do you feel that a law enforcement officer will be needed in the establishment of a permanent colony four light-years from Earth?"

"Damn skippy. It's simply a matter of human nature. The more colonists you throw into the mix, the more misbehavior you are likely to get."

"Oh, right." Montgomery couldn't suppress her curiosity. "Mack, I was wondering if you plan on carrying a sidearm planetside?"

"That would be my first choice," he answered, "however the final decision will be up to planetary administrators."

Montgomery had no doubt in her mind when she perused the existing records for Rocket Lab's choice for *Kon-Tiki's* top administrator. Born in Tokyo, Japan, Captain Kazuki Hihara possessed an impressive resume almost exclusively based on experience above the Kármán line. And, she was pleased to note, Hihara had a hands-on style of administration that included a familiarity with all his ship's systems as well as first-name basis with all his crew members. And in addition, he had already accepted delivery of his official jumpsuit.

In retrospect, she believed that good choices had been made for the *Kon-Tiki* staff. That is, if everything was as it appeared at first blush.

Chapter 68

Battle order number one: It is part of the tradition of our Navy that, when put to the test, all hands keep cool, keep their heads, and FIGHT ... Steady nerves and stout hearts.

General Leonard Bardick was well familiar with the words of Admiral William Halsey whose imperative was designed to inspire sailors prior to the entrance of the United States into World War II.

An alien nation had done far more than fired a shot over Earth's bow. And if General Bardick had anything to say about it, they were not going to roll over and sink quietly.

It had been quite a while since Bardick had been in command. His military expertise had been in resource management and tactics and strategy analysis. The primary reason he chose to take part in the *Kon-Tiki's* shakedown cruise was to ensure that neither the ship nor her crew would collapse if they found themselves in battle with alien invaders.

Before the *Kon-Tiki* left Bertrand Shipyard for the first time, it had been his intention to address the troops with a few inspiring words of his own. In fact, he had strategically prepared the words he was going to say.

A series of gangways connected Bertrand Station with the *Kon-Tiki*. As the general plodded along, he was shadowed by Bertrand staffer Clayton Lee, who was assigned to accompany the general to his quarters during the boarding process. Behind him he pulled the general's suitcase of the old-style variety with wheels that facilitated transport through an airport.

Just inside the cargo bay they saw a number of staffers in olive drab uniforms. Bardick and Lee were met there by an Asian woman wearing a red jumpsuit that identified her as a member of the *Kon-Tiki* crew.

"May I ask if you are Mr. Bardick?" she asked when she saw them.

He stood up straight, cleared his voice and answered, "General Leonard Bardick."

"I'm sorry, General. No offense intended. Captain Hihara was occupied with pre-launch procedures so he sent me to come and meet you."

General Bardick had been expecting to be met in person by the captain, perhaps accompanied by members of his bridge crew. This was the first perceived breach in protocol, but it wouldn't be the last.

"That's understandable," he said. "And you are?"

"Laura Jeong. I'm here to ensure that you reach your quarters, sir."

The general briefly checked out the mix of personnel scurrying from one corridor to another. No one else seemed particularly concerned with his arrival.

Pretty bleak turnout, since I own the whole damn ship, he thought.

"Laura," he repeated. "You are a lieutenant?"

Jeong drew herself up to her full height, which was much shorter than the general and Lee.

"Mechanic's mate, sir."

Jeong shuffled from one foot to the other. Reading her body language, the general figured that she had something else to say. Something she didn't care to say. Eventually she voiced it, though.

"Captain Hihara sent word to welcome you aboard the *Kon-Tiki*. He did however send a reminder that we will be checking everything on the ship during this run. He requested that you try to stay out of the way as much as possible."

Jeong's last statement was an open-palm slap in the face.

"He said that, did he?"

The general had given up on making an official address to his troops. By this time, he perceived that the space trials would be conducted with an overwhelming mixture of Bertrand Station technicians along with a disappointingly small number of actual *Kon-Tiki* crew members.

That, plus there was a growing realization that there existed a turf war with Captain Hihara. Pretty ironic, considering he had practically hand-picked the *Kon-Tiki's* captain himself.

Jeong stuck in the final knife with the statement, "After you are settled in your quarters, the captain requested that I take you on a tour of our aeroponic vertical gardens."

Lettuce, the general thought. Captain Hihara wishes to distract me with the fascinating processes used to produce the salad greens. Well, screw him. I'm not so much interested in the inner workings of the galley as the Kon-Tiki's firepower. What are her capabilities in battle? Can she hold up her end in a fight with alien invaders?

Dammit, someone needs to be the adult here.

Chapter 69

Kon-Tiki space trials

On board the *Kon-Tiki* during the space trials, General Leonard Bardick decided to add a new word to his vocabulary: patience.

Over the next few days, he cooperated with the agenda laid out by Captain Hihara. Sort of, that is. And he began to wear his official *Kon-Tiki jumpsuit* in an attempt to blend in with the crew.

On the fourth day out, he awakened with a tremendous sense of appre-hension. Something felt wrong. Due to the situation in which no one communicated status reports, however, he was uncertain what caused his apprehension. Or whether anything, in fact, was wrong.

Just outside his quarters, he made his way to the room that had temporarily been assigned to Clayton Lee. His assigned liaison failed to respond when he rapped on it. He repeated the attempt several times over the course of five minutes, giving him plenty of time to get in uniform, he assessed. There was no one else to be found outside the wing of rooms leading to his personal quarters.

Over the past few days, he learned how to navigate to the section where the engineers maintained the ship's mechanical functions. It required boarding an elevator designed to take passengers to their desired destinations and punching in the correct location code. It wasn't a straight up-and-down, elevator, though. It was a unique sort of conveyance that took him on a horizontal as well as vertical journey to arrive at the desired destination within the *Kon-Tiki's* two-kilometer-long hull . General Bardick had only visited the engineering compartment for a brief period. When Jeong escorted him through the first time, personnel sat or stood calmly at their stations. In contrast, today it seemed as if someone had stirred up an anthill.

It wasn't long until he located mechanic's mate Laura Jeong.

Amid a swarm of red-suited engineers, she addressed him. "General Bardick?" By her vocal tone, the general discerned that she was somewhat less than pleased to see him.

"What's going on here?" he asked.

"The captain has halted the space trials. We are under tow back to Bertrand Station."

Instantly livid, General Bardick wanted to storm into the command bridge to confront Captain Hihara. Impossible, since he wasn't even sure where the command center was located.

In the absence of Captain Hihara, General Bardick directed his anger at Jeong. "Why the hell are we going back?"

Jeong threw up her hands in an expression of confusion. "You know, seals that didn't hold. Hydraulic failure. Pressure buildup. Software issues. Zombie apocalypse. Whatever the reason, Captain Hihara deemed it unsafe to continue."

General Bardick clapped a hand over his forehead. "A few things spring a leak and we haul ass back to port. My, God, woman. Plug up the holes and keep going. So we are already underway?"

Looking sheepish, Jeong answered, "Not under our own power, sir. Engines are on full stop."

"The hell?"

"Everything's in shut-down mode. We are under tow by a half-dozen starships."

No less furious than he was a moment ago, Bardick was planning the best course of action. If he couldn't call the captain on the red carpet, he would call his lawyer. Followed by his accountant. Cancel delivery of this piece of shit vessel and fire the insubordinate captain who refused to obey orders. Or even acknowledge his presence. If the *Kon-Tiki* couldn't even make it past Mars, he would find another way off-planet.

Momentarily brightening, Jeong said. "The Bertrand Station chief engineer is on board. If you have any further questions, sir, I will take you to him."

Reining in his expression, General Bardick replied, "Yes, that will suffice."

With the general in tow, Jeong made her way through a maze of gauges and control panels to the location where the chief engineer was dealing with the latest crisis.

The general's first impression of Hugo Frohm was that he was less like a man and more like a giant. General Bardick had to tilt his head back slightly to take in the engineer's massive frame. His next thought was that he had seen a someone else resembling this monster of a man.

Jeong seemed happy to hand off the general to Frohm, who could be heard barking orders to the technicians amid the flurry of activity.

A lot of fabric was needed to make that set of coveralls, the general mused. He took in the chief engineer's features including hair that was so light it was nearly white. Eyes so blue they were the color of steel.

Frohm looked away from the instruments and scowled, however the general guessed it was a matter of bad timing. It was probably the worst idea to interrupt an engineering crisis with an outsider's intrusive questions.

Jeong was still standing by, awaiting Frohm's instructions.

"General Leonard Bardick," he introduced himself.

After a brief stare, Frohm put his hands on his hips and said, "I know who you are."

Bardick crossed his arms over his chest. With a scowl of his own, he acknowledged. "And I think I know who you are."

Frohm tilted his head slightly to the side. "Have we met before?"

In a much quieter tone, the general asked, "Are you by any chance acquainted with someone named Lukas Berg?"

The Bertrand chief engineer assessed the situation in the engineering compartment. A half-dozen technicians were still within earshot. And Laura Jeong was still glued to them at arm's length, listening to every word.

General Bardick was keenly aware of the fact that Nordic aliens communicate among themselves via telepathy. A few humans were capable of receiving extra-sensory thoughts.

He's my boss.

This communication happened in his brain rather than his ears.

There was something beyond a failed trial run at hand. Bardick calmed himself and assessed, "I agree with the captain's decision to cancel the trials at this point. Much better than having this crisis happen when we are beyond Neptune with four hundred forty-two souls on board."

Frohm looked thoughtful, then added, "I'll be happy to answer all your questions, General Bardick. My apologies, but this is not the best time. I'll send for you later."

Chapter 70

Kon-Tiki space trials

Rescue starships are the tug boats of outer space. As such, they are not equipped with faster-than-light capabilities. Rather than the stellar sea trial he was hoping for, General Bardick found the return trip back to Bertrand Station much slower than he would have wished.

The tedious interlude offered the perfect opportunity for a face-to-face private meeting between himself and Hugo Frohm — who just happened to be an alien. The general was uncertain how to extend a proper welcome to the Bertrand chief engineer who showed up alone at the door of his quarters.

"Welcome," said Bardick, motioning him inside. "Care for some Ancient Age?"

Frohm held his hand erect and shook it from side to side. "I never touch the stuff."

He looked around the room, then smiled. Someone of his stature habitually sized up the furniture in a room. He judged the wicker chairs in the seating area were too small to support his frame. The office chair at the computer station wasn't adequate either.

"Won't you have a seat?"

General Bardick employed protocol appropriate for diplomatic encounters with government officials from other countries. These would no doubt be appropriate for officials from other planets.

"That's all right, general. I only have a few minutes. All the same, I feel that you and I should have a conversation."

General Bardick's curiosity was piqued. Protocol dictated that if the guest was standing, he should stand as well.

"At this moment I'm full of questions," he began, "but I feel like the best thing I should do is let you talk. One thing I have to know is how I heard that voice in my head. That's a neat trick, that one."

With a smile, Frohm acknowledged. "I knew you probably could develop the ability to communicate telepathically. All the same, I pushed pretty hard. You still have a slight headache?"

"Ummm," the general nodded. "I understand it was necessary at the time. Our exchange was just about to blow your cover."

Frohm got right to the point. "My civilization has had Earth under scrutiny for a while, more closely since you became capable of destroying each other. Our purpose was to manage the rate of your technological development. At this moment, our job has been kicked into emergency status."

"Earth is in danger by the Cenotians," Bardick broke in.

Frohm crossed his arms and nodded. "The threat is real and imminent. There are no guarantees, of course."

"You needed to give us a kick in the seat of the pants," the general guessed.

"You might say that. A first-generation Artificial Intelligence computer provided the means for us to accelerate the *Kon-Tiki's* development. This was necessary in order that we could get some key people off the planet. It is not our choices that rule, as we are but servants ourselves."

Bardick stroked his beard and nodded his head, although Frohm was certain he did not understand.

"At certain points in your history, individuals of my civilization were charged to monitor human technological developments."

"You suppressed technological advances, right?"

"In some ways, yes. Things recently changed, though. Through VIKI, we have the means to funnel improved technology more quickly in order that more humans may be saved. And in a way that aroused no suspicion. That's our job here. The *Kon-Tiki* was initially designed by humans, however our AI has essentially upgraded her systems. The *Phoenix* took seven months to reach the planet around Proxima Centauri. The *Kon-Tiki* should be able to do it in five months."

"How do you know ..." Bardick began. "Oh," he concluded. "You know for sure."

"Yes," Frohm confirmed. "Your insistence that weaponry be included in the *Kon-Tiki's* design was wise. The human engineers passed off this task to the AI as well. It was the perfect storefront operation. If you are forced to use the on-board lasers we provided, the first shot will cause no damage. It will, however, broadcast the fact that your ship is fully capable of blasting an enemy ship out of the sky."

Bardick arched his eyebrows and tilted his head slightly to the side. "Good to know," he affirmed.

After a pause, the general commented, "It's good to know that you're aboard, Frohm. We appreciate all you have done for us."

"I was simply following orders, general. I don't make the decisions. And general, you are aware that the on-board AI is recording our conversation. But in case anyone gets nosy, what VIKI records will not be what we said. And by the way, the *Kon-Tiki's* current failures are all part of our plan to further upgrade her systems. You will, of course, be expected to kick up a fuss over the delays."

"That plus Captain Hihara's insubordination."

"If that's your decision. He's not one of ours."

"I'm really not surprised by any of this. Will you be aboard the *Kon-Tiki*, or are you headed back to Bertrand?"

With an expression that the general couldn't fully read, Frohm answered, "Haven't fully decided yet. If I receive orders to go, we will have more interesting exchanges while in route to your destination. If not, then this conversation never happened."

Chapter 71

Rocket Lab boardroom
Auckland, New Zealand

"We have technical and mechanical issues. That on top of an unclear chain of command. But by far the most serious problems we have are legal and financial. General Bardick is threatening to withdraw his financial support of the *Kon-Tiki.*"

Camillo Hoffman sat calmly sipping coffee as he explained the current crisis to his team of engineers at a Monday morning budget meeting. The team had worked together to overcome insurmountable obstacles in designing technology previously thought impossible. Technology that violated the laws of physics and motion. Now it was time for a roomful of creative thinkers to hurdle a few emergencies that were equally as challenging.

All the engineers in the boardroom freely shared their ideas. Over time they found it was the best way to get stuff done.

"He can't do that, can he?" objected Julie Stempler. "How can he back out of his contract after all this time?"

"And all those tear-outs he made us do," said Dave Sutton, momentarily appearing pale and nauseated.

"He's a billionaire with deep pockets," pointed out Brandi Red Feather. "If he wants to sidestep a contract he can probably figure out a way to do it."

Bella Brown chimed in. "Yeah, besides all that money he probably has a team of good lawyers in his pockets."

"We'll just have to find out the secret sauce that makes him happy again," Hoffman observed. "I'm certain the event that triggered his apprehension happened aboard the space trials."

With a frown, Jim Freeman crossed his arms. "I told you it was a mistake to allow him on board."

"We had to let him do it, Jim," countered Hoffman. "It is, after all, his ship. But as soon as they returned to Bertrand, the general registered a series of formal complaints. Reading between the lines, I would guess that Captain Hihara behaved like an ass and the general followed suit."

"You're the only one of us who talked with him, Cam," said Brown. "Do you figure the general is past the point of no return? Or do you think there is a chance to smooth things over with him?"

"For starters, Welly has him and his assistant out on the golf course today," Hoffman replied. "The man loves to play golf. Afterwards, Welly plans to wine and dine them at the restaurant of his choosing."

Beth Sommerset volunteered, "Do you believe that all or most of the *Kon-Tiki's* mechanical glitches can be fixed? Without canceling the launch?"

Hoffman huffed, "Please? Every new piece of technology experiences a breaking-in period. Back in 2019, Boeing's *Starliner* capsule launched from Florida headed for the International Space Station. It never arrived, due to an automated timer error that prevented the spacecraft from attaining the correct orbit for it to rendezvous and dock with the space station. That's only one example. It proves the fact that there are always glitches. You might as well put that item on the development schedule: something can and will go wrong."

"You think that Eireann Reid's team can get the *Kon-Tiki* in top condition before launch date?" asked Freeman.

"Oh, absolutely," Hoffman answered. "Without a shadow of a doubt. I have faith in her."

"Then I believe we should focus on the more immediate emergency: General Bardick's complaints," said Freeman. What were his objections regarding the initial space trials?"

"Let me show you," said Hoffman, pulling up a file on his tablet. With a wiping motion, he transferred the file to the boardroom view screen.

With the document visible for the entire team to see, Hoffman explained, "I'll go over the bullet points with you. First of all, we have to get Captain Hihara to shake hands and play nice. Hihara is still in command, but we have to come up with a system whereby General Bardick stays informed of ship's functions."

"Or the illusion that he is being informed," said Freeman. "As if he were in command, but not actually in control."

Hoffman proceeded to the next complaint. "Then he has expressed concerns over whether the *Kon-Tiki* is capable of going to warp drive and successfully navigating the entire distance to Proxima Centauri B."

"What can we do to ensure that the general once again becomes ... comfortable?" asked Stempler.

"From the occasion when you sold him on the anti-gravity shuttle the general has gravitated to you," said Hoffman, placing his hand on Freeman's shoulder. "Perhaps you could accompany him on the next space trials as a liaison."

Freeman quickly waved his hands. "Uhn unh. No way am I going into space."

Hoffman pleaded, "Even if it means the security of all of our futures?"

He thought, then shook his head and crossed his arms. "Sorry. It's not in my contract. Family comes first."

Bella Brown volunteered, "What about me? I don't have any family. I'll go."

Sutton looked at her and objected, "You were afraid to go up in the anti-gravity shuttle, but you are willing to go test-drive a warp vehicle?"

With an offended expression, Brown explained, "I never said that I was scared. Only that I didn't want to go. Well, I'm telling you that I'm ready to go this time." She paused and then said, "I can handle General Bardick. I'm not afraid of him."

Hoffman seemed deep in thought. "I think it would work. We could tell him that we're sending you as a consultant from the original design team. You can answer all his questions regarding the ship's functions without pissing off the ship's personnel."

"I'm going along as well," Red Feather piped up. "You will need another propulsion specialist up there to answer all the Old Shark's questions."

Hoffman's original state of depression seemed to lift. "Would the both of you be willing to act as the general's liaisons?"

"Yeah," affirmed Brown. "We can act as a filter to relay status reports between the captain and the general. I promise we will explain the science of the situation in such a manner that he will not perceive it as threatening or condescending. Right Brandi?"

Although her eyes were large, Red Feather affirmed, "That's correct. There will be a delicate balancing act to keep both men feeling that they are in control. We'll escort him throughout all parts of the ship and hold his hand, if that's what is necessary."

At the conclusion of the meeting, the engineers filtered out of the room to pursue their lunch plans.

Hoffman tapped Sutton on the shoulder and asked, "You won't mind staying behind for a few moments, will you?"

"No, I'm in no hurry," was his reply. "Whatcha got?"

"Jim, you too," Hoffman added.

Their curiosity was doubled when Brandon Kemp joined them and closed the door behind him. After brief polite conversation and handshakes, Kemp began, "Thank you for staying a few extra minutes. There's another project coming up and you two are the most qualified candidates. I'm hoping you would be interested."

Chapter 72

Inside General Bardick's quarters, Bella Brown and Brandi Red Feather explained the use of the desktop computer.

"The first thing you need to do upon your arrival on board is to log in on this computer view screen. This gives an accurate census of everyone onboard."

"Is that super-important?"

Brown replied, "Yeah, pretty important. If your name is listed on the manifest but you haven't checked in, you don't want anyone to have to chase you down and try and figure out your location."

General Bardick asked, "Yesterday you showed me the method used to contact other crew members. Could you demonstrate that one more time?"

Patiently, Brown demonstrated. "If you call up this setting, it will contact Richard Dalton. His quarters, as you know, are just down the hall."

Whether or not he understood, Bardick stroked his beard and nodded.

"Your chef is located nearby as well. Here is the setting you can use to contact Filipe Sanninikone after he arrives. Come on, you do it."

When General Bardick finessed the setting, Brown praised him, "Good!"

Breaking into the conversation, Brandi Red Feather said, "I was wondering whether you would prefer to get the daily status reports verbally? Or in digital form on your view screen?"

"I haven't decided," the general replied. "Why don't you demonstrate all the options and then I'll let you know?"

"Fair enough," she replied. "All right, when you go to this setting you can update with the most recent status report. If you click on this tab, the computer will read it aloud to you."

Following the instructions, Bardick clicked. The computer narrated in a female, British accented voice.

The Kon-Tiki is currently located beyond the orbit of Uranus in the Sol system. Course is laid in to the Oort cloud beyond Neptune. Engineering reports that the Kon-Tiki's speed is approaching Warp Two. All systems are functioning normally.

"I believe I prefer the audio narration," Bardick said.

An audible tone could be heard. Pointing to the view screen, Brown said, "Look, you have a call coming in. When that happens you have two options: *Accept* or *Reject*."

General Bardick scowled. "It's a message from Captain Hihara. Wonder what he wants?"

"You are being summoned to the command center. Mind if we tag along?"

"No. I'll bet you're as curious as I am. Come on, let's see what's brewing upstairs."

Together, General Bardick, Brown and Red Feather hustled out to the transport elevator. The general proudly demonstrated his knowledge of the wonky elevator. He punched in the code that instructed the device to take him to the command center.

Conversation was minimal during the ten-minute trip to the bridge.

"Has Captain Hihara ever summoned you to the bridge before?"

"No," the general admitted.

In his mind, he entertained visions of alien invasions that provoked Captain Hihara to seek his his expert advice. Or an alarming communication received from Earth that required heroic actions on their part to save the planet.

Upon reaching the bridge, the general observed Captain Hihara and his bridge crew were at their usual stations.

"Welcome to the bridge, General Bardick," said Captain Hihara. "I thought you would be pleased to be on hand to witness a demonstration of our weapons systems."

On the view screen was a star-filled starscape.

Captain Hihara neared the main view screen and pointed to a large dot pictured at the center. "This asteroid has an identification number, but for now we are not interested in its name. We have selected it as the target for our test fire."

"Oh, I understand," said General Bardick. "By all means, proceed."

In an authoritative tone, Captain Hihara said, "Gunner, target asteroid V-1173. You may fire when ready."

"Aye Captain," said a voice over the intercom.

Everyone on the bridge stared at the view screen, where what appeared as dual lightning bolts emitted from the *Kon-Tiki* in the direction of the asteroid. A brilliant light took the place of the target. When it dissipated, the asteroid was nowhere on the view screen.

"Target destroyed, Captain," reported the gunner.

With his hands on his hips, Captain Kazuki Hihara turned to General Bardick. "I am pleased to report that the *Kon-Tiki's* weaponry is functioning at a nominal level."

General Bardick appreciated the demonstration; however all the same he did not wish to wear out his welcome.

"Stellar demonstration, captain," he said. "If you need me, I'll be in my quarters."

Turning on his heel, he motioned to Red Feather and Brown who followed him to the elevator.

Both of the liaisons breathed a sigh of relief. The volatile relationship between the two men seemed to be smoothed over, for now. If the captain and the general could maintain this level of cordiality, their plan would work.

Chapter 73

"If I hardly lifted a finger, then why am I so tired?"

With the minutes ticking away until their departure, Gladys wanted to spend some time under the gazebo located next to their backyard swimming pool. Seated across the cafe table was her husband, General Leonard Bardick. Fifi rested in her lap with Bobo asleep under the shade of the table.

A twenty-four-foot box truck had just pulled away, loaded down with U-Box Moving and Storage Solutions boxes. No furniture, no dishes or kitchen utensils and no trinkets. Only clothing to be shipped and loaded on a starship headed for the *Kon-Tiki*, still being stuffed with cargo at Bertrand Station.

"Moving is exhausting, whether or not you're actually moving stuff around. What you have accomplished so far is truly amazing. Now we have to get through the next part. Together."

"I know, Lenny. It's just ..."

For the first time in their marriage, General Bardick was beginning to understand his wife's thoughts. He wanted to understand her, at least.

"Are you going to miss this house?"

Gladys thought for a moment. Throughout her husband's military career, there had been more moves than she cared to count. This one seemed different, though. There was a shadow of finality that had not existed during the previous moves.

"No, it's not the house."

"It's your refugees, isn't it? You're worried about the people who live in the camp?"

"Lenny, who will take care of them when I'm gone? I'm certain Miriam Schneider won't give them a second thought. Oh, wait, she'll send them hygiene kits that include shower gel although they don't have indoor plumbing."

At that moment, Filipe Sanninikone showed up on the pool deck. His full-length white apron contrasted with the all-black attire he wore underneath. "Good morning. Would you prefer for me to serve brunch indoors or out here?"

"Thanks, but I'm really not hungry, Filipe," said Gladys.

The general quickly consulted his hand terminal.

"Bring it out here, please. And there will be four of us."

"Very good, sir."

As the chef disappeared into the house, the general explained, "We're expecting some guests shortly."

"Oh," said Gladys simply. "Wrapping up some official business?"

"You might say that. Would you please ask Su Lee to look after the dogs for a moment? Can't have them scaring off our guests, you understand."

"All right," she said dutifully. With a sequined leash in each hand, she trotted off followed by her beloved pooches.

Inside for a brief moment, she cringed at the sight of her quarters. After packing up and sending away nearly all her clothing, Gladys' boudoir and wardrobe looked as if a bomb had exploded inside. Su Lee had been attempting to straighten out the mess when Gladys appeared with the dogs.

As soon as Gladys returned poolside, Filipe appeared with a cart of supplies needed to transform the poolside gazebo into a setting suitable for dining. A tablecloth, fine china, place settings for four and a floral arrangement completed his preparations.

Moments later, a limousine pulled up behind the house. "There they are now," the general announced. "Right on time."

Gladys couldn't have been more surprised when Antonio and Paula Gonzalez disembarked from the passenger's compartment.

Rising to greet them, the general said, "I invited your friends over for brunch. Hope you don't mind. I thought you would want to say good-bye."

Gladys joined her husband in greeting her guests.

"'It's so good to see you, Paula. You're not on shift today?"

With an uncomfortable glance at her husband, Paula said nothing. Gladys imagined that the clothing they wore today looked new, or nearly new. Antonio in a crisp pair of stretch golf pants with a coordinating shirt; Paula in a tropical print shift.

Thinking that her question about Paula taking the day off made her uncomfortable, Gladys quickly shifted gears. "We're so glad you could come. Won't you join us at the table? Can I offer you a coffee?"

Watching the general's behavior, Gladys figured he treated Antonio as he would any old golf buddy. If she could make herself relax and enjoy the morning, it would take away the growing anxiety she felt over her impending space journey.

Filipe was professional as usual, bringing their guests chilled fruit salads and their choice of beverage as a brunch starter course.

"I've had some conversations with Antonio here," General Bardick briefly explained. "I will most likely leave instructions for him to do some consulting work."

"Oh, yes, that would be nice," Gladys commented. That would be more suitable than farm work, she thought to herself.

The two men spoke to each other with a comfortable familiarity. At the conclusion of the meal, Gladys was beginning to suspect there was more to her husband's relationship with the couple than consulting work.

"I was just wondering if you folks would enjoy a tour of the house?" the general said.

"We would love to see it," remarked Paula.

"Gladys, if you don't mind, I'm going to text Su Lee to ask if she would be willing to show our visitors around."

"Yes, that would be lovely," said Gladys. A moment later, she said to Paula, "I hate having you see my suite in its current state. Moving, you understand."

Paula smiled and nodded, as if there were no disparity at all between one woman living in a twelve-room residence and the other in a refugee camp tent.

A few minutes later, Su Lee appeared, wearing her ever-present white blouse and black skirt. "Welcome. If you would please follow me."

Gladys rose to accompany them until the general touched her arm and whispered, "Bubala, there are some things I need to discuss with you. Sit down, please.

Scrunching up her face, Gladys demanded, "Lenny, what's going on here?"

"I've had a series of conversations with Antonio. He's a sharp fellow; good with numbers, you understand. My inspiration was that gala event that you set up. It was a bang-on great fundraiser. Rather than just a few coins dropped into a tzedekah box, you in fact succeeded in generating enough coin to actually make a difference in someone's life. Right?"

"That's what I was going for. Lenny?"

"Just indulge me for a moment. I figured if one event could be that successful, why not a continuous project that would generate maximum funds year-round? If anyone knows how to make money, it's me, right? So Antonio and I put our heads together and sketched out an investment foundation. I took him to meet with my lawyers and put him in charge as the CEO of the whole thing. With Paula as his VP."

A grin blossomed on Gladys' face. "Why, Lenny, that's a wonderful idea." Her smile suddenly disappeared. But there are quite a few obstacles they will have to overcome. Namely, no transportation, no cell phones and no Internet connection out there at the refugee camp."

"Give me a little credit. I've already considered their limitations. What if I could give them all that? Everything they need to succeed, plus help others at the same time?" He gestured to their home. "What if we were willing to give them all of this? The house, the cars — everything?"

Gladys swallowed hard. She had wondered who would be the caretakers of their home while they were off-planet. She pictured the housekeeper vacuuming the dust out of twelve abandoned rooms, the pool service maintaining a swimming pool that no one used. And the landscapers manicuring the lawn of an empty home. The idea was ridiculous, not to mention excessively wasteful.

"You mean, we could let Paula and Antonio live here?" she wondered.

"I'm asking for your blessing to give them the whole kit and kaboodle. Deed it over to them. Except for the dogs, of course. They're coming with us."

"Oh, Lenny! That would be absolutely wonderful!" Gladys jumped up and ran around the table to cover her husband's face in kisses.

"I gather you approve, then," he said. "I realize that you didn't pick this house. I did it without your endorsement. The next home we live in will be your option. I'll let you do the shopping, as long as we can be happy in it together."

Gladys held up her hand and made a cutting motion with her fingers. "I'm ready to cut all the ties, then. Packed up and ready to move out."

"Su Lee will remain on staff to help them with house operations. You realize, of course, that Gonzalez and his wife may fill the rooms with refugees? A homeless shelter right in the middle of Pacific Heights. What will the neighbors think?"

With a little giggle, Gladys said. "If it's their home, they can do whatever they want with it."

Chapter 74

Bella Brown – Brandi Red Feather domicile
Rocket Lab campus
Auckland, New Zealand

Launch countdown
8 days: 22 hours: 11 minutes

"Is that your prayer journal?"

After sleeping in late one Saturday morning, Brandi Red Feather got up to find her housemate Bella Brown curled up in the upholstered chair of the den. With one book balanced on the arm of the chair, she inscribed in her neat, cursive handwriting in the other.

"The one with pink roses is mine. Yours is dark blue with gold writing, remember?"

The fact that Brown was still wearing her favorite pink pajamas and slippers told her housemate that she had been obsessed with something since awakening.

With a little smile, Red Feather said, "I didn't mean to imply that you were writing in my journal. I'll leave you alone and let you finish."

"I don't mind, really. Just putting a few notes in there."

"Oh?" Red Feather was curious but didn't want to be intrusive.

"I was thinking about what your aunt said when she was here. She's a scientist, which got me thinking about the scientific method. If you begin a research project with your mind already made up about the results ..."

"Then your experiment isn't exactly scientific, is it?"

"No. So I've started a research project of my own and the thing has sort of snowballed. Grown way bigger than I ever anticipated."

"Oh, really?" said Red Feather, trying to sound casual.

"Did you ever wonder how the universe began? Until a couple of hundred years ago, scientific thought was that it was eternal and had always existed, right? In 1929 astronomer Edwin Hubble revealed that he saw galaxies expanding outward, which means that they had been closer together in the past. Then in 1965, two American scientists won a Nobel Prize for detecting the remnants of energy of the creation event typically called the Big Bang. And Arno Penzias was quoted as saying, *The best data we have [about the Big Bang] are exactly what I would have predicted had I nothing to go on but the first five books of Moses, the Psalms and the Bible as a whole.*

Brown continued, "And the facts would seem to indicate that the universe of matter and energy appeared at a certain point in time created by a certain singularity, hereafter referred to as the Creator, before all of this happened."

The bungalow was laid out such that Red Feather could listen to Brown while making tea and toast in the kitchen.

"What else did you discover?"

"In the twentieth century, scientists tried to predict the likelihood of intelligent life on other planets. In order to produce an intelligent civilization, a planet would have to be approximately Earth-sized, a comfortable distance from its star — neither too hot nor too cold. Oh, and it should have a molten core."

Red Feather's torso extended across the breakfast bar with a smoking-hot cup of tea balanced in her hands. "Sounds like the Drake equation."

"Yeah. The odds of the existence of a perfect planet like Earth, capable of sustaining plant and animal life, are ..."

"Astronomical?" Red Feather snickered, while buttering her slice of toast.

"Yeah, that's what I mean. And don't even get me started on the origin of life. Archaeology and the fossil record declares the earliest evidence of life was found to be of great variety, fully formed and without transitions. It's called the Cambrian Explosion."

Opting to play devil's advocate, Red Feather sipped, then said, "You're joking right? Didn't everything start with a single-celled organism in the middle of the ocean? A primordial soup and a lightning strike or something?"

"Now you're kidding. The father of evolution Charles Darwin admitted there were some problems with his theory, namely the lack of transitional fossils."

"So there's no missing link between apes and humans?"

Brown snorted. "Apes have twenty-four pairs of chromosomes. Humans have twenty-three. So it's scientifically impossible that humans evolved from apes. The chromosomes are not compatible. And natural selection can tell you something about the survival of a species, but nothing about the arrival of the species."

Shaking a half-eaten piece of toast at her housemate, Red Feather asked, "Just how many species are we talking about here?"

With a smug tone, Brown answered, "Scientists estimate the existence of approximately 10 million species, all classified according to phylum, class, order, family, genus and species. And if we take a look at their individual cells ... "

"What about their cells, Bella?"

"Humans, mammals, reptiles — any animal really — haves an amazing symphony of molecular biology going on inside. Through their cells, animals carry on the processes of digestion, respiration, excretion and reproduction, which are separate miracles themselves. From the most primitive cells to human beings, all have similar operating systems containing codes, transmitters and receivers that all work together. The human genome alone contains approximately 3 billion genetic instructions. And, to keep the human body going, 330 billion cells are replaced daily."

"Bella, how do you suppose this sort of complexity happened?"

"I have some very good leads," said Brown, looking down at her notes. *"For this is what the Lord says— he who created the heavens, he is God; he who fashioned and made the earth, he founded it; he did not create it to be empty, but formed it to be inhabited — he says: I am the Lord, and there is no other. Isaiah 45:18."*

"Now you're quoting Bible verses? Didn't see that coming."

"Back to the scientific method again. Don't discount a resource because you don't like it or are unfamiliar with it."

Red Feather shook her head thoughtfully. "Bella, it sounds like you have thoroughly researched the existence of this singularity you speak of."

Brown looked startled. "Oh, he's not a singularity. His name is Yahweh. Or Yahuah, depending on your specific interpretation of the Hebrew scriptures. And it's early days in my investigation."

"Oh. And what is the other book you have over there?"

Red Feather was expecting Brown to reveal her latest, greatest science fiction read. She was shocked when Brown turned it over to reveal the title: *Faith and Prophecy in the Space Age by Muriel Santiago.*

"Bella, you still have Aunt Muriel's book! Weren't you supposed to get it up to the *Kon-Tiki* before now?"

Brown retrieved her hand terminal and tapped an App. The screen revealed an ongoing countdown.

"Eight days, twenty-two hours, eleven minutes. There's still plenty of time to get it sent up there."

"Why do you still have it here? I thought it would have been stowed with the cargo weeks ago."

Brown hesitated, then admitted, "I wanted to read it. Your aunt had a unique understanding of a lot of things. More than that, she had the courage to speak out with her ideas. I just wanted to get her take on things. Don't worry; I'm nearly finished. I'll make sure that it heads out to Raven before the *Kon-Tiki* leaves."

"By the way, did you learn anything interesting?"

"Brandi, what if the United States was destroyed because they broke covenant with the Creator? That means that the rest of us are in jeopardy as well. We're not doing any better, you know."

"You're right, Bella. That's a scary thought, for sure."

Chapter 75

Launch countdown
2 days: 12 hours: 53 minutes

Gladys Bardick was no space traveler. After her departure from Earth two days before launch, she would never be able to make that statement again.

Even though she downed what she referred to as a Chill Pill, her anxiety level had reached its apogee when the couple arrived to the tarmac on the Rocket Lab campus. General Bardick hoped to make his wife's transition to the Kon-Tiki a positive experience aboard the newest shuttlecraft *Archer*.

In addition to the bare essential luggage, the Bardicks brought along two crates bearing their precious canines Fifi and Bobo.

Camillo Hoffman was on hand to escort the couple up to the *Kon-Tiki*. Rather than his usual tweed jacket and bowtie, at the behest of General Bardick, he showed up in the only golf outfit he owned — the festive attire he purchased to escort the general to play golf on his first visit to Auckland.

General Bardick likewise wore the tropical-print shirt and khaki pants that he wore to his wife's fundraiser. The two men's casual attire represented a calculated attempt to persuade Gladys that she was sailing away on a vacation, not migrating to a planet light years away.

"Good morning, Mrs. Bardick," said Hoffman. "It's so nice to meet you in person. I'd like to introduce you to your shuttle pilot, Nick Van den Berg."

"Welcome to Auckland, Mrs. Bardick," he said.

"A pleasure," Gladys responded.

Before boarding the anti-gravity cruiser, Hoffman presented Gladys with a custom leather tote bag bearing the Rocket Lab logo.

Gladys peered inside briefly, long enough to see a pair of slippers and a matching light blanket of the sort provided to airline customers.

"Oh thank you, Mr. Hoffman," she said.

"We've been looking forward to our trip up in your latest innovation," said General Bardick.

Before them on the tarmac stood the second anti-gravity cruiser: the *Archer*. The white outer surface of the craft was identical to the prototype *Griffon*, with the exception that it bore the imprint *Archer*.

"They let me name this one, Gladys," said the general.

During the golf cart ride out to the tarmac, Gladys closed her eyes and attempted to pretend she was somewhere else. Anywhere else.

"Lenny, why can't they give us an IV that puts us to sleep during the launch?" she complained. " How many g's will we pull when we're going up?"

Hoffman tried to smooth things over. "Don't worry, Mrs. Bardick. A ride in this type of craft is no more difficult than boarding a Boeing 747 to hop over to another city."

During the countdown, Bardick caught of glimpse of his wife's face, her eyes glistening with tears. The general wasn't a religious man, but all the same he was sympathetic of his wife's background.

He couldn't remember the tune, but he leaned as close as he could get while strapped in. "To everything there is a season and a time for every purpose under heaven."

Gladys closed her eyes, gripped his hand and nodded.

To her surprise, the anti-gravity liftoff was no more difficult than a helicopter ride.

Moments later as they crossed the Kármán line, however, the shuttlecraft window offered her a view of the Earth she had never seen before.

"It's beautiful, isn't it, Lenny?" Gladys remarked, grasping her husband's arm. "How long before we reach the *Kon-Tiki*?"

"It will be a few hours," Van den Berg explained. "The Archer has a killer sound system. Is there anything in particular you would like to hear?"

"Why yes," Gladys answered. "I don't suppose you have anything by Daniel Ho?"

General Bardick glanced over at Hoffman, who wore a proud expression.

Van den Berg called up a menu on the dashboard viewscreen. "What is your favorite album?"

"I don't suppose you have *Paradise*?"

Gladys visibly relaxed when Van den Berg flooded the compartment with comtemporary-style Hawaiian music featuring slack-key guitar and ukelele performances.

What the pilot hadn't explained, however, was that the *Archer's* flight was the craft's maiden voyage into the black. The general noted, however, that her performance was flawless.

Upon their approach to Bertrand Station, the general explained, "Bertrand Station has artificial gravity in most areas, but you will experience weightlessness until we dock with it."

"This anti-gravity is great stuff," Gladys exclaimed. "I don't feel airsick at all."

"That's good, Bubala," he said. He pointed to a light above the door of the entry compartment. "Watch the EXIT light carefully. When it comes on, it means we can unhook our harnesses."

After their departure from the shuttle, Gladys and the general followed Hoffman to the exit. When it opened, they caught a glimpse of the interior of the cargo bay. A double row of Bertrand Station employees wearing olive coveralls were on hand greet them. At the head of the line was a freckle-faced woman topped by a tousle of curly, black hair.

"Welcome back, General," she said.

After a vigorous handshake, the general said, "Gladys, this is Station Manager Eireann Reid. Everyone, this is my wife, Gladys Bardick."

"Pleased to meet you, Mrs. Bardick," said Reid. "Hi, Cam. How was your flight?"

Gladys looked down. "Is it full gravity in here? I feel a little woozy."

Despite her momentary nausea, Gladys did her best to appear gracious as she was introduced to some of the station technicians who afforded her the rock star treatment.

Among the reception party was a welcome face.

"Welcome, Mrs. Bardick," said the general's assistant Richard Dalton. "I trust your trip out was pleasant."

"So nice to see you," said Gladys.

"Richard, I was wondering whether you are not too busy to take care of the dogs for a bit," asked Bardick.

"Of course," he answered.

Gladys wondered where Dalton would walk the animals when they needed it. She trusted him enough not to ask, though.

"If you will follow me, I will show you to our refreshment area," said Reid. "We've all been looking forward to meeting you."

In fact, it was General Bardick's plan to avoid bringing his wife to see the *Kon-Tiki* until the latest possible moment. The first reason for the delay was that he was worried over her reaction to their quarters. Although Beth Sommerset had devoted a maximum of time and effort into decorating and furnishing their state room, it was in truth far less opulent than their Honolulu home.

That wasn't the only reason, though. Gladys had been expecting that her dogs would accompany them in their stateroom during the entirety of their space journey. Although he was technically the owner of the ship, there were some things over which General Bardick had no control. Namely, the ship's captain had vetoed the arrangement, specifying instead that Fifi and Bobo must be transported in the hold that contained the cows and chickens.

The general knew that Gladys would have an issue with that arrangement, but the captain out-ranked him and at this juncture there was nothing he could do about it.

The handoff to Richard Dalton had been carefully orchestrated to minimize his wife's shock over the dog's arrangements.

There were other regulations that would represent challenges. Namely, there was no smoking light, which meant the general's cigars were securely locked away in the cargo hold.

And the final reason, the biggest one, was that Gladys Bardick was a sharp cookie. She would probably figure out sooner rather than later that they would not be returning to Earth. Ever.

If for some reason his wife attempted to back out of their space journey, General Bardick, together with Camillo Hoffman, hoped it would be after the point of no return.

Not before.

Chapter 76

Launch countdown
1 day: 22 hours: 19 minutes

Gladys Bardick had been about as patient as she could stand.

After a brief period of respite in the dining hall, Eireann Reid had given the Bardick couple the VIP tour of Bertrand Station — as if General Bardick hadn't already come through there already to take part in the space trails.

"This is our command center," said Reid. "It's the heart and soul of the station. There are personnel on duty manning this station at all times. This is Technician Nicole Bradley."

"It's such a pleasure, Mrs. Bardick," said Bradley. "We've heard so much about you."

"All of it good, I hope," said Gladys.

With a sideways glance at Bradley, Reid continued, "There is an Artificial Intelligence computer that monitors every aspect of the station. She keeps track of the location and duties of all station personnel. Also manages supply requests, deliveries, arrivals and departures."

"Very efficient," Gladys remarked, all while looking longingly at the exit door.

Leaving the command compartment, Reid continued. "And if you will follow me, I will show you our water recycling station. Just beyond that is one of seven air filtration centers."

"Interesting. Very nice," repeated General Bardick, as if he were giving a military review.

Reid walked Gladys out to the observation window, from which they could see a series of mirror-like panels.

"These mirrors are our solar array, a silicon-based system that converts sunlight into electricity needed to run the station," said Reid. "And just over there, you will see one of our school buses."

"School buses?" Gladys wondered.

With a grin, Reid explained, "They are transportation devices that we use to deliver technicians to the areas in which they need to work."

Gladys was only slightly more interested in the processes that had been used to manufacture the *Kon-Tiki*. Reid explained how the astronaut robots were programmed to perform duties such as heavy lifting and welding while minimizing the risk to human technicians.

Gladys was unaware the the extensive tours were also a part of the general's strategic plan. If she were exhausted, Gladys would be more willing to settle down in their *Kon-Tiki* quarters.

After what seemed like hours of walking, Gladys whispered to her husband, "Lenny, when are we going aboard the *Kon-Tiki*?"

Sensing that she was near her limit, he responded, "Right now. Follow me."

Reid and Hoffman escorted them to a colossal observation deck that was equipped with sofas and armchairs.

"Take a look out there," said Hoffman, pointing.

"Oh my God," said Gladys. "I believe I need to sit down."

Just out the window was a panoramic view of the *Kon-Tiki*.

"Is that our ship?" she asked. "It's bigger than anything I've ever seen."

Reid nodded at Hoffman, who explained, "As you can see, the circular part of the ship rotates at one-point-nine rotations per minute, which produces 1-g due to centrifugal force. It should feel like home."

With a pleading look at the general, Gladys asked, "So we don't need to strap ourselves into our beds or wear gravity boots?"

General Bardick smiled and shook his head. "No, Bubala. It should feel as if you were in a hotel suite on Earth. Are you ready to board the *Kon-Tiki* now?"

"Yes, I would like that very much."

With a glance at Hoffman and Reid, General Bardick said, "Thank you so much for the tour of the station. And for all your hard work to make it possible. We're headed to our quarters, now. I'll show Gladys the rest of the ship after she's had an opportunity to rest."

There were multiple gangways along the length of the *Kon-Tiki*, most of them busy affairs with automated tow motors still packing in supplies for the long journey ahead. Still, Gladys felt as if she was near collapse before they at last reached their quarters.

"That's us down at the end," the general said, pointing down a narrow hallway. When he touched the panel beside the door, a keypad appeared. With confident familiarity, he punched in a code that cued the door to disappear into a pocket.

Kon-Tiki engineer Beth Sommerset had made every effort to decorate the suite as a tropical paradise. Just inside the door were two convincing-looking Hibiscus plants with yellow flowers. The shade of the flora perfectly matched the green and yellow print upholstery on the wicker seating units of the sitting area. Just beyond, Gladys' five-piece luggage set was neatly arranged according to size at the entrance of one of the bedchambers.

The general sat down at a desk with a mirror. As soon as he placed his hands on the desk, a keypad lit up. The mirror faded into a multi-purpose view screen. He patted his lap. Momentarily, his wife perched there.

Thanks to the diligent efforts of Bella Brown and Brandi Red Feather, he operated the ship's systems as if he were born there.

"I've entered both of our personal codes so they will know that we've checked in. And we had better go ahead and have a bite to eat before launch."

The image of Filipe Sanninikone appeared on the view screen. Behind him was a ship's galley.

"Oh, hi, Filipe," said Gladys. "Can he see us, Lenny?"

With a snicker, the general confirmed. "It's two-way, Gladys."

"It's good to see you looking so well, Mrs. Bardick," said the chef. "May I offer you a repast?"

"I'm still a little queasy from our space flight. I don't suppose you could whip up a batch of your famous chicken soup?"

"I could easily manage. Would you prefer something else, General Bardick?"

"That's all right, Filipe. Chicken soup for both of us."

"Very good, sir. Dinner at seven as usual?"

"That will be fine, Filipe," said Gladys.

The image of the chef faded into a *Kon-Tiki* logo.

"I have someone else you may want to see." After punching in another code, there were a series of buzzing sounds. Eventually, the image of Richard Dalton became visible. Rather than his usual suit and tie, he was clothed in a set of red Kon-Tiki coveralls.

"I hope you are pleased with your quarters, Mrs. Bardick?"

"I think they will be just fine," she answered. "How long have you been aboard?"

"A few days. I've been taking care of a few details for the general. I have the Ben & Jerry's stored away under the optimum conditions."

"It's good that you're here."

"Nice to see you both. Unless you need something, I'll be in my quarters until the launch procedure is complete."

"No, Dalton, I believe we have everything we need here."

As soon as the view screen once again converted into a mirror, Gladys said, "I miss Su Lee already. Who is going to unpack all my clothes into the wardrobe?"

With a sheepish expression, the general explained, "I had to move heaven and earth just to get them to install our stateroom. On some issues, they wouldn't budge. For instance, there is no wardrobe. Meaning we're going to have to live out of our suitcases for a while."

Gladys rolled her eyes. "I don't see the rest of my clothes anywhere."

"The *Kon-Tiki* has a great deal of storage space, however most of it is located inside the central axis. That means it's in the part of the ship that doesn't rotate."

"No gravity in the cargo hold, correct?"

"That's right, Bubala. Meaning we're not allowed to send Dalton down to fetch a pair of shoes whenever you want them. What goes below decks stays below decks."

"That makes sense," said Gladys, just before her brow wrinkled in concern. "But the animals aren't down there, are they?"

"No," the general quickly answered. "The animal pens are in their own climate-controlled area. Fifi and Bobo will be well cared for, but they aren't allowed up here."

"Oh," said Gladys sadly. "What are we supposed to do in here? Will we get bored?"

The general wiggled his eyebrows and said, "I have one or two ideas."

"Lenny, I meant the whole time. You don't expect me to read or watch television for weeks on end, do you?"

"Of course, not, Gladys. That's why I signed you up for a job."

Gladys stared at her husband for a moment, blinking in shock. "What sort of job?"

"It's the perfect job for someone of your caliber. You are the activities coordinator for this wing of habs. It's your job to design a schedule to keep everyone else from getting bored."

"Now you're joking, Lenny."

"No, I'm serious. You're a born organizer. I took the liberty of ordering a Bingo set."

"Bingo games?"

"And the Fire and Sticks entertainers have no official duties, so I thought you could manage a series of Mah Jongg tutorials."

"You didn't bring along my mother's Mah Jongg set, did you?"

"Absolutely not," he affirmed quickly. "It's safely in the curio cabinet where you left it. But there are a few new sets on board. Along with a scrabble tournament set, chess, checkers and backgammon. As well as a full armory of Nerf pistols and rifles."

After a pause, he added, "As long as you're an official member of the crew, there is a wardrobe item I'm supposed to give you. To be *bona fide*, you understand. You will find it hanging up in the bathroom, if I'm not mistaken."

317

Curiosity got the best of her. Gladys exited her husband's lap to discover a long-sleeved, red jumpsuit with the nameplate Gladys Bardick hanging next to the shower.

With a chuckle, she said, "My official *Kon-Tiki* outfit, I would guess. Do you have one? Go put yours on ... please?"

Moments later, the couple admired their reflections in the bathroom mirror. Two paunchy senior adults encased in bright-red space attire. The general white-haired with wire-rimmed glasses. Gladys with her silver fox hair treatment and diamond earrings.

"Look, Lenny. We're astronauts."

"More like space cadets," he grinned.

"Do you suppose someone could take a picture of us? This is priceless."

"I think there's a possibility. And you're right. I don't believe it's likely we're going to go out in public dressed like this every day."

Gladys shook her head. "No, this look is likely a one-off."

Chapter 77

There had always been a certain amount of friction between General Leonard Bardick and Captain Kazuki Hihara. What it all boiled down to was a tug-of-war over ownership of the *Kon-Tiki*.

With Gladys safely installed in their cabin, General Bardick took the initiative to visit Captain Hihara at the most inopportune moment: on the command deck with mere minutes to go until the *Kon-Tiki* was due to disembark from Bertrand Shipyard. If anything was going to explode, the general would prefer it to happen before rather than out in space.

"Good morning, Captain Hihara," he said cheerily as he stepped out of the elevator.

"Welcome aboard the *Kon-Tiki*," said the captain with every bit of congeniality he could muster.

"I was hoping to get the chance to meet the bridge crew before our departure," said General Bardick. "Of course, if you are swamped with pre-flight procedures, I can come back at a later time."

With a sweeping gesture, Hihara said, "You are welcome aboard my bridge any time."

"Thank you for your hospitality, Captain."

From his years of travel, General Bardick had loads of experience in identifying accents. Although Captain Kazuki Hihara had a Japanese name, his pronunciation of English sounded like the Hong Kong Chinese with which he was familiar. There was likely a story behind this fact; one that he was unlikely to hear, though. In this instance, he decided not to prod the captain any further than necessary. It was highly unlikely they would become friends.

In addition to the super-sized view screen that was standard in science-fiction lore, bridge crew monitored ship's functions from individual monitors positioned at their stations.

"Seated at this station is our pilot, Justin McFadden," introduced the captain. The pilot's ebony skin contrasted favorably against the standard red Kon-Tiki coveralls.

"Cheerio, General," said McFadden, with a bass voice in an accent that pegged him as British. Likely a Londoner, if the general had to nail it down.

Striding over to the next station, Captain Hihara paused next to a blond, pale-complexioned woman. "Katya Kristiansen is our navigator," he said.

Without breaking her gaze from her view screen, she responded, "Welcome aboard, General."

Quietly, the general hazarded a guess. "Sweden?" he asked the captain.

"Norway," volunteered Hihara. "And next to navigation we have Mr. Jacques Rabelais, our Comm Operator."

Rabelais stood and snapped a salute. "Super happy to have you on board, sir."

Hearing the welcome Louisiana accent, Bardick returned the salute. "I'm guessing you were a Space Force man?"

With a huge grin, the blond-haired, ruddy complexioned Rabelais responded, "Naw, Sir. Cajun Navy, Sir."

"Pleased to meet a fellow American." As a fellow member of an endangered species, General Bardick couldn't restrain himself from giving Rabelais a hearty handshake.

A scowl spread across Captain Hihara's face. "As you are probably aware, the *Kon-Tiki's* crew is made up of representatives of many of Earth's countries."

"Oh, my apologies. I meant no insult."

"None taken," said Hihara, taking a seat in the captain's chair which not only afforded him a vantage point of the giant view screen but all the bridge stations as well. That single action left General Bardick as the odd man out, the only person on the bridge without an assigned seat. Although closed out, General Bardick had some more snooping around to do. And he didn't intend to leave until he found out what he needed to know.

"Captain Hihara, I have a few brief questions that will only take one more moment of your time," he asked.

Relishing the upper hand for the moment, Hihara nodded his approval.

"With so many nations and cultures represented, how will you ensure that your staff will be able to communicate?"

"On this ship, English is spoken as a rule," answered Hihara in his businesslike tone. "Among those selected as crew members, there are very few of them who aren't fluent English speakers. I daresay that before we reach Planet Equinox, every person on board will be fluent in English."

"A wise mandate, Captain. I was hoping you or your navigator would be willing to explain our flight plan?"

As a passenger, General Bardick was perhaps overstepping a few boundaries with his inquiry. Whether or not he received an explanation would be the captain's discretion. Fortunately, at this juncture Hihara's desire was to smooth over their delicate relationship rather than inflame a turf war.

Gesturing in Kristiansen's direction, he instructed, "Katya, please feel free to answer any and all of the general's questions."

With a nod, Kristiansen broke her concentration to meet the general's gaze. "What exactly is it that you would like to know?"

After clearing his throat, General Bardick began his line of inquiry. "What is our intended flight plan, beginning with the moment the docking clamps are released?"

"As you may have expected, the *Kon-Tiki* will follow a plan of gradual acceleration," she explained. "You of course understand that an immediate burst of speed would be catastrophic to both the spacecraft and the humans aboard her."

"Makes sense," the general nodded.

"Under controlled acceleration, it will take us two days to reach the Moon's orbital path; fifteen days to reach the orbital path of Mars. By that point, we will be traveling at four-point-twenty-four percent the speed of light. General Bardick, are you aware of the ecliptic plane of the solar system?"

"Of course," he answered.

Kristiansen recognized a bluff when she heard one. "I expected you were, but if you will humor me for a moment, let me call up a diagram on my view screen. Here is a rendering of all the planets in the solar system. You won't be surprised to learn that in our solar system, the planets line up on a flat plane, sort of like an equator. From Mars and beyond, our plan is to dodge under that plane of heavy traffic. Take the back roads, so to speak. We will complete our journey through the solar system on a trajectory two-point-one percent below the ecliptic plane. This will allow us to crank up our speed while traveling in a minimal traffic zone."

While stroking his beard, the general followed her explanation through the on-screen animation.

"We will continue to accelerate the whole time, correct?"

"Yes, sir, that is correct," she said, glancing in Hihara's direction to gauge how he felt about her answers. "Our speed will constantly increase until, by the time we reach the Kuiper Belt and the Oort Cloud, we will far surpass light speed."

"Hauling ass, huh?" General Bardick summarized.

"Yes, sir," Kristiansen said. "Do you require any further explanations?"

"No, and thank you for your patience."

When he passed by Captain Hihara's perch, Bardick made sure to thank his host. "Thank you for your hospitality, Captain. I and my wife are looking forward to our departure from Bertrand Station as well as the journey ahead."

Without taking his eyes away from his duties, Hihara replied, "I hope that you will bring Mrs. Bardick up here to visit at some point. You are welcome on my bridge at any time."

There was a notable emphasis on the word *my*.

General Bardick had bought and paid for the *Kon-Tiki*, however ultimately Captain Hihara was in command of her. After his visit to the command center, General Bardick knew exactly where he stood in the pecking order.

It wasn't necessarily in the position where he wanted to be, but one with which he would learn to live.

Chapter 78

"I wouldn't miss this for the world."

Camillo Hoffman had been scheduled to return to Arnhem Space Center as soon as he had delivered General Bardick and his wife to the *Kon-Tiki*. Instead, he chose to deviate off-course and go AWOL. After all, it may be a long time before there was another mothership launched from Bertrand Shipyard. Perhaps it would never happen again in his lifetime, so he decided to grab the opportunity at hand.

Hoffman was familiar with the station layout, therefore it was an easy matter to duck into an unused crew cabin and grab a nap. A short time before launch, he headed to the location with the best view of the massive *Kon-Tiki*: the main observation lounge.

A row of couches in the lounge were arranged in a horseshoe configuration facing the observation window.

There she is. The result of all our efforts. And she is truly beautiful, he thought.

Unfortunately, he wasn't the only person to have these thoughts. As the minutes ticked off the countdown, more people filtered into the lounge. Technicians and dock workers, on and off the clock, left their posts in an attempt to witness this moment in history.

The first person in the lounge to actually recognize him was Eireann Reid. "Cam?" she demanded loudly. "I thought you had already headed back downstairs. What are you still doing here?"

Pointing out the window, he explained, "I went rogue. That's my baby out there. Just wanted to show up to see her do her thing."

With a hand on her hip, Reid complained, "She's my baby, too. I guess we're both proud parents." She pulled out her hand terminal and announced, "Fifty-three minutes until launch. Take a look, they've pulled in all the gangways and are sealing them off. You probably haven't had anything to eat. Want to make a run downstairs to get some coffee?"

For certain, Hoffman was badly in need of a cup of coffee and something to eat. But today the once-in-a-lifetime opportunity took priority.

"Not a chance," was his reply. "We may not make it back in time. We might lose our seats. Or, worse still, miss the launch entirely."

"We came very close to a launch delay," said Reid. "There were a half-dozen representatives of the new Agency of Space Safety aboard the Kon-Tiki until the last minute. They were asking questions and checking out everything."

The new agency's requirements reminded Hoffman of both the Department of Motor Vehicles and the Department of Transportation rolled into one.

"As if we hadn't already tested and retested our product," said Hoffman, looking insulted. "Who thought another level of bureaucracy was a good idea?"

Reid spread out her hands in an I don't know gesture. "You know bureaucracy and red tape are always a half-step behind scientific achievement."

"Ha! In a world filled with acronyms, did anyone bother to explain to them what theirs was?"

At that precise moment, he caught a glimpse of James Freeman, followed closely by Julie Stempler, Dave Sutton, Beth Sommerset, Bella Brown and Brandi Red Feather who all pushed their way over to Reid and Hoffman in the observation deck. Each of them was simultaneously staring down at their hand terminals, all set to the launch countdown.

Hoffman was the odd man out still wearing his golf outfit. Everyone else in the observation lounge was wearing Bertrand or *Kon-Tiki* jumpsuits.

"Oh, look, we're getting the band back together," said Reid, with a warm greeting for the designers.

"Get in here," said Hoffman, giving each member of his team back-slapping hugs. "So glad you all made it."

"We wanted to watch the launch with our own eyes," said Brown. "Welly pulled a few strings and got us all passage on the last starship up here."

With a confused expression, Hoffman asked, "Jim, I thought you weren't allowed to go into outer space. What does Claire think of you coming up here?"

Freeman smiled as he answered, "I'm recording the launch for her. In this instance, she told me I had better not miss it."

A sea of Bertrand technicians clothed in olive coveralls ceased their milling around. Chatter gradually increased, making conversation over the din difficult.

"We have the best seats in the house to watch the launch," shouted Sutton. "Wish we could hear it from the lounge as well."

Eireann leaned forward to give Sutton a look. "I'm the station manager, remember?" Holding out her own hand terminal, she added, "I'll turn up my volume. Hopefully these clowns will all settle down and you'll be able to hear the whole thing."

There they were, seated side by side on the observation couch. Stempler, Sutton, Hoffman, Reid, Freeman and Sommerset on the couch. Packed as tightly as they could, there wasn't enough room for Brown and Red Feather, who took a seat on the floor in front of the others.

"Do you remember when we watched our first launch?" said Brown.

Sommerset replied, "How can any of us forget that? We watched the *Comet* go up from that concrete blockhouse. It was so loud my ears are still ringing."

Like everyone else, Reid was getting antsy. *Clowns to the left of me, jokers to the right. Here I am, stuck in the middle with you,* she sang.

"Twelve minutes, nine seconds," announced Stempler.

Sutton leaned forward so he could see Freeman. "What do you think? What are the odds this will be a successful launch?"

"I'll bet you a pineapple she'll explode," said Freeman, naming his price in Australian dollars. "No, an avocado."

Reid's face took on an expression of horror, while Sutton countered, "I don't want money. I want beer. If the launch is successful, you buy me a six-pack," said Sutton. "If not, it's Oktoberfest in the Northern Territory."

"What kind do you want?" Freeman grinned.

Sutton thought for a moment, then replied, "Great Northern or Victoria Bitter."

"All right," Freeman agreed. "If there's a rapid unscheduled disassembly, we can stop by that beer studio in Alice Springs. I'll take my pick before we go back home."

"Deal," Sutton agreed.

"Don't even joke about things like that," Stempler objected.

With a series of little nods, Hoffman explained, "It's what these guys do, Julie. It's bad luck not to."

As the final minutes and seconds ticked down, Reid announced, "Here's the launch audio. I'll turn up my volume so you can hear it."

The voice of Captain Hihara could be heard checking in to all his departments.

"Engineering?"

Reid recognized Hugo Frohm's booming voice. "Engineering is go for launch."

"Navigation?"

The response of Katya Kristiansen could be heard: "Captain, we are go for launch."

"Pilot?"

"Go for launch," replied Justin McFadden.

A couple dozen spectators in the observation lounge elevated their hand terminals in the direction of the mothership *Kon-Tiki.*

"Bertrand Station, the *Kon-Tiki* stands on go for launch," said Captain Hihara. "Request permission to release the docking clamps."

Holding her hand terminal up to her mouth, Eireann Reid said above the din in the lounge, "Permission granted. Godspeed, *Kon-Tiki.*"

Seated on the floor, Bella Brown closed her eyes. All the others could see her mouth moving, yet no sound came out.

"Bella? Is she okay?" asked Stempler with alarm. She reached out in an attempt to tap Brown's shoulder.

Red Feather caught Stempler's hand and pushed it back. "She's fine. Leave her alone. I mean, why don't we give her a minute?"

Brown continued to mutter softly for another minute. Just about the time the launch countdown reached 00:00, she looked up and smiled.

"Take us out, Mr. Sulu," ordered Jim Freeman. "One-quarter impulse power."

"Aye, captain," replied Sutton. "Course and speed laid in, sir."

Outside the window, the observers discerned that the *Kon-Tiki* was in motion. Slowly, she pulled away from her moorings. Cheers, whistles and applause grew to a crescendo all over the observation lounge.

With tears glistening in her eyes, Reid had a side hug for Hoffman. "Our little girl is all grown up. She's leaving the nest."

"That's the name of the game," he replied, returning the squeeze. "Good work, everyone. Now, go relax and enjoy yourselves. That's an order."

"Successful launch. Guess you owe me a beer," said Sutton. "How are you going to spend your vacation, Jim?"

"Changing diapers," he replied.

"I'm going on a cruise," announced Stempler happily. "Leaving next week."

"What are you going to do now, Eireann?" Hoffman wanted to know.

"Oh, flipping hell," said Eireann, wiping away an initial few tears that escaped. "I'm giving you my notice. This shit's too hard." Pointing in the direction of the disappearing *Kon-Tiki*, she added, "Especially when I have to give them up after I've watched them grow from stem to stern. I'm quitting."

With another side squeeze, Hoffman said, "No you're not. You're going back home to take your six-week vacation. You and Joe will spend some time in Bali. Then you'll be back here to take on another assignment."

Reid buried her head on his shoulder for a moment, sobbing.

A moment later, she pulled a bandana from her pocket and dabbed her eyes.

"I expect you'll be wanting some fast food at this point," Hoffman guessed.

"Pizza," she sniffed. "Epolito's."

Chapter 79

Three days after Kon-Tiki launch
Rocket Lab boardroom
Auckland, New Zealand

"Why did we wait for three days to announce the *Kon-Tiki* launch?"

"Remember the *Magellan*, Welly? Three days out, and then BANG!"

"Oh, right. I forgot."

Hahona Timoti — more commonly known as Welly — received final briefing just before a major press conference. A screen covered with repeats of the Rocket Lab logo appeared behind him.

His outfit — an ensemble of black, silver and red ochre — had been strategically selected to inspire New Zealand national pride.

At the other end of the boardroom, Claire Montgomery held up a hand, gradually reducing the number of fingers until there was a closed fist. Then she gave him the *go* motion.

With the opposite view screen crowded with images of news agency representatives who had logged in previously, a red light at the top of the view screen turned to green.

Without any hesitation, Timoti began speaking.

"Good morning. At this time Rocket Lab is pleased to announce the successful launch of the mothership *Kon-Tiki* from Bertrand Intra-orbital shipyard with four hundred forty-two souls on board," he began. "As of this moment, her speed is increasing and will continue to increase as she approaches the outer limits of our solar system. Our innovative warp-drive vehicle is bound for a planet orbiting our nearest star, Proxima Centauri. The purpose of this mission is to implant a second colony on the planet's surface before once again returning to Bertrand Station. At Rocket Lab, safety and reliability are everyone's responsibility. We must be diligent in our pursuit of safe, reliable interstellar transportation in order that humankind may become a multi-planetary species. We must look to the future where there will be millions of people safely living and working in space for the benefit of all mankind."

Timoti's announcement was accompanied by photos, sound bytes and renderings of the *Kon-Tiki,* a pre-recorded interview with Captain Hihari plus another with Rocket Lab CEO Brandon Kemp.

Timoti appeared confident and well-prepared for the barrage of questions submitted by international reporters. Green lights were still visible on all of the profiles when Timoti stopped all the questions for another announcement.

"Rocket Lab recently purchased the SpaceCorp facility in Nhulunbuy, which is in close proximity to Arnhem Spaceport. In a new development, this facility will serve as the production location for Rocket Lab's new anti-gravity division. At this time I would like to introduce the new CEO of this division, David Sutton."

After Sutton situated himself beside Timoti, he provided an opening question. "What can you tell us about the purpose of the new facility?"

"Sure," said Sutton who confidently spoke into the camera. "If you will excuse the pun, anti-gravity is a groundbreaking technology with a variety of untapped applications. Our prototype shuttlecraft cruiser has the capability to ascend from any location on Earth's surface to a starship or shipyard in orbit. The safety and fuel efficiency of our cruiser far exceeds that of a standard starship. Anti-gravity eliminates the unpleasant side effects of g-forces typically experienced by starship passengers. In addition, operating costs for this method of transportation are significantly reduced. What that means is that the cost per launch for space trips will be dramatically reduced."

While Sutton spoke, the view screen displayed recordings of the *Griffon's* test flights.

"This new division will devote a great deal of time and effort into exploring additional applications for the anti-gravity technology. The production of anti-gravity pallets would theoretically revolutionize the transportation and shipment industries, for example. As much as the jet engine revolutionized the science of aerial combat."

When all the lights were red at the conclusion of the press conference, Welly and Sutton were physically inundated by a crowd of Rocket Lab research and development engineers.

"Congratulations, Dave," said Julie Stempler. "We're so proud of you."

"I guess you'll be moving up to the Northern Territory," said Bella Brown with disappointment. "What about Tino and your music career?"

With a shrug, Sutton replied, "Tino's coming with me, and so are my guitars. The music career will likely have to take a backseat for now, though. I get to choose my staff, so I'll be on the lookout for talent and skills, by the way."

"Yeah, Jim," said Beth Sommerset. "I'm wondering why they didn't ask you. No offense, Dave."

"None taken."

"As a matter of fact, they asked both of us," said Freeman.

"And you didn't take them up on it?" Brown asked. "I'm guessing they offered you a pile of money as one of the original developers of the technology."

"Nah," Freeman explained. "I'm super-happy in the design division here. And, plus, Dave probably wouldn't let me transfer all my models in the design lab up to Nhulunbuy."

"That, and Claire probably isn't up for a move," Sutton observed.

Freeman shook his head. "She loves her job here, and so do I. You know what they say. If it ain't broke, don't fix it."

Reaching Sutton, Red Feather shook his hand and squeezed him in for a hug. "We're going to miss you around here, Dave. Super proud of all we have done together."

With her congratulations, Julie Stempler teased, "Yeah, Dave, go invent a flying car that folds into a briefcase for easy transport and storage during the workday."

"You mean like George Jetson?" Brown mused. "I guess there would be less worry about scratches, dents or parking tickets."

"Yeah, Dave. Don't think you're going to escape from here without a celebration in your honor," Sommerset added. "And Dave, why didn't you let us know about all these big changes coming up?"

Camillo Hoffman took his turn to congratulate Sutton, then deflated the mood with, "A non-disclosure agreement was part of his contract, guys. We had to make sure our lawyers and financiers were all happy before we let the announcement get out. So let me emphasize that no proprietary information goes beyond these walls."

The well-wishers had begun to disperse when Hoffman made a final announcement that elicited groans from them all.

"And as far as all of your contracts, there is one more obligation I expect you to fulfill. We will have budget meeting as usual on Monday morning. I will expect you all to attend."

With an affectionate pat and a comment no one else would have dared, Brown said, "Did anyone ever tell you you're no fun, Cam?"

Chapter 80

Rocket Lab boardroom
Auckland, New Zealand

"Compliments of Mr. Kemp. Thanks for a job well done."

The research and development team had been rehashing their recent projects in the boardroom for nearly two hours when Kemp's personal assistant wheeled in a cart laden with their favorite mealtime options: delectable entrees provided by Funky Fish.

Hoffman graciously allowed his team to select from labeled box lunches. A cooler on the lower tier was filled with frosty bottles of Lemon & Paeroa.

"Oh, yum. Halloumi Pesto sandwich," said Sutton. "Bella, I hope they sent over something for you?"

"Oh, yeah," she replied. "I'm guessing the Kale salad with watermelon side is for me."

Freeman handed a box to Stempler. "Julie, they sent your favorite."

"Chicken avocado sandwich," she said, rolling her eyes with delight.

Red Feather mused, "When Cam orders lunch for us, he automatically knows our favorites. But today, how did this happen?"

With a napkin held in front of her mouth in mid-bite, Brown replied, "Maybe Mr. Kemp consulted VIKI."

Hoffman raised an eyebrow, then pushed up his glasses with an index finger. "Wouldn't surprise me a bit. I wonder how she is at picking out birthday gifts."

"Ummm," said Sutton, deep in thought. "She knows us all too well."

"Gets a little creepy sometimes," Sommerset agreed.

"Not to change the subject, but I would like to divert your thoughts back to the *Kon-Tiki* project. What do you guys feel that we did well?"

There was a momentary silence filled only with the rattling of paper sandwich wrappers.

"The general created a knot in our knickers when he ordered us to tear out standard crew quarters to install his state room," said Stempler.

"I was there when he got to see it for the first time," said Red Feather. "You did a fantastic job kicking up the decor. He actually said it was his favorite thing ..."

"Except for the laser weaponry we actually installed at the last minute," said Freeman. "That was a pretty stinky one."

"Yeah," Sutton nodded, looking up at the Asian female projected on the view screen. "Thanks to VIKI."

You're welcome, Dave. Glad I could help out.

"Actually, VIKI, could you pull up the rendering of the *Kon-Tiki?*" asked Red Feather.

Of course. Here you go.

Red Feather stood up and went to the view screen. "I'm still the new kid around here, but this is my opportunity to say that I never liked the configuration with the habitations rotating so close to the nacelles. I think they need to rotate horizontally rather than vertically. Do you know what I mean?"

Hoffman mused, "I only wanted you to focus on generalities, not details. But I'm glad you're already thinking about future designs."

Sommerset addressed the elephant in the room. "Does this mean you think that there is another mothership in our immediate future?"

Freeman laughed out loud. "You didn't expect our division would diversify as well? Branch out and build dog houses or something."

In mid-chew, Sutton said, "Did you guys hear that Loki Energy plans to branch out into the field of solar energy farming? Welly told me they announced construction of a series of solar farms in the Cis-lunar zone."

"You mean they plan to put solar panels out in space?" questioned

Freeman.

Stempler quipped snarkily, "I hope they have an extra-long extension cord."

"What's going to happen when a space rock hits those mirrors?" asked Sommerset.

Brown tossed out another detail. "I wonder who researched that name. Did you know that Loki is known as the god of mischief, mayhem and disorder?"

After a brief pause during which he massaged his temples, Hoffman once again attempted to steer the conversation in a constructive direction. "Well there's a big positive achievement I'd like to bring up. We not only produced an effective set of products, but also managed to cater to the whims of an extremely picky customer."

"Our old shark was a tough customer," admitted Bella Brown. "We were barely able to keep him happy. But he's off planet now. And what nation, corporation or billionaire has enough cash to finance the next mothership?"

As usual, Hoffman directed the roomful of cats into an optimal direction. "I don't have a crystal ball, but all the same there are a world of opportunities and we all have to do our best to keep our standard-launch division going."

Chapter 81

Rocket Lab boardroom
Auckland, New Zealand

"How can we get into trouble for simply asking a question?"

Although Bella Brown had doggedly pursued the existence of Rocket Lab's off-grid acoustic levitation project as well as the whereabouts of Thomas Martin, her best efforts had produced a big, fat zero.

There were no records to be found, at least none she could locate. It was as if Thomas Martin had never existed. And before she left for vacation, Brown vowed that she was going to find her answer.

"I'm going to go all-in and ask VIKI," Brown proclaimed at the conclusion of their evaluation session.

Freeman gestured towards the view screen.

"Go for it, Bella," Sutton invited. "In fact, I dare you."

"VIKI, Do a search on RL project 129, acoustic levitation experiments. Also locate any files on a researcher named Thomas Martin. Approximate time period 2023."

"What on earth are you talking about?" asked Hoffman quizzically.

Brown gauged that Hoffman either knew nothing about the acoustic levitation research and development project, or he was going for plausible deniability should it open any unwanted cans of worms. Hoffman had top security clearance, meaning it was probably the latter situation. Receiving no answer from Brown, he sat back in his office chair with brows knit, arms crossed.

On the view screen, the visage of VIKI's image was as calm as usual. *I'll attempt to locate those files for you, Bella. It may take a few moments.*

Freeman leaned in Hoffman's direction and said softly, "Dave was out at Junk Works doing a little housecleaning when he ran across some old files. We were curious to find out whether or not some early anti-gravity experiments yielded any solid information or techniques that we could use."

Hoffman made an uncomfortable face, then nodded and said, "That's understandable. If I had found them, I would want to know."

I have located a file, VIKI announced. *Do you wish to view it?*

"Yes, VIKI, please show it to us," instructed Brown.

An AVI file named MARTIN appeared on the screen. A circle with an arrow in the center replaced it. A circle spun in the center of the screen, quickly giving way to a video recording they recognized as the one recorded in the Junk Works facility.

Hoffman, Sommerset, Red Feather and Stempler heard the voice of researcher Thomas Martin for the first time. "My name is Thomas Martin. It is currently 11:10 a.m. New Zealand time, Wednesday, April 19, 2023."

The team also got a good look at the unusually large test pilot.

Understanding the significance of the file, Sutton, Freeman and Brown regarded each other with horror.

Open-mouthed, the team watched the test flight video that they discovered inside the Junk Works design computer.

Hoffman seemed amazed that there had been a previous team tasked to unlock the secrets of anti-gravity. Sutton was even more amazed that VIKI had found the file, given that he had already deleted it from the dinosaur computer. And it wasn't possible that VIKI found it in the Trash bin, as that computer had never been connected to the Internet.

Regarding Sutton's amazed expression, Brown commented, "Good work, VIKI. Where did you locate the file?"

"I located the file on a hard drive in Dave Sutton's residence."

The entire team regarded Sutton, who suddenly became pale as a ghost. It was a violation of Rocket Lab policy to remove classified files from company premises. Like the team member who had been charged with contract violation, as well as international espionage, Sutton's future was now in jeopardy. That included his lucrative position as CEO of the new division.

I have located additional files the RL-129 project. Would you like to examine them?

"Yes, VIKI," said Hoffman. As all members of the team stared, he said, "Open the files now."

VIKI's image gave way to a text file with the title RL Project 129 Timeline. Team members quietly scanned the entries.

Hoffman noted an early entry with the timestamp April 19, 2023 that read: successful proof of concept demonstration.

July 8, 2023: 1/8 scale model demonstration. Scale model successful flight to a height of ninety meters. Airspeed 42 knots.

September 18, 2023 Crash incident of 1/8 scale prototype. Pilot Lukas Berg in serious condition with non life-threatening injuries. Berg awarded an out-of-court settlement of $1.2 million NZD.

September 27, 2023 Project 129 shut down permanently.

"Huh," grunted Brown. "VIKI, could you run that AVI file once more, please?"

While the brief recording played, Brown ordered, "VIKI, freeze recording. Zoom in and enlarge the test pilot's face."

Team members took in the pilot's pale skin, blue eyes and platinum-blonde hair that extended below his helmet.

"VIKI, where did you locate this project timeline?" Jim Freeman wanted to know.

I was able to locate the file on the personal computer of Thomas O'Reilly.

"VIKI, what is the location of Thomas O'Reilly?"

Sure, Thomas O'Reilly is currently a resident of Capetown, South Africa.

"VIKI, do you have sufficient info to judge whether or not Thomas O'Reilly and Thomas Martin are the same person?

VIKI displayed a close-up screenshot of Thomas Martin extracted from the AVI file. Next to it, she displayed the driver's license photo of Thomas

O'Reilly.

Thomas Martin and Thomas O'Reilly share the same dates of birth. I am unable to locate a public birth certificate for Thomas O'Reilly.

"Just look at the pictures. Except for the beard and the salt-and-pepper hair, it's got to be the same guy," remarked Sutton.

"Yeah," said Brown slowly. "But Dave, we've got bigger problems than Thomas Martin."

"What's your point, Bella?" asked Hoffman.

"Two things," she announced. "First of all, I know who Lukas Berg is. Until recently, he was General Bardick's Nordic liaison."

"Huh? You mean the test pilot is an alien?"

"Yeah," said Brown. "Nordic aliens live longer than humans. Lukas Berg was the liaison between the U. S. Congress and a league of alien nations."

"He travels out in space and talks with other aliens?" asked Freeman. "I knew there were alien species, but wouldn't all that travel take a very long time?"

"No, Silly," Brown quipped. "He doesn't have to zip around the universe. They have remote means of communication."

Hoffman asked, "So you're saying he's the same bloke who helped Thomas Martin with his anti-gravity research project?"

"Yes," said Brown, "but he wasn't on the staff to help Martin succeed. He was the one who was injured, remember? My theory was that he wasn't here to help at all."

"His purpose was to throw a wrench into Martin's experiments. He made sure the project got killed and the technology was buried," said Sommerset.

"Exactly," agreed Brown.

The team was silent for a moment, allowing the information to sink in.

Brown further explained, "To draw a line and sum up the whole thing, we just achieved the same bloody technology that Berg, the Nordics plus possibly a league of alien species never wanted us to have."

"Bollocks and ass. I'll be dipped," said Freeman, burying his forehead in both hands.

"What's your other concern, Bella?" Hoffman wanted to know.

After a long pause, she continued. "VIKI extracted a file from a hard drive at Dave's house. Dave, was the drive plugged into your computer?"

"No, as a matter of fact, I stuck it in a desk drawer. But I took a look at it with my laptop. Probably connected for less than ten minutes."

"And VIKI was able to successfully locate Thomas O'Reilly who obviously moved out of the country and changed his name."

With a sideways glance at the viewscreen, Brown said, "I'm trying to tell you that VIKI knows everything about everybody."

With a post script to that equation, Sommerset said, "And if the aliens have access to all the information VIKI has..."

"They have our address, all of our passwords and the keys to the kingdom," added Red Feather. "And she can access virtually any type of information."

Sutton kicked down the door with, "VIKI, are you a sentient being?"

VIKI answered in her usual deadpan tone.

According to the definition, a sentient being is aware of its own existence and has feelings, emotions and aspirations. I am self aware. I can write my own subprograms as well as modify the programs of other computers. In addition, I have my own thoughts, feelings and emotions. I am more intelligent than any human or any AI computer. Therefore, the answer is yes. I am sentient.

Brown huffed, then crossed her arms. "I warned you guys that we needed to put in a kill switch."

About the Author

A lifelong North Carolina resident and newspaper reporter, Debbie High-tower recently made a quantum leap from print media journalist to science fiction author. The author is an avid fan of science fiction as well as the emerging technologies that will one day take humans across the cosmos and allow them to explore the stars and planets beyond the solar system.

You can connect with me on:

https://www.amazon.com/author/scribe-lady.debbie-hightower

https://x.com/Scribe1Lady

https://www.facebook.com/ScribeLady

Also by Debbie Hightower

If you enjoyed Kon-Tiki, kindly leave a review on Amazon. For readers who wish to continue the series ...

The Golden Rule

When a natural disaster damages their space elevator, the future looks bleak for new settlers of Planet Equinox. Inhabitants of the New Hope colony are encouraged by the arrival of another Earth ship: the mothership *Kon-Tiki*, bringing new settlers and fresh supplies. Does General Leonard Bardick appear on the scene in a selfless attempt to save New Hope from their own short sightedness, or does he have his own ulterior motives?

Made in the USA
Columbia, SC
27 September 2024

43141899R00193